TAINTED EVIDENCE

RACHEL GRANT

JANUS
PUBLISHING

This one is for Paula Johnson

It's been 29 years +2 days since our friendship began. From those first minutes in the van on the drive to archaeological field school and our first-ever dig, to dig bumming, volunteering at NB, that weekend in Montana when we both fell in love (with our now-husbands!), through grad school (for you), and moves to DC and Hawaii (for me), bridesmaids and births (two each), to owning our own businesses in different fields. This has been an amazing journey made possible thanks to your friendship.

Love you!

Chapter One

Troutdale, Oregon
July

Some people might freak out at the prospect of being alone in a crypt with over two hundred skeletons—remains of people who had good reason to be pissed off at the living, no less—but not Madeline Foster. No. Maddie would give anything to be alone in this spooky, hellish basement right this very minute.

Bring on the haunting of angry bones if it meant peace from the living, breathing, flesh-covered Troy Kocher.

She took a deep breath and tried to quell the shaking of her hands as she opened another vault, knowing Troy was watching her every move. Inside the vault were bones identified as B-14, collected from a rockshelter in the Palouse Canyons region in 1923, according to the yellowed note card in the vault with the remains.

The skull had wispy hair and an open mouth with yellow teeth. Hair was extremely rare on skeletons, but rockshelters offered excellent preservation, so this wasn't surprising. Now, if the note card said "Painted Hills," she'd have questions about the accuracy of the card's information.

A DNA test—the kind that didn't destroy bones—would be possible thanks to the intact hair roots, but that wouldn't be necessary in this circumstance. It was obvious these remains were ancient and indigenous.

From the slope of the forehead, she guessed this person was male, and from the closure of the cranial sutures, he was probably over thirty-five at the time of death, but she wasn't skilled enough in that area to make more than basic guesses. Her job was to inventory the collection and research the remains to determine where they'd been originally buried. If she could show the remains had been removed from federal land, these bones and any associated funerary objects would be repatriated to one of several Native American tribes. Not all the remains had a handy note card like this one, but there were file cabinets upstairs full of field notes that would aid her research and—even better—piss off Troy.

The actual physical remains wouldn't be analyzed for anything beyond trying to determine which tribe had the right to repatriation of the bones so they could be laid to rest again, after having been looted by the Kocher family patriarch, Otto Kocher, eighty to a hundred years ago. The jury was still out on which Kocher was the more vile, Otto or Troy.

Maddie was betting on a hung jury on that score as Troy, who happened to be Otto's great-grandson, was now acting as security guard, supposedly protecting his great-grandfather's legacy, but the only threat that concerned him was clearly Madeline herself, who, thankfully, had federal law on her side as she dismantled Otto's legacy and collection bone by bone, artifact by artifact.

Troy wore a full utility belt—gun, Taser, big-ass flashlight —all to guard a museum that had closed to the public a year ago. She knew exactly who he'd donned the belt to intimidate, and it wasn't the bones in the crypt. He wanted to scare Maddie, and, unfortunately, he was doing a damn good job.

Troy, his sister Anne, and a half dozen Kocher cousins Maddie hadn't met yet, were angry, first at the closure of their inherited privately owned museum, and then at the fact they were subject to the Native American Graves Protection and Repatriation Act at long last.

In Oregon, it was illegal for human remains to be put on display. The Kochers had circumvented that law by storing all the skeletons in these vaults and claiming they never used human remains in the upstairs exhibits. But everyone knew they rotated exhibits in the back room, which was always magically closed when tribal members or other authorities showed up. But with the advent of social media, tourists couldn't resist the skeleton selfie—horrifying photos of museum visitors playing with the bones as if they were movie props and not human beings who'd been stolen from their final resting place.

Enough photos appeared online that the state of Oregon could no longer look the other way. After more than six decades of operation, the museum closed for good.

Now the family wanted to sell the house, but they couldn't sell a house with a basement full of human remains that weren't part of an historic or otherwise legal cemetery, burial ground, or crypt. So they'd decided to donate the entire collection of artifacts and remains to the Columbia Legacy Museum, another small, privately owned museum, but on the Washington side of the river. Conveniently, Washington didn't have a law on the books that prevented displaying of human remains.

The Kochers had managed to avoid a NAGPRA reckoning when the federal law was enacted in 1990, but once the papers were signed with CLM, they discovered that the donation made the collection subject to a NAGPRA inventory because CLM had just been awarded a federal grant to upgrade their climate control system. Once federal dollars were in play, museums—even privately owned ones like CLM and the Kocher Collection—became subject to federal law.

Hello, NAGPRA. Goodbye displaying human remains like trophies for tourists. At least she hoped that would be the case. If she could show the remains had been collected from federal land, then federal agencies—in this case likely the Bureau of Land Management—would be forced to repatriate the remains to culturally affiliated tribes.

Oregon and Washington tribes had been trying for decades to reclaim the remains of their ancestors from the Kocher family, but NAGPRA had no bearing on private collections. Now, at last, Maddie could help see justice was done.

Ironically, it was the Kochers themselves who'd hired her. They'd had no choice and were paying a hefty price for the inventory that would dismantle the collection. To say the Kocher family was not pleased was putting it mildly. They felt they *owned* the bones—to which they had no genetic tie—and returning them to the tribes was theft of *their* property. Bones Otto had stolen from the ground.

So yeah, Maddie wasn't a fan of Troy, or any of his klan with a K. And now, on day one of her inventory, he was doing his best to scare her, even to the point of wearing a gun and Taser and sneaking up on her in the quiet crypt.

She'd be working in this house alone with him for at least ten more days, and the hell of it was, she *was* scared. Any guy who'd wear that kind of weaponry in this situation probably wouldn't hesitate to use them and claim his actions were justified.

He hovered over her shoulder. She could feel his breath

on her neck. "You get nightmares after handling so many bones all day?" he asked.

While instinct would have her stepping to the side and ceding the territory to him, she wouldn't retreat or he'd end up backing her into a corner. She elbowed him as if by accident and ran the note card through her portable document scanner, annotating the file with a quick count of how many bones were in the vault and a checklist of which elements were present.

Her goal today was to have a look inside every vault and scan any documentation. She wouldn't put it past the family to have removed remains if they thought they could get away with it, so she needed a baseline inventory.

Starting tomorrow, she'd do a more detailed catalogue, with a goal of recording the contents of at least twenty-five vaults a day. She would record every last button and bead in this museum.

Troy moved too close again as she scanned another card from another vault. She stepped on his foot, not accidently.

"Ouch."

"Sorry," she lied. "You're standing too close. I need room to do my job." He didn't move or say a word, so she turned to face him and held his gaze. She didn't smile or pretend she didn't know exactly what he was doing. "You need to step back and let me work."

He glared at her, then finally stepped back. He looped his fingers through his utility belt, one hand close to the gun, the other by the Taser. "You didn't answer my question. You get nightmares?"

"No. I don't scare easily, Mr. Kocher." That was a damn lie. She was scared of Troy, and he'd likely seen her shaking hands. She'd claim it was due to hunger—which was partially true. She had at least forty more vaults to open before she'd be done and could get out of here. She wouldn't stop to eat a protein bar. Anything that prolonged this time with Troy looming over her wasn't worth it.

"We'll see about that," Troy said.

She set down her tablet and faced him again. "Are you threatening me?"

His eyes went wide and fake innocent. "What? No. Of course not. I just meant you might get nightmares tonight."

"Mr. Kocher, this will go much faster if you leave me alone."

"Why do you care if this goes fast? Aren't you paid hourly? Take your time."

"I'd think you'd be eager for me to finish for the day so you can go home."

"Darlin', this is my home." His gaze raked her from head to toe. "And I like having you here." He gave her a mocking grin. "Usually, it's just me and the stiffs."

Her scalp tingled as her fear ratcheted up a notch. "Well, my boyfriend will be upset if I'm late for our date tonight." The lie came easily. Anything to let the guy know there was someone out there who knew where she was and who expected her at a particular time.

He cocked his head. "Boyfriend? Too bad."

What did he mean by that? Too bad that she had a boyfriend? Or too bad that she would never leave this crypt alive?

She pulled out her cell phone. Given that this was a real, underground crypt beneath the 1890s-era Victorian mansion in a rural area with spotty cell phone service, she had zero bars down here. "Speaking of, I'd better call him and check in. He's eager to hear how my first day is going."

She headed for the stairwell to the exterior exit before Troy could stop her and hurried up into the sunlight. Her mind raced as she tried to figure out who she should call besides her boss. She didn't want to freak out Sienna Aubrey

Vaughn, co-owner of Aubrey Sisters Heritage Preservation, because the woman was on bed rest for the last weeks of her pregnancy. This stress wouldn't be good for mother or baby.

Unfortunately, Larkspur Aubrey, Sienna's sister and co-owner, was out of the country for the next month. Maddie needed to handle this herself.

She stepped outside and held out her phone, divining for cell service bars. She glanced to the north, toward the driveway, shaded with giant trees that predated the house by fifty years, and the high riverbank to the east. She opted for the river in hopes that the lack of trees would deliver a stronger signal. She glanced back and saw Troy had followed her outside and now stood watching her from the porch of the old house.

At least he was too far away to overhear.

She scrolled through her contacts list. She considered calling her brother. He probably had a staffer he could send to play boyfriend. But she'd never asked Alan for a favor like this before and didn't like the idea of starting now. The rift might be new, but it was wide and deep.

Inspiration struck when she saw Trina's name. She quickly hit the call button and turned her back to the house so Troy couldn't read her lips. It was seven p.m. in DC. She prayed Trina would answer. Leaving a message wouldn't be enough.

Relief rippled through her when she heard her old college friend say, "Hey, Madds! What's up?"

Maddie wasn't a casual caller, so the concern in Trina's voice was warranted. "Hey, Treen. I'm in a bit of a bind." She glanced over her shoulder and confirmed that Troy remained on the porch, watching her. "You know that Raptor operative who just moved to Portland, the one you were hoping to fix me up with?"

"I wasn't—"

Maddie shook her head and smiled. "Yes, you were, but it's cool. I sort of need him, if he's available, to show up at this place where I'm working and pretend to be my boyfriend. I've got a security guard slash angry looter's descendant who's giving me the creeps."

"Is this that NAGPRA project for the looter museum?"

"Yep. The security guard is Troy Kocher, Otto's creepy great-grandson. Today is my first day, and he's setting off all sorts of alarm bells. I'm stuck working here for the next ten days and then have months of follow-up work, so I need to shut him down now. I'll pay whatever Raptor's rate is for this kind of thing."

A few weeks ago, Trina had told her the guy had moved to Portland because he was opening a Raptor office in the city. She'd never be able to afford an actual bodyguard, but surely she could cover a one-hour fake-boyfriend drive-by?

"If Josh isn't busy, I'm sure he'll do it for free."

"No way. This is business. Aubrey Sisters will reimburse me." She was fairly certain this was true, but Maddie really didn't want to worry Sienna to confirm. She'd tell Larkspur as soon as she was back on the grid, and if the cost wasn't authorized, so be it.

"I'll call Josh and tell him the situation, see if he's available. You need him tonight?"

"If he could, yes. Otherwise, tomorrow or Friday? The sooner the better."

"Got it."

"Give him my number, but tell him I've got no reception in the crypt, so I won't get calls or messages while I'm down below."

"What's the address?"

She gave Trina the address and described the exterior basement entrance so he could find her if he was able to stop by tonight. Even if he couldn't stop by, she'd told someone she was uncomfortable with Troy. It gave her a sense of security.

She watched the man as she tucked away her phone. He stared at her, his gaze unwavering. The back of her neck tingled, as if she could feel his anger across the long expanse of lawn.

He *knew* she'd shared her concerns, and he didn't like it.

Her phone vibrated, and she smiled at the creep as she pulled it out to see the message. Trina had sent Josh Warner's cell number. Maddie saved him in her address book.

Josh. My boyfriend's name is Josh.

She added a heart emoji next to his name and deleted Trina's message, in case Troy should get a look at her phone.

Too bad she didn't know anything else about Josh other than that he worked for Trina's husband, CEO of Raptor, a private security and military training company. Well, that and Trina had wanted to fix them up—which meant he was single.

Maddie hadn't been keen on the fix up because she'd been through too many excruciating blind dates after a nasty breakup. Her friends were determined to help her by forcing her back on the horse. And while their hearts might be in the right place, their screening methods were for shit.

Until a few weeks ago, Trina hadn't been on the fix-up bandwagon, but then, they hadn't lived in the same city since they were roommates at Ohio State, so the woman hadn't had any prospects to throw at Maddie to see if they would stick. That changed when Josh Warner moved to Portland several weeks ago.

After a year of crappy dates with men and women who were equally unhappy to be roped into a fix up, Maddie had shot Trina down without breaking a sweat. *No, thank you.*

Except today. Today, she'd take Josh and be grateful. She tucked her phone in her pocket, silently praying he was available to play white knight. The tribes had literally been waiting a hundred years for this day. She wasn't about to fail them because one slimeball made her nervous.

*J*osh pulled into the horseshoe driveway and stared at the huge gothic mansion and museum with a **FOR SALE BY OWNER** sign out front. The house would be stunning if he didn't know there was a crypt full of stolen Native American remains beneath it. With that knowledge, it looked creepy as hell.

Seeing Trina's number in caller ID had sent him for a loop, but Keith was fine. Owen was fine. Trina needed a favor, and it was business. Not that he'd expected anything else coming from her. Her friend, Madeline Foster, felt threatened, and there was no way Josh could say no to Trina.

He'd spent an hour getting up to speed before driving east. He'd checked out both the museum website and real estate listing and ran a financial and criminal background check on the Kocher family and museum.

No doubt the mansion would sell for several million, creepy or not. Over five thousand square feet, southern exposure, situated on five acres above the Sandy River a few miles from the confluence with the Columbia. Even though it was on the river, the valley was deep here, and the house was well above the hundred-year floodplain—which was why it stood in pristine condition nearly a hundred and thirty years after it was built by a logger baron whose son was a grave robber.

Josh had grown up in a small town in eastern Oregon. He'd gone to school on a reservation with Umatilla and Cayuse tribal members. He knew what looting meant to Native Americans on a personal level, but it didn't take growing up with tribal members to know that grave robbing was bad. And this museum had operated without consequences for the last sixty years.

He'd had to rearrange his schedule to make this field trip, but Trina had made the request, and when she'd told him why her friend was here, he couldn't say no.

He texted Madeline to let her know he was here, but Trina had explained it was unlikely she'd receive it. He circled the building and found the open door with brick steps leading down into darkness, as described.

Josh descended the stairs, being careful to make no sound. He reached a landing where the steps made a ninety-degree turn and paused, staying out of sight of those in the crypt below. A man's voice carried up to him. "You don't have permission to do that."

"My job is to inspect the entire collection, Mr. Kocher. You're permitted to be here as security guard, as this is your home, but you're not to impede me or my research. This collection no longer belongs to you, and the Columbia Legacy Museum cannot accession any artifacts until after repatriation of all human remains and associated funerary objects has occurred."

"You'll damage the brick."

"I don't care about the brick. I care about the human remains inside."

"This house is on the National Register—"

"I promise, prying open a vault won't alter the exterior of the house or in any way mar the integrity of the historical nature of the property. I can assure you I know the National Historic Preservation Act chapter and verse, and there is no adverse effect. I'm working within the parameters of the agreement. You were informed that every vault was to be accessible *today*."

"I won't let you."

"Get your hands off me, Mr. Kocher." The woman's

voice sounded more angry than alarmed, but still, adrenaline surged through Josh.

Josh hurried down the last flight of stairs. The rectangular room was about fifteen feet wide and at least fifty feet long, lined with brick on either side. Small metal doors—each one slightly larger than a license plate—were mounted in the bricks at regular intervals. Presumably, these were the vaults. Dozens of doors. More than a hundred. More than two hundred?

Midway down the length of the room, a large man— several inches above six feet and thick with muscle—had his back to Josh. The guy wore a tricked-out belt, like he expected a riot any moment. He gripped something—or rather someone—blocked from Josh's view.

"Madeline?" Josh said. "You down here?" He was careful to pronounce her name *Mada-lynn*, not *line*, as Trina had instructed. A boyfriend would know these things.

The guy jerked around, dropping his grip on her.

"Josh!" She darted around the guard and ran to meet him at the base of the stairs. He found his arms full of woman as she threw herself at him.

He leaned down as any boyfriend would and kissed her, brushing his lips over hers, pausing with their mouths pressed together a beat longer than necessary to sell the boyfriend charade. He raised his head and got his first look at her. He usually tried to see a woman's face before he kissed her for the first time, but apparently, that wasn't always possible.

He smiled as he met her relieved gaze.

Thank you, she mouthed.

Trina had said Madeline was gorgeous—which he'd taken with a grain of salt given that she'd been angling for a fix up —but Keith's wife hadn't been exaggerating. In fact, Madeline reminded him a bit of Trina in that she was nearly a foot shorter than him and had big eyes—blue, not hazel like

Trina's—framed in purple metal-rimmed glasses. She had delicate features, high cheekbones, a button nose, soft pink lips, and flawless skin. In another life, Madeline Foster would catch and hold his attention.

In this life, he didn't have time or attention to give.

But still, her short, light brown hair was pulled back in a bright orange headband that made her look younger than thirty-four or thirty-five, which was how old she'd be if she were close to Trina's age. She had a sexy Velma-from-Scooby-Doo kind of vibe, and Josh had always been a Velma fan.

And here they were, in a haunted crypt. All that was missing was the Great Dane jonesing for treats. He smiled down at her and wondered why he'd resisted the fix up when he had the chance.

But he knew why, and it wasn't just because he was here to open a new Raptor office, get Owen settled in at the wounded warrior retreat center, and provide a stable home for his teenage niece. He didn't have time for big blue-eyed distractions, superficial flings, or meddling crime-solving kids, dog or no dog.

"You ready to go, sweetheart?" he asked as he cupped her nape in one palm, like he held her this way all the time.

She gave him a crooked smile. "Twenty minutes? I've got a few more vaults to inventory before I can quit for the night." She blinked rapidly, not in a batting-eyelashes sort of way, but in a way that telegraphed alarm or annoyance.

He pressed a kiss to her forehead. "Sure thing. I thought you'd be done by now."

She glanced over her shoulder. "Several vaults aren't accessible. I was about to use the flat end of my tire iron to pry them open."

She nodded to a table set up to one side of the room. On top was a laptop, a portable scanner, a camera, a heavy-based magnifying glass with light, and a stack of papers and note-books. Next to that was a tire iron and an assortment of other tools: flathead screwdrivers, hammer, a pointed flat trowel, a thick file.

"I raided my car toolbox and dig kit for anything that might work, I think the tire iron is the best bet. The latches won't budge."

"Maybe I can help. If your tire iron doesn't work, I've got a beefier one in my SUV."

He waited for Kocher to object, but the man said nothing, which was telling. He was only willing to block her from opening the vaults when she didn't have a witness.

He met the man's gaze. "Josh Warner." He didn't offer his hand, he just cocked his head and waited for the man to offer up his name.

He was bigger than Josh, and his posture—and belt full of weapons—was meant to intimidate, but Josh didn't scare easily after a decade in the military and another five in high-end private security and paramilitary operations.

After a long pause, he said, "Troy Kocher. This is my house."

"Yours and about a half dozen other people, right?" After looking at the real estate listing, he'd checked out the museum's website. It was officially down, but he'd managed to find a cached version. The "About" page had described the Kocher cousins, who shared ownership of the museum, house, and grounds.

Kocher's eyes flattened as he crossed his arms. "Yeah. I'm the caretaker. The one who does all the work."

The way he said it made Josh wonder if this guy was stealing from his relatives as well, considering it his due. Not Josh's problem. The entire Kocher family had happily prof-ited from putting human remains on display. Screw them and their internal disagreements. He only cared if he could use

Troy Kocher's dishonesty with his cousins to Madeline's advantage and for her protection.

Josh crossed to the table and picked up the tire iron. He scanned the vaults. "Which one?" he asked Madeline. Or Maddie. Trina had used both names; he needed to find out what she preferred. Seemed like a boyfriend ought to know that, and from the vibe in this nightmare of a room, this wasn't going to be a one-time gig.

How long would she be working here? Given the number of crypts, he guessed weeks. Maybe even months?

None of the archaeologists he'd met through Trina did NAGPRA work, so he had no clue what a project like this entailed. All he knew was he probably didn't have time for this. Ava would start her junior year in a month. Owen was flying in tomorrow. He needed to get the office off the ground, and today's meeting had been a bust.

His priority list was full before he added a charity case in the form of Madeline Foster. It was extremely unlikely the woman could afford Raptor's base fee, let alone the under-cover boyfriend experience. But here he was.

The vault popped open easily once he applied pressure in the right spot. No damage to the bricks; only the rusted latch paid the price.

"Thank you," Madeline said.

Josh studied the dark void. "It's empty."

She frowned, then cast a glance over her shoulder. "Where are the remains?"

The security guard shrugged. "Don't know."

"The donation form you filled out stated there were remains in every vault, some containing more than one individual."

He shrugged again. "It was probably on display in the museum at some point, then put in the wrong vault afterward."

From what Josh could find on the internet, the fact that human remains had been on display in the first place was the reason the museum closed last year. Guess there was no point in Kocher denying it now.

She closed her eyes and took a deep breath as if her patience neared an end. "It had better turn up." She then pointed to five other vaults and asked Josh to open them. He made quick work of their rusted latches, and thankfully, each one contained a skeleton inside.

He set the bar on the table and grabbed a seat so he could watch as she did her thing, scanning any papers in the vault, taking photos of any objects that weren't bones, and writing notes on the contents of each one.

Twenty minutes came and went, and it was clear to Josh they wouldn't be leaving any time soon. He spent the time counting vaults.

Two hundred and thirty. And all but one held at least one skeleton. Had this creepy basement been designed this way from the start, or were the vaults added later?

He studied the brickwork and tried to guess if it had been done in phases, or all at once. He didn't know much about Victorian mansions, but it seemed as if wealthy families would have their crypts in a separate building, not in their own basement. It's not like this was Winterfell.

But…these also weren't the remains of Kocher family ancestors. These were the bones of indigenous people, kept as trophies.

From the website, he gathered that Troy was the grandson or great-grandson of the looter. He studied the man, then nodded toward the vaults. "How would you feel if someone dug up Grandpa Otto and kept him as a trophy?"

"My great-grandfather was cremated."

Yeah, the old man probably insisted on that to make sure he didn't suffer the same fate he'd inflicted on so many others.

Josh watched Kocher watch Madeline. This part was familiar. He'd done bodyguard duty for the last few years for Raptor. Prior to that, he'd been a SEAL, on the same team with Raptor CEO Keith Hatcher. Trina's husband. His best friend.

A few months ago, Josh had submitted his resignation—he needed to move to Portland to take guardianship of his niece while she finished high school. He wouldn't make the girl move to a new school because her dad was an asshole. But Keith had a better idea. He'd long wanted a West Coast office and had been looking at LA, but Portland would be a lot cheaper to get up and running, and there was a chance they could develop a new training compound on the east side of the state. Cheap land and a desert environment, filling gaps in their existing training facilities.

Josh had two years to make it happen, and his best friend to thank for the opportunity. He was a lucky man, but there was guilt in accepting Keith's offer that weighed on him.

Madeline closed the last vault door and returned to the table and began packing up her laptop. Josh joined her, gathering the tools strewn across one end of the table.

"Sorry that took so long," she said.

He shrugged and dropped a kiss on her cheek, deep in the role of relaxed, indifferent boyfriend. Usually, he met the client first, and, if it was warranted, they'd plan body language and kiss/touch boundaries. But given that he wouldn't be able to be around much as she worked this job, it was a good idea to lay it on thick. She played her part well, reacting as if his kisses were natural and welcome.

Madeline headed for the stairs without a word to Kocher. Josh made a point of meeting the security guard's gaze before following. "I watch out for what's mine," he said in a quiet voice.

The man's gaze hardened, but he didn't say a word.

"I know you can't sell this property as long as the bones are here. They aren't your ancestors, and this isn't your family crypt. This isn't a graveyard or a cemetery. It's not sacred ground in any way, shape, or form. And this place is costing you a fortune in taxes. You interfere or hinder Madeline's work again, and she can drag this into the next tax year. And I know for a fact you can't pay last year's tax bill, let alone this one or the next. I recommend you back off and leave the rent-a-cop utility belt upstairs in your playroom. Attempting to intimidate Madeline will only hurt you in the long run. I will make sure of it."

Josh turned before Kocher could respond and ascended the stairs. He caught up with Madeline on the central landing, her eyes wide with surprise. Guess she hadn't known about the tax issue and how very desperate the Kochers were for cash.

It felt good to be on the job. Helping someone. Doing what he did best. Plus, she was pretty, and it had been years since he'd looked at another woman and thought that.

He shook his head. He was done with impossible, destructive fantasies.

He took her hand and squeezed it, then they climbed from the crypt together.

Chapter Two

Adrenaline still coursed through Maddie's system when she pulled into her driveway twenty-five minutes later. She parked in the garage while Josh parked his SUV in the driveway behind her.

She wanted more than anything to go inside and pour herself a stiff drink and soak in the tub as she processed the day, but she owed the man a huge thanks, and it was too soon in their fake relationship to jump into a tub together.

But damn, the thought of him submerged in bubble bath was enough to turn her mood around. Trina had said he was hot, but that came with the territory of the fix up and usually meant average—which was fine; there was nothing above average about Maddie either—but Josh Warner was heat-wave-scorching, five-alarm levels of hot.

She shook her head at the path of her thoughts. He was a security professional who showed up to help her out, nothing more or less. What a bizarre and disturbing day this had been.

She stepped into the driveway as he climbed from his vehicle, which still sported a Virginia license plate.

She wondered what his deal was. Guys who looked like Josh Warner and carried themselves with his confidence didn't need blind dates to meet people. But then, he was new in town, and Trina had claimed it wasn't a fix up. Right. Single, thirty-seven-year-old male friend, meet single, thirty-five-year-old female friend on the wrong side of a bad breakup. His interests are protecting women caught in weird situations at work, hiking, and skiing. Her interests are, oh, will you look at that…hiking and skiing. Plus, occasionally being rescued by handsome men who aren't afraid to announce a claim on total strangers and lay down warnings.

She smiled and shook her head, remembering the shiver she'd felt when he'd called her his.

He cocked his head. "What's so funny?"

"You watch out for what's yours?"

He grinned. "It was warranted. That guy sends off some creepy as shit vibes."

"Agreed." She sighed and offered her hand. "It's a little late, but I'm Madeline Foster. Thank you for coming to my rescue."

He took her hand. "I enjoyed our initial meeting just fine. I've never jumped straight to the kiss hello like that before." He pulled her toward him, and her heart fluttered as he exhibited extreme hot-guy confidence and competence, which was pretty much her weakness. "Josh Warner, at your service."

She thought he was going to kiss her lips again, but he shifted at the last moment, and his lips brushed her cheek. Then he moved to her ear and whispered, "Your creepy friend followed us most of the way here. He turned off when we passed the shopping center, but I wouldn't be surprised if he rolls down this street any moment. We need to take this conversation inside."

His words killed the heady buzz that had been triggered with his performative flirting. The guy was damn good at his job, and she needed to wrap her brain around the fact that this was an act for him and remember why she'd called him.

That creep Troy followed us?

She shivered. "Of course." She glanced toward the street.

Josh touched her cheek. "Don't look. That's my job." He brushed his lips over hers again and said, "Does he know your address? Is it on your contract?"

"No. The company I work for is based in Seattle."

"But he has your name, so he could google you."

She nodded, her belly churning at the idea. "But I've only lived here a few months, and it's a rental."

"Let's go inside."

She led him in through the open garage and into her tiny rental home. Months ago, she'd been thrilled to find a place she could afford on her own. She'd always had roommates. Thirty-five years old, and it was past time to have her own space. But knowing the creep had followed them on the drive, suddenly living alone didn't sound so great.

She led him through the small kitchen and entered the living room. One glance toward the big front window, and she shivered. Damn. She'd never felt like this room was a fishbowl before.

Warm arms surrounded her. She felt a rush of needy relief and pleasure. He smelled good. Felt safe. But of course, this was just a performance for the front window.

"I'll order curtains tonight," she whispered. "They'll be here in a few days." She didn't have time to drive into the city to shop. Two-day delivery would have to suffice.

"Where can we talk that's private?"

She nodded toward glass-paneled French doors. "My office has a love seat. And curtains." She started to lead him in that direction, then stopped. "I'm going to have a glass of wine. Can I pour you a glass?"

He glanced at his watch. "Sure. But I need to make a call first."

"Of course. Make yourself comfortable in the office."

She was in the kitchen before she realized she'd forgotten to ask if he wanted red or white. His voice carried from the other room. He was already on the phone. Not wanting to interrupt, she decided to open a good bottle of pinot noir. It was from West Arch Estate, her favorite Willamette Valley winery, and at sixty bucks a bottle, she'd been saving it for a special occasion. Tonight wasn't what she'd been thinking of as special, but there was no denying she deserved the good wine.

She'd opened vaults that contained the remains of over two hundred men, women, and children today. They'd been stolen from the ground by a man who would never have desecrated a white burial ground in the same way. Not surprisingly, Otto Kocher had been a Nazi sympathizer in the thirties and forties. Maddie would bet her next paycheck Troy Kocher was a branch from the same racist tree.

The early pioneers of her profession hadn't been far removed from the Otto Kochers of this world. For decades, archaeologists had collected remains and funerary objects and shipped them off to museums, which were still full of the ill-gotten gains. She would do what she could to make up for that and make sure the Colville, Umatilla, Nez Perce, Cayuse, Walla Walla, and other tribes of the region got their ancestors back.

She poured the wine in the good glasses. After all, good wine deserved a nice presentation, and these glasses had been a wedding gift—one she'd kept after being dumped a week before the big day. They were beautiful, handblown, and hand painted, a gift from Trina, who knew the whole sordid story and had urged her to keep the present and use them to toast future triumphs.

Today had been more trial than triumph, but in the end, she'd survived, so she'd call it a win.

Her belly rumbled, and she remembered that she'd skipped lunch. She needed food. Fortunately, her cheese addiction meant she was prepared.

It took a few minutes to arrange a platter with four kinds of cheese, two kinds of crackers, olives, and prosciutto. Odds were this would be her dinner, but she wouldn't admit that to the hot man in her office.

When you hit thirty-five, you were supposed to have moved beyond the appetizers-for-dinner stage, right?

She loaded the cheese platter, crackers, and wineglasses on a tray and crossed the living room to her office. She could hear Josh on the phone and hesitated, but the tray was heavy, and if she spilled two glasses of her favorite expensive wine, she might lose it in a way that was out of proportion with the loss. She pushed the door open.

"Not cool, Ava," Josh said into the phone.

She kept her gaze averted as she set the tray on the coffee table.

Is he arguing with his girlfriend?

Her heart sank, and she realized she'd been harboring a little fantasy from the moment he kissed her in the crypt. An unconscious hope it would turn into some sort of meet-cute, a story they'd later tell friends when asked how they'd met. He must've met someone since he moved to Portland. It wasn't like he was required to keep Trina updated on his relationship status.

He flashed a smile and picked up his glass from the tray, raising it in silent toast before taking a sip. After drinking, he paused and looked at the glass, then raised a brow, cocking his head toward the hand that held the wine and giving a nod of approval, even as he said into the phone, "I'll be home in a couple of hours. We'll talk then. Love you."

Already at the casual "love you" stage? Damn. It was a fun hour while it lasted. Her brief crush was entirely based on Josh swooping in like a white knight and making her feel safe. She hadn't minded the kiss or the hug either. Or the way he'd brushed his lips over her temple. And told Troy he protected what was his.

She was pathetic. And Josh Warner was way too good-looking.

Damn Trina. Couldn't she have sent a nice but unappealing guy to rescue her?

He tucked his phone in his breast pocket and said, "This is a *very* good wine."

She smiled in spite of her disappointment as she dropped onto the sofa, trying to give him as much room as possible, wishing her office could accommodate something larger than a love seat. "I figured I deserve it after today, and you deserve it for coming to my rescue." She took a sip from her glass and enjoyed the rich, herbal bouquet and earthy finish. She'd made the right call in the wine department, at least. She met Josh's gaze over her glass. "You know wine."

"I lived in Portland for a few years before I joined the Navy. Hung with a group of people who did wine tastings nearly every weekend. It's one of the things I've been looking forward to doing again since moving back, but I've lost touch with all those old friends and haven't made the time."

"I go once a month." She hesitated to say what she was thinking. He might believe she was asking for a date, and that would make everything awkward. "With a group of friends," she added in a rush. "It's a standing date."

He smiled. He could probably guess at all the confused

thoughts that raced through her mind. He was a handsome man who put off the best kind of protective, manly vibes. She'd bet clients threw themselves at him all the time. "If you ever have room for one more," he said, "I'd love to join you."

She felt a little flutter, but reminded herself he just wanted to go wine tasting, make new friends. His friends from the past were all gone. "Sure. We can always make room. Most of my friends are archaeologists or historic preservation specialists. We're wonderfully nerdy, if you can handle that."

He laughed. "I'm used to hanging out with archaeologist- and historian-types thanks to Keith being married to Trina. Plus, my friend and coworker, Ian, married an underwater archaeologist, and Rav—the owner of Raptor—married an archaeologist. I've met their friends who work for Naval History and Heritage Command. You're all kind of hard to get away from."

She smiled. "Yeah. We run in packs. Trina and I met in undergrad. I minored in history, and we ended up sharing an apartment our senior year and during grad school with two other history geeks."

"Trina's husband, Keith, is one of my best friends. He and I were on a SEAL team together once upon a time."

She'd only met Keith once in the years he'd been with Trina, when she was in DC to conduct research at the National Archives and extended the trip a few days to visit with her old friend. It was before the couple had eloped, but it had still been more than clear they were the together-forever types. She was happy for Trina, even if she'd felt a little lingering envy.

She'd returned to her boyfriend in Portland and wondered if they had the same contentment and passion. One week before their scheduled wedding she'd discovered the answer to that was a definitive *no*.

"Trina didn't mention you were a SEAL." No wonder she'd felt all those badass but protective vibes from him.

He nodded. "Eight years on the teams before I left the Navy."

There was so much she wanted to ask him. Why he quit, why he'd opted to move back to Portland. Who Ava was…

But this wasn't a date, and none of that was any of her business. After finishing a cracker, she said, "That will be sure to scare the crap out of Troy after your parting comment. He might be big, but I don't think he's had any sort of security guard training."

He nodded. "I have the feeling he's relied on using his size and weapons to intimidate and get his way." He leaned forward and plucked a slice of cheese from the tray. "Thanks for the wine and food."

"It's the least I could do. Thank you for dropping everything and coming to my rescue."

"You going to be okay tomorrow?"

She bit her lip as she considered his question. After a long moment she said, "I think so. Now that he knows I have someone watching my back, I think he'll retreat."

"I'll try to show up a few more times to keep him on his best behavior. I want you to tell me if he steps out of line again."

"I'll be at the house for the next ten days or so, but after that, it will be sporadic."

He glanced toward the living room. "I don't like that he followed us most of the way here—but it's possible he was just going to get groceries." He leaned forward. "Have you reported this to your boss?"

She took a sip of her wine, then explained why she couldn't tell Sienna. "I can't add to her stress when this all could be in my head."

"I get your concerns. For what it's worth, I don't think this is in your head."

She closed her eyes and took a deep breath, then opened them again and met his gaze. Damn, he had great eyes. Warm brown. But even more than that, they were caring. Concerned. "Thank you. It means a lot to hear that."

"I'll do what I can to help."

"I'll pay out of my own pocket. Aubrey Sisters will reimburse me, most likely, and if they choose not to, that's fine. It was my call to bring you in."

He shook his head. "No. This is on the house. My rate is…probably way more than you can afford, and we have minimum number of hours required for contracts like this that are cost prohibitive. Easier if we keep it off the books."

"You have to let me pay you for your time."

He smiled and took a drink. "This wine is payment enough. You know how long it's been since I had something this fine?"

She appreciated the offer, but it wasn't right. "This is your profession. I'm not comfortable asking you to work for free."

"It would be different if I were needed to guard you twenty-four seven. This is me showing up and calling you sweetheart and looking intimidating. Not exactly taxing, and not worth the amount I bill out for. If it makes you feel better, you buy the wine when you take me to a tasting."

Was he asking her out or just being kind?

She needed his help and didn't want to screw it up by asking questions that could make him regret his offer.

"You should be concerned," he said. "I have expensive taste when it comes to wine." He popped an olive into his mouth.

She laughed. "Okay. Deal for now. We'll renegotiate if necessary."

"Good. Before I leave, we're doing a walk-through of the

house so I can evaluate your security and come up with a plan. You don't have an alarm system. If he hadn't followed us on the drive, that wouldn't concern me too much, but I think you need one."

She nodded. She'd been thinking the same thing. "I'll research it tonight and make calls tomorrow."

"I don't like that you're without cell coverage in the crypt. I don't suppose the house has Wi-Fi and you can use Wi-Fi calling?"

"No. I'm sure the house has internet—he lives in the turret tower—but he's not sharing."

"We could hack in, but that wouldn't exactly be legal. Plus the Wi-Fi probably can't penetrate the bricks anyway." He piled a cracker with cheese and an olive and closed his eyes as if it hit his palate like a gourmet treat.

Damn. Even watching him eat was hot. She wished she hadn't blown off Trina when she first called. Now it was too late.

"When you're done at the house, what will your work entail? I'm not familiar with NAGPRA-related work."

She explained the research phase, which would take weeks—probably months—visiting archives and consulting with tribes and historians and visiting the sites where Otto Kocher was known to have dug, in addition to trying to find information on the digs he didn't record. "My primary job is to identify where the remains were collected from, because that will determine if a federal or state agency has jurisdiction. Second to that is to determine if there are groups of remains that can be repatriated together, as each location is its own repatriation. Third is matching artifacts that are funerary objects to the remains they were buried with, because funerary objects are also subject to repatriation along with the remains."

She would have stopped there, but he asked questions

about how she'd conduct that particular research, so she gave him a quick overview of the process, surprised when he continued to ask questions, like he was really interested in her work.

Part of her wondered if it was a sign he was interested in *her*, but she quashed that thought. It wouldn't be good to get her hopes up. She'd missed her chance, or maybe she'd never had one.

"Often, looters will label artifacts in terms of the burial they found them with," she continued in her lengthy explanation. She'd been on dates with people who worked in a related field who would have begged to change the subject by now, but not Josh. "The most common way they did that was to use the abbreviation 'B' for burial. So if I find an artifact labeled B3-10, I will assume it's the tenth artifact found with the third burial at a particular location."

"People really wrote that stuff down when it was illegal?"

"Federal laws started being more strict in the 1970s, and by 1974, when the Archaeological and Historic Preservation Act was enacted, the writing was on the wall…and many collectors chose to cover their tracks. They burned their notes to prevent anyone from proving they had collected from federal land. Plus, you'll find a lot of people who sell on eBay are super cagey and vague about provenience. You see a lot of 'Collected from the surface' or 'Collected in the 1960s.' Much of Otto's collecting was documented in the twenties and thirties—and therefore is not subject to NHPA, AHPA, or NAGPRA, unless he'd taken from federal land—and the family claims that was the end of it. But given his obvious obsession, I have a hard time believing he didn't continue collecting until the stroke that disabled him in the seventies."

His eyes hadn't glazed over, so she continued. "I fully expect he burned the most incriminating of his notes— anything that indicated he dug on what was then federal grazing land. Even if the land is no longer under federal ownership, all that matters now is who owned it when Otto collected there. My best hope is looking for correspondence with others who might not have been so careful. My first order of business is figuring out who his friends were and hoping their descendants have letters they're willing to share."

"So it's detective work you'll be diving into?"

"In a sense. I might actually have luck in Otto's case—there's a good chance his correspondence was saved, but it's going to be brutal. He was a vocal Nazi sympathizer and corresponded regularly with other sympathizers in Portland and across the country. I'm not looking forward to reading his lengthy writings praising the Third Reich."

She caught Josh's slight shudder. "That's gonna suck."

She nodded. "So much." Then she squared her shoulders and dug deep for a smile. "But, on the flipside, if it means proving Otto was digging on federal land and the bones will be repatriated, it will be worth it. I want Otto's so-called legacy to be destroyed and would love it if the entire collection was returned to the people he stole from. I just wish the family had paid a price sooner. I wish there was some sort of restitution."

The conversation flowed from there to her planned trips into the Painted Hills and other areas in Oregon, Washington, and Idaho she'd likely visit. He spoke of the town in eastern Oregon where he grew up—which was on her list of places where Otto had looted—and said to let him know when she was headed that way. He hadn't been back to visit in over a dozen years, and maybe he could join her.

She told herself it was nothing more than the convergence of his past, her job, and his willingness to help her with this project, but still, she couldn't help but open the door to a little fantasy.

He finished his glass of wine, then suddenly made a face and pulled his vibrating phone out of his pocket again. "Sorry. I need to take this." Into the phone, he said, "What's wrong, Ava?"

He closed his eyes and pinched the bridge of his nose.

Hmm. Maybe Ava wasn't a girlfriend.

"No. I'm not on my way. I told you, I'll be home in a couple of hours." He opened his eyes and gave Maddie an apologetic look. "I know, but something came up." He paused, then said, "No, it's not a date. I'm working." He grimaced at the wine and cheese, and she suspected he felt guilty. He wasn't lying—this was work, but it would look like a date if Ava walked into the room.

"Yes, she's pretty," he continued, "but that doesn't mean it's not work. You know I don't keep normal hours."

She cocked her head even as she smiled and her belly fluttered.

He thinks I'm pretty?

But more importantly, who was this Ava person?

He rolled his eyes, clearly exasperated. "The longer we're on the phone, the longer I'll be here." After another pause, he said, "Order pizza. I'm not sure when I'll be home." He hung up and shook his head. "Sorry. My niece. She worries about everything. Tonight, she seems to think you're a threat to her status as the number one woman in my life."

Okay, now her heart was melting a little bit. Ava was his *niece?*

"How old is she?"

"Just turned seventeen. She's in a rough place." He cocked his head. "Did Trina tell you why I moved here?"

"She said you're opening a new Raptor office."

"That's only part of it. I mean, it's my job, but I needed to move here, and Keith gave me the time and budget to get an office up and running so I wouldn't have to quit. Which is good, because I can't afford to lose health insurance now that I'm the guardian of a seventeen-year-old with mental health issues.

"My brother—Ava's father—is an asshole. A shitty parent. And a thief. He was caught embezzling from his company. He worked in demolition. You know how before a building is brought down, they clean it out and sell everything that's worth anything? My brother was selling some of those materials on the side. He got caught because Ava was confused by junk he was storing in the garage at their house. He was bringing copper pipes and sinks and all kinds of stuff home that isn't found in a normal person's garage. Ava got fed up and called the company. She left a long message on the main phone line asking her dad when the company was going to get their stuff and why they didn't just pay for a storage unit. The office manager played the message for the owner, and within an hour, the police were at the house. They didn't have a warrant, but it didn't matter, because Ava let them in.

"Pretty much the only thing my brother did right was plead guilty to save the expense of an attorney and a drawn-out trial, but it all happened fast. Three months from arrest to him serving time and me needing to get my ass out here to take care of Ava. She spent those three months in foster care." He closed his eyes and let out a deep sigh before adding, "Two and a half years ago, her mom committed suicide."

Maddie gasped, her heart aching for a girl she hadn't known existed until a few minutes ago.

He frowned at his glass. "Ava blames herself for her dad being in jail, and I'm pretty sure she blames herself for her mom losing the battle with depression. I considered having her move to DC, but I couldn't make her start over in a new school after everything she's been through. So, here I am."

"You moved across the country for your niece? That's…amazing."

He shook his head. "I regret not doing anything sooner. I knew what a fuckup my brother is. After Lori's suicide, I should have moved here or insisted they move to DC."

"And your brother's mistakes are no more your fault than they are Ava's."

"Oh, I know. But I'm good at taking on guilt."

"On the plus side, it sounds like Ava is really attached to you."

He nodded. "That's the only part of this that's working. She's not a surly teen, even though she has every right to be. She's sweet—but full of anxiety. She's afraid she's going to lose me too. She knows my job can be dangerous—thank God I'm not in the Navy anymore—but tonight is a new one. Now it seems she's afraid I'm going to meet someone and choose them over her. She doesn't trust that I won't abandon her."

He couldn't be more clear: he wasn't emotionally available right now. He had a teenage girl who needed him. Maddie understood that, but maybe she could enjoy a little harmless flirting that went nowhere. Because she felt good with him. Everything about this evening felt natural. "You're a good man to put her needs first."

"Someone has to. I know what Lori did was about depression. I know she never would have abandoned her daughter if she'd been capable of making a different choice, but that doesn't mean I'm not also angry for Ava's sake. I mean, she left her daughter with my dipshit brother."

"How long will he be in jail?"

"He'll probably be out in another eight months, but he's not getting Ava back. I insisted he sign away his parental rights. I'm her legal guardian and responsible for her until she finishes high school. I'm probably going to need to get some kind of court order to keep him away from her once he's out, but I'll deal with that when the time comes."

"Will you move back to DC after she graduates?"

"It'll depend on how building the Portland office goes. If it's not self-supporting by then, I'll need to move back and will hope she's willing to move with me if she isn't attending a four-year university here or elsewhere."

"It's pretty great that Keith found a way for you to move and keep your job." She'd known Trina had married well, but this solidified her opinion that Trina had landed a good one.

"Keith saved my ass with this solution, and I'll be forever grateful, but it's the owner who makes it possible—Senator Alec Ravissant has been adamant that Raptor doesn't have to make money, it just needs to break even. So Keith is always looking for ways to invest profits back into the company. With me here, there's the potential of starting up a new training ground in eastern Oregon. That's the long-term goal. Training military personnel is our number one priority. The personal security and operations part of the business prevents operatives like me from getting rusty and keeps the satellite offices afloat, but the training program is the heart of the company."

He gazed into his empty wineglass with disappointment. "I'd like to ask for another glass, but I feel guilty. On the one hand, I want to be there for Ava and keep building her trust. On the other, when I tell her I won't be home for a few hours, I don't want her to think she can manipulate me into running home for anything short of a real emergency. This could set a bad precedent."

He waved a hand at the table. "And this sort of undermines my argument that this is work only. But it's been months since I had a chance to enjoy an evening with another adult, and I like it." One corner of his mouth kicked

up, and he gave her a look that could only be described as…
deliberate. "I like *you*."

Heat flooded her. There was no mistaking his look or
meaning. He was interested, and that was mighty convenient
given her gathering lust. But only he knew the ins and outs of
his relationship with Ava. She couldn't pressure him either
way. "I'm happy to offer you another glass of wine if that's
what you want, but the decision to stay or go needs to be
yours alone."

Chapter Three

Josh met Madeline's gaze, his heart beating at an inexplicably rapid rate. What did this attraction mean? All he knew was his desire to stay didn't have anything to do with not setting a bad precedent for Ava.

Was this merely a shared taste in wine and respect for the work she was doing at the Kocher Mansion? Or because she was a foot shorter than him with brown hair and glasses? She was a close match to his idea of perfection. But he knew that even having an idea of perfection was beyond messed up. People came in all different shapes and backgrounds, and idealizing one type over another was wrong.

Still, knowing it was wrong didn't change what he was attracted to, and Madeline pressed all his good buttons, and a few of the wonderfully bad ones. He lifted the glass from the coffee table and held it out to her. "I'd like to stay."

Her eyes lit up, and she gave him a sweet, sexy smile. "Let me refill your wine, then."

She returned with the bottle and poured them both a second glass, then dropped onto the sofa beside him, an inch or two closer than she'd sat before. She plucked an olive from the tray and popped it in her mouth, relaxed now. The tension had left her shoulders. "Want to see pictures of Trina from when we were in college?"

He startled, completely caught off guard by the question. Trina at twenty? He sort of did want to see that. But he shouldn't. Wished he didn't. He took a sip of wine as he searched for a response. "Hard to imagine Dr. Sorensen as an undergrad."

"Right? But she was. Cute as a button too. I can prove it." She rose from the love seat and crossed to a shelf full of photo albums. The woman had actual photo albums, with printed pictures and everything. He didn't know anyone who still did that.

She returned to the sofa, and this time, she sat so close, he could feel her body heat. She placed the album between them. Opened, it was wide enough to cover both their laps.

"We met during summer term before our junior year. We were both taking history courses—her to get a jump on her major, me on my minor. The classes were small in the summer, and we shared notes and ended up pulling all-nighters studying together, quizzing each other."

She flipped the pages, and there was Trina, looking exactly the same as she did now. When he first met her, he'd been surprised to learn she was thirty—she'd looked like she was twenty, twenty-five tops. Now thirty-five, she was still carded regularly. But in these photos, Trina really was twenty. She wore different glasses and her hair was longer, and she gave the camera flirty looks.

There were photos of the two women dancing, laughing, drinking. Playing board games. At an amusement park on Lake Erie called Cedar Point. As the pages turned, he realized the entire album was devoted to Dr. Trina Sorensen in all her moods.

He focused on a picture, tight on Trina's face. She was

beautiful, as always, but this photo said more about the photographer. He spoke his thought as it formed. "You were…in love with her?"

"Yes. For a while."

He lifted his gaze from the Trina buffet. "And Trina? Did she love you?"

Madeline smiled and shook her head. "Not in the same way. We only kissed once. She…didn't like it. I did." She flipped the page, and there were pictures of the two of them in a restaurant, cheek to cheek, smiling for the camera. "It was thanks to my feelings for Trina that I realized I was bisexual. But she isn't, so all we could be was friends."

"Your feelings for her didn't cause problems in your friendship?"

"At first, there was tension, but she wasn't available to me in a very clear and final way. I had to accept that and figure out my own self. Plus, we didn't pretend nothing had happened. We talked about it after the kiss that went nowhere."

She smiled and leaned back against the cushion, lifting her arm to rest her elbow on the low back of the couch in the small space between them. "After that, every time she went on a bad date, she'd come home to our apartment and we'd watch a movie and eat Rocky Road ice cream, and she'd usually say something like, 'Sometimes, I really wish I were gay.' And I'd say, 'Me too.' But it was a joke, because I'd moved on. I dated women and men and did my best to figure out what I wanted."

"And what did you learn?" His voice had gone husky at the intimacy of their position and conversation.

She leaned her head on the hand, bringing her face close to his. "That I can love both men and women, and betrayal hurts no matter the gender of the partner."

"You've been burned. At least twice."

"Yes."

"Are you seeing anyone right now?"

"Nope. My last serious relationship ended a year ago." She cocked her head. "So, tell me about you, Josh. What do you look for in a woman, assuming you aren't gay?"

He smiled and leaned closer. "Not gay. Nor am I bi. In general, I like women who are short—like about a foot shorter than me. Brown hair. And who wear glasses."

Her grin deepened. "That's…very specific."

"What can I say? I have a type. And you, Madeline? When it comes to men, do you have a type?"

"Tall, muscular. Maybe a bit badass and protective. Brown eyes. The kind of guy who will show up at a moment's notice to help out a woman in distress."

It was his turn to grin. "So, when you kissed Trina, did you ask first, or did it just happen?"

"I asked first."

"Show me. How you kissed her. That one time." His words came out in a husky whisper.

Her eyes flared hot, and she hesitated for the barest moment, then she leaned forward, closing the small bit of distance left between them, and pressed her mouth to his.

Her lips were soft as they brushed over his. Gentle. Welcoming but not demanding.

He parted his lips, and she did the same. The kiss started soft and languid, but the heat and taste of her lit a fire in him, and he cupped the back of her head as he took the kiss deeper, his tongue invading her warm mouth, stroking and tasting. He no longer thought of Trina or any other woman. Just Madeline, who tasted like a fine pinot noir and woke his body from a long coma.

His cock thickened, nudging at the photo album that remained open across their laps. He wanted to move the bulky item to the table, but didn't want to end the kiss.

Madeline made the decision for him and inched closer, causing it to slide to the floor. He placed a hand on her waist and pulled her to him, until their bodies were as flush as possible given their positions on the couch. He left her mouth and ran his lips over her jaw and neck before finally raising his head and saying, "There must be something wrong with Treen, because you are a really excellent kisser."

A laugh burst from her, her whole face alight. God, she was beautiful. He wanted to make her laugh like that again. Wanted to watch her face as he made her feel all sorts of emotions and sensations.

"Thank you. You're a fine kisser yourself."

He gripped the back of her hair and kissed her again, long and deep, resisting the urge to pull her onto his lap. He wouldn't bring her into contact with his heavy erection unless she wanted to be introduced.

Her hands stroked his shoulders and moved down his chest, exploring. She made sexy sounds as she ran her hands over his pecs, then shifted to his biceps and triceps.

Damn, he couldn't remember how long it had been since he'd had a surprise make-out session with a beautiful woman. He wanted to savor this like a fine pinot. Sip her slowly. Enjoy the bouquet and complex flavors. She was crisp, sweet, and hot. He chuckled as he kissed her, remembering the term *hot* when applied to wine meant overly alcoholic. That might be apt here, because the longer they kissed, the more likely he was to get drunk on this feeling.

"What's so funny?" she asked as her hands made their way to his abs.

"You are even more fine than the pinot."

Her laugh was light, joyful, and utterly sexy. "I wish I hadn't blown Trina off when she suggested we meet."

His lips grazed her neck. "Same. But we've fixed that now."

Her hand inched south, and he took that as permission to do his own exploring. The hand on her hip shifted to cup her ass. She had generous curves—very different from his previous preference—and felt so damn good in his arms.

Her exploring fingers reached the waistband of his slacks. She pulled at the fabric of his shirt, untucking the button-down and sliding her warm hands up beneath it to touch his bare abs. He copied her movements, sliding a hand under her top and grazing her ribs on the way north. His thumb brushed over her bra, finding a nipple, when the phone in his breast pocket vibrated.

She felt it too, and they separated, removing hands from under clothes, as if someone had walked into the room and they were breaking some sort of rule. They were both out of breath, and God, he was so damn hard, his dick pressed against his belt. He'd been able to ignore the pain of the restriction when forward progress was in the works, but now he had to shift to relieve the pressure before he could check his phone.

Ava. *Damn.*

"Sorry. I have to take it."

She nodded. "I understand." She pulled back, retreating as far as she could into her corner of the love seat—which wasn't very far at all.

He smiled at her, liking how she looked all disheveled. Her chest rose with a hint of heavy breathing and her hair was mussed, with headband skewed, thanks to his fingers. He wanted to take a picture to add to her photo album. This was how she looked after a sudden and intense make-out session. Imagine how she'd look after he gave her an orgasm.

He intended to find out.

He shook his head and ran a hand over his face. Time to be Ava's guardian, not some rando who wanted to bang a woman he'd met less than two hours ago.

"What's up, Ava?"

"I have a pain in my side, and I looked up the symptoms, and I think it's appendicitis."

He blew out a breath. This was a new tactic. "Describe the pain."

"It started suddenly around my navel. It gets worse when I cough. Oh. And it…shifted to my lower abdomen." Her words were stilted, like she'd read them online.

He closed his eyes. "Left side or right side?"

"Left. I mean right! Definitely right."

"I'll be home in an hour."

"But—I have a fever. A hundred and four!"

"You should have led with that. A hundred and four is serious. Tell me, where did you find the thermometer?"

"It was in the drawer in your bathroom, with all the old man stuff like the Bengay, hair dye, and hemorrhoid cream."

He laughed. She knew she was busted and was smart enough to deflect with humor. God, he loved her. His brother might be a dipshit asshole, but his daughter was amazing.

"I'll be home in an hour." He hit the End button and met Madeline's gaze. "We should do a walk-through of your house, make sure you're secure."

She nodded. "She okay?"

"She's fine, but I should head home. I'm sorry."

"Don't be. She comes first. I get that. And we can…pick up where we left off later."

He smiled. "I'd like that. A lot."

He regrouped and returned to full business mode as he checked out her home. It took twenty minutes, and he made several recommendations for both her home security system and general personal protection.

By the time they reached her front entryway, it was as if they'd never had a make-out session on the couch. "I'm more concerned about the back door than the front. I know light pollution sucks, but you need a bright light in the back—all night long—for the duration of this project."

"Will do. Thank you."

"I'm glad you called Trina, and not because you have amazing taste in wine. Listen to your instincts on this. Troy Kocher is bad news."

"It means a lot to hear you say that. I spent the day wondering if I was nuts."

He tucked her hair behind her ear. She'd taken off the headband after getting a glimpse of her hair in the bathroom mirror during the house tour. Free of restraint, her short hair had more curl than he'd realized. She was ten different kinds of gorgeous—sultry, girl next door, brainiac, to name a few. He liked every facet.

He gave in to impulse and cupped the back of her head, then stooped to kiss her even as he nudged her back to the wall. The heat level of the kiss went from spark to conflagration in seconds.

Without realizing how it happened, he found her legs wrapped around his hips and his arms beneath her ass, supporting her weight as he ground his erection into her center. She fit into his arms so perfectly, her short frame molded to his.

She moaned. He groaned. If he had a condom handy, he had no doubt he'd be shoving aside her panties as she opened his fly.

But he didn't want a quickie by the front door. He wanted her spread out on his bed. He wanted his mouth on her. Her mouth on him. He wanted slow and hot and to act out every fantasy he'd harbored for the last five years.

He jerked back, the last thought a kick in the gut.

What am I doing?

He blew out a deep breath as he set her on her feet.

"Lock up behind me. Call if you hear anything odd. I don't care if it's nothing. Better safe than the alternative."

She looked up at him with those big, beautiful blue eyes framed in sexy glasses. She nodded and said, "Promise."

"Good. Call me tomorrow night. I want a full report, and we can decide next steps for handling Kocher from there."

"'Kay."

He brushed his lips over hers in a soft goodbye, then opened the door and stepped outside into the warm summer night air. "Night, Madeline."

Her eyes held a happy, sexy heat as her mouth curved in a warm smile. "Night, Josh."

Inside the car, he pressed his forehead to the steering wheel. He liked her, a lot, but what if…what if she was just a mental replacement? Was he the kind of asshole who would use her that way?

The drive home took twenty minutes, and he didn't have any answers as he pulled into the garage of the house he'd purchased with the help of his best friend and boss.

"Did you have sex with her?" Ava asked the moment he stepped into the kitchen.

He frowned at her and mentally counted to three. He would never yell at her, but he'd grown up in a house with parents who yelled—a lot—so the instinct was there. It was a default setting he had to remember to reset. "That is none of your business."

"You did! You had sex with her! Otherwise, you'd deny it."

"No. I refuse to answer inappropriate questions, and my sex life is not open for discussion with you."

"You like her. That's why you were gone so long."

He fixed her with a look. "How's the appendix?"

She crossed her arms. "I guess it was just something I ate."

"Suuure."

He sighed and took a step forward, then enfolded her in his arms. She went willingly and, a moment later, let out a sob. "You're going to fall in love with her, and she's going to hate me and be like every wicked stepmother ever and try to send me away, and you'll let her because I'm not your daughter and love makes people assholes."

"Ava, no such thing will ever happen. I would never let anyone send you into foster care again. You know that."

"You say that, but you'll feel differently once she gets her claws into you."

He couldn't help it, he laughed. "Why are you so certain she has claws?"

"It's not funny!"

"It is. And if you'd met Madeline, you'd think it was ridiculous. She's a nice woman who needed help. She's working in the creepiest crypt and studying human remains that were looted over eighty years ago by a Nazi named Otto. And his great-grandson is big, mean, and intimidating. He wears a gun on his belt and spent all day, before I got there, standing way too close to Madeline. Imagine how that must have scared her."

But Ava wasn't ready to hear it. "Nuh-uh. You're making that up. There weren't Nazis in the US."

"There were plenty of Nazis in the US in the thirties, just like there are Nazis here now. They call themselves names like Proud Boys, Alt-Right, or White Patriots, but they're white supremacist, neo-Nazi hate-mongers just the same. And odds are Otto's great-grandson, who was with Madeline in the crypt hovering too close and scaring her, is one of them."

She pulled away from his hug. "You were stuck in a crypt with a Nazi with a gun? Does he know you're Jewish?"

"Well, I didn't point it out, but my nose probably gave me away."

"You can't go back there."

"I can take care of myself, Ava. I was a SEAL, and I work in private security. I can handle one pathetic troll."

"But it's the trolls who are the worst. They're the ones who're most likely to shoot up a school."

Josh knew the active shooter drills and false alarm lockdowns at her school had ratcheted up her anxiety even further.

He'd been in his early twenties and in the Navy when he first started training for that sort of thing, because it was his actual job. Ava had been eleven. Her job had been sixth grade.

"One of the trolls at school threatened Marcus last year," she said softly. "The guy was suspended for the rest of the semester, but with the new school year, he'll probably be back. If that happens, Marcus will probably homeschool, and I'll be all alone." Tears rolled down her cheeks again, and she swiped at them. "I mean, I know it's selfish to think of me when Marcus could be in danger. He needs to be safe. But I —I can't face a year of having lunch alone."

Marcus was Ava's best friend since second grade. Last year, he'd come out as a trans male and begun transitioning. Josh didn't even know what Marcus's cisgender name had been and didn't need to know. He was Marcus, one of the few rocks in Ava's life.

Not surprisingly, Ari—Ava's dad—had been awful. Ari had forbidden Ava from hanging out with Marcus and had accused his daughter of turning him in out of revenge for that. Another reminder of why this girl needed Josh's undivided attention.

There was so much damage to undo. Meds and therapy were helping, but they could only do so much. She needed Josh's unwavering support more than anything.

The time he'd spent with Madeline—the minutes that

hadn't been about the job—had been among the most enjoyable he'd had in a long time. But that's all it was. Sexual attraction. Fun. An escape. Things that couldn't—shouldn't —be a priority right now.

And the connection he'd felt, it could have had more to do with similarities rather than genuine attraction.

No matter how he looked at it, it was a mistake. He couldn't pursue anything with Madeline Foster right now. Not until Ava could trust he wouldn't let her down.

Ava needed to come first. Period.

Two hours later, Josh was in the master bathroom, stepping into his shower. What an insane day.

He'd finally gotten a prospective client interview with the big-man-billionaire CEO. Within thirty seconds, it had been clear that the man had hoped hiring Raptor would give him access to Senator Ravissant. When Josh made it clear that there would be no quid pro quo access, the CEO had cut the meeting short.

It was par for the course when the owner of Raptor was an extremely rich politician who refused donations of more than fifty dollars. Rav couldn't be bought, so the rich and powerful searched for a back door and thought Raptor would be the key. But Rav was a firm believer in the Emoluments Clause and made sure there was no pollination between his role as a senator and the clients of the company he owned.

Josh had been irritated at the wasted time. The billionaire should focus on buying a senator closer to home. But then, this was a Senate election year for Oregon, so maybe Cliff Nielsen was hedging his bets.

Prior to that failure of a meeting, Josh had gone to his daily workout at the nearby gym—usually the highlight of his day—but that last hour with Madeline won today's popularity contest, hands down.

Jesus. She'd been so hot and sexy, and the sounds she'd made as he kissed her… He could have come right then and there. The hot water from the shower sluiced down his back, and his erection thickened as he relived each touch and taste. He stroked his cock. He closed his eyes and saw Madeline's face. His hand moved slow at first, but with her soft pants and her firm, sexy touch in his mind, he quickly passed the controlled, measured stage.

He imagined her in the shower with him. First, he'd drop to his knees and lick her. He'd stroke his cock as he was doing now, as he made her come on his tongue. Then, if he was very lucky, she'd be on her knees before him, taking his cock into her mouth.

He braced a hand on the shower wall as he thrust his hips as if he was fucking her mouth, jerking his penis with slick, firm strokes. His orgasm came hard and fast. Powerful.

He sagged against the shower wall. The hot spray washed away his semen, and he caught his breath. For the first time in years, the face he'd envisioned as he stroked himself to orgasm was not Trina Sorensen's. Not his best friend's wife. And that was a relief and release all its own.

<h1 style="text-align:center">Chapter Four</h1>

osh's muscles burned as he breathed out and pushed the dumbbells upward. One more rep of dumbbell shoulder presses and he'd switch to weighted sit-ups for the abs phase of today's workout, then a quick jog on the treadmill, and he'd be done with Friday— AKA shoulder day—in his weekly rotation.

Owen Bishop sat on the next bench over, doing his own reps and keeping up just fine. He'd arrived yesterday without a hitch, and they were already back in their familiar routine of working out together. From the way Owen handled the reps, he'd gotten stronger in the months since Josh left Virginia.

Josh had gotten spoiled by living in Raptor's Virginia compound for the last two years. He'd had a cafeteria and on-site gym with on-call personal trainers. Free room and board, no cooking, no cleanup, zero commute, and daily workouts to keep him in top form.

His first order of business after the move, besides finding a house within her school district that could accommodate him, Ava, and a business office, had been to find a gym that could handle regular daily sessions for him and any personnel he hired. With Raptor, daily workouts were part of the job.

He'd found the perfect gym—Bond Ironworks—just ten minutes from his house. Arthur Bond, the owner, was a tall Black man with massive muscles. Josh was no slouch in the muscle department, but Arthur was next level. They'd hit it off immediately, and Arthur had agreed to set up special Raptor sessions once Josh had enough clients to support five employees—which was the goal he and Keith had set for the first year.

Arthur had wasted no time recruiting Josh to volunteer once a week to spot and mentor young men who'd recently gotten caught in the legal system and were trying to get back on their feet. Arthur opened up Bond Ironworks to these guys from two to three o'clock each weekday.

Josh suspected some of the men were homeless; the gym was a safe space, complete with showers. Plus, there was always food. A local grocery store donated produce and day-old bread, and there were stockpiles of peanut butter and protein bars donated by gym members. It wasn't a balanced diet, but it was a meal they could count on.

After today's workout, Josh would put in his hour for the week with Owen's help. Owen had gone through his own legal issues thanks to self-medicating after suffering a traumatic brain injury years ago. The track marks on his arms were readily visible, and seeing the health, muscles, and vibrancy Owen now sported would be a good example to the young men as far as what could be overcome.

Today would be Josh's fourth session as mentor, and it was one of his favorite hours of the week. By the time they were on the treadmills finishing their cardio, the guys started to arrive. Josh recognized a few of the men he'd trained before. Some were hardened, angry, and trying to dig their way out. Others were scared and likely saw the daily workouts as a way to reclaim power. A few remained jovial, high-fiving Arthur and offering bets on who would finish the workout first.

This kind of work spoke to Josh. He'd been an at-risk youth once. He could have turned into an asshole like his brother if not for the mentors and friends he'd picked up on the way.

It was the same reason he looked forward to taking Owen to R&R and meeting the soldier who'd founded the retreat for wounded warriors, which was situated on a lake near the Oregon coast. It was icing on the cake that Owen was on that path now—after years of needing help, he could pay it forward and be there for other soldiers dealing with the physical and mental damage of combat.

Cardio complete, they grabbed their water bottles and met with Arthur to go over the roster of students today. Because it was Owen's first time, they would work together and oversee the workout of six men who were midlevel skilled with the weights and machines.

Arthur and another volunteer would each have four men in their groups.

Josh and Owen led their group in a free-weight workout designed to build upper body strength. As the guys lifted, they talked and joked, keeping the conversation light, for the most part. All except Desmond, a nineteen-year-old Black man with a young face but jaded eyes. He was having none of the smile-and-pretend-everything-is-fine shit.

"You know what pisses me off," Desmond said as he raised the barbells. "There's another damn White Patriot rally in the city this weekend. Can't we have one weekend without racist white boys being assholes?"

"No way, man," Javonte responded. "White boys gotta white." He flashed a grin at Owen and Josh. "Present company excluded, of course."

Josh laughed. "The only time you'll catch me near something like that is providing security for the counterprotest. Owen and I worked several of those in DC and Virginia."

"I was thinking of going to the counterprotest," Desmond said. "But the cops always target us. Like *we're* the problem."

"We could go over techniques for safe civil disobedience," Owen suggested. "How to protect without presenting as threatening."

"You can do that?" Javonte asked. He looked at his arm as if noting the skin color, then rolled his eyes. "That sounds like a white privilege thing."

"It is, for the most part," Josh said, "but if you're with an organized group, it works. Safety in numbers and presenting a united front."

"Like a Guardian Angels sort of thing?"

"Yes. Anti-fascist, Guardian Angels, whatever you want to call it. Basically, standing against crime and racist demonstrations."

"But we've already got records. What if the cops come after us?" Javonte asked.

"It's a risk," Josh couldn't sugarcoat this. "A really big one. I don't know. This is probably a terrible idea."

"But what if I *want* to take the risk?" Desmond asked. "I'm so damn tired of White Patriots getting a free pass and making us feel unsafe in our city."

Josh nodded. Some White Patriots brazenly wore swastikas on their arms. It was impossible to see that symbol without feeling a deep sense of fear and loss. Fear for Ava's future. Immediate fears of pending attacks on synagogues. Heartache for his great-aunt Ethel who, along with his late grandmother, were the only members of that branch of the family to survive the Holocaust, only to see a rise in anti-Semitic violence in what should be her golden and peaceful years.

It burned that groups like the White Patriots were granted permits to gather for rallies—which news outlets then broadcast nationwide, allowing the organization to use it as a propaganda film to recruit even more members—and the Portland Police Bureau had to spend taxpayer dollars protecting *them*.

He looked at Desmond. Black, brown, and Native American people were the primary targets for White Patriot hate. Desmond and the other young men here would risk far more than Josh did if they showed up at the rally, and that was before factoring in their police records.

Josh was a decorated veteran and former SEAL employed by a wealthy US senator. His job was secure, and he'd have Raptor's attorneys to help with legal issues that might arise. He risked only physical safety in the moment. If these guys were willing to risk everything to make a stand against white supremacists, he would damn well show up and use his privilege to aid them.

"It's dangerous, and you would be risking a lot," Josh said. "But if we present as protectors of the peace and control the narrative with our actions, it's hard to argue we're the instigators."

"You'd show us what to do and stand with us?" Desmond asked.

Josh looked to Owen, who nodded.

"Yes. One hundred percent," Josh said. "We can probably get my company to provide T-shirts—a uniform that would make us look official and another way to control the narrative —and Senator Ravissant could make a statement in support of communities standing up against fascism and racism."

"Might be better to get one of our Oregon senators to do that," Javonte said.

"Or the candidate, that Tisdale guy who's all over the internet," Desmond said.

Javonte scoffed. "No way would Tisdale support us."

Josh was inclined to agree with Javonte there. "I don't know either current senator or Congressman Tisdale, but I do know Rav, and he'd speak up in support of this."

Arthur, who'd clearly been listening as they talked, crossed the rubber-mat-covered floor. "You can train my boys here to provide protection and not get arrested at the rally on Sunday?"

"I can't guarantee the not-get-arrested part, but as long as no one here initiates confrontation or throws the first—or even the second—punch, it's possible. This kind of protection work requires patience and taking more blows than is reasonable. But it's foolproof in proving the other guy started it when cameras are rolling—which is guaranteed to be the case at a White Patriot gathering."

"So, you're saying no fighting back? We're just punching bags?" Javonte asked.

"No, but…" He paused and searched for an example, then said, "Did you see the movie, *42*? About Jackie Robinson? How he was told he had to brace himself and hold it in, because his response to racist shit would become the story? He would be the problem if he fought back? This is similar, but on a lesser scale. You don't have to eat *all* the bullshit. Just two or three punches before you can fight back. Enough for cameras to capture who the real aggressor is. It's shitty, but it works."

"You up for taking some blows if necessary?" Owen asked.

Javonte, Desmond, and the others glanced at each other, then nodded almost as one. "We've been dealing with this shit our whole lives," Desmond said. "As long as we *can* fight back, I'm in."

Josh cocked his head and scanned the group. "Okay, then. Let's come up with a plan."

*A*t the sound of footsteps on the stairs, Maddie glanced up, expecting to see Josh and Owen, but sadly, the person who entered the crypt wasn't Josh. It was a tall, blond-haired, blue-eyed white man. Handsome. Fortyish. He reminded her of Peter O'Toole in his younger years.

"Oliver!" Troy said. "Thank you for stopping by."

Oliver had to be Oliver Shields, the curator of the Columbia Legacy Museum, which would become the new home of the Kocher collection once Maddie's work was complete. She pulled off the surgical gloves she wore for handling remains and offered the curator her hand. "Mr. Shields, it's nice to finally meet you. Madeline Foster."

"Yes, I'm sorry I wasn't able to meet with you sooner."

"I am envious of your trip. How was Norway?"

"Wonderful, as to be expected. I just wish I'd had more time to explore, but the symposium was successful."

"Glad to hear it."

"How is your inventory going?"

"It will take me at least seven more days to inventory the house—I'll be working through the weekend—then the research phase will begin."

"Do let me know if I can help. We're eager for the collection to be transferred to the museum."

Legally, he couldn't help with the inventory. It was a conflict of interest as her work would lead to the repatriation of—she hoped—a large number of the remains along with their associated artifacts. He'd been eager to acquire the entire collection for his for-profit private museum giving him motive to undermine her work.

Shields had a degree in museology like she did, and his willingness to take on a looted collection confused her. But then, a job was a job, and the artifacts needed a home. The family had been clear they would never return any part of the collection to the tribes. And in the private museum, at least they'd be curated and cared for and, for the first time in eighty years, if Maddie could identify where the items were taken from, they could actually contribute to the knowledge of the prehistory of the region. Without provenience, they were old tools that contributed nothing to the archaeological record.

"I'm wondering if you've worked up a valuation for the collection?" Shields asked.

She took a step back, caught off guard by the question. "Surely you're joking?"

"I told you we need a valuation," Troy said.

She glared at him. "Yes, and I told you that's impossible." She turned to the curator. "And I'm shocked you would ask for it. You know placing a value on artifacts is unethical." To say nothing of putting a value on human remains.

"Unethical or not, I need to provide the family with some sort of receipt."

"You do you, but leave me out of it." Dammit, did she have to be in an adversarial position with everyone involved in this project? She'd held on to a sliver of hope that Oliver Shields would be a professional.

"I will take you to dinner, and we can discuss this," Shields announced, as if she had no say in the matter.

"No, thank you," she said. "There's nothing to discuss."

"She already has plans." The voice came from the stair-well, and she turned to see Josh just rounding the bend in the stairs, sending a warm flutter loose in her belly.

He wore a tight T-shirt that showed off his impressive biceps. He'd looked handsome on Wednesday in his business attire, but today's look was pure hot athlete. And he'd brought a friend, hot athlete number two.

Owen Bishop was white, tall, and wiry. His blonde hair was trimmed close to the scalp in a military buzz cut. Trina had warned Maddie about his scars, most of which would be on the back of his head.

Maddie crossed the short distance to meet Josh and Owen at the base of the stairs. Josh leaned down and kissed her, a faint brush of his lips over hers, then spoke to Shields while looking into her eyes. "She has plans with me."

Owen cleared his throat. "*And* me."

She laughed. "It's great to finally meet you, Owen." Because it was how she rolled, she hugged him. He hugged her back, friendly. Easy. From the way Trina had described him, it had been a long road to get here.

"You ready to go?" Josh asked.

She frowned at the table in the middle of the room. "I found a bag of bones in a closet upstairs today when I was searching for notes on a particular burial. It threw me off schedule. I need to finish up with it and document the contents of one more vault to hit my quota for the day. Twenty more minutes?"

"Last time you said twenty minutes, it was more like forty-five." Josh winked at her.

She flashed a grin. "Thirty minutes. I promise."

He tweaked her nose like they were longtime lovers. "You got it." He and Owen leaned against the brick wall between the vault doors.

"Creepy place," Owen commented.

"Who are you?" Shields asked.

Josh smiled. "You first."

Maddie choked down her laugh. She'd wondered about Shields when she'd signed on for this project, and it had taken only a few minutes for him to show his colors. He wanted a value placed on artifacts?

Nope. Nope. Nope.

"I'm Oliver Shields, curator of the Columbia Legacy Museum."

"I'm Josh. This is Owen."

"And you are?"

"Madeline's boyfriend. Former SEAL. Current security specialist."

Troy's head jerked to the side at that, and Maddie hid her grin as she pulled her gloves back on and resumed cataloguing the skeleton on the table. An older male based on the cranial sutures and shape of the forehead and jaw. The note card indicated it was stolen from the Painted Hills region, as were many of the skeletons in Kocher's collection. There was a good chance this was collected from federal grazing land, which would now fall under Bureau of Land Management jurisdiction.

The back of the card listed other burials found in the vicinity—useful information for determining groups of remains that could be repatriated together—and included the name Clifford Nielsen as a "guest" excavator. That had to be none other than Clifford Nielsen the first, son of the founder of Nielsen Steel, and great-grandfather of the current CEO. This could potentially be a big lead for her research, as Nielsen Steel had an extensive archive where she might find more information.

As far as this particular skeleton went, most of the small bones were missing. All they had were the cranium, pelvis, both scapula, the long bones, plus a few ribs and vertebrae. Hand and feet bones were missing, as was most of the spinal column. Two of the long bones—a femur and ulna—were broken, the femur in three pieces and ulna in two, but all the broken ends fit together, making a complete bone. They'd probably been broken by Otto—or maybe even Nielsen— eighty-plus years ago.

She'd tuned out the conversation around her for the most

part, but her attention was caught when Shields said, "As a security guard, you're in the same line of work as Troy here. Troy will join the museum security staff when the collection is moved there."

That was news to Maddie, but the detail clicked into place. Troy had a lot riding on this deal going through, including future employment. It was possible the overdone utility belt was to impress his future boss. But his wearing it when Shields wasn't around made that excuse unlikely.

"Not that kind of security," Josh said. "We protect people and events—public figures with credible threats or other strong need for security. Politicians, CEOs of Fortune 500 companies. Raptor is more along the lines of Secret Service with a touch of special forces. We have advance teams to secure and pave the way, and an operational detachment should a situation escalate. In addition, our operations branch provides hostage rescue and other services home and abroad when the US government isn't willing or able to step in."

Maddie tuned them out again as the conversation turned to Shields asking Josh questions about Raptor. Much as Maddie wanted to know more about his work, she had her own job to do.

As she was finishing with the skeleton, Josh stepped up to the table. "This is the one you found upstairs?"

She nodded. "The number on the note card with it indicates it came from the empty vault you pried open on Wednesday." She avoided giving Kocher an accusatory glance. "The rusted latch could be the reason the remains weren't returned to the vault after being on display upstairs, but my guess is they were put in the closet out of laziness."

A sideways glance showed Kocher had stiffened. "The bones could have been in there for decades. My parents, and later my sister, were in charge of rotating the displays."

"What's with the red marks on the collar and shoulder bones?" Josh asked. "Is that some kind of stain?"

She nodded. "Yes. Sometimes the soil or items buried with the individual will cause staining when it decomposes. I've worked with protohistoric remains here in the Pacific Northwest in which the person was buried wearing a copper necklace and the bones have a greenish tinge. The red could be iron, I suppose, but that would be unusual for this area."

She studied the bones laid out on a large tray on the table. She'd placed them in the shape of the man to estimate his height, but without the spinal column, she didn't have enough data for a better than ballpark estimation. The red mottling on the clavicle and scapula was a stark contrast to the otherwise yellowed bones. If she couldn't confirm through Otto's notes where these remains came from, maybe she could get a pollen sample from dirt adhered to the bones that would explain the staining. But that was a last-resort sort of test, and her goal was to be minimally invasive of the remains. She made a note about the staining and potential for pollen analysis, then carefully placed the bones in the box she'd pulled from the empty vault.

Shields said goodbye and left the crypt as Maddie returned the box to its vault and pulled the last box for the night.

"Now that your future boss is gone," Josh said, "I'm going to give you some advice." Maddie paused in her work to watch Josh give Troy a once-over.

"For starters, the full utility belt hurts your cause. Flashlight, Taser, knife, and gun? Over the top and makes you look scared, especially when you go to such extremes for a closed museum. You afraid of the bones? Sorry, pal, but lethal force won't help you there."

Troy opened his mouth, but then his jaw snapped closed. He must realize anything he said would only make him look ridiculous. Or he'd have to admit his plan was to intimidate her all along, and now he knew Josh was a former SEAL and perhaps guessed that Owen was the same.

"Security isn't about a show of force," Josh continued. "It's about being observant. All those weapons won't help you if you aren't watching everything at all times. Your best weapon is your eyes. Look a potential threat in the eye, and ninety-five percent of the time, they'll back off. Let them know you see them. You're watching them.

"Sometimes, you don't even have to be in the room to make this point." Josh took a step closer to Troy and stared the man down. "Like, I know you've spent the last three days hovering over my girl to intimidate her. That stops now, man. Because I see you. She's here for another week, and you need to remember that even when I'm not here, I know the shit that's going down. You lay a finger on her, I know about it. You keep trying to intimidate her, and we're going to have a problem. I protect what's mine. I told you that two days ago."

Troy's face flamed red, but he said nothing, just glared at Josh. What Troy didn't know was Josh had her install a special panic button app to her phone, so he really would know instantly if Troy scared her again. One touch, and Josh —and everyone at Raptor—would be alerted to her distress. It was only to be used if she was physically threatened, and she was thankful to have it.

She knew for a fact it had saved Trina's life once. She'd never thought in a million years she'd have reason to have the Rap App on her phone, but here she was.

It would even work in the basement because Josh had a Raptor portable Wi-Fi device configured and overnighted to her. Now, anytime she was in the basement, she'd leave the booster in the shrubs by the open exterior door, as she'd done this morning when she arrived.

She returned her focus to the bones on the table. She

needed to finish so she could put this place behind her and enjoy a few hours off. She wished she hadn't scheduled herself to work tomorrow, but she wanted to get this phase over with as fast as possible. She'd also requested access to the collection on Sunday, but Troy had refused on religious grounds.

As a result, she'd push herself to do thirty skeletons each day next week so she could move on to the research phase, which was always when the job got interesting. The week after next, she'd drive out to the John Day Fossil Beds National Monument and access the archives in the Thomas Condon Paleontology and Visitor Center. She already had special permission to access areas usually off-limits to tourists in the Painted Hills Unit of the National Park to find several burial locations, if possible. The tribes would likely prefer these remains be returned to where they'd been taken from, and now that the monument was a protected area with limited access, they would be safer from people like Otto in the future.

But nothing was foolproof. Sites within the monument had been looted just last year, and the looters hadn't been identified. Maddie wanted archaeological looting to be classified as a hate crime—in the western United States it was always directed at Native Americans, and there was an essential racism behind it, but doubted that classification would be a deterrent. Looters, like all criminals, were always certain they wouldn't get caught.

And much of the time, this was true.

She finished documenting the skeleton and returned it to its vault, then said to Josh and Owen, "Done." She packed up her computer and snagged the portable Wi-Fi device from the bushes on the way to her car.

In the driveway in front of the mansion, Owen took Josh's

keys and waved to Maddie. "I'm just dropping Josh off. You two enjoy your evening."

He drove away, and Maddie climbed into the driver's seat of her sedan. "Where am I taking us?" she asked as Josh buckled his seat belt.

"I'd like to take you to dinner, but we've got business to discuss that we shouldn't talk about in public. Your place first, then dinner out?"

She nodded and pulled out onto the two-lane highway that paralleled the river. He was quiet as she drove, and the silence went from being comfortable to…awkward. Not what she expected after they'd spent over an hour on the phone last night discussing not just her situation, but also inconsequential stuff like movies and food and what it was like to move back to Portland after fifteen years away. It had been a comfortable, easy conversation that flowed like good wine. But now, alone for the first time since she'd had her tongue down his throat, maybe the awkwardness was understandable.

Five miles down the road, he spoke. "There's something I need to talk to you about, but I didn't want to say it on the phone."

She tightened her grip on the steering wheel and kept her eyes on the road.

"I shouldn't have kissed you. I should have kept it professional. It was wrong to act interested like that."

Ouch. "Because you aren't interested."

"No! I'm…shit. I suck at this." He ran his hand over his face. "Ask Keith, he'll tell you. I'm great at my job. Hopeless in my personal life. And right now, I can't have one. A personal life, I mean." He sighed. "The truth is, I like you, Madeline, or rather—"

"Maddie," she corrected. "I prefer Maddie among friends."

"Maddie," he said. "And that just underscores my point. I like the *idea* of you, but we don't really know each other. And I'd like to get to know you, but I can't do more than that, not when Ava needs my full attention."

He faced forward, his body stiff. "She was jealous and freaked out the other night because I dropped everything for you, then came home late. Some people would probably say she's being selfish and immature and needs to grow up, but I'm not one of those people.

"I mean, she might be those things, but she's earned it the hard way. She lost her mother in one of the most painful ways possible and blames herself. Her asshole father blames her for his situation. She's latched on to me as a lifeline, and I *will* be that for her. I can't let her down." He sighed. "And now Owen is here. I don't know how much you know about Owen?"

"Trina said he was injured in combat and suffered a traumatic brain injury eight or nine years ago?"

"Yeah. He self-medicated after that, and he's been in and out of rehab. I've been helping him out, keeping an eye on him, and he's been clean for over three years now. You saw him today. He's doing great. But we were worried that with my move, he might relapse. Keith's been there for him too, but I've been Owen's anchor. So I helped him find a job at a retreat for wounded warriors. The place is called R&R. It's near the coast. He starts in two weeks. He came early to help me with some Raptor stuff and to have time to adjust. We've learned with his injury that big things—like moving across the country and starting a new job—need to happen in stages. Once he's settled in, I'll need to drop in on him periodically, make sure it's a good fit."

"Sounds like it could be great for him."

"Yeah. He's been doing wilderness training work at Anderson Lake in Virginia for Raptor for the last year, but this will be more his speed. Not prepping men and women for returning to combat, prepping them to return to life."

He reached across the console and placed a hand on her knee and gently squeezed, then released. She felt a flutter in her belly, but knew it didn't mean what she wanted it to mean.

"I want to continue what we started the other night, but between Ava and Owen, building a new branch of Raptor, and…today, I sort of took on a volunteer project working with guys at the gym who want to protect counterprotesters at White Patriot rallies. I just don't have the time or emotional energy to do more than scratch an itch."

Damn. It was hard to argue with that. She didn't know much about Josh, but now she understood one thing: the man was a caretaker. Ava. Owen. Her. He'd dropped everything to move across the country for his niece. He'd dropped everything to race to Maddie's aid with zero notice. He couldn't leave his SEAL buddy behind. And he'd signed on to help a random bunch of guys at the gym who were embarking on a noble cause.

She guessed he wasn't the scratch-an-itch type because he didn't know how to do casual, which made sense given that whole caretaker thing. Like, he could probably do one-night stands with strangers, but someone he needed to be on call to help for the next several weeks—maybe even months—was off-limits because he couldn't give his caretaking all while keeping it simple.

It was good that she was driving the car, because otherwise, her impulse would be to hug him—after all, who took care of Josh?—but given the sparks that went off when they'd touched the other night, it probably wouldn't stop at a hug, and he didn't need that kind of pressure from her.

"Thank you. For your honesty. And for your help. You're a good man, Josh, and if you need someone to talk to at the end of your long days taking care of everyone but yourself, I'm a phone call away. No pressure, no strings."

"I think I'd like that."

She turned into her neighborhood. "If you have a few hours free next Saturday afternoon, my friends and I are going wine tasting. You're welcome to join us."

"Next weekend is no good. Planning to take Owen and Ava to R&R for a day trip to check it out."

"Maybe next month, then."

"I'd like that if I can swing it."

After a left turn, she reached her street and pulled into her driveway in the middle of the block. She opened the garage door, then drove inside and shut off the engine before closing it.

Josh had performed a miracle when yesterday he'd convinced an alarm company to install a system this morning before she left for the Kocher Mansion. She punched in her new security code on the car remote.

"Did he follow us this time?" She'd noticed him watching even as they talked and she drove. Josh had been alert. *Your best weapon is your eyes.*

"No tail. You're sure he didn't follow you last night?"

"I didn't see him. And I didn't drive straight home, like you suggested."

"Good." His gaze fell to her lips, and she felt the air thicken, like he wanted to ignore everything he'd just said and make out like teenagers in the car. Which was pretty much exactly how she felt.

It was a little insane, this attraction. But she'd been wound up since Wednesday, imagining his mouth, his fingers, his cock as she teased herself to orgasm. She wanted to ask him if he'd done the same thing, if he'd come while thinking of her.

She cleared her throat and reached for the door handle. She needed to respect his words, no matter what his eyes said.

He opened his own door and slipped out of her car. "Let me see this new security system of yours." His voice was even. All business. He was in protector mode again.

She guessed Josh didn't rest much.

They entered her house, and she punched the buttons to bypass the alarm while keeping it activated. The alarm would be on twenty-four seven for the foreseeable future.

While checking the system, they found the packages she'd ordered Wednesday night—curtains and a rod for the front living room window—on the front porch. "I can help you hang those," Josh offered.

She shook her head. "I'll do it later. Let's have a glass of wine in my office while you wait for your ride."

He paused. "You don't want me to take you out to dinner?"

She *did* want to have dinner with him, but the temptation would be too much. She was hopelessly attracted to him, and spending more time with him would only make it worse. "I think it would be a bad idea. I'm respecting the boundaries you've set. Dinner would muddle that."

He gave a slow nod, and she couldn't help but wonder if he'd hoped she'd push back against his limits. Take it out of his control. Maybe not consciously, but unconsciously.

They settled on the love seat with a glass of wine each while he ordered a ride. "Fifteen minutes out," he said with perhaps a tinge of disappointment.

She felt it too, but it was necessary. She was not going to encourage him to break promises he'd made to himself or to Ava. She wanted to be a person he enjoyed, not a responsibility. And, with him helping her with Troy Kocher, she'd already become a responsibility.

He took a sip of his wine, this one a pinot blanc she

particularly loved and had chilled knowing he'd be over tonight. As before, he smiled into the glass. "Damn. You have good taste in wine."

She felt a flush of warmth. At wine tastings, she never paid attention to the details the server always gave—the direction of the wind on the vineyard that season, when the first frost came, the ritual sacrifices made to determine harvest date—but she knew what she liked, and it pleased her that Josh shared her tastes.

They chatted about his plans to train young men from the gym to defend counterprotesters, how it had spontaneously come about from a conversation in the gym just a few short hours ago, and already Keith was onboard and Senator Ravissant would make a statement, and T-shirts were being printed.

"And this all happened *today*?"

"Crazy, right? But I've done this kind of stuff for Raptor for the last year—ever since Rav showed up at that rally last fall. You might have heard of it?"

"Yeah. Trina was there and told me about it."

He nodded. "Basically, Keith saw it as an opportunity to start an advocacy program to counter fascism and white supremacists. And we've got that rule about not making a profit, so it was a good place to sink resources. So I was given the green light today without hesitation. It's volunteer work, but Raptor will provide headsets and T-shirts, and I'm going to spend all day tomorrow prepping the guys. After the rally, we'll establish a training schedule because there will be more marches in Portland between now and the election in November."

She felt a jab of guilt thinking of the coming election. She should be a team player and volunteer, but it was the last thing she wanted to do. However, a counterprotest was different. Plus it was something she could try to fit into her schedule. "That's happening Sunday? Since Kocher won't let me into the museum, I was planning to use the day to go over the notes I've managed to copy and start putting together a map of estimated burial locations. But I could—"

Josh shook his head. "It's your call if you want to show up and protest the rally, but I'm going to be busy. I wouldn't be able to talk to you at all."

"You won't think less of me for not stepping up?"

"Of course not. It's likely to be dangerous. I've got a bad feeling about what the White Patriots are planning."

"What do you mean?"

"Given my work for Raptor and the current political landscape, I've been studying up on the white supremacist movement in the US. All the experts who follow the movement think they're planning something."

"What do you mean, like an attack?"

He nodded. "Yes. An attack to signal other groups to rise up."

"Like Oklahoma City? Wasn't that supposed to be a signal to other militia members to start the revolution?"

"Yes. Exactly."

"That's…terrifying." She sipped her wine. "I'm glad you'll be there and helping. Making it possible for others to be there."

"I just hope none of the guys get hurt or arrested."

She studied his face. Earnest, warm brown eyes, prominent nose, firm jawline. His face was bold and friendly. Like an actor who always played the nice guy on TV and then suddenly was cast in an action movie, making his deep and utter hotness undeniable and obvious to everyone.

But Josh had shown up like an action hero, so she was never fooled by his nice-guy looks. Everything about him was genuine, including deflecting her praise—she'd bet it didn't come from modesty or insecurity. He simply didn't view this volunteer job as being about him at all.

"It's probably just as well that I skip it," she said, unable to hold back her sigh. "My mom will kill me if I miss family dinner again."

"You have Sunday dinner every week?"

"Once a month, but I've missed the last three in a row." For *reasons*. But she wasn't about to spill that tea with Josh.

"How big is your family?"

"Mom, Dad. Brother and his wife."

"You close? To your brother?"

"Not really. I mean, we're not like you and your brother. Just…distant. He and I are fifteen years apart in age. I worshipped him when I was a kid, but things are different now." She missed the brother of her childhood. Alan had been fun and caring, and she'd counted the days between his visits home from college.

He glanced at his phone. "Car is about a minute away."

She was a little relieved, as it saved her from having to explain her family dynamics. Things were strained between her parents, her brother, and herself, but in the end, they all loved each other. That was more than Josh had.

She walked him to the front door and paused the alarm to step outside. He faced her, the intensity in his eyes sending a shot of heat straight to her center. "I wish we could start something."

"Me too." She didn't think she'd ever said a truer thing.

He held her gaze. A car pulled up in front of her house, but he didn't move. He stared at her for a long moment, then said, "Fuck it," and his hand was behind her neck, pulling her forward. He leaned down and gave her a hot, deep kiss. His tongue invaded her mouth, and she took him in and stroked him with her own.

The kiss was intense, amazing, and utterly unexpected.

A horn honked.

Josh raised his head. He gave her a slow, sexy smile. "G'night, Maddie."

She smiled back, giddiness radiating outward until even her fingertips tingled. "Night, Josh."

He crossed the front walk and climbed into the waiting vehicle. She was back inside and had just reset the alarm when her phone buzzed.

JOSH

I shouldn't have done that.

MADDIE

I know.

I'm not sorry.

I'm not either.

Chapter Five

Josh lowered his sunglasses and scanned the crowd. The White Patriots were on the green grass next to the pond, a sea of pasty skin burning in the hot noon sun.

Not that Josh wasn't pasty, but those guys took it to a whole new level.

He swatted at a mosquito and wished it wasn't too early for the tiki torches to come out. The mosquitoes were ripe thanks to the heat wave and ponds that dotted the park. Citronella would be handy about now.

The White Patriots were made up of several white supremacist demographic groups that were fairly easy to identify. The oldest White Patriots were the Vietnam vets, but there were also skinheads, old-school KKK, swastika-wearing neo-Nazis—he was damn glad Ava was nowhere near this park—and some guys who looked like they belonged to the eastern Oregon militia movement crowd.

Josh steeled himself against reacting to the symbols and signs, and studied his team. He, Owen, Arthur, and two other trainers from the gym wore bright green Raptor/Bond Ironworks T-shirts. They were the commanders of the volunteers. All five of them had served in one branch of the military or another, and Arthur had also been special forces—a Ranger —in his Army days. The volunteers—foot soldiers in this makeshift army—all wore blue shirts with the same Raptor/Bond logos.

The Raptor logo had always looked a little malevolent to Josh, but also a bit badass in a don't-mess-with-the-bird kind of way. On the back of the shirt it said "Security Volunteer" in big letters.

The shirts made a promise: *Follow our lead, and we'll keep you safe.* Claiming authority when officially they had none, but Josh did his best to smooth the way, meeting with the police prior to the event and having all his volunteers submit to inspection. No one carried weapons. They were here to protect peaceful counterprotesters using peaceful means.

Satellite trucks lined the street at the edge of the park. They weren't in downtown, but still, this rally would garner attention and the media was out in force. As the White Patriots filled the park, reporters approached Josh and the other green shirts to request interviews. The real story here was the reaction of city residents to the gathering of white supremacists in Portland.

Josh and the others refused on the grounds that talking to the press meant they couldn't be vigilant for threats. The reporters moved on, zeroing in on the blue shirt volunteers.

They'd rehearsed this yesterday, and one by one, they all refused, nor did they rise to the bait of being questioned on whether or not they were here to start violence. The not so subtle message presented by the reporters being: *Who is the real terrorist organization here? The one with the nice white boys, or the one with all the brown people led by the Black guy and the Raptor operative?*

Josh ignored it all and scanned the crowd. Everyone on

the team wore Raptor headsets, and they were spread out amongst the counterprotesters, checking in and alerting others if they saw anything suspicious as the rally shifted into full swing.

A face in the park caught Josh's eye, and he spoke into the radio. "Owen, see the guy to the right of the stage about five meters, yellow shirt, blond hair?"

"No…I—wait. Yes. *Motherfucker,* it's the wannabe security guard, isn't it?"

"Yes. Troy Kocher."

"Not surprising given his great-grandpa was a bona fide Nazi," Owen said.

"Damn, I think that's the curator with him. Oliver Shields." Josh studied the two men. They were grinning and laughing. Having the time of their lives at a hate rally. "Now we know why Kocher refused Maddie access to the collection today. 'Religious reasons,' he'd said."

"Asshole," Owen grumbled.

"Who's Maddie?" Javonte asked.

"Josh's girl," Owen said before Josh could kill the conversation.

"You got a girl?" Desmond said, "Man, you been holding out on us. I bet she's hot too. Even though you've got an ugly mug, I hear chicks dig SEALs, even old-man former ones."

Josh laughed. "Old man? That's not what your mother said."

There was laughter over the radio, then Javonte said, "Weren't you a SEAL too, Owen? Why don't you have a girl? Can't be the scars. Chicks dig those too."

Owen had several scars on the back of his head from his injury and subsequent surgeries. They'd be hidden, except he chose to wear his hair military short. He laughed into the radio, and Josh could have wept at hearing the genuine amusement in his voice as he said, "I only arrived in town on Thursday. Gimme a few days, at least."

"Desmond's got a sister," Javonte said. "He won't let me near her, but—"

"And for our next lesson, gentlemen," Josh said, "we will discuss how you are not the keeper of your female siblings, and they can date whomever they damn well please. But for now, we should focus on the rally—"

"She's fifteen," Desmond said.

"Oh. Never mind, then. Javonte, you go near her, and I'll come after you myself."

Desmond, at nineteen years old, was the youngest of the volunteers. The rest were between twenty and twenty-three. He thought of Ava, barely seventeen and about to start her junior year in high school, and nope. No way. He wouldn't tell her she couldn't date, but her pool was limited to high schoolers. Nineteen years old max.

Josh kept his gaze fixed on Troy Kocher's bright yellow shirt as he slipped through the crowd. Where was he headed?

"I'm gonna follow Kocher," he said into the radio. "Desmond, take over my spot on the front line."

"Yes, sir."

Josh wove his way through the crowd, keeping his eye on Kocher, who stopped and spoke with one man, exchanged high fives, and moved on.

Josh tucked himself into the counterprotest crowd and cast his gaze down as Kocher paused to scan their gathering. The guy had sensed he was being watched. He might have the instincts for security after all.

Kocher left the gathering on the lawn and slipped between news vans. Josh followed at a distance, catching a glimpse as he entered a narrow alley between two buildings. Josh reached the alley and hesitated. This was the perfect place for an ambush.

But that would give Kocher credit for planning that was beyond him. After all, he couldn't have known Josh would be here today. Hell, Josh hadn't known until two days ago.

He radioed the others and alerted them that he was entering the alley and gave the location.

"You want backup?" Owen asked.

"No. Just giving the heads-up."

He walked slowly, making no sound. His gut said the alley was empty. Kocher wasn't behind a dumpster, and he doubted the guy had climbed into one. He reached the far end of the alley and found doors on either side. One building housed a restaurant, the other a clothing boutique. Kocher must have entered one of the businesses through the back door.

With nothing more to learn here, he headed back to the entrance of the alley. He reached the street as Javonte said, "Guys, is it just me, or are the marchers surging this way?"

"Not just you," Arthur said. "The speaker just called us terrorists trying to steal their homeland."

Shit.

"Guess they've never heard of Native Americans? Sorry, Darrell."

Darrell was a member of the Confederated Tribes of the Umatilla Indian Reservation. He responded, "Oh, they've heard of us, but they believe they're entitled to our land."

Josh scanned the alley behind him and the street ahead as Arthur said, "I don't like the look of that guy, Dez. On your left."

A bunch of unintelligible chatter sounded, and in the distance, he heard the crowd noise rise. Josh broke into a run.

"Shit! That fucker has a knife!"

Josh couldn't be sure who spoke, but thought it might be Arthur again.

He reached the counterprotest area to find chaos. People

were screaming and running toward him. There were barricades to prevent cars from entering the protest and counter-protest vicinity, so they must be running from the man wielding the knife.

By the time his path cleared, only a handful of counter-protesters remained, plus a dozen blue shirts and the other four green shirts. In the center of it all was Desmond, with his knee pressed to a white man's back, the man's arm wrenched behind in a basic restraining hold they'd practiced yesterday. The right side of his face was pressed to the sidewalk, his mouth locked in a sneer or snarl, or maybe pain. It was hard to tell, but he didn't make a sound.

Blood dripped from Desmond's arm, the short sleeve of his blue shirt split open and a bloody knife rested on the sidewalk, just out of the white man's reach.

Police officers moved in, and Desmond was surrounded by no fewer than six officers, all pointing their guns at him as he held down the man who'd slashed open his arm.

"He was going for the kid next to me." Desmond's voice rang out over the crowd. "I had to act." His voice shook with fear. Understandable given the guns pointed at him.

Desmond had a conviction on his record. The cops could decide he was the problem here, not the guy with the knife.

"You did good protecting the others," Josh said into the headset radio. "How's your arm?"

"Stings like a bitch. I think. I—I'm not sure."

Josh understood. Adrenaline could do that. Mess up perceptions of pain or mask it altogether.

"Put your hands on top of your head," one of the officers shouted.

A half dozen cameras were recording the standoff. This was playing on live TV locally, and probably on the national cable news channels.

Running footsteps sounded behind Josh, and he turned to

see the senior officer overseeing the safety of the rally running toward the standoff. A white man in his late forties, the officer had over twenty years' experience with the bureau. Josh had spoken with him yesterday on the phone and today in person, before the rally started, and his gut said the man was solid.

"Tell your officers to lower their guns," Josh said. "They're making this worse."

"We have a report that your man has a gun."

"That's bullshit, and you know it. We submitted to searches when we arrived."

"He could have picked one up after the search."

"He stopped a guy with a knife from attacking a counter-protester, and you're going to make him the villain here?"

The officer let out a heavy sigh. "We need to do our jobs."

Josh waved to the cameras. "The optics on this won't look good for your department once the footage reveals the White Patriot was the only one armed."

"Get your guy to cooperate, and we'll get his statement."

"You won't arrest him."

The officer looked at the cameras and back at Josh. "We won't arrest. Not in front of the cameras."

"Not at all."

"If footage shows he was armed or he initiated the fight, we'll arrest him."

The footage would show nothing of the sort. He'd searched the guys himself, and they were too smart to obtain weapons after that. The stakes were too high for them. Into his radio, Josh said, "Dez, I need you to very carefully raise your hands. Announce it before you move."

"They're gonna arrest me," Desmond said.

"No, they won't. They're going to interview you and review the recording. Your cut will be looked at by a medic."

"Don't let me go back to jail, Josh."

"I won't." He hoped to hell his words were true. Guilt

swirled through him, and he had to force it back. He'd let it strangle him later, after Desmond was safe. Josh never should have agreed to train them. They were risking too much.

Desmond announced his movements as instructed and slowly raised his hands and rose. He stepped away from the man he'd pinned to the ground, and one officer approached, gun still out, and ordered Desmond to lie on the ground.

Josh turned to the commanding officer. "Stop this shit now, or I will make sure the media crucifies you for lying and endangering everyone."

"Stand down, Officer Thomas!" the man said, stepping forward.

"He's got a gun," Thomas said, not lowering his weapon.

"He disarmed a man with a knife, and he's wounded. His hands are at the back of his head as instructed. He does not need to lie on the ground. He's the *hero* here. What you need to do in this situation is holster your weapon, pat him down, then get him to a medic." The commanding officer stepped in front of Desmond.

Officer Thomas lowered his weapon the moment his commander stepped into the line of fire, but Josh watched his face. He was pissed at the reprimand. Pissed he didn't get to make an example of Desmond.

The commander patted Desmond down, but none of the other officers stepped forward to arrest the guy with the knife.

Owen must've caught the movement before Josh did. The white guy inched across the ground, forgotten, as everyone watched Desmond. Before Josh could react, Owen was there, stopping the man from grabbing his knife by planting a foot on the hand as it covered the handle.

All at once, two white officers noticed and stepped in, pulling the White Patriot to his feet and slapping handcuffs on him. Josh turned to one of the cameras and caught the eye of the woman filming. He raised an eyebrow and nodded toward the scene. Had she gotten all of it?

She grinned and nodded, giving him a thumbs-up.

Josh smiled back as relief swamped him. The local police would have their hands full explaining how they'd managed to zero in on the hero of the hour as the villain and nearly let the guy with the knife slip away.

But Josh had also screwed up. If he hadn't followed Kocher, Desmond wouldn't have been on the front line. He'd left the young man at risk, and for what? Did it matter where Kocher had gone?

He'd been thinking of Maddie and not the job he was here for, not the men he'd promised to keep safe.

A microphone was thrust before him, and much as he wanted to say, "No comment," and walk away, this was his one chance to frame the narrative and make it clear that Desmond was a hero for protecting others.

Because they wore Raptor shirts, he'd cleared his talking points with Keith yesterday, and thankfully had his opening comments memorized, because his brain was a jumble.

The confrontation had effectively ended the rally, and by the time his interview was complete, the crowd had dwindled down to police, press, a handful of counterprotesters, and a few dozen remaining White Patriots.

Josh scanned the remainder and spotted Kocher among them. Josh waved and smiled like he'd spotted an old friend. Kocher glared at him and turned his back.

"Daaaamn, snubbed by a white supremacist," Owen said. "How will you ever get over the heartache?"

Josh laughed as his phone buzzed. He glanced at the screen.

MADDIE

You're on the news.

JOSH

Did they capture my good side?

MADDIE

Not yet. Turn around.

He laughed as his phone chimed again.

Is the guy who was cut okay?

Josh glanced over to the ambulance, where Desmond was having his wound stitched by an ER doctor who'd tagged along with the medics on his day off in case things got out of hand. As he watched, the rear door of the ambulance opened, and Desmond shook the doctor's hand then jumped down.

He's all stitched up. Should be fine.

One of the networks got footage of the WP guy pulling the knife. They keep replaying it in a loop. You can also see he has a gun in his sock. It was knocked out when they fought and disappeared in the grass.

Josh glanced to where the struggle had taken place and saw two officers pacing the area, clearly searching for something.

Looks like someone picked it up. Cops are searching. Thank God the news caught it on film. Hard to argue with that. WP probably intended to plant it on Desmond.

Is he going to have trouble with the police?

JOSH

I don't think so, but the WPs will try to pin it on him. BTW—Kocher is here. With that curator guy.

MADDIE

I wish I were surprised. Religious reasons my ass.

Next time you go to the house, I want to be with you. All day. I've got a bad feeling.

Thanks, but I need to be able to do my job— and you need to do yours. I can't afford Raptor's fees.

She was right, but still, he was worried.

Maybe we can work something out. Thanks for the updates.

Welcome. Ohh. There's a hot guy on TV. Gotta go.

He smiled. He shouldn't have kissed her. Shouldn't want to spend more time with her. And he really shouldn't flirt with her. But still, he typed another message.

Hope they're showing his good side.

Don Lemon doesn't have a bad side.

A laugh burst from him.

He looked up to see Owen shaking his head. "You've got it bad, man, if you're sexting *now*."

"Not sexting." But Owen had a point, and he did have it

bad. "Maddie's watching the news, and there was a gun in knife guy's sock. Caught on camera."

"I thought something like that might have happened. Cops started searching the grass a few minutes ago."

"That gun is long gone," Josh said.

"Yeah. Question is, did one of his buddies retrieve it, or did a counterprotester grab it?"

Josh blew out a breath. "I don't like any of this." He nodded to where the remaining White Patriots were gathered. "This was clearly a setup to make it look like the counterprotesters were the problem."

"Straight from the false flag playbook. Blame Desmond and the rest of us for starting the violence. Basic game plan."

"Maybe that's the goal of knife guy and the other stooges, but there's always a bigger goal. Oklahoma City was supposed to signal other white militias to rise up. It was supposed to be the start of a revolution. The frequency of marches now makes me think they're building up to something bigger."

Josh stared across the lawn at Troy Kocher and wondered if he was a pawn or a knight in the White Patriot army.

Chapter Six

After a week in the crypt, it was a relief to finally be aboveground. All the remains in the basement had been documented, and now Maddie could go to town on the data that mattered most: Otto's notes.

With the exception of the kitchen at the back of the house, the museum filled the ground floor of the mansion. The front hall, all three sitting rooms, library, living room, and dining room had all been converted decades ago to display the artifacts. A second staircase led down into the crypt, which had also been open to the public. Supposedly, all the vaults had remained closed, but that was another lie the family got away with for far too long.

Adjacent to the kitchen, next to that staircase, was a study that served as the museum office. It was in there that Otto Kocher's notes and maps were stored and where she'd found the misplaced bag of bones last Friday.

Now Maddie was settled into the office with new appreciation for tall windows and sunlight. And cell service. Not to mention it was a lot harder for Troy to find excuses to stand too close.

She took a deep breath of the fresh air wafting in from the open window. The heat wave had ended, and it was a perfect summer day, the last of July. She'd spent at least an hour on the phone with Josh every night since she'd last seen him a week ago, and today, he would stop by the house for a midday visit just to remind Troy he was still paying attention.

Troy hadn't hovered quite so close in the crypt this week, and Maddie suspected seeing Josh at the rally had rattled him. There had been no shortage of interviews of Josh, Arthur, and Desmond as the days passed, and with every replay of video from the rally, Josh looked like a calm-headed leader, Desmond was a hero for protecting several counterprotestors from a man with a knife, and the White Patriot who'd assaulted him was facing more assault charges by the day. The officer who'd held the gun on Desmond after being told to stand down had been suspended, and there was a call to review all his arrests, examining for racial bias.

All in all, it was a win for the good guys, and Troy Kocher was pissed—but he was keeping his distance, which was all that mattered to Maddie.

She did her best to ignore him as she fed Otto's papers into the document feed of the full-size scanner. There were too many pages to mess around with the portable scanner she'd used in the crypt, and she hoped to finish making copies today so she could put this house in her rearview mirror.

The nightly calls from Josh had been the best part of her days. Even though she knew it couldn't go anywhere right now, she still enjoyed the flirting. The man.

Every night as she drifted to sleep, she relived that last good-night kiss and the one on the first night by the door, which had been pure wild heat.

She focused on the papers in front of her. She didn't need to read them now, she would spend the next weeks combing through them, but it wouldn't hurt to redirect her thoughts and get a jump start on the next phase.

Otto's wife, Sally Kocher, had done much of the note-taking while Otto dug. Her handwriting was distinctive and, thankfully, easy to read. Flipping through the files, which had been ordered chronologically, Maddie noticed there were big gaps in the years. Otto was extremely wealthy for his time—the family logging business was booming, and hired managers ran the business. With loads of free time and plenty of money to support his habit, he spent his summers adding to his collection. Newspaper articles were written about him as if he were a swashbuckling adventurer.

She knew the newspaper articles were a product of their time—and it wasn't as if her own professional predecessors were much better—but it was still disturbing.

The multiyear gaps in the notes were likely because Otto had been digging on federal land and the documents were destroyed in the seventies. As she scanned what remained of their papers, Maddie skimmed the pages, looking for references to previous excavations—as sometimes the woman noted similarities between finds. She also studied the news articles looking for references to specific digs and their time-frame. NAGPRA only required a preponderance of evidence to show an item was subject to repatriation. She didn't have to worry about "beyond a reasonable doubt" and a passing reference to a dig would add the data needed to fulfill the preponderance requirement.

The name Clifford Nielsen snagged Maddie's eye. She'd been looking for it after spotting it on the back of the burial card a week ago. This had to be the steel magnate. Nielsen Steel had been a major employer in Portland in the first half of the twentieth century, and the company had only grown and expanded since then, with revenues in the billions. Clifford Nielsen's great-grandson, known locally as C-IV—which had to be a play on the explosive C-4—was CEO now and one of the city's wealthiest residents. Given that he was in his midforties, handsome, and recently divorced, local news treated his private life like tabloid fodder.

It made sense that Otto Kocher would know Clifford Nielsen Sr.—C-I—given that they were both second-generation wealthy men of industry in the region in the thirties, their fathers having founded the family business before either man was born. She'd suspected, after reading the card last week, that Nielsen had gone on digs with the Kochers.

Maddie flipped through Sally's notes, looking for more concrete details. She found a reference to Nielsen admiring a mortar and pestle as it was removed from the ground. Proof Nielsen had been with them in the Painted Hills.

More important to Maddie, however, was the question: would there be references to fieldwork with the Kochers in Clifford Nielsen Sr.'s papers? A few years ago, she'd researched Nielsen Steel while preparing a history of Oregon industries for the Oregon Heritage Commission. The company had an excellent archive in their posh corporate office, a Nielsen Steel-owned high-rise in Portland's Pearl District.

She'd finish going through Sally's notes this weekend in prep for a trip to Nielsen Steel's archives next week. If Clifford I had looted with the Kochers, perhaps the gaps in the records—where the Kocher family had likely burned their notes—could be filled in thanks to correspondence with the Nielsens.

She felt energized with this find. Outside corroboration of where the bones were stolen from would add to the preponderance of evidence.

"Whatcha looking at?" Troy asked.

Crap. He must've noticed from her body language that she'd found something. "Nothing. Just skimming your great-grandmother's notes." She wasn't required to tell him anything about her work or process, and he knew it. But still he pushed at every turn.

Her cell phone pinged, and she pulled it out to see the message. She smiled.

JOSH

#1 boyfriend check-in. How's it going today?

MADDIE

Counting the minutes until I'm done at the house. Current # = 292. Hmm. Just realized #2 boyfriend hasn't checked in in days.

I didn't want to mention it, but he took one look at me and surrendered. There will be no other boyfriends.

She laughed at that. It was all ridiculous and silly. Their texts had to keep up the charade just in case Troy grabbed her phone, but that didn't mean she didn't like reading the possessive words. Not because she liked possessiveness, but because they came from Josh, and he…was so damn appealing.

It was nice to feel wanted, and she knew it wasn't all pretend.

Are you going to be able to stop by today?

Yes, but only for an hour, then I need to head back to the city. I've got a meeting with a potential client.

So there was no chance for a not-date tonight. She felt a trickle of disappointment, but she'd deal. They needed to keep their distance anyway. Josh had to prioritize Ava and Owen and his work. There was no room for Maddie in his life except as a volunteer protection side job, and she was grateful he was making the time for that.

MADDIE

Glad you got a meeting. Hope it goes well.

JOSH

I'll be there in an hour or so. Want me to bring lunch?

She considered the protein bars she'd grabbed for lunch today because she forgot to go to the grocery store last night.

I'd kill for a Cubano from Bunk, if it's not out of your way.

No need to kill. I'm on it.

You make a great #1 boyfriend.

Wait until you see what else I'm good at.

She laughed. Oh, if only she would have the chance to find out. But his surprising good-night kiss a week ago changed nothing. Their flirting changed nothing. They were keeping their distance to limit temptation. Today's visit to the house would serve the purpose of reminding Troy that Josh had her back, but also being here, it would prevent them from sharing a hot kiss against a wall that went too far.

She set her phone on the table—why go to all the trouble of staying in character and not give the creep a chance to see?—and returned to her job of copying Otto's and Sally's field notes.

If she wanted to let go of her Josh fantasies, she should consider starting to date again. Her friends were always trying to fix her up. Just yesterday, Jasmine had messaged her about a guy who was a paramedic in Troutdale, and Andrea asked if she could invite a woman who worked in the Portland Planning Department to tomorrow's wine tasting because she was sure Maddie would like her.

But one thing about the boyfriend ruse—it wouldn't work if Maddie was seeing other people, and…she didn't *want* to see other people.

But she would find it impossible to get over this crush if all she did was pine for Josh Warner. She grabbed her phone again and told Andrea to extend the invite. It wouldn't hurt to meet someone new.

*M*addie wore makeup today, and her hair was pulled back with a clip—Josh suspected to keep it out of her eyes while she bent over the old journals that were stacked on the desk beside her. Her hair was glossy and curlier than the last time he'd seen her, and he wanted to thread his fingers through it as he plundered her mouth.

His ego couldn't help but wonder if the makeup and hairstyle were for him, because she knew he'd planned to stop by the Kocher Mansion today. He might have taken extra care with his appearance this morning too, come to think of it. After all, it had been a week since they'd seen each other.

She rose from the desk and approached him. Taking advantage of Troy Kocher's unrelenting presence, he dropped a light kiss on her lips and took in her scent. He forced himself to pull back and held up the bag of sandwiches. "I hope you're hungry."

Her eyes lit and she took a deep breath, a dreamy expression on her face that was damn hot. "Oh my God. Those smell so good. You're the best."

"Where shall we eat?"

"I have a blanket in my car. We can picnic on the flat above the river."

That would take them far away from Troy, a plan he approved of so they could talk, and it was a beautiful summer day. They needed to enjoy it while they could.

"Perfect."

Maddie led the way, and minutes later, they were seated on the blanket in the sun. The river rushed below, and flowers bloomed on the opposite bank. "This really is a sweet piece of property," Josh said before taking a bite of his Italian sandwich.

"It's a shame it's tainted." Maddie nodded toward the house. "I mean, the mansion is utterly gorgeous and a perfect example of the architectural style. And it makes my skin crawl. And I work in historic preservation."

"If ever a gothic mansion should be haunted, it's that one."

He studied Maddie, sitting there in the sunlight, and felt the warmth settle into his belly. Warmth from the summer heat, warmth from being near her. They'd chatted on the phone at length every night since they met over a week ago, and that filled an ache, but it was nothing like sitting beside her on a blanket in the sunshine.

"What will you do next week, when you finish at the house?"

"Monday, I'm heading to the State Historic Preservation Office to look up site data. I think on Thursday I'll visit John Day Fossil Beds—several of the burials are from the Painted Hills. Oh, and this morning I found another reference to Clifford Nielsen the first—it appears he went on digs with the Kochers—so I'm planning to visit Nielsen Steel's archives. If I remember correctly, the archive is open without an appointment on Tuesdays."

"I met C-IV last week—the day you and I met, actually."

"Wow. You move in impressive company, and you didn't even brag about it."

He shrugged. "It was a business meeting. He only agreed to meet with me because he was hoping to pocket a senator, but Rav doesn't play that way, so it was something of a bust. The guy has some tricky security issues, though. If I'd landed that contract, I'd immediately need a team of six to eight operatives, which would exceed my goals for the first year."

"How would you hire that many people so quickly?"

"I'd probably bring down three from Alaska, and grab one or two more from other offices, and hire the rest locally. Over time, all the transplants would be replaced with locals so our seasoned employees could return to their preferred posts. But for a contract like that, we'd need to start with our best and brightest and fold in new hires as they prove they can handle the job."

"Well, I hear Troy Kocher is entering the private security business," she said dryly.

Josh spewed the water he'd just sipped, then laughed. "I think I'm gonna pass on that one."

"But he has his own Taser. Think of the money Raptor will save." She flicked her gaze back to the house.

Josh looked over his shoulder and saw Kocher sitting on the wraparound porch, watching them. That dude was creepy as hell. Like Stephen King-movie kind of creepy.

Thank God, Maddie would be done here after today.

"You said you'll go to Nielsen on Tuesday? Let me know if that works out. I've got a meeting in the Pearl District and could meet you for drinks at the end of the day."

"Works for me."

Okay, so maybe he didn't have a meeting in the Pearl District, but he'd set one up if he had to. "I can meet you in the lobby around five p.m. There's a wine bar near Nielsen Tower I've been wanting to try." Yeah, he definitely shouldn't be doing this, but then, there were a lot of things he should probably do or not do when it came to Maddie Foster. He'd missed her this past week, and his weekend was booked solid between Ava, Owen, and training volunteers for the next rally —which he'd just been informed was scheduled for two weeks from Sunday.

"It's a date, then," Maddie said. "Or, um, two friends getting together after work."

He met her gaze and smiled, knowing they were both thinking the same thing. It absolutely was a date, even if neither of them would admit it.

Chapter Seven

"Madeline Foster, welcome back to the archives," the woman behind the desk said when Maddie entered the Nielsen Steel archives, located on the twenty-first floor of the tower.

That the woman knew her name wasn't a surprise—she'd provided her ID in the lobby to get an elevator pass, as floors ten and up were restricted—but the "welcome back" threw her off. "You remember me?"

"Absolutely. The work you did for the Oregon Heritage Commission showcasing Nielsen Steel's role in the history of Oregon was great PR for the company. C-IV even dropped by the archives to thank me for facilitating your research. It's not every day the CEO drops in to thank me for simply doing my job."

Maddie laughed. "I'm glad it was beneficial for you. I enjoyed the research on that one."

"How can I help you today? You working on another project that'll make me look good?"

She kept her smile bright even though this research could

get dicey. Over the weekend, she'd found references to the Nielsens having Nazi ties in the 1930s. The family had done a decent job of burying that part of their history, but there were old newspaper articles that couldn't be erased. "I'm not actually researching Nielsen Steel at all."

She explained about her project and potential for correspondence between the Kochers and Nielsens, then used the computer tablet on the counter to identify which boxes she needed pulled. Tasks complete, she settled in at a corner table in the empty archive. When the archivist delivered a dozen boxes on a rolling cart, Maddie dove in.

Ninety minutes later, she hit pay dirt in the form of letters from Sally Kocher to Clifford I and his wife, Gladys. With six boxes yet to be explored, Maddie used her phone to photograph the letters without reading. She wasn't permitted to scan the documents with her own equipment, but would submit a request for the archivist to scan them for her. The fragility of the papers had to be taken into account. Photos would work if these were deemed too delicate for scanning.

An hour after that, she had gone through all of C-I's personal papers. He died in 1946, and C-II took over the company for the next four decades. C-III's run went from 1985-2012, and now they were in the era of C-IV. The archives contained papers through 2000, as recent documents were housed in an active work repository on another floor of this building. There was no reason for Maddie to believe she'd need access to any of those papers, but she would be back to look at the records from C-II's era, as Otto Kocher had survived into the 1970s and it was possible correspondence between families had continued through the generations.

For now, she had what she needed, plus, it was nearly five o'clock and she had a date.

Well, sort of.

It *felt* like a date. So much so that she'd turned off her inner flirt at Saturday's wine tasting, even though she'd been attracted to the woman Andrea had invited to meet her. Flirting would've felt dishonest.

She packed up her notes and glanced at her phone. She had five minutes to get to the lobby to meet Josh so they could sit in a dark, romantic bar and flirt shamelessly.

At the archivist's desk, she thanked the woman for her help and submitted her request for high-resolution scans of the letters from the Kocher family, and notes and journal entries by Gladys Nielsen.

"I'm sorry, but before I can provide you with the PDFs, I was told we'd need more information on why you're researching Clifford Nielsen the first." The woman's face flushed red. "Sorry. I just received a request from one of our executives." She lowered her voice to a conspiratorial whisper and added, "He said the request came directly from C-IV. He's…protective of his family's legacy."

Maddie knew it had been too easy. "I can forward you my scope of work, and you can let your boss—or Mr. Nielsen— know I'm more concerned with the Kochers' work and travels. I found letters today that show C-I and his wife, Gladys, corresponded regularly, and C-I joined them on a few of their digs in eastern Oregon. The research I did today will go a long way to making sure we have a satisfactory outcome with the tribes, and they will be so pleased with Nielsen Steel's aid in my research."

"Yes. Well, Nielsen is always pleased to be able to assist the tribes." She grimaced. "I'm sorry, but I probably shouldn't have let you photograph the family papers without permission. I've…never received this kind of notice before— not with a professional researcher working on a government contract, anyway."

Maddie didn't want to get this woman fired, but she also wouldn't delete the photos. Not until she knew they'd been backed up to the cloud, at least. "If Mr. Nielsen is concerned about his great-grandparents being associated with looting, he should know even the Kocher family isn't in any sort of legal trouble for looting, and they robbed hundreds of graves. I will keep Nielsen Steel out of the public report. This will have burial location information so it's all protected data and not subject to the Freedom of Information Act."

The woman smiled. "That's a relief. Thank you. I'm sorry I had to say any of this."

"I understand. It's a sensitive issue."

She left the archive and checked her phone as she waited for the elevator. The doors opened, and she glanced up to see a lone man in a suit. She stepped inside and returned her gaze to her screen, smiling as she read Trina's texts.

Twenty floors later, she stepped out into the ornate lobby with a forest of plants, a quarry of marble, and an ocean of fountains. A dozen people stood in a swarm in front of the elevator, eager eyes on the lift's other occupant. She frowned and glanced over, then realized he was none other than the mega-rich CEO of Nielsen Steel, Clifford Nielsen the fourth.

He cast her a faint smile before stepping out to deal with the swarm, probably missing the quiet of their shared elevator ride.

She wove through the crowd—how did they know he'd be on that elevator?—and made her way to the fountain where she and Josh had agreed to meet. She stared at the flowing water, which poured from delicate-looking metallic roses linked by an intricate network of thorny metal vines.

Like wine, she didn't know much about art, but she knew what she liked, and this design landed in a sweet spot. The oxidized copper that made up the rose petals and vines was a pretty matte green that contrasted sharply with the stark white of the marble basin. The discoloration made her think of the skeleton with the red staining on the clavicles and scapulae. Odd that it wasn't green from copper.

She shook the thought aside. She was off work now and staring at a lovely fountain. No more thoughts of Nazis and looting for the night. She focused on the roses, finding the choice of green copper to be interesting for a steel company. They could easily have chosen industrial steel artwork that would also have worked, but it would have been bland compared to this, which brought to mind the impenetrable barrier in Sleeping Beauty combined with the perfection of a rose in bloom. In places, the water dripped instead of poured, like rain or tears.

She felt hands on her hips, and a man spoke softly in her ear. "Hey, beautiful." Lips touched her neck, and she shivered from Josh's kiss. "C-IV is staring at you as he talks to some suits across the lobby. What's that about?"

She turned and cupped his face in one palm, while her other hand settled on his hip. If they were being watched, she'd play her part as girlfriend and enjoy every second. "No idea. I shared the elevator with him, but didn't notice because I was reading texts from Trina."

His nostrils flared, and he pulled back a tiny bit. The movements were small, but she'd felt his body stiffen beneath her hands.

"How's Treen?" he asked.

Did he and Trina not get along? If so, it was one-sided. Trina only ever said good things about him. Plus, she never would have suggested they meet if she didn't like the guy. "She's fine. She was just checking in."

She wanted to ask what was up, but this wasn't the place or time. Over Josh's shoulder, she could see C-IV making a beeline for them. She rose on her toes and brushed her lips over Josh's. "Incoming," she whispered.

He slipped an arm around her waist and turned to face Clifford Nielsen the fourth.

The CEO reached the fountain and stood beside them, as if the waterworks had been his goal all along. "Mr. Warner, you're quite the celebrity now. And here you are with the lovely Ms. Foster."

Maddie startled at the fact that he knew who she was, but clearly, he'd been alerted to her presence in the archive. He'd probably been given a copy of her driver's license photo, which had been scanned into the system by security.

Both Josh and C-IV shifted to face each other. "Maddie," Josh said, "meet Clifford Nielsen the fourth. Nielsen, this is my girlfriend, Madeline Foster."

"A pleasure to meet you, Mr. Nielsen." She offered her hand, and he took it, holding on a bit longer than customary. Like he was making some sort of point.

"Likewise. I understand you're researching my grand-parents."

"Your great-grandparents, actually, and in only a round-about way. I was searching for correspondence between Gladys and Clifford the first, and Otto and Sally Kocher, of Kocher Lumber Mills.

"Ah yes, wood and steel. Between our two families, we built most of Portland."

"And your family business is currently among the Fortune 500, while Kocher Lumber Mills is long gone."

"Well, Otto was short-sighted and for several decades didn't plant trees after he cut them, while Great-Grandpa Cliff included steel recycling in our business model during World War II and never went back. Their product is rapidly disappearing, and ours is reusable." He frowned. "I want to review your report before you submit it to the government and tribes."

She'd expected him to ask her to delete her photos. This

request surprised her. It was customary for archives to request copies of resulting reports as part of their research access policy, but that didn't grant right to review prior to publication. She'd signed the Nielsen Steel Archive Access Agreement on the tablet when she submitted her box requests, and a PDF receipt had been emailed to her on the spot. "I will, of course, adhere to the access agreement."

Did he know what that meant?

His blue eyes turned a flinty steel worthy of the family business, and she took that to mean he did. She was glad she was on solid legal ground, because C-IV could make her life miserable if he had a loophole to exploit.

He turned to Josh. "Convenient to find you here today. After you were all over the news last week, I dug a little deeper into both your background and your proposal to provide personal security services for our key personnel. I'm intrigued by what Raptor has to offer. I'd like to meet again and discuss it further."

"Senator Ravissant will not attend any such meeting, Mr. Nielsen."

"Please, call me Cliff. And I understand Ravissant won't be involved. Get Hatcher here for a meeting in two weeks, and we'll talk."

"I'll ask him, but usually his travel is planned far in advance."

"I'm looking for a company that can handle on-site security for this building along with my other assets across the globe. Nielsen Steel is one of the US's biggest steel manufacturers, and our European and African affiliates remain China's biggest competitors on those continents. Now we're looking at expanding into Indonesia. This will be a worldwide and extremely lucrative contract for a company like Raptor."

"I'm surprised you aren't attending the security symposium on the island of Nabat in Indonesia this coming week-end, then."

"No time. I have business in Japan next week. Besides, I can choose my security team from Portland." The CEO cocked his head. "Will Keith Hatcher be on Nabat?"

"No. Actually, I was supposed to go, but my priorities changed, so Keith decided to send another senior operative from our DC offices."

"Then a trip to Portland two weeks from now shouldn't be an issue. Three o'clock, Monday. My assistant will set it up." The CEO nodded to them both, then turned and walked away.

Maddie didn't dare say what she was thinking about the man's presumption while they still stood in the lobby of his high-rise building. Instead, she turned to Josh and said in a falsely cheerful voice. "Shall we get some wine, then?"

Josh's eyes narrowed as he watched the retreating CEO. "Wine. Yes. I definitely need wine."

*J*osh wanted to be excited by the offer from Nielsen —after all, hadn't he met with the guy two weeks ago, hoping to cut a deal just like this? But something didn't sit right.

It was just too easy, given how fast Nielsen had shut him down when he realized access to Rav wasn't part of the package. So what was the angle now? What did Clifford Nielsen the fourth want from Raptor?

The only thing that had changed since their meeting was Josh had been on the news defending a young man who was set up to appear dangerous. But that was off-the-clock volun-teer work. While Raptor had lent their name and logo to the T-shirt—like a Little League team sponsor—the project was basic charity. Hell, there wasn't even a tax write-off in it for Raptor except for the cost of the shirts, because no one was getting paid for anything.

But Nielsen was right about one thing: Keith would fly out for the meeting, no question.

This was what Josh wanted, wasn't it? He needed some big clients to get the Portland office off the ground. Nielsen Steel was as big as it got in the Portland area.

Maddie discussed the wine with the waiter and ordered while Josh texted Keith and shared the news.

Keith's response was immediate.

KEITH

Wow. Great job. I'll have to look at my calendar when I get to the office tomorrow, but I can probably shift things around to make a trip that way happen.

JOSH

We can probably push it back if needed. His insistence on the date was just a power play.

We'll play his game for now.

A moment later, he texted again.

I hear you and Maddie are hitting it off. I'll see if Trina can get time off work and join me. She'd love to see Maddie.

Josh's heart rate kicked up at the thought of seeing Trina again. One of the perks of moving here was getting away from her. Away from the guilt that had eaten at him for years.

He wanted to say no, but that would just raise questions he had no intention of answering.

He looked at Maddie, who sat across the table from him,

patiently waiting for him to put down the phone and show her some attention.

He'd woken up this morning with her on his mind, his heart racing just knowing he'd see her today. Knowing he'd probably break all his rules and kiss her again. And she'd kiss him back, making those soft noises that drove him wild.

And now, with Trina in the conversation, he was again reminded of the physical similarities between the two women. Both short, fair, brown hair. Sexy glasses. Similar professions.

Was Maddie just a replacement for Trina in his mind? Was the rush of excitement he felt when he looked at her just an extension of his desire for a woman he could and would never have?

"What's wrong?" Maddie asked.

He shook his head. "Everything's fine. Just confused by Nielsen's sudden about-face." He glanced at his phone. "Keith's going to try to swing the trip. He suggested he bring Trina with him, if you'd like a visit with her."

Maddie's face lit up. "That would be wonderful!" Then her brow furrowed. "Unless…you don't like Trina? I sort of sensed some tension in you when she came up earlier."

"I think Trina's great." That was true enough. "Keith is a lucky man." He didn't want to overplay it, so he left it at that.

She studied his face for a long moment then said, "Tell Keith I'd love to see her." She slowly smiled, "So I can pump her for information on all the women you've dated."

He forced a laugh. "You can try, but she won't be able to tell you much."

The truth was, for the last four years, his love life had been little more than a series of one-night stands. He'd compared every woman to Trina, which was a lousy thing to do, but he hadn't figured out how to shut down that part of his brain. In the end, he found he wasn't interested in anything beyond superficial, and he'd made damn sure the women he dated were fine with that arrangement.

No one got serious, and no one got hurt.

Now, for the first time, he found himself comparing yet another woman to Trina, and Maddie was…ahead, for lack of a better word. But was it simply because Trina wasn't here? Because they were similar? Or was Maddie Foster the person he'd been seeking all along?

The waiter arrived with the bottle of wine, and while Maddie went through the motions of tasting and approving, Josh texted Keith, letting him know Maddie was eager to see Trina. Task complete, he set aside his phone and focused on the woman before him.

"How is Desmond doing?" she asked.

"The media circus around him has finally died down, but just this morning, the Portland Police Bureau let him know he's not under investigation—while the officer who refused to stand down is. He has ties to the White Patriots. As for Desmond, thank God for all those rolling cameras."

"It's weird how the White Patriots didn't consider the cameras."

"I think they didn't consider that we'd have people there who would know how to fight unarmed. I think they were counting on Desmond—or any of us, really—to be carrying a weapon. And let's face it, if he'd had a weapon on him, even if it never came out, that would be the story right now."

"I'm glad he's going to be okay."

"The publicity has been positive overall. We get more people showing up at the trainings every night we have one." It was one of the reasons he'd been unable to see Maddie in the evenings. He was taking tonight off, though. He needed a break. Needed to see her.

"That can't be a bad thing."

"Not bad at all, but it requires screening everyone to make sure there are no Trojan horses, or glory hounds."

"Oh jeez. I didn't even think of that."

"Nature of the business." He shrugged. "How did your research go today?"

"Pretty much as described to C-IV. I found letters by Sally Kocher to Gladys Nielsen, and Gladys kept a journal, while C-I's notes are sporadic, he did keep most of the letters he received, as far as I can tell. I haven't had time to read through any of it yet."

"What's next?"

"Painted Hills. I'll be researching at the visitor center archives and visiting some of the places where Otto dug."

"The Painted Hills are amazing," he said. His take was far from original, but it was true. The rolling multicolored hills were one of his favorite places in his home state, and he hadn't visited the region in far too many years.

"This is my favorite part of my job. I love research. I love discovering new sources of information. Even today at the archives was exciting. You never know what you'll find when you open a box."

She was beautiful as she spoke with such enthusiasm. Eyes bright, smile wide. He ached with the pleasure of being with her. This feeling wasn't a substitute reaction.

He liked her. Not the idea of her. *Her*. Maddie.

"Will you come home with me tonight?" Her jaw dropped in a way that was both endearing and made him shake his head. "Sorry. I meant…I'd like you to meet Ava."

"Are you sure that's a good idea?"

He covered her hand with his on the table. "I am. But… she probably won't make it easy."

She held his gaze. Her mouth moved in the slightest of smiles. Invisible except to the most observant person. Or to someone who was fascinated by her. "Okay."

He couldn't help himself and leaned forward and brushed his lips over hers. "Thank you."

She gripped his shirt in one hand, holding him close to her, and kissed him, her mouth soft and sweet. "We aren't getting involved," she said against his lips.

"Nope," he whispered. "Definitely not." He slipped his tongue between her lips in the briefest of kisses.

"Good," she said in a husky voice. "Now, take me to meet your niece."

Chapter Eight

Ava Warner was not pleased to meet Maddie. At all.

She did that thing where she glared at Maddie whenever Josh or Owen weren't paying attention. It made Maddie laugh because the pretty, willowy teen was so sincere in her annoyance and so very bad at conveying it in a less melodramatic way.

"Uncle Josh tells me you hang out with Nazis. You know we're Jewish, right?"

"Ava," Josh said in a warning tone. "I also told you Maddie has no choice but to deal with Troy Kocher so the bones can be returned to the tribe."

"Troy is a piece of work," Maddie said to Ava. "I don't know if I've ever so thoroughly disliked someone from the moment I met them."

"Yeah, I wonder what that's like," Ava said, heavy on the sarcasm.

Maddie burst out laughing as Josh turned to his niece in horror. "Ava!"

But Maddie kept laughing, and after a pause, a laugh escaped Owen too.

Ava glared at Owen across the dinner table—they were eating Thai food Maddie and Josh had picked up on the way home—but when she looked at the big, scarred former SEAL, Ava's lips started to twitch, and a beat later, she was laughing too.

Josh sat there, shaking his head as the rest of them laughed.

When her laughter subsided, Maddie said, "Seriously, though, I don't think I've ever met someone who would go to a racist rally without a hood before. I wake up in the middle of the night sometimes and wonder what is happening to our country. And I wonder if it's better that the hoods are off."

"I think it's better without the hoods," Josh said. "Like I told Troy, a security specialist's best weapon is our eyes. We see them. We can fight them."

"Yet even when the cameras are running and they're surrounded by cops, that guy who cut Desmond almost got away," Ava said.

"We've got a long, ugly fight ahead of us," Owen said. "Racism is built into the system, and some cops will focus on the Black man as the aggressor even when the white man— who is openly attending a white supremacist rally—came into the counterprotesters' safe zone."

"The purpose was to scare more counterprotesters from showing up at the next rally," Maddie said.

"It's having the opposite effect," Josh said. "As I mentioned earlier, Bond Ironworks has had dozens of calls from people who want to stand up to the White Patriots. Every training includes more people. Honestly, it's given me more hope than I've felt in a long time."

Maddie wrapped a wide, flat noodle around her fork. "When is your next training session?"

"Tomorrow night, then we'll take a few days off because Thursday, Owen and I are going to R&R. I won't be back until Saturday. Then we'll do another training on Sunday midday and more in the evenings next week to prep for the rally on the following Sunday."

"Are you going to be able to continue with the volunteer work once you're working for R&R, Owen?" Maddie asked.

"Not until I get a car. Can't have Josh driving me back and forth all the time. But I wanted to see if R&R is a good fit before I get a vehicle." He fixed his gaze on Ava. "Sometimes having a car—the freedom of it—is too much for me. I need to be certain I won't slide back into temptation."

"Why are you looking at me?" Ava asked without hostility.

"Because you're young and going to high school." He held up a hand to cut off what she was about to say. "I know you're a smart girl. I know you can—and want to—make the right choices. I also know you've dealt with some shit, and self-medicating will hold a special appeal. It's a slippery slope. I didn't start with heroin, but I almost ended with it.

"Before I came out here, I told Josh I'd be a hundred percent honest with you about how drugs took over my life." He held out his arm, showing her the track marks. "My addiction still owns me. I'm still afraid I'll lose the battle. Even after three years clean, I can't be trusted with a car. I honestly don't know if I can ever be trusted with that kind of freedom. Learn from my mistakes. Let me be your cautionary tale."

Maddie's eyes teared at the raw honesty and vulnerability shown by this former SEAL. She'd bet the military man inside him hated showing this weakness. Yet here he was, sharing his greatest regret and shame in hopes it would prevent a troubled girl from following the same path.

Ava nodded and cleared her throat. "Thank you. I won't forget."

Owen nodded. "Good."

A sharp buzz sounded, and both Owen and Josh looked at their phones. Josh cursed. "Raptor alert from one of our techs. Aww, fuck. Voigt Forum doxed us. Desmond too."

A jolt of fear ran through Maddie, and her gaze jerked to Ava. The blood drained from the girl's cheeks, her pale skin looking ghostly against her long dark hair. "What does that mean, Uncle Josh?"

Josh jumped from his seat. "We need to see what they posted."

They all followed Josh into his office. He dropped into the chair and woke his large desktop computer. In seconds, the alt-right conspiracy theory website, Voigt Forum, filled the screen. The home page featured photos of Josh and the others lined up to protect the people who'd gathered to protest the white supremacist gathering. The article was about Raptor and Bond Ironworks and their plan to continue providing protection at future rallies. It included not just Josh's address, but also a photo of the house they were currently inside.

"Why would they do this?" Ava asked.

"They're afraid if too many counterprotesters show up, they won't be able to use the rallies to recruit more members," Josh said. He reached out and squeezed the girl's hand. "By posting our address, they're trying to scare me off. Stop the training sessions at the gym." He turned back to the monitor. "I need to contact the police. Seattle has a registry for people in danger of swatting attacks, but I don't think Portland does. It's time to change that."

"Swatting?" Ava asked. "Is that when people call the police to report fake crimes so SWAT teams will be called in?"

"Yeah. It's basically attempted murder, but getting the cops to pull the trigger," Owen said.

Josh ran a hand over his face. "Ava, you're going to need

to come with us to R&R on Thursday. I can't leave you here alone."

"I don't need a babysitter."

"This isn't about you. It's about them." Josh pointed to the computer screen.

"But I have plans with Marcus on Friday. I haven't been able to see him all summer, and we were going to the lake with Casey and the others."

"I'm sorry, Ava. It's too dangerous."

Maddie put her hand on Josh's shoulder. "Ava can stay with me."

"Aren't you going to the Painted Hills?" Josh asked.

"I'm going to the visitor center on Thursday. I'll be gone all day but home that night."

"Troy Kocher might know where you live. And he knows you're associated with me. Ava might not be safe alone at your house either."

"Then she can come with me to the Painted Hills, and Friday, I can drop her at the lake with her friends." She glanced at Ava, who clearly wasn't sure if she liked this idea but wasn't ready to shoot it down either. "If you haven't been there, the Thomas Condon Paleontology and Visitor Center has some great exhibits. You can explore while I work."

"Sounds boring," Ava sighed. "It's just a bunch of old rocks."

"You can learn about hell pigs," Maddie said.

"What are hell pigs?"

"Come with me, and you'll find out."

Ava looked from Maddie to Josh. "I don't know."

"It's either go with Maddie, or come with us to R&R."

Ava pursed her lips. Finally, she huffed out a sigh and said, "Fine. I'll go see the old rocks."

Josh cleared his throat and fixed Ava with a stare.

Ava wrinkled her nose, then offered Maddie a smile that might even be genuine. "Thank you. For the offer."

Maddie smiled. Thursday alone with Ava was bound to be interesting.

*J*osh hung up the phone after speaking to an officer with the Portland Police Bureau. Alerts would go out informing officers that any 911 calls that indicated violence at his address were to be handled with caution—phone calls would be made to Josh and Ava first to confirm the report. Officers sent to the scene would be informed of the likelihood of it being a false alarm.

He left the office to find Maddie watching TV with Owen and Ava. She smiled when he stepped into the room, and his heart squeezed. It was crazy, this attraction. And the timing was terrible.

In theory, he barely knew her, but they'd spent hours on the phone in the two weeks since they'd met, and he felt like he knew her. Like he'd known her forever. Plus, she was a Pacific Northwester—had grown up in the same state he had, graduating from high school two years after he did. She felt familiar to him. They had a similar history, even though they'd never met.

She rose from the couch. "All set?"

He nodded. "The police chief was personally informed, and she's taking the situation seriously." He smiled. "The irony of being in the high-end private security business and having to turn to the police for this."

"It's because of me, isn't it, Uncle Josh?"

He couldn't deny Ava's question, much as he wanted to. If he were the only one at risk, he'd contact the police, but it would be handled differently. He should have considered her safety when he signed on to train the volunteers. When he'd calculated what he was risking, he hadn't factored in Ava. So much for putting her first. He was a failure as a father.

He'd quit now if it wasn't too late.

And it sucked that Voigt Forum was counting on that reaction. Not only to scare him away, but to discourage others from stepping into his place.

His hand curled into a fist. "I won't let anyone hurt you, Ladybug."

Her mom had started calling her that when she was one and wore a ladybug raincoat and boots to play in the rain. Josh had picked it up, and it had been her nickname for years, but he realized when the name slipped out that he hadn't called her that since he'd moved to Portland.

He knelt in front of her. "And I won't send you to live with anyone else. Ever. I promise."

Ava swiped at her cheek. "'Kay."

"But I need you to help me out. I will need to know where you are at all times—not because I don't trust you, but because it's the only way to protect you. I'm going to put a tracker in your purse. You are *not* under surveillance. You understand?"

She nodded, and he kissed her forehead. "We'll talk more in a bit. Right now, I need to walk Maddie out."

Ava nodded and Josh rose.

Maddie stood as well. "I'll pick you up Thursday morning at seven," she said to Ava.

Ava groaned. "It's summer vacation. I should get to sleep in." But it was a good-natured grumble.

Josh followed Maddie out the door and down the front walk to the driveway. When she would have paused by her car, he placed a hand on her hip and pulled her into the shadows next to the garage. "Thank you for taking Ava on Thursday and letting her stay with you through Saturday. She hasn't been able to see her friends much this summer, and she needs that connection."

"You're welcome. I'm glad I can help."

"I think she'll be nicer than she was at the start tonight."

She placed a hand on his cheek, her fingers stroking the stubble on his jaw, and he leaned in to the touch. "It's fine if she's not. I can take it. There's nothing Ava can say that would hurt me. I know what she's gone through and that it's not really personal."

"But still, don't let her get away with being a brat. She's better than that."

"Deal."

She continued stroking his jaw, and he felt all sorts of things he shouldn't be feeling when he had so much on his plate.

"Josh? Owen is on the right path and you're doing great with Ava. But you're forgetting someone. Promise me you'll take care of yourself too, okay?"

He held her gaze, his stomach tight. "That's a luxury I can't afford."

"But you need to. Listen, on Thursday, when Owen is busy with R&R paperwork or whatever, grab a kayak and paddle to the center of the lake, and then…just breathe. Or fish. Or whatever relaxes you. Just promise me you'll give yourself some silence. Take a time out."

He'd mentioned to her how much he loved being out on the water during one of their phone calls. Now he closed his eyes and imagined what she described and slowly nodded. "Deal," he said, echoing her. He cupped her face in his hands. "There's something else I want to do. And it's very, very selfish."

"Oh yeah? What's that?"

He lowered his head and took her mouth with his, his tongue diving deep as she gripped his shoulders and kissed him back, her response just as fierce as his kiss. He pressed her to the side of the garage, his hand on her neck as his other found her breast.

She threaded her fingers though his hair, her mouth nipping his lips, her tongue meeting his as she made the sounds he imagined late at night as he stroked himself. Now he pressed his erection to her belly, and her hand left his hair to slide between their bodies and caress him.

Layers of clothing separated them, but it didn't matter. Her touch triggered the best kind of ache. "I want to be deep inside you," he whispered. "To make you scream as you come. To lick every part of you."

She bit his earlobe. "That doesn't sound selfish at all."

"Oh, but it is. I want you splayed on my bed and utterly abandoned to my touch. All mine."

"You're killing me, Warner."

"I think about you," he continued, "as I slide my hand down my cock and imagine how you'd feel. How you'd look when I make you come with my mouth. If I could do one thing that was selfish, just for me, it would be you."

She gave a husky laugh. "Your kind of selfish sounds amazing." She kissed him, then pulled back as far as the wall at her back would allow, which was only about a half an inch. "It's a shame we can't get involved right now."

"A damn shame," he said, his mouth on her neck, pressing openmouthed kisses on her smooth skin, trying to get his raging lust under control.

"So, when are we going to not see each other again?"

He smiled against her neck and took a deep breath, trying to make sense of their schedules for the next few days while the ache in his balls tried to eclipse rational thought. "Saturday night. I'll take you out to dinner after you deliver Ava home. A thank-you for helping out."

"Okay. It's not a date, then."

He stepped back and brushed his hands down her clothes, straightening the top where it had ridden up thanks to his groping hands. He threaded his fingers through hers and led her back to her car. He paused and cupped her face, brushing his thumb over her lips—full and lush from his kisses—and his brain went straight to wondering how swollen her other lips might be. He pressed his mouth to hers one more time. This time, he was gentle, mouth closed, an almost proper good-night. "Text me when you get home so I know you're safe."

"Will do."

He stood in the driveway, watching as her taillights disappeared into the darkness. Teasing aside, he had no idea how he was going to balance this thing that was definitely happening with Maddie and the rest of his responsibilities. Wanting her was selfish and wrong. But he wasn't even going to pretend to fight it anymore.

Chapter Nine

$\mathcal{A}$va slept for the first hour of the drive as they left Portland and headed east. Maddie listened to Morning Edition to keep herself entertained. The rally in Portland eleven days ago might have faded from national news, but the local affiliates were still covering the story as the city braced for another rally in ten days. Portland's police chief was interviewed, and she spoke at length about the rising number of what were essentially planned brawls breaking out in parts of the city.

The factions involved were usually some form of white supremacist group versus another group aligned to defend against fascism, but the anarchists never wanted to be left out. When questioned as to whether or not the Raptor/Bond Ironworks-sponsored group was involved in the brawls that plagued the city, the police chief stated she'd spoken with Josh Warner, Arthur Bond, and Raptor's CEO, Keith Hatcher, and been assured that the newly formed group's only goal was to provide security for people who protested the increasingly active white supremacist movement in the Portland area. They would not in any way engage in brawls with the

White Patriots, KKK, or other groups. Their goal was simply to show up and make it a safer place for other people to show their opposition to the racist rallies that were occurring with alarming frequency.

The Raptor-Bond Alliance, as the news was now calling it, was created on the simple hope that with safety, more would show up and demonstrate to the white supremacists in the region that they were far outnumbered.

They played portions of an interview with Josh and Keith. When asked if Raptor's owner, Maryland Senator Alec Ravissant, supported the volunteer project, Keith stated that Ravissant was pleased with Josh's initiative and reminded the interviewer of the counterprotest the senator had attended last October.

"Senator Ravissant," Keith continued, "is a firm believer in free speech and understands that cities like Portland must issue permits that make the events possible, but he also believes firmly in the right to oppose hate groups like the White Patriots, and the only way to send a message is to let them know they're outnumbered."

"Keep in mind," Josh said, picking up the thread of the interview, "these rallies aren't harmless free speech exercises. They are about recruitment, more soldiers for their white army. The next step is arming and training, and then armed conflict. They want nothing less than for white people to use violence to—in their words—'take back' our country from Black Americans, from Native Americans, from Asians and brown people. From Jewish people like myself. They say they're concerned about immigration and they just want to stop more brown people from coming in—reprehensible enough, but that's their slippery slope. They want nothing less than eradication. The fundamental goals of the White Power movement haven't changed since the founders of the movement returned from Vietnam and began organizing.

"It hasn't changed since Oklahoma City—which McVeigh had hoped would be the signal to start the next war. Read the manifestos, listen to the scholars who've been studying the movement for decades. This current group is simply following the old playbook. What we're doing is the first line of defense, to try to halt recruitment in their tracks. Let them know we see them and won't stand idly by and politely let them use our parks and streets to recruit for their army of hate.

"Plus," Josh continued, "there's a darker side that goes hand in hand with these rallies, which is using the gatherings —and the brawls that the police chief mentioned—to further accelerationist goals."

"Could you define 'accelerationist' for our listeners who are unfamiliar with the term?" the interviewer asked.

"Accelerationism relies on the idea that Western governments are irreparably corrupt. Some white supremacists believe the best thing they can do is accelerate their demise by sowing chaos. You'll find accelerationist ideas cited in manifestos written by mass shooters and referenced in white supremacist chat rooms. Accelerationist literature is frequently found in the browsing history of white men who've committed random acts of violence. This isn't confined to the US by any means. The shooter in New Zealand specifically cited accelerationist ideology."

"Uncle Josh is really smart."

Maddie startled and pressed her hand to her heart. "I didn't realize you were awake." She returned her hand to the steering wheel and kept her gaze on the road as she added, "And yes, your uncle is very smart. He's been researching the White Power movement for some time."

"I'm scared for him," Ava whispered.

The NPR interview ended, and Maddie turned off the radio. "These are scary people." She searched for reassuring words, but the truth was, Maddie was scared too. Doxing and the risk of swatting was nothing to wave away. "But one thing your uncle knows is how to protect himself and others. I heard a rumor he got medals for that kind of thing when he was a SEAL."

"He doesn't talk about being a SEAL with me."

"I don't think he can talk about the missions. They're probably classified."

"Yeah. I guess." Maddie felt the girl's gaze as she shifted in her seat. "What's up with you two? Are you dating or just sleeping together?"

Maddie took a deep breath. The first question was reasonable, the second she suspected was intended to trigger a reaction. "We're not sure where this is going but agree it was bad timing for us to meet."

"So you're just fucking him."

She gripped the steering wheel and studied the white lines on the two-lane highway. This was a seventeen-year-old girl who probably knew little of sex or love or dating and who very much wanted to put Maddie in her place. "Whether your uncle and I are sleeping together or not is really none of your business. Just as your sex life is none of mine."

"I don't have a sex life. I'm not a slut."

"Honey, having sex doesn't make you a slut. Having sex with ten people doesn't make you a slut. Because there is no such thing as a slut. Slut shaming is a construct meant to control women and their bodies. Men are not condemned for the same act. It goes both ways, or it's not a thing. If it's wrong for a woman to have sex, it's wrong for a man too."

"Men don't get pregnant."

"Men cause one hundred percent of pregnancies. Every single unwanted pregnancy was the result of male ejaculation. It is literally impossible to accidently get pregnant without a penis being involved."

"Artificial insemination—"

"I said accidently. No one gets pregnant accidently through artificial insemination. And even with in vitro pregnancies, a guy ejaculated at some point."

"My dad says women who have sex before marriage are sluts, and my mom wasn't a slut."

"Your mom made her own decision about her body and her relationship, and you can honor that, but your dad is flat-out wrong about the rest. Did your dad have sex before he married your mom?"

"He never said."

"And he didn't because he knew it invalidated his entire argument because it would make him a slut." She sighed. "Listen, sex is not something to be taken lightly—unless you're on good emotional ground and can handle a light relationship. You're young, and the last few years have been horrible. This would be a terrible time for you to wade into the physical aspects of relationships. But when you're ready, when you know who you are and can continue to be that person even after physical intimacy—because sex changes relationships, don't let anyone tell you otherwise—then it can be wonderful, whether you're in a committed relationship or just fooling around. But it's your body. Your call."

"Are you sure Uncle Josh would want you to have this conversation with me?"

"If your uncle is a slut shamer, then he's not someone I would ever want near my vagina."

Ava let out a squeal that sounded like a shocked laugh.

Maddie smiled but added, "I'm serious. Don't ever let anyone touch you if they don't respect your personhood. And anyone who would have sex with you and then call you a slut doesn't see you as equal."

A few miles went by in silence, then Ava said in a quiet voice, "I sometimes wonder if I'm gay. But there was a senior

at my school last year, and when I was around him, I definitely didn't feel gay. But he was such a jerk too. Like a total
pig when it came to girls. So why did I like him?"

Emotion flooded Maddie. She remembered her own
questions at that age, but she'd had reasonable parents and
good friends to turn to for answers. Ava had lost her mother
at fourteen, and her father, according to both Josh and now
Ava, was seriously lacking.

"For the second part, some attractions can be purely
physical. A certain look or manner can speak to something in
you. It's like having a crush on an actor or musician. You
don't actually know them, but you find them appealing. The
senior last year, he did that for you, but you knew him just
well enough to see below the surface and know there wasn't
anything worth having. Enjoy the crush, but for your own
emotional protection, don't let it go further than that."

She cleared her throat. "And to speak to the first part, I'm
bisexual, and it took me a long time to figure that out."

"You are? Does that mean you'll cheat on Uncle Josh?"

Maddie wanted to pull over for this conversation, but had
a feeling that would freak Ava out and that she'd only been
able to bring it up because Maddie had to focus on the road.
"Just because I'm sexually attracted to both men and women
doesn't mean I don't believe in monogamy. I've never cheated
on anyone—male or female—I've dated. The idea that
bisexual people can't commit is put forth to stigmatize us and
strip us of our allies."

"Oh. I guess my question was kind of offensive."

"A little, but you get a pass. I realize you have your own
questions and your father wasn't the most open-minded of
souls." She would assume Ava hadn't been trying to hurt her
in hopes of driving a wedge between her and Josh, especially
given that so far, Ava had been straightforward on the
aiming-to-hurt front.

"How did you know you were bisexual?"

"After wondering for years, I fell in love with my best friend in college, and it became clear the feelings weren't in any way platonic."

"So you dated your best friend?"

"No. At the same time I became certain I was bi, she became certain she wasn't."

"That must have been…awkward. Did you stop being friends?"

"No. We talked about it. A lot. And once I knew it couldn't happen between us because Trina wasn't wired the same way, I moved on. I had to. Our friendship recovered."

"Figures it would be Trina." Ava sighed. "Uncle Josh is in love with Trina. Has been for years."

Maddie stiffened, her whole body going rigid as she gripped the steering wheel.

Ava flushed and, seeming to realize what she'd said, slapped a hand over her mouth. "Shit. I didn't mean—"

"You shouldn't share things your uncle told you in confidence, Ava."

"He didn't—I mean, I…" Her voice trailed off.

Was she lying in hopes of driving Maddie away, or had Ava blurted out a simple truth? She couldn't ask. If it was true, it was violating Josh's privacy. But if it was a lie…

She remembered Josh's reaction to seeing her photo album of Trina. How he'd flirted with her and kissed her after looking at the album. Had he imagined he was kissing Trina? In college, friends had commented often enough that they looked like sisters.

Was Josh's interest in her simply based on the fact that she made a decent substitute for a woman he couldn't have? A woman Maddie had loved once too?

"A few weeks ago, when Uncle Josh was out, I found a letter he wrote but never sent to Trina."

"You mean you were snooping."

"Yeah. I just—my uncle I barely knew was suddenly my guardian. My dad said so much nasty stuff about Uncle Josh. I needed to know who he was."

Those might be the only words the girl could say that exonerated her in Maddie's mind. Plus, she remembered what it was like to be a teenager. She wasn't proud of the snooping she'd done in her brother's and parents' stuff at fourteen.

"In the letter, Josh said he'd always love her—"

Maddie kept her focus straight ahead, trying not to read Ava's body language even with her peripheral vision. "I don't need to know what the letter said." Much as she wanted to know, it was the right thing to say. To do.

"But I need to talk to someone, because I found out that Uncle Josh didn't move here for me, like he claimed." Ava's voice cracked, and Maddie realized the girl was crying. "He did it to get away from her because he couldn't have her. That's how I know he's going to fall in love with you or someone else and leave me all alone again. Or you'll break his heart, and he'll leave because he's not here for me at all."

The shoulder was wide on this rural highway, and Maddie pulled to the side and put the car in Park. She reached across the console and took Ava's hand. "Your uncle loves you, and no matter what he wrote in that letter, he came here for *you*."

"You don't know that. You don't know him."

"And you just admitted you don't know him either. So all we can do is base our conclusions on the man's actions and our conversations with him. This is what I know: the moment Josh knew you were in trouble, he moved well over two thousand miles and became your guardian. Also, he didn't rent an apartment for you both when he got here—which would have been reasonable, given the situation. No, he bought a house.

You probably don't know what a commitment and investment that is, but I can tell you, I'm only two years younger than your Uncle Josh and I haven't bought a house here, and this is where I *know* I want to live for the rest of my life. He bought it for you because he wanted you to know you have a home with him."

"Keith helped him buy it. Probably because he knew Uncle Josh is in love with his wife and wanted to get rid of him."

The words stung every time Ava said them, but Maddie shoved the feeling aside. "Keith gave Josh the job security needed to get a mortgage and committed to Raptor paying rent for the home office to offset the mortgage. That is not Keith forcing Josh away, and you're making a lot of assumptions. Listen, your uncle and I have been talking a lot late at night. He's told me all of this, and he told me why he moved here. He told me he can't get involved with me because you're his number one priority."

"But see, that's another lie. You're dating."

"Would you believe we're trying not to? Something just… happens when we're together. But technically, we've never been on a date."

"Tuesday was a date."

"No, it wasn't. He had a meeting in the Pearl District, and so did I. We met afterward because it was convenient. He's helping me with my creepy client problem."

"Wow, you're more clueless than me. Uncle Josh did not have a meeting in the city on Tuesday."

She cocked her head at the girl. "How would you know that?"

Ava pulled out her cell phone. "Shared calendar. He puts all his meetings on it. You were the only person scheduled on Tuesday. Everything else he did by phone or computer."

Maddie felt a small flush of pleasure—an offset to the

idea that she was a mere replacement for Trina—and then ruthlessly shoved all her invading thoughts aside. None of this was about her. Ava was a confused and hurting young woman who needed to know there was one adult in her life she could count on.

"He's not going to abandon you, Ava. Ever. But he is going to be hurt when he finds out you went snooping in his things."

The girl's eyes grew big with alarm. "Please don't tell him. He'll hate me."

She reached out and pushed the girl's dark hair from her face. "Honey, he could never hate you. He'll understand, but he'll be hurt. You'll have to talk it out. Trust needs to go both ways."

"You *are* going to tell him."

Tell the man I want to have wild, wall-banging sex with that I know he's in love with his best friend's wife? Oh, hell no.

She shook her head. "You'll do it."

"Are you mad he's in love with Trina?" The words were a soft whisper. When the conversation started, she'd wondered if Ava's agenda was to run Maddie off, but now she guessed Ava feared that outcome.

"Josh's unrequited feelings for someone else are none of my business." And she had no doubt on the unrequited part. She and Trina might have grown apart due to the miles that separated them, but she knew Trina, and the woman was crazy in love with Keith. She was the kind of happy that made Maddie envious, but also served as a reminder that that kind of love did exist, and Maddie should settle for nothing less for herself.

She touched the back of Ava's hand. "Whether you like it or not, I'm sticking around. And if things don't work out between your uncle and me, that won't mean you can't reach out to me if you need a woman to talk to."

Ava swiped at her eyes, and Maddie thought she was going to say something along the lines of thank you, but instead, the girl just shrugged. "I'll figure it out."

Maddie let out a soft laugh. Oh, to be seventeen and to have no clue how much you didn't know. "Fine. Just don't rely on Reddit for everything, 'kay?"

Ava gave her a friendly glare, and Maddie put the car in gear and merged back on the highway again. After ten minutes of silence, Ava said, "Does Uncle Josh know you're bi?"

"Yes."

"How many people have you had sex with?"

"At the same time? Seven."

"Seven!"

"No. It's none of your business, Ava. Listen, I'll be honest with you about sex as a concept and relationships in the abstract. I'll help you find a gynecologist if you want information on birth control, but given that I'm sort of maybe involved with your guardian, specifics about me and my history are off-limits."

"It's not like you're going to be my stepmom."

"Maybe not, but my relationship with your uncle needs to remain private between us. And if, after we get to know each other, it feels appropriate to share information about my past relationships with you, I will do so. But I'm not going to answer your sex-history quiz at this stage without a damn good reason. We need trust between us too."

Josh had warned her today wouldn't be easy. Good Lord, he had no idea. And she couldn't tell him about the Trina/snooping part of the conversation at all. It was going to be a difficult debriefing.

"Did you download playlists like I suggested?" Cell coverage would get spotty as they drove through hills and windmills, making streaming music difficult. Maddie wasn't about to risk nearly eight hours in the car round trip without music to entertain the girl.

"Yes. I loaded some audiobooks too."

"Great. We're two hours from the visitor's center. Show me what you've got."

Music cut off the need for conversation, and they settled in, reaching the visitor's center at eleven as planned. Maddie wanted to walk through the exhibits with Ava, but she had hours of research to do. If she finished early enough, they'd drive through the Painted Hills and go on some of the trails. She gave Ava her car keys so she could sit in the car and read or listen to books or music when she was done exploring the small museum.

Maddie settled into the back room, having been given free range of the files. The work was tedious for the most part, but it always felt like a treasure hunt. Somewhere in here could be the gem that proved where the burials came from. The remains could be returned to where they'd been stolen from.

So maybe it was the opposite of a treasure hunt. It was about putting the stolen artifacts and bones back where they came from.

She found what she was searching for buried deep in an archive box from the 1960s, but it wasn't what she'd expected. Correspondence between Otto's son and Clifford II. So, the family association had continued into the next generation. And both families were still looting.

She scanned the files and kept searching, quickly finding more papers that dated right up to the establishment of John Day Fossil Beds National Monument in October 1975—after the passing of the National Historic Preservation Act of 1966 and the Archaeological and Historic Protection act of 1974. If she could find proof the families were digging on federal land, or after the passing of either act, she'd have more leverage to break up the collection. She was certain notes had been burned to obscure the provenience of the collection.

If she could show the remains had been taken from federal lands, she would have a strong case for repatriation, because federal agencies had to comply with the law, no matter when it went into effect. And under NAGPRA, federal agencies *must* repatriate.

All those pretty, intact baskets that must have come from a rockshelter or other dry site. If they'd been taken from federal land, they'd be returned to the government and couldn't go on display in Shields's museum. No one would put a price tag on something that should never be in private ownership.

That had to be Shields's reason for insisting on a valuation of the collection. The man wanted to deaccession—the formal process of removing items from a museum collection —artifacts through private sales. The Kocher family couldn't sell their mansion, worth several million given the size, condition, and land values, as long as it contained the human remains. So they'd convinced Shields to take the remains, but to do that, they had to give him everything, all the artifacts collected by the family over the decades.

The price of the donation was giving Troy Kocher a job as a security guard, with kickbacks after the artifacts sold to follow.

For Maddie, ensuring much of the collection could never be sold would be deeply satisfying.

Invigorated, she continued combing through files, skipping lunch, which she'd planned to eat with Ava at a picnic table in the parking lot. She texted her and told her to eat without her. The sooner she was done, the sooner they could move on to the looking-at-the-pretty-hills part of this exercise.

She'd planned to visit some of the areas where it was known Otto had dug, but that would wait for another day, when she didn't have Ava with her. For now, she had what she needed. At three o'clock, she stretched and cracked her joints. She was starving, tired, and her brain was utterly fried.

But she had hundreds of pages of correspondence that showed a long, ongoing association between the Kocher and Nielsen families. A glorious preponderance of evidence that was outside both families' control.

Were the Kochers and Nielsens still close? Had their unholy alliance continued into this generation?

Troy Kocher was a White Patriot. What about C-IV? Was he a white supremacist in billionaire clothing? What could she find if she searched in the Nielsen archives but focused on the 1990s and early 2000s, instead of the 1920s and 1930s?

Chapter Ten

Josh paddled to the middle of the cold, calm lake. Stars faded as the sky lightened in the last minutes before dawn. The morning was cool, but it was expected to hit ninety degrees today, and this new heat wave would continue through the weekend.

He was supposed to be in Indonesia right now for the symposium he'd mentioned to C-IV, but his schedule had changed when Owen was hired by R&R. He'd discussed it with Keith, and they'd agreed getting Owen settled was the priority, and Tricia Rooks had been tapped to go in Josh's place.

It was a great opportunity for Tricia, and she'd pitch the new Portland branch along with the other Raptor offices with the same gusto Josh would have. Indonesia would have been fun, and a kind of break from his sudden fatherhood that had him spinning half the time, wondering if he was doing it right, but in this moment, Josh didn't want to be anywhere other than here, in this kayak, on this lake.

Maddie had been right. This was the break he needed, and it didn't require flying halfway around the world. He'd only needed thirty minutes of peace with the breaking dawn. He rested the paddle across the cockpit opening and tilted his head back to gaze up at the fading stars.

A thousand thoughts and worries filled his mind, and he took a deep breath to silence the noise. He focused on inhaling and exhaling, nothing more complex than that.

This place was a good fit for Owen. The founder/director of R&R, Jake, was a great guy, and Owen would have plenty of support. Josh would head back to Portland today with one less worry. Owen would have his new beginning without further interference. He didn't need a babysitter, and it was time for Josh to let go of that role, for both their sakes.

Ava had begged for permission to sleep over at Marcus's house tonight, and Josh had agreed after a lengthy discussion with Marcus's parents. Ava needed time with her friends, and, after Josh had been doxed, Marcus's home would be safer for her.

It hadn't escaped his notice that the sleepover meant his evening was free from the responsibilities of guardianship, and he and Maddie had a date lined up. Really, he should use the time to go over the proposal for Nielsen Steel, or talk to Arthur about the volunteer training tomorrow. Or, hell, he could binge-watch TV.

When was the last time he zoned out and watched something mindless?

But an evening with pizza, beer, and free rein with the remote control didn't appeal as much as it would have three weeks ago. Now, all he wanted was to spend time with Maddie, to wine and dine her and see if this thing that simmered between them was real.

He wanted it to be real and worried he was using her to replace a woman he couldn't have. When he talked to her on the phone or pressed her against a wall and kissed her, he didn't worry about these things. The doubts only crept in when she wasn't near.

His parents' marriage had been an unhappy one, and their hostility with each other had extended to their two sons. Josh had witnessed his brother Ari's controlling behavior toward Lori and his takeaway had been that Warner men were too messed up for real relationships. Best not to ruin someone's life by getting serious—or having sex without a condom.

The philosophy had carried him through his years in the Navy and beyond. Now he was thirty-seven years old, and he'd never attempted a serious relationship before, but there could be no half-assing this thing with Maddie.

First of all, he didn't want to, but equally important, the moment he'd introduced Maddie to Ava, he'd known there was no going back to trying to keep it casual. He wouldn't have a random string of women parade through Ava's life. She needed to know she could count on Josh, and that meant showing commitment in everything he did. His work, his friendships, and his love life.

If he'd wanted to casually sleep around, that was fine, as long as Ava didn't know about it. Ironically, Ava would probably prefer if he slept around and she never met the women involved, as it would mean she remained the number one priority in his life, but he also believed that if she gave Maddie half a chance, Ava would become attached to her too.

His stomach clenched at that idea. What if he screwed up this thing with Maddie, and Ava lost another adult?

He never should have kissed Maddie. He shouldn't want to keep kissing her. But it was too late now. His niece and potential girlfriend had spent two days together, and they'd both been positive when he spoke to them on the phone. Ava had even admitted Maddie was kind of okay.

He smiled thinking of the lukewarm, grudging compliment.

A fish jumped nearby, breaking the silence of the dawn. He pulled out his cell phone and snapped a picture of the sunrise above the trees and sent it to Maddie.

JOSH

You were right. This is what I needed.

He didn't expect an answer—it was just before six a.m. on a Saturday, after all—but his phone buzzed a minute later.

MADDIE

Beautiful. Glad you're taking time for yourself.

He typed a reply, hesitated, then hit Send.

This is great, but not quite the selfish moment I want right now.

Maddie smiled as she stared at the text, remembering exactly what the word "selfish" meant to Josh.

MADDIE

Word on the streets is Ava is spending the night at a friend's tonight.

JOSH

The streets are accurate as usual. I promised to take you out to dinner tonight. Change in plans. Instead of a restaurant, let's eat at my place, 6:00. I'll cook.

Heat flashed through her, and she grinned as she typed her response.

MADDIE

Hmmm… Can you cook?

JOSH

I'm no chef, but I make a mean MRE.

She laughed.

Meals Ready to Eat? Hard pass.

Damn. Okay, how about mini-Beef Wellingtons with roasted veggies and au gratin potatoes?

That's more like it. I'm in. But you won't possibly have time to make a welly.

That's where the mini part comes in. It'll be fabulous, I promise. You bring the wine.

Deal. Can't wait.

See you tonight. Arrive hungry.

She hesitated, then decided to go all in on the flirting.

I've been hungry since the night we met.

You might want to pack an overnight bag. I mean, a freak snowstorm might hit, and you'd be trapped at my place with no toothbrush.

She laughed. They were in the middle of a rare heat

wave, with temperatures expected to go above ninety in the city today.

MADDIE

I think an earthquake or volcano eruption might have higher likelihood.

JOSH

Mt. Hood has been jealous of the attention St. Helens has been getting for 40 years…

When you put it that way, I'd be foolish *not* to pack a bag.

See you at six. And Maddie, thanks for letting Ava stay with you. I know she can be difficult, but it meant a lot to her. And to me.

I'm glad I could help you both. She's a sweet young woman. You're doing a great job by her, you know.

Thanks. I hope I am. I feel lost half the time.

Keep doing what you're doing. You're on the right track. She feels loved, and that's the most important thing. Security will come over time.

Thanks.

Now get back to relaxing.

Yes, ma'am.

She set her phone on the nightstand and lay back on the pillow. Her belly was fluttery and excited at the thought of their date tonight—complete with overnight bag—but the feeling was tempered by what Ava had revealed on Thursday.

She wished she could set the concerns aside, but it popped into her mind every time she thought of Josh—which was about four times a minute.

She believed Josh was genuinely attracted to her, but how much of that attraction was built on similarity?

And really, could she blame him? She'd been attracted to Trina too, and had always considered the comparison a compliment.

She closed her eyes and breathed deeply, remembering her mother's words: *"Don't go borrowing trouble."*

Was she looking for reasons for this heat that flared between them to flash out and disappear? Or was the concern justified? She didn't think she could take rejection after her last relationship had ended with humiliation and heartbreak.

Telling her friends and family, including her perfect brother, *after* the invitations had been mailed that the groom had decided he preferred the maid of honor had been devastating.

It's just a date, she reminded herself.

She took another deep breath and allowed herself to remember how it had felt to be pushed up against the side of Josh's garage as he kissed her. The heat had been blistering.

Josh wanted *her*.

And tonight, he'd get what he wanted.

*M*addie startled at the sound of her ring tone, a shrill sound that mimicked the push-button landline phones of her childhood and teen years. After dropping Ava off at her friend Marcus's house, she'd settled in to work on transcribing the documents she'd photographed in the Nielsen Steel archives on Tuesday. She'd been engrossed in the task for hours, her house silent but for the fan she'd set up in her office, and the loud ring pulled her mind out of eastern Oregon in 1937, as if she'd been dragged through a time warp.

She shook her head, taking a deep breath in the twenty-first century, and glanced at the phone. Caller ID was an unknown Portland number. Usually, she'd let unknown numbers go to voicemail, but she was responsible for Ava until Josh returned to the city even if the girl wasn't physically at her house, so she answered. "Madeline Foster," she said, using her business voice.

"Ms. Foster, this is Cliff Nielsen."

Surprise rippled through her. C-IV didn't even make the top five hundred list of people who might call her on a Saturday afternoon.

"Mr. Nielsen." She paused to find the words. "How can I help you?"

"Cliff, please. I'd like to discuss my great-grandparents' papers with you. I'm flying to Japan tomorrow, so my time is limited. Tonight, I'm attending a charity auction—a private reception at a local history museum catered by one of Portland's finest chefs to benefit the Columbia River Historic Preservation Commission. They're raising money for several museums and to restore a half dozen properties in the Portland area. I've purchased a ticket for you to attend as my date."

She pulled the phone away from her ear and frowned at it. She didn't know much about the one percent, but even she knew these kinds of fund-raisers were more about society than the cause. And he wanted her to be his *date*? Then there was the fact that he seemed to think she'd go all fluttery and fail to notice the command in his words.

She was neither fluttery nor in the mood to be

commanded. "I'm sorry, was there a question in that sentence?"

"It's important you understand I'll be gone for several days. Tonight is the only option."

"Try again." She held her breath to hide her nerves. Even though she was in the right, this felt dangerous. He was the richest man in Portland, possibly even the whole state of Oregon, and with money came power. He could bad-mouth her to the State Historic Preservation Officer. She could be quietly removed from the roster of Secretary of the Interior qualified archaeologists to do NAGPRA consulting.

"I'm screwing this up," Cliff said. "I'm sorry. There's a reason my assistant usually handles my calendar, but as this is a social event, I thought I should call myself."

She said nothing into the silent pause.

Finally, he said, "Will you attend the fund-raiser with me tonight?"

As victories went, it was a small one, but it still made her smile. "No."

"Please?"

"I'm sorry, Cliff, but I have a date tonight. With my boyfriend." She'd feel guilty about repeating the boyfriend lie, but Josh had called her his girlfriend to the man's face, so she would run with it.

"Surely you can reschedule."

"I don't cancel plans to go out on dates with other men. Not even with billionaires."

"I'm not *quite* a billionaire," he said with a chuckle.

Interesting that he didn't deny asking her out on a date— but then, he'd called it a date when he mentioned the ticket, so it wasn't a great leap on her part.

"Have your assistant call me to set up an appointment to meet at your office when you get back from Japan."

He let out a sigh. "What if I got a ticket for Warner to come too? Will you go, then?"

"We'll *both* be your date?"

He laughed. "Wouldn't that make an interesting photo for the paparazzi? No, I'll find another date. Too bad, though. I think we'd have made an interesting headline."

She frowned. What did that mean? Did this have anything to do with her brother, Alan? The two had almost certainly met at some point. She wanted to ask, but delving into potential motives C-IV might have for asking her out was the sort of ego beating she didn't need.

Josh liked her for who she was. At least, she hoped so.

Damn, the dating landscape was riddled with land mines.

"I'll ask if Josh is willing."

"It'll be good to have Warner there. We can talk about the contract between Nielsen Steel and Raptor."

C-IV was a baffling man. Now he spoke of hiring Raptor as if it were a done deal. "I'll get back to you after I speak with him."

"He won't say no. I'll have a courier deliver the tickets to Warner's home. See you at seven. The event is formal—if Warner doesn't have a tux, I can have one sent over. You'll need a dress. I can get you an appointment at a shop down-town in the next hour—"

"I have a dress," she said. She wished she could say no, but she would likely need access to his archives again.

Cliff hung up, and she let out a sigh before dialing Josh. He picked up on the first ring. "Hi, beautiful, good timing. I'm just pulling into the grocery store parking lot."

She imagined the delicious mini-Wellington he'd planned to seduce her with. It *so* would have worked. "Sorry, Josh, but we've got a change of plans."

Chapter Eleven

$\mathscr{M}$uch as he'd hated having their dinner plans ruined, Josh had to admit seeing Maddie in a sexy violet evening gown might be worth having to put up with C-IV for a few hours. Her hair was sleek and smooth, the curls tamed and styled in a simple way that made her look like a fifties-era film star like Grace Kelly, while the gown also had simple, elegant lines—narrow off-the-shoulder sleeves with a heart-shaped neckline that clung to her full bust. Cinched tight at the waist, the gown flared out below the hips. Mermaid style, if he remembered correctly.

His coworker Tricia had worn a gown with a similar cut to several black-tie events they'd worked in DC. She'd told him she liked the style because she could easily conceal a gun just below her knee thanks to the flare of the fabric. There was even a slit in the seam so she could grab it in a hurry. Above the knee, there was no room to conceal anything.

Tricia was a beautiful Black woman with blue braids, flawless smooth skin, and perfect, toned curves. She always stunned in her evening wear—and no one ever guessed she was undercover security and packing heat.

He hoped she was enjoying the symposium in Indonesia. He'd meant to check in with her, but he'd spent his time at R&R enjoying…a little long-overdue R&R.

Now he was picking up his date for a black-tie event he didn't want to go to, wearing a tux he'd donned many times to work security events with Tricia. No doubt tonight would be work—he wasn't providing security, but he'd have to schmooze with C-IV—yet it was still a date. Hopefully, they could slip out before the auction began and go back to his place for a real dinner with dessert.

His gaze swept down Maddie's body as she twirled to show off her dress. With her petite frame, he could pick her up and make love to her without need for a wall to provide support. He'd had that fantasy on repeat for days.

Yeah. He couldn't wait for dessert.

She set her alarm, grabbed her overnight bag, and locked the front door.

He took the bag from her as he led her down the path to his SUV. He tucked the bag in the backseat, then faced her. "All set in case of volcanic or other seismic activity?"

She laughed and leaned into him. Rising on her toes, she whispered in his ear, "Oh, the earth is definitely gonna move tonight."

He grinned and wrapped his arms around her, pulling her body flush with his. "You're stunning in that dress, but still, I can't wait to strip it off you."

"I'm thinking the same thing about your tux." She stroked the silk of his lapel. "You sure you want to do this? We can come up with an excuse."

He shrugged. "I've got to go. If I get Nielsen as a client, it would be a huge step toward making the Portland office viable. I owe it to Keith. I can't blow it by being a no-show, even if the prick did ask you out."

"I'm not one hundred percent sure that's what he was doing, if that makes a difference."

Josh cupped her cheek. "I might need him as a client, but I won't put up with any more bullshit. Keith will understand. If he comes on to you in any way, tell me. Some guys with his power and money get off on making their subordinates submit—either themselves or their significant others. I don't know if C-IV does that, but it doesn't look good so far."

"But why would he need to do that? He's, what, in his midforties? Single. Attractive. Obscenely wealthy. Why take people by force when he could get it willingly?" She frowned. "I mean, I *know* why. Rape is always about power and control. It's never about sex. But with some people, it just boggles the mind."

"I think for some, when you grow up with all the power and control, you need to find new ways to get off." He smiled and kissed her forehead. "I sure wish I could have seen his face when you demanded he actually ask, then said no."

She flashed her teeth at him. "Yeah. Me too."

He reached to the side and opened the passenger door for her, and gave her a hand as she stepped up to the high seat in her heels and dress. After she settled in, he pulled the seat belt across her lap, his hand unnecessarily running across her body as he did so. He secured the buckle and leaned in to kiss her bare throat, taking a deep breath and catching the faint scent of perfume.

She'd texted him an hour ago to ask if he was allergic to perfumes. Now he was glad he wasn't, because the scent was subtle, sexy, and enticing.

He couldn't wait until the reception was over and he could take her home and finally explore every inch of her.

"So, I looked up what I could find about the fund-raiser, and the tickets cost five grand each," Maddie said as Josh drove to the museum, which was in an old renovated warehouse in the Pearl District. "Plus, we're expected to bid on things so we'll look generous to the other attendees."

"I'm not worried about looking cheap among the Portland elite. I donate to charities when I can, but it's not for recognition or any other kind of cookie."

"Darn, I had my eye on a diamond bracelet in the catalogue that's only thirty-five thousand dollars."

"Jesus. What I could do with thirty-five grand."

"Right?"

"College for Ava, for starters."

"Damn, I didn't even think of that. It's right around the corner, isn't it? She'll be taking the SAT in a few months."

"Yeah. She says she isn't sure she wants to go to college—which is fine if it isn't right for her. I mean, I didn't go to college, and that was the right call for me, but I think she's saying it because of money. I don't blame her for not wanting to mortgage her future. It's another reason I need to get this Portland office off the ground. Job security for me is security for her."

She squeezed his knee. "I promise I'll be nice to C-IV tonight."

"Not too nice, though. He doesn't get a pass for being a prick if he comes on to you."

"That's fair. No passes for passes."

They arrived at the historic building and parked. The museum had gone all out on the high-brow frills. There was even a red carpet leading to the entrance. Josh presented their tickets and they were led inside, past the rustic front rooms with historical exhibits about the Oregon Territory and into a ballroom that could have belonged to a wealthy lumber—or steel—baron.

Maddie guessed there were around two hundred guests, the men in dark tuxes with bow ties and the women in a sparkling array of colors. Thankfully, the old-fashioned ballroom had a very modern air-conditioning system, because the room would be sweltering in this heat wave.

A jazz quartet played softly in the corner as people mingled, cocktails in hand. Servers circulated with platters of hors d'oeuvres. The guests were a sea of white faces—which shouldn't surprise her, given Oregon's history—but still, it was jarring. She'd attended similar events with her ex-fiancé—he'd been an attorney with political aspirations—but the crowd had never been quite this pale.

Of course, she and Josh were as pasty as the rest of them, but still, it seemed odd.

She and Josh both plucked glasses of champagne from a tray carried by a passing server and clinked glasses in a silent toast. "At least for the price tag, the champagne is free." She sipped the bubbly wine and smiled at the glass. "And it's *good*." There were several Willamette Valley vineyards that made excellent sparkling wine. She'd be sure to check the vintage before they left tonight.

"We still haven't found time to go wine tasting," Josh said.

"My group doesn't go again for another three weeks, but you and I could go. Next Saturday?"

He gave a short shake of his head. "I'm doing a final training that day before Sunday's rally. It was a mistake for me to spend so much time at R&R. I should've been here, training the volunteers today." She could see the tension in his shoulders, and he held the champagne flute in a tight grip. That quickly, his stress level had shot up.

She leaned close to him. "You don't have to be a superhero. You deserve a break too."

He gave her a weak smile. "I'm trying to convince myself of that, but there's something about the timing of these rallies that makes me anxious. Like, I'm already too late in starting these trainings. Something is imminent."

And just like that, his worry became hers. She believed Josh had good instincts, plus he'd spent the last few years studying white supremacy and militia movements to try to gauge their next move. If he was worried, there was reason to be.

"You're training tomorrow?"

"Yes. And every night this week."

"I'd like to go. To train."

He frowned. "I'd prefer if you didn't."

That…didn't feel great to hear. She tried not to let hurt—or anger—take over her tongue. "Are women not…*allowed*?"

"No. Hell no. Of course women can train with us and participate in the counterprotest protection. I just don't want *you* to do it because…I'd be distracted. I might lose my focus checking on you more than the others. I had the same conversation with Ava—aside from the fact that she's under eighteen and we aren't training anyone who isn't a legal adult, it would be terrifying for me to have her at a protest." He slipped an arm around her waist and whispered, "I care about you, Maddie. I can't risk splitting my focus when things can get dangerous."

"That's fair," she said, her throat going a little dry at the emotion in his eyes. "Can I at least train? Self-defense is never a bad thing."

"Can I think about that? Not give an answer right now?"

She nodded and scanned the crowd, searching for C-IV. Her gaze landed on a familiar face, and she let out a soft gasp of surprise.

Good Lord. She really should have considered *this* possibility. She huffed out a breath. At least *now* Cliff's invitation made sense. He'd made it clear to Josh he wanted to buy a senator. This was the next best thing.

"What's wrong?" Josh asked.

"I'm such an idiot. I can't believe…" She let her words trail off. He was making a beeline for her. Had he asked Cliff to invite her? All because she'd refused to be in public with him or do anything that might be considered an endorsement?

This was *so* not going to be fun.

He reached her before she had a chance to say anything to Josh. He kissed both her cheeks and gave her an awkward hug. "Maddie, such a surprise to see you here."

"A surprise for us both," she said, inwardly cursing C-IV for this ambush. If she'd realized, she could have warned Josh.

He turned to face Josh and held out his hand. "I'm Alan Tisdale."

"Congressman, it's nice to meet you. Josh Warner." They shook hands. Josh's gaze flicked to hers in question. All she could do was give him a sorry smile.

"I recognize you from the news," Alan said. "Such disturbing business with what happened at the rally."

Maddie moved closer to Josh. "It's thanks to Josh's team of volunteers that only one person was injured."

"Your campaign has yet to make a statement," Josh said, and Maddie let out an internal cheer. She'd told Alan the same thing on Sunday night. He needed to make a statement disavowing the White Patriot's assault on Desmond. "While your opponent reached out to me within hours."

Alan stiffened. "My team is still weighing the evidence provided by the police bureau."

Josh put an arm around her and cinched her to his side. "So, how do you know my Maddie?"

Alan gave her a baffled look, and she couldn't suppress a

laugh. It *was* ridiculous that she hadn't told Josh about Alan and vice versa, but the moment was funny thanks to the look on Alan's face.

"*Your* Maddie?" Alan cocked his head. "Who is this guy to you? And why haven't you mentioned him?"

She let out a soft sigh. This wasn't how she'd planned this introduction. Not that she'd planned it at all, but this definitely wasn't how she'd have wanted it to happen. "Alan, this is my boyfriend, Josh." At least this was less of a lie now than it would have been a week ago. "The relationship is new, so I didn't mention him at dinner last week. Josh, Alan is my brother."

Now it was Josh's turn to give her a confused look. "Your brother is congressman and Senate candidate Alan Tisdale, and you didn't mention it?"

Alan gave her a pained look—upset that she hadn't seen fit to tell her boyfriend about her famous brother—but his feelings didn't matter to her in the way Josh's did. She hadn't considered how her omission would hurt her sort-of-fake boyfriend. "Yes. Sorry I forgot to tell you."

Josh laughed. "*Forgot.* Sure."

She gave him a sheepish grin and shrugged. "It didn't come up?"

His smirk combined with the light in his eyes said she'd be answering his questions later, which was totally fair. "So you're…half siblings?"

Maddie nodded. "Different dads." To Alan, she said, "Where's Sharon?"

"She isn't feeling well and decided to sit this evening out."

Maddie had no doubt the campaign had been grueling for her sister-in-law, considering her brother used the woman as a prop. But when asked about it, Sharon denied there was a problem, and Maddie wasn't about to make it worse by pressing her to stand up for herself. Perhaps taking the night off from a public event was a start.

"Be sure to give her my love," Maddie said.

Alan's gaze bounced from Maddie to Josh and back to Maddie. "How did you two meet, anyway?"

"Josh is best friends with Trina's husband."

"Ah. Yes. The Raptor CEO." He gave Josh his best politician smile. "It's uncanny how much Maddie and Trina look alike, isn't it?"

Maddie stiffened. It was a natural statement to make—everyone commented on it at one point or another—but now, knowing what she did, it felt awkward.

Josh's arm at her back also tensed. "I noticed the resemblance at first, but now, when I look at your sister, I only see the beautiful woman I'm crazy about."

She couldn't stop herself from studying his face, searching for truth in his words. She hated knowing his secret.

Alan broke into her tangled thoughts. "Mom's going to love this one, Madds." He glanced around. "Listen, I've got to work the room, and since you're here, you can fill in for Sharon. Show a united family front."

And that, right there, had to be why C-IV had invited her here tonight. What were the odds that Alan asked him to get Maddie to force her to publicly join his campaign?

Maddie represented the demographic where he performed most poorly: women between eighteen and forty-five on the western side of the state. Alan and his staff had been after her to campaign for him for months, to show a family-centric side of him and convince women voters that Alan would be good for the women of Oregon and the nation. He didn't have children to use as props, so he wanted Maddie to step up.

The problem was, she knew he wouldn't be good for women if he won. And not because he had any personal beliefs, but because his views were informed by whatever was most politically expedient.

"Sorry, Alan. This is a date and not a political event for me." She looked up at Josh, who smiled down at her, his arm tightening around her in support. "We're here to speak with C-IV about my research for the Kocher project. Then we're out of here."

"You know Troy Kocher is here, right?" Alan said.

Maddie glanced around the room, and her gaze landed on Troy. She recognized the woman by his side as his sister. Next to Anne Kocher was the curator, Oliver Shields.

She should have realized they'd be here. Shields's museum would probably receive grants from the historical society. This event could help fund his museum. Yet another reason to skip the diamond necklace.

Did Anne know about Troy's tricked-out security belt? Did she know about his intimidation tactics? Anne had negotiated the NAGPRA contract, and Maddie had the sense she was eager to get it over with so the house could be sold. She might not be pleased to know her brother had done everything he could to slow the work down.

It might be worth talking to the woman. Maybe she could rein her brother in.

"Troy Kocher approached me before you got here, complaining about your work," Alan said in a pained voice.

"Troy knows I'm your sister?"

Alan shrugged. "Guess you aren't hiding it as well as you thought."

"I'm not *hiding* it, Alan."

"Yeah, you're just not acknowledging it." His voice was hurt.

There wasn't anything she could say to that.

Once upon a time, she'd worshipped her big brother, and his approval had meant everything to her. But that ended when he won his party's nomination. It wasn't his political affiliation that mattered, it was what he'd done to win.

"It's *your* campaign. Not mine. When you change your stance on women's health care, we'll talk."

"I wouldn't have won the nomination if—"

She crossed her arms. "Maybe it wasn't worth winning if you have to betray your beliefs." *And your sister.*

She turned away from him. This wasn't the time or place for this.

She headed for the cash bar. The champagne might be good, but she wanted a real drink. Josh kept pace with her as she wove through the crowd. "I'm sorry," she said. "I should have told you about Alan." All those evening phone calls, when their conversation had flowed so easily, she could have mentioned her brother. But—she'd enjoyed those conversations so much, and talking about Alan hurt these days.

"I think I understand."

"I promise, I'll tell you everything later."

"You don't have to. I mean, eventually, yes. But not before you're ready."

She stopped and turned to face him. "I really, really like you, Josh Warner."

He leaned down and brushed his lips over hers. "Same," he whispered. He glanced around the room and kept his voice low. "I don't know why I had it in my head you were part of some idyllic family. Mental image corrected."

She gave him an apologetic smile. "To be fair, I never said anything one way or another. Not even after our very awkward family dinner two weeks ago. Family can be so complicated."

"Tell me about it."

"Yeah, you probably win there." She spotted Alan talking to a couple on the far side of the room. He was laughing and probably being his undeniably charming self. There was good reason he'd gotten as far as he had in politics. "I know Alan loves me, and truth is, even though I'm hurt, I love him. He'll always be that larger-than-life big brother who swooped in and played with me when he was home from college. I cherish those memories. But I'm not sure if I like him anymore, if that makes sense."

"So much sense. I struggle with childhood memories versus who my brother Ari has become on a daily basis. We *were* close as children, just two years apart in age and allies against our father."

She got a fruity cocktail from the bar. They circled the room after that, looking at the history exhibits and silent auction items. "Oh, good Lord," Maddie said when she found the Kocher family's contribution to the event. "We can host a party of ten to spend the night in a haunted mansion and enjoy a séance in a crypt, where we will speak with the Native Americans housed in the vaults."

"Wow. That's crass. And horrific. Can they *do* that?"

"If the party is scheduled before my work is done, there's nothing I can do to stop it."

"No one's bid on it, though," Josh said.

"Thank goodness for small mercies."

"Are you saying it wouldn't be a good choice for my donation?" a man asked from behind Maddie.

She turned to face C-IV. "It's another exploitation of remains his and your great-grandparents stole. I don't care if it supports curation and museums. It's wrong."

"You don't believe in gray areas, do you?" Nielsen asked.

"I know there are gray areas in this world, but this isn't one of them."

His gaze scanned the tables. "So which silent auction item should I bid on?"

Josh put a possessive arm around her waist again and said, "Depends on what you need."

"I'm the wealthiest man in this room. I don't *need* anything."

"Not even a senator?" Maddie asked.

Nielsen's eyes narrowed. "I don't believe those are up for auction. Unless you know something I don't?"

"That's why I'm here, isn't it? A path to my brother?"

"No, actually. I *do* want to talk to you about your research into my great-grandparents." He met Josh's gaze. "And once she told me she had plans with you tonight, I realized this would be the perfect opportunity to make the announcement."

"Announcement?" Josh asked.

C-IV turned toward the front of the room where a photographer was taking photos. "We'll have our photo taken for the paper, then we can talk," Cliff said.

They had no choice but to follow as he turned to cross the room.

"What announcement? And why are we having our picture taken?" Maddie asked.

"Nielsen Steel is hiring Raptor for all our security needs. The photo will be good PR for us both."

Josh stopped in his tracks. "We haven't negotiated the contract yet."

Cliff paused and faced Josh. "The details don't matter. We'll make it work. We can get a photo now. It will look good in the news."

"What happened to your contract with Apex?"

"My needs have changed. They no longer suit."

"In less than two weeks, your needs have changed." It was a statement, said with a tinge of disbelief in Josh's voice.

"Yes. I want Raptor taking over security at Nielsen Tower within the next ten days. We'll discuss my personal security when I get back from Japan. I'd ask you to start tomorrow and accompany me, but I realize that's too short notice."

"Are you doing this for the PR? Because of my work with Bond Ironworks?"

"I'm doing it because I got ahold of your military record, and I'm impressed." He paused. "And I have concerns about Apex."

"If you're so eager to hire Raptor, why did you ask my girlfriend out instead of calling me?"

Maddie was surprised he asked the question, given how much he wanted this contract. Her belly did a little flip. Who knew integrity was such a turn-on?

Nielsen's gaze bounced between them. After a pause he said, "When Maddie showed up in my archives asking about my great-grandparents, I did a background check and discovered the connection to Congressman Tisdale. Almost immediately after, I spotted her in the lobby of my building with a contractor I'd decided not to hire. You claimed to be a couple, so I called Tisdale and asked if you were dating Warner. He said you weren't."

"Why would that even matter?" Maddie asked.

"I wondered if it was all a lie. If Warner was using you and your connection to Tisdale to get to me."

Maddie startled and stepped back. "Josh didn't even know Alan is my brother."

Josh's hand curled around her hip. "Our relationship might be new, but it is quite real. And if you ever make a pass at Maddie again, ruse or not, you can take your contract and shove it. People are not pawns to test and manipulate."

Nielsen grinned. "Good. I needed to be certain you wouldn't be a drone of a yes-man, even willing to sell out your girlfriend for a contract. That's one of the reasons I'm firing Simon Barstow and Apex. His entire staff are ass-kissers. That's no way to protect someone in my position. Plus, no one at Apex is willing to take a risk to do what's right, like you're doing to protect counterprotesters. I need someone with balls to watch my back." He leaned toward Josh and said in a low voice, "I've been getting threats…and I think these ones are serious."

"If that's the case, you should cancel your trip to Japan tomorrow."

"I can't do that. But before I leave tomorrow morning, I'm going to have a contract couriered to you authorizing you to do a thorough vetting of the security at Nielsen Tower. I want you to be ready to take over tower security in ten days. And within twenty days, I want you in charge of my twenty-four seven personal security team. Can you do that?"

Maddie could practically see Josh weighing Ava's need for college money with his desire to push back against what had to be impossible demands.

"I can get started assessing tower security by the end of the week."

Nielsen nodded. "It's settled, then. Now, let's get our picture taken, then we'll have a stiff drink to celebrate."

The photographer had Maddie stand between the two men in the photo. Right as he began snapping, Josh's phone let out a loud odd beeping sound.

"That's quite the ringtone you've got there," Cliff said.

Josh frowned and pulled the phone from his breast pocket. "That tone means it's an emergency call from Raptor headquarters." He ignored the flashing camera and jabbed at the touch screen. "What's happening, Keith?"

All the color drained from Josh's face, and he took a step backward, bumping into a table. "Tricia? But how——?"

The photographer kept taking photos, capturing the horror on Josh's face. Maddie glared at the man. "Do you mind?"

He shrugged and lowered the camera. "Sorry. I'm a photojournalist who got suckered into this job tonight. Whatever is going on with your friend is a helluva lot more interesting than this."

It was a cold statement, and she turned her back on him, catching Josh's words to Keith. "Okay. Keep me posted. I can fly—"

Josh had shown worry and concern many times in their short acquaintance. She'd been there when he found out he'd been doxed, after all, but nothing compared to his expression now.

He hung up the phone and said, "The symposium, the one I mentioned before," he nodded to Cliff. "The one in Indonesia that we talked about."

"What happened?" Cliff asked.

"There was an attack on the hotel. It was a slaughter, apparently. They're saying everyone—over a hundred people, hotel staff…everyone…they're all dead."

The photographer gasped as the reporter by his side pulled out her cell phone. "Mr. Warner, can you tell me what symposium you're talking about?"

"You were supposed to go to that, weren't you?" Maddie asked, ignoring the reporter.

"Yes." Josh closed his eyes and looked as close to breaking as Maddie had ever seen him. "Tricia Rooks went in my place."

Chapter Twelve

$\mathcal{J}$osh paced a small office that was just down the hall from the ballroom. Maddie had dragged him out of the room before he could let loose on the reporter and photographer.

"Let's head to your house, so you'll have access to Raptor servers," she said.

He nodded. The night had shifted gears with the speed and pain of whiplash. One moment he was meeting Maddie's brother—and discovered he was the US congressman running for the Senate—then he was offered the job he'd been hoping to land for weeks, and then…

No. It wasn't possible.

"I'll drop you off on the way home," he said. "Sorry our date is ending early."

She crossed her arms. "You shouldn't be alone right now." She stepped forward and grabbed his arms, stopping his pacing. "The date part of our night is over, yes. But let me keep you company. Let me make you dinner. Let me take care of you."

Was it wrong that he wanted to say yes? That he wanted to fall apart and let Maddie do the heavy lifting?

He *never* fell apart. Not when Owen was injured in Somalia. Not when their coms were shot out in Afghanistan and they had to hike five miles through Taliban-held territory to get to the backup exfil point. Not when he was fourteen and his dad beat his mom to within an inch of her life and it fell to Josh to get her to the hospital because Ari—the one with a driver's license—refused on the grounds that if cops knew what happened, they'd both end up in foster care.

So why did *this* feel like a breaking point?

Probably because in this instance, he was helpless. He couldn't do a damn thing. Keith would never send him to Indonesia to track down the terrorists who attacked the hotel, not when he had Ava to consider. And Sean Logan was already en route on the company jet to claim Tricia's body.

He couldn't even do that service for his friend. She'd gone to the symposium *in his place*. Josh should be the one who was dead right now.

He didn't harbor illusions that if only he'd been there, it would be different, that he could have stopped the attack. Some of the best security professionals in the world had attended that conference, and Tricia was right there among them. Now they were all dead.

"Josh? Please. Let me take care of you."

He met Maddie's gaze and gave a slow nod. "Will you drive? I need to make some calls."

"Of course."

They bypassed the ballroom as they left, and Josh settled in the unfamiliar passenger seat for the drive home. He spent the entire trip on the phone with various coworkers—asking questions of some, and with others, they just shared pained silence before hanging up.

Tricia had lived in the Virginia compound for the last year. There was a special bond between the group of senior operatives who lived in the compound. They'd all ended up in freshman-type living quarters for their own reasons. Nate, because it was the only job Raptor offered when he transferred from the Alaska compound. Chase, because he'd needed people to watch out for him after the trauma of what happened to him in Alaska. He'd tried living on his own and hated it.

Josh had moved in when Owen was finally stable and took a job as a trainer that came with housing. Living in the compound, Josh had been able to look after both Owen and Chase.

Tricia had moved into the compound because she wanted to save money for a down payment on a house. Living in the compound saved a lot of money. No rent. No food costs. No utilities. Hell, Raptor even provided their cell phones and vehicles.

Trish had joked that the longer she lived in the compound, the more square feet she could afford, and she loved not having to cook or do dishes. She was a social person and enjoyed the communal areas—she was always up for games and movies in the lounge and had been teaching half the operators the fundamentals of tennis on the indoor court. She crushed them all on a regular basis, but Josh had finally learned how to score the game.

She was vivacious, cheerful, smart as hell, and seriously badass. She'd been a police officer in DC before taking the job with Raptor, and she enjoyed the more even tempo of security work after the brutal intensity of working vice.

Tricia had plans for her future and was doing everything right to make it happen, and now, she was…gone.

"Keep me posted," he said to Nate after a long silence

neither of them had a clue how to fill. "And give Leah a hug from me."

"Will do," Nate said. "Take care of yourself, Josh. I mean it."

He glanced sideways at Maddie. Had she somehow mind-melded with Nate?

"I will." He hit the End button and noted they were only a block from his house. There was no point in making another call, so he tucked his phone in his breast pocket. "Nate wants me to take care of myself."

"Sounds like Nate knows you."

He managed a faint smile. Apparently, Maddie knew him too.

They reached his house, and Maddie hit the button for the garage door. Josh deactivated the alarm system with a remote in the SUV. She shut off the engine as the door closed behind them. They were alone at last, but this was nothing like he'd imagined it would be to return here when they'd set out this evening.

Josh leaned back in his seat and took a deep breath. "I'm sorry this isn't the date we planned."

"And I'm sorry about Tricia, and everyone who was at the conference. Over a hundred people? The scale of that is… unfathomable. A massacre."

He nodded. He was having trouble wrapping his brain around it himself. It wasn't a battle in a war zone. It was a gathering of people in business suits enjoying the cocktail reception on the last night of the conference. Tricia might even be wearing her mermaid gown.

He closed his eyes. His brain immediately delivered up images of a hotel in flames.

When he'd talked to Trish about taking his place, she'd made a joke about it being a male-dominated event, and maybe she'd finally meet someone worth her time in Indonesia. She'd found dating difficult in DC—too many men were threatened by her job and badassness, and she would be in a gathering of men in her field.

"Is there…any hope? Do you know for certain Tricia is dead?" Maddie asked.

"No. But given what we do know, it's highly unlikely she survived. They hunted everyone down and shot them, and set fire to the hotel to draw out anyone hiding in their room. One call made it through to report the carnage, and they witnessed people being shot as they fled the flames."

She let out a gasp. "That's…horrible."

He gave a sharp nod. He couldn't dare hope Tricia had somehow survived. Hope only made it that much worse when the truth was confirmed.

He opened his door and slipped from the vehicle. He circled around to help Maddie down from the high seat—a hazard of her short stature and the big SUV—but she'd managed on her own and reached in to grab her clutch from the center console. She couldn't reach it, though. Even in heels, she was too short, so he leaned in behind her, his body pressed tight to hers as he grabbed her bag.

He'd figured his sex drive was dead for the night, but the feel of her round ass against his upper thighs stirred something.

She leaned back against him, and he wrapped his arms around her and just held her. A moment of silence and peace.

He was glad he wasn't alone tonight, and even more glad the person he was with was Maddie. He pressed his face into her neck, her soft perfume filling his senses. "Thank you for insisting on keeping me company."

She turned in his arms and hugged him. They stood there in his closed garage in the open vee of the car door and held each other. It was somehow exactly what he needed.

Tears welled, and he didn't fight them. Tricia was dead. She deserved his tears and grief.

"I'm so sorry," she whispered.

He said nothing, just held her tight and allowed his emotions to flow.

His phone vibrated. Maddie's cheek was pressed against it, and she pulled back, ending the moment too soon.

He was in no shape to answer the call. Tears in front of Maddie was one thing.

When he made no move to answer the call, she gingerly pulled the phone from his breast pocket. She showed him the screen. It was Keith. "Do you want me to take it?" she asked.

He nodded. If Keith was calling now, it was important, but he doubted he'd be able to choke out even a greeting.

She hit the speaker button and said, "Hi, Keith, it's Maddie."

"Maddie. Is Josh available?"

She met his gaze. He gave a short nod but made no move to take the phone.

She nudged him back and stepped forward, closing the car door with her elbow before leaning against the side of the vehicle. "He's listening."

He smiled. Her answer was somehow perfect.

"Great. I've got news he needs to hear. We just received confirmation from Indonesian police who were the first on the scene. There were two survivors recovered from the grounds who were transported to a hospital in Jakarta. One of the survivors is a Black woman with blue braids."

Josh let out a gasp that was half sob. How many Black women with blue braids had attended the symposium? Odds were, only one.

"She has a chest wound and possibly head trauma as well," Keith continued. "She's unconscious and is in a medically induced coma at this time."

She wasn't out of the woods, but she was alive. There was hope.

"Thanks, Keith. That means everything," Josh said, not bothering to hide the emotion in his voice.

"I know. Trina and I have been crying since we first got word she might be dead, and now we're crying with hope. Sean will know more when he gets to the hospital tomorrow. We've already changed his flight path to Jakarta. If things go well, he'll be flying Tricia back to DC in a few days."

"I want to go to Jakarta," Josh said. "I can help with the investigation."

"No can do. The FBI is all over this one. One of their negotiators is likely one of the dead. Sean will offer Raptor's assistance, but we don't want to screw with their investigation. Besides, you need to be there to handle this new contract with Nielsen and to train the volunteers. Rav is really pleased with the initiative you've taken there. It's meaningful work, with the added bonus of great PR for us."

Josh nodded, not caring that Keith couldn't see his response. "Okay, but if things change, I'm the first to go to Jakarta."

"Deal," Keith said. He cleared his throat. "And um… what happened to Tricia brings it all home again, so I'll just say it: you are my brother in all but blood. Love you, man."

Josh also cleared his throat, finding it hard to breathe and speak. Finally, he managed, "You've been my best friend for a decade, and we've been to hell and back more than once. Love you too."

"Trina sends you and Maddie her love too."

He could no longer speak, so he just nodded, and Maddie said, "Give Trina a hug from me. I'll take care of Josh."

"Thanks, Maddie. I'll call if I get more news. Night."

Maddie hit the End button and met Josh's gaze, a beautiful watery smile on her face.

He took his phone from her hand and slipped it into the back pocket of his trousers. He didn't want the hard rectangle between them when he held her this time. "Well, tonight has been an emotional roller coaster." He wrapped his arms around her and pulled her snug to his chest again.

She nodded and swiped at the tears that rolled down her cheeks. "I don't even know Tricia."

"And the good news is, you *will* get to meet her."

"I can't wait," she croaked in a teary voice.

Josh kissed her, a soft kiss. Sweet, comforting. Not asking for anything. She kissed back with the same sweetness.

They drew apart, and he stared into her eyes, which were still wet with tears, and he knew his were the same. She smiled at him, and his heart did a little flip. In such a short time, she'd taken over his fantasies. They'd spoken on the phone every night since they met, and he'd spent his days looking forward to the nightly call. The important moments of each day had been accompanied by planning in his head how he'd tell her about it that night and imagining her reaction. And when he couldn't wait to share a tidbit, he'd shot off a text and gotten a warm rush with every reply.

He wanted this relationship to continue. To deepen. To have a partner to face the highs and lows of life together, as she'd been here for him tonight.

"I'm crazy about you," he whispered.

The automatic garage door light chose that moment to shut off, leaving them in inky darkness, robbing him of seeing her face at his declaration.

She laughed, and then her mouth was on his, and the kiss wasn't sweet. It was hot and demanding and everything he wanted from her. He hiked up her dress and scooped her from the ground, not breaking the kiss as she wrapped her thighs around him. He navigated the dark garage to the stairs, kissing her every step of the way.

She lifted her head and asked, "Is that…a gun under my calf or…do you have a tail?"

He laughed. "Inside-the-waistband holster specially tailored for this tux. In DC, I provided undercover security for a lot of formal political events and needed to carry concealed."

"That's…hot."

He laughed and kissed her again. With her arms around his neck and legs wrapped around his hips, it was easy for him to support her with one arm under her ass as he gripped the rail to climb the short flight of steps to the interior door. The garage opened into the laundry and mudroom. He didn't bother with the light switch as he breezed through with her clinging to him.

The living room was dark, with curtains closed thanks to the doxing. He made a beeline for the plush L-shaped sofa that faced the fireplace in the large, open-plan room. He set her down, his mouth still on hers as he knelt before her.

After a long and very thorough kiss, he raised his head and met her gaze in the dim, ambient light. "I want to make love to you."

She reached for his shirt and pulled on the tail of his bow tie, then began opening buttons.

He chuckled and said, "Tell me you want me too." He wanted to hear the words as much as feel her hands on him.

"I want you, Josh. I want to feel you deep inside me as you come. As you make me come."

He reached behind her and tugged down the zipper of her dress just low enough to loosen the bodice. The cut didn't allow for a bra, and her full breasts were revealed. He slipped a hand into the top, making the opening wider, then he took her nipple into his mouth and sucked on one while his hand cupped and gently squeezed her other breast.

She made a breathy noise, and her fingers slipped into his

hair, holding him there. He released her just enough to say, "What else do you want?"

"This," she said. "Exactly what you're doing."

He switched to the other breast. "Go on."

"I want to taste you. I want your face between my thighs, your tongue on my clit. I want you to fuck me, and I want you to make love to me. I want one to blur into the other. I want dirty, and I want sweet. I want wild, and I want sensual. You make me feel all these things emotionally. I want the physical version too."

She'd somehow managed to put into words everything he'd been thinking and feeling. He wanted everything she'd described and more.

He rose to his feet and doffed his jacket and cummerbund, then finished unbuttoning his shirt.

She leaned forward and said, "Leave it on. Your bow tie loose around your neck like that and your shirt open and partially tucked in, it's fricking hot." She opened his fly and freed his cock, stroking him from base to tip, then down again, following her hand with her open mouth and wet, warm tongue.

He gasped at the suddenness of the sharp, intense pleasure of being in her hand and mouth.

She tilted her head up and met his gaze. The head of his penis between her lips, she sucked and released him, her lips brushing the tip as she whispered, "This. Is. So. Hot. I never knew a disheveled tuxedo could be so wildly sexy." And then he was deep in her mouth again, his cock pressing the back of her throat.

"You look"—he couldn't hold back a gasp as her tongue ran along the underside of his cock—"so damn hot too." His view of her mouth on him, the open top of her dress that gave him glimpses of her full breasts and hard nipples, which bounced as she went down on him, was perfection. She leaned forward, moving to the very edge of the couch, her head blocking his view of her breasts, but now he could see her backside with the sexy dress hiked up to her hips. She wore sheer dark lace panties, and he itched to get his hands on her ass again.

He threaded his fingers through her hair, mussing the sleek style, and that was sexy too. He rocked his hips, taking all the pleasure she gave him, then gently pulled back, leaving the heat of her mouth. "My turn."

He nudged her back so she lay on the cushion and slid his hands up her dress and tugged down the small swath of lace. He reached her knees and moved back and guided the panties over her stilettos. "It's crazy hot that you're still in your dress and heels."

He pushed the dress up higher, clearing her hips to her waist so he could spread her legs wide. He stared at her center, enjoying the view of her, tight, dark curls, and pink lips, wet with arousal. "Beautiful," he whispered, then he leaned down and licked her from vagina to clit.

She let out a sharp groan, so he did it again, then grazed the sensitive spot with his teeth. She gasped, and he sucked on her, licked her. Explored her folds and wet heat, dipping his tongue inside her, followed by his finger. Her body tightened around him, coiling with the intensity, and he groaned in sympathetic pleasure as he used his fingers and mouth to wind her up.

Watching her, feeling her body's reaction to his attention, hearing the sounds she made was glorious.

He was rock hard and completely lost. This was the pure selfish moment he'd told her he wanted. Needed. The best kind of self-care.

A crash sounded, and he jolted just in time to see an object hurtling through the front window. He grabbed

Maddie's hips and yanked her to the floor as the object hit the arm of the couch near where her head had been.

He covered her body with his own. She yelped as another crash was followed by another hurtled object. A white gas billowed out. *Shit!*

"Close your eyes and hold your breath! It's tear gas."

Chapter Thirteen

Josh pulled Maddie to her feet, then tucked himself back in his pants one-handed as he closed his eyes and pulled her through the harsh gas toward the back door. This was a case of the blind leading the blind, but at least he knew the way. His eyes burned and his lungs ached. He threw the dead bolt.

He pulled his gun from the holster at his back, thankful they hadn't stripped or he'd be scrambling for clothes, gun, and phone before they could escape outside. He shoved the door wide, opened his eyes, then stepped into his fenced backyard, scanning for intruders. Tear gas was designed to get people out of buildings, which meant an ambush could be waiting.

He didn't bother with the alarm. It would signal the police in ten seconds—an extremely short interval thanks to his current risk level.

Maddie followed him through the door, her dress no longer hiked up, but her breasts remained exposed as she took a deep breath and coughed. The alarm blared behind him right on schedule as he studied the patio, lawn, and garden, gun pointed in all the dark corners in turn.

The sun had set only twenty minutes before, and shadows were deepening, offering limited concealment. "Stay with your back to the wall," he whispered to Maddie, then approached the storage shed in the far corner, looking for signs it had been breached or someone was concealed behind the small structure.

His eyes still burned, and his nose ran. His reaction time had been slow because his attention had been consumed by the need to make Maddie come, and they'd been too close to the grenades when they went off to escape unscathed. He ignored the pain in his eyes, nose, and lungs, and checked the shed. The lock was secure, and a quick circuit of the structure revealed no one lying in wait.

The backyard was empty, for the moment. He returned to Maddie's side, keeping his gun out, but pointed down. He helped her zip her dress, then touched her cheek. She coughed again. Her eyes were red and teary, her nose running as the gas did its job of irritating the mucus membranes of the eyes, mouth, nose, and lungs. He'd left the tuxedo jacket in the house, or he'd have a handkerchief to give her. He pulled off his open shirt instead and offered it to her.

"Thank you," she said between coughs. She must have gotten a lungful right before he told her to hold her breath.

She wiped her face and handed the shirt back, and he cleaned up his own face, then pulled his phone from his back pocket, thankful it was there and not in the jacket. In five minutes, it would be safe to go inside and retrieve belongings, but he needed to call the police and Raptor now.

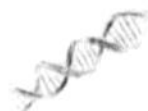

*M*addie paced the backyard. She'd given up on the stilettos in the lawn and paced barefoot, her mermaid tail dragging in the grass and twigs. A Black female uniformed officer stood by the back door, guarding Maddie while Josh went over the scene with a male detective and more uniformed officers inside.

The scene. Josh's living room was now a crime scene. She shivered in spite of the muggy air.

Josh stepped outside, followed by the detective. Both men crossed the patio to where she stood in the grass. He put an arm around her and said, "You ready to answer questions?"

She nodded. "There's not much I can say. I didn't really see anything. I was in the middle of the best sex of my life, and then everything went to hell."

Josh glanced at the detective. "Can you make sure to put that in the report? Maybe highlight it in a bold font?"

Both the detective and Maddie laughed. She leaned into Josh's embrace and pressed her nose to the T-shirt he'd donned when he went back into the house. It smelled of fabric softener and not the peppery scent of tear gas she'd been trying to expel from her nose and lungs for the last thirty minutes.

He kissed the top of her head, then released her. She turned to face the detective. "Where do I start?"

The detective was tall—he had to be at least six-four. A handsome Black man, he had the air of authority one wanted in a police detective. "You, um, don't have to go into detail about your activities before the grenades were thrown. I think I got the gist."

Yeah, her panties on the floor had probably been a big clue.

"Whew," she said with a half laugh. "There's really not much to say. I was…distracted. I heard glass break, but I'm not even certain the sound registered right away. Next thing I knew, Josh pulled me off the couch and covered me—I presume to protect me from broken glass or whatever had broken the window." It had all happened so fast, and his protection had been instant. Instinctive.

She glanced at him. "You didn't get cut, did you?"

He gave a sharp shake of his head.

She turned back to the tall detective. "Then Josh said to close my eyes and hold my breath. It was too late, though. I got a lungful and opened my eyes when I stumbled getting to my feet. Josh pulled me to the back door, and we got outside."

Her exposure to the gas was mild compared to how bad it could have been. She'd been better within minutes of stepping outside. There'd been no need for paramedics to examine either her or Josh. Really, what she wanted more than anything was a shower.

She answered the detective's last questions, and he returned to the inside of the house.

"There's little evidence to go on," Josh said. "Aside from tracking the tear gas grenades. If we hadn't been—"

He stopped short, and she realized what he wasn't saying. "If we hadn't been in the middle of having sex, you'd have gone out the front and tried to identify them."

"No. I needed to get you out safely. That was the top priority."

"But still, you wish you'd been able to do both."

"Of course I wish I could have protected you and caught them. I'm an operator. My job has always been to jump into the fray. It's ingrained so deep, it's instinctual."

"No. Your instinct was to cover me, to protect me." She gripped his shirt and pulled his head down so his lips were a scant centimeter from hers. "Tell you what, next time, you go after the bad guys and I'll get myself out. I know the way now. I'll be fine."

"One, there won't be a next time, and two, protecting you always comes first. Period."

He said it with such authority mixed with emotion, she felt a giddy thrill. He brushed his lips over hers, then raised his head and met her gaze. His eyes were sad and intense. "Listen, I shouldn't leave here tonight, not with the front windows shattered. I already had a contractor lined up to switch out the windows for bulletproof glass next week. I'm going to see if he'll be able to jump on it in the next day or two, but until then, I'm not comfortable with you being here."

She'd longed for him to hold her tonight as she slept, but his words made it clear that wasn't going to happen. "If you're worried about Ava, she can stay with me if she's willing."

"Thank you. I'm sure she'd rather stay with Marcus, but that might not work out for his family."

She'd met Marcus and his parents when she dropped Ava off. She'd realized right away that Marcus was probably trans and only a few months into the hormone therapy, but it wasn't her business, and she wouldn't ask for confirmation. She was just glad to see the boy had parents who embraced their son and suspected the support Marcus and Ava gave each other was mutual and deep, as both of their worlds had undergone a major shift in the last year.

She envied their friendship, having felt somewhat adrift after losing her fiancé and her closest friend on the same day a year ago.

When she got home tonight, she'd call Trina...except there was a three-hour time difference, and Trina had gone through her own trauma tonight along with her husband. Keith needed her far more than Maddie did.

She bit her lip. Josh needed her as much as Keith needed Trina. And equally important, she needed Josh. "Please, can I stay the night? I don't…want to be alone. And you shouldn't be alone either."

"It's too dangerous."

She cupped his face. "They had their fun. They scared us. Got us running outside half-naked. They won't come back, and if they do, you'll be ready for them. I heard the officers say they'd drive by every thirty minutes tonight. Your house is probably safer than mine right now."

"I can't. We can't. I need to be alert for intruders."

"And you need to sleep because you aren't a machine. Listen, sex is off the table, I know that. I might be too traumatized for that anyway. Oral sex might never be the same."

He cupped her cheeks. "No way. I will personally devote my life to healing that scar, even if it takes years of practice until you enjoy it again like you did tonight."

She smiled and whispered, "It might take decades of endless oral sex until I'm fixed."

His brown eyes lit with humor. "I'm here to help you heal. But not tonight. No sex, no distractions tonight."

Warmth bloomed in her chest. "I can stay?"

"You can stay. I mean, you were prepared for a volcano eruption or earthquake. Shame to let that preparation go to waste when we *did* have a terror attack."

"Is that what this was? A terror attack?"

"Did you feel terror?" Josh asked.

She nodded.

"The whole point of gassing us was to make us afraid, so yeah, that's what it was."

"You're still going to train people to protect counterprotestors, right?"

"Hell yeah. I won't let them scare me off. It's their end goal, and I won't let them win." He brushed her hair out of her eyes. "And I've made a decision on another question you asked too. Tomorrow, I want you and Ava to attend the training—not because you'll be at the protests, but because I want you both to learn self-defense."

⸎

Josh held Maddie in his arms for a long time after they crawled into bed. He was so thankful he wasn't alone, that she'd pushed him to let her stay. After the cops had left, Maddie made dinner while he boarded up the front windows with plywood he robbed from one of the walls in the unfinished basement. Finishing it and painting the walls was on his very long to-do list, but right now, he was glad he hadn't gotten around to it.

Task complete, they'd eaten tacos in his office while he checked in with the night shift at Raptor headquarters, giving the full report of the incident. While they were at it, decisions were made on who would fly to Portland to help out with the new Nielsen Steel contract. He needed help here by midweek or sooner, if possible.

After dinner, Maddie had showered, then crawled into bed while Josh took his turn in the shower. Much as he wanted to shower with her, the potential for distraction was too high.

Clean, all tear gas residue removed from his skin, he'd donned boxer briefs and a T-shirt and crawled into bed with her, and now they held each other in silence. It filled some missing piece in his heart. He'd never done this before, or at least not without sex being involved at the beginning or the end of the holding part.

He wondered if she had. There was so much he didn't know about her. Starting with her family. "Will you tell me about your brother?"

She stiffened in his arms, then relaxed. "I suppose now is as good a time as any."

"No. Not if you don't want to."

She scooted back and stared at him. She was more shadow than light, and he found even her silhouette beautiful. "I'm sorry I didn't tell you about Alan. I mean that. I just—it was really nice to *not* have that as part of our conversation, because it hurts, more than I can tell my parents. More than I can tell him."

"What happened?"

"Nearly two years ago, I was in a serious relationship, and we had a birth control fail. I was on a prescription that negated the hormones and didn't realize it. My doctor caught it, and called me. I went straight in to her office and got a test and learned I was pregnant. I was reeling, trying to figure out what I wanted. My boyfriend proposed. I was in love with him and knew if I didn't say yes, there would be no recovering from that. So even though he didn't propose because he *wanted* to get married, we got engaged. Told everyone—but didn't tell anyone about the pregnancy. I was only four weeks, after all.

"Then…I got sick. I ended up in the emergency room and discovered the pregnancy was ectopic. Not viable, and killing me. My fallopian tube ruptured, which required major surgery. They had to remove the ruptured tube—which, of course, included the fetus. I lost a lot of blood and needed a transfusion."

Josh sensed she didn't want to be held and took her hand in his instead and squeezed. "I'm so sorry."

"Thank you. I barely had time to adjust to the idea of having a baby before it was gone, but my fiancé started talking about trying again as soon as we got the go-ahead from the doctor after the wedding. So the wedding plans moved forward, like a tractor beam. It was like…we couldn't take it back even though there wasn't going to be a baby. I was all kinds of messed up and didn't know if I wanted to marry him or not. I mean, I *loved* him. But, was it a marriage kind of love or a for-now kind of love?

"Then, a week before the wedding, my maid of honor told me *she* couldn't go through with it. And…I was confused, because she'd always liked him." She let out a bitter laugh. "Boy, did she. So it turns out that while I was still in the hospital after emergency surgery, she told my fiancé she was in love with him, and now that there was no baby, he could leave me and be with her. And…he said he couldn't leave me while I was recovering, but he had no problem having sex with her."

"Oh, Maddie."

She sat up and pulled her knees to her chest. "I guess he kept stringing her along, telling her he couldn't dump me, and we found ourselves planning a wedding in which my maid of honor was banging the groom and I was utterly clueless. Finally, she couldn't take it anymore and told me. I confronted him, and he admitted everything, and now they're married and have a kid on the way. I think she was trying to get pregnant in the months leading up to the wedding as a way to seal the deal. Anyway, I'm better off without both of them, and I got to keep all our mutual friends in the breakup so…yay?"

"I'm so sorry they both betrayed you so badly."

"I am too, and yet, I realize I dodged a bullet. I could be *married* to that cheating sonofabitch. I could still be confiding in my ex-bestie." Her smile was only faintly visible in the darkened room. "And then I wouldn't be here with you now."

He pulled her hand to his lips and kissed her fingers. "And I'm so thankful you're with me here now."

She let out a heavy breath. "But…none of that explains my current relationship with my brother."

"I'm thinking I might be able to guess."

"Go for it."

"I've listened to several of his speeches. I know his talking points. His stance on abortion is cold. He doesn't view reproductive rights as health care and thinks it should be outlawed in all instances, even when the woman's life is in danger."

"Bingo." She shook her head. "The worst part is, I know him, and I know that he doesn't actually *believe* any of that. He sees it as necessary to getting elected, and it's so nice to know my own brother would let me die if it meant more power for him. My mom argues that he doesn't mean it, and that hurts too. My own mom. A woman. And she's so eager for the golden boy to be…I don't know…the next president of the United States, so she's willing to look the other way instead of listening to the words that come out of his mouth. She and my dad have always doted on him. She was thrilled when he was elected to congress—which I get, of course— but she doesn't look at the cost of his stated views.

"Alan is pissed I won't campaign for him…but why would I? He's betrayed me and every woman in this country when he refuses to acknowledge my bodily autonomy, that I have a right to live that supersedes that of a six-week-old bundle of cells."

"Can I…hold you?"

She leaned against him, snuggling into his chest and he wrapped his arms around her. "One of the hardest parts in all of this is I lost both of my best friends on the same day, and then my brother started campaigning and saying the most hurtful things, and I lost my family too. I have my wine-tasting friends, but…it's not the same level of closeness. I felt so utterly abandoned. It's a horrible thing to have to wade through intensely emotional waters alone. Trina helped, but she was thousands of miles away."

Josh tensed at hearing Trina's name, but then relaxed. He was past worrying about mixed attractions. He could bury his secret shame and move on. "Thank you for sharing this with me." He stroked her back and kissed her forehead. "I'm here for you now."

She ran a hand over his stomach, under his shirt. A caress not meant to be arousing, but it was Maddie, so he got hard anyway. "Have I mentioned how much I like you, Josh?"

"I was getting a solid idea of your opinion of me when we were on the couch earlier." He paused, then added, "So, the best sex you've ever had? And I have a witness, so you can't deny saying it."

She laughed. "The best. And we hadn't even gotten to penetration yet."

"Hmm. Kinda adds a layer of pressure I wasn't counting on."

"I have no doubt you will live up to the fantasies I'm having now."

"Right now?" His hand ignored his brain and slipped lower to cup her butt.

"Well, not *right* now. I'm kind of exhausted and maybe a bit emotionally wrung out."

He kissed her forehead again. "Me too. We should get some sleep."

"We should."

Neither of them moved. They just went back to holding each other in silence, but then finally, her eyes drifted closed. Their position was awkward for sleeping, so he loosened his hold and she rolled over and scooted back against him. He tucked his knees behind hers, spooning her back to his front, and held her that way until her breathing evened out and she drifted to sleep.

He lay awake, holding her, wondering how in the hell he was going to be able to keep her and Ava safe from the White Patriots who had targeted him, all while protecting an entitled billionaire and facing off with her ambitious brother, who he suspected was an active member of the White Patriots.

Chapter Fourteen

$\mathcal{M}$addie drove Ava to Bond Ironworks and couldn't help but smile at the packed parking lot. "Your uncle has managed to get a lot of volunteers in such a short time." She pulled into the last employee-only spot, thankful he'd reserved it for them.

"With all the TV interviews he did, there'll probably be a lot of women. You might be in for some competition."

Maddie laughed. It seemed unlikely a horde of women would sign up for such a dangerous task just to meet a man. But then, the man was Josh, who had looked damn compelling on TV. "Good thing I met him before he became famous, then."

"You aren't worried?"

She put the car in Park and shut off the engine. "Not even a little bit. Besides, if Josh is the type of guy to lose interest at the next pretty face, he's not the guy for me." *Been there, done that.*

"Are you still going to make me tell him about reading his letter?"

The words were a sharp jolt to the heart after the night she and Josh had shared. They might not have finished what they started, but it still had been intensely intimate.

Josh's clear feelings had nothing to do with her resemblance to Trina. "I think you should come clean. It's important for trust to go both ways. And you're worried Josh isn't committed to being here for you, partly because of what you read in that letter. I can tell you until the end of time that he is, but you need to clear this air with him to be able to let it go."

"Are you trying to make him mad at me?"

"Ava, the last thing in the world I want is a wedge between you and your uncle. If I wanted anything along those lines, I'd lose, because you're Josh's number one priority. As you should be."

"You don't resent that?"

"Of course not. If you were his biological daughter, I'd expect nothing less. The fact that he puts you first just makes me like him more. He's a *good* man." She glanced at her watch. "And we're going to disappoint him if we're late."

They grabbed their gym bags from the backseat, and Maddie locked the car, then they headed into the gym.

The space was full—there had to be over eighty volunteers ready to train. It was a good thing the gym was in a large open former warehouse, because it was at capacity.

Josh was in the back corner, talking with the big, exceedingly muscular man who Maddie recognized from the news as Arthur Bond.

Maddie and Ava crossed the crowded room to the two men in charge. Josh's face lit with a big smile at the sight of them. He gave Ava a crushing hug. He hadn't seen her since Maddie had picked her up on Thursday morning, and it was clear he'd missed her.

After hugging Ava, he turned to Maddie. They'd said goodbye this morning at eight a.m., when he drove her home before his early meeting with Arthur to prep for the day's training session.

Her belly did a small flip at seeing the warm light in his eyes. The heat and intimacy between them was tangible. Sweet. And hot.

He slipped an arm around her waist and kissed her. A real kiss, barely on the side of appropriate for public view.

A few catcalls made it past the sound of blood rushing to important places.

He raised his head and said, "Just making sure to stake my claim."

She laughed. "It goes both ways, so works for me."

He released her and pointed to the end of the front row. "You and Ava take the end there. We're going to divide into groups of ten based on skill level."

The next three hours were a mix of workout and lessons. In the center of the room, Josh and Arthur demonstrated techniques, taking turns as aggressors and using volunteers to play victim. Each ten-minute demonstration was then followed up by twenty minutes of practice, with Bond Ironworks employees leading the groups and Josh and Arthur circulating the room.

As they neared the end of the session, Maddie was exhausted and covered in sweat. Ava looked the same, but there was a light of exhilaration in her eyes. It didn't hurt that their beginner circle was next to an advanced group, and Ava had her eyes on Desmond.

The news had reported Desmond's age: nineteen. With Ava barely seventeen, they were within reasonable—even legal—age to get involved. Would Josh balk at Ava dating if something developed between the two of them? Because one thing was certain: Desmond noticed Ava too.

A buzzer sounded, and everyone turned to face Josh in the center of the room. Someone new stood with him. He was white. Taller than Josh, but shorter than Arthur, he wore a tight Raptor T-shirt that matched Josh's.

Maddie really liked the fit of those T-shirts.

"We've got one last demonstration for everyone today. This is Chase Johnston. Chase has been with Raptor longer than I have, and he has the distinct honor of being the only Raptor employee to have never been a police officer or serve in the military to be named to our elite Falcon Team. Today, you're going to see why Chase made the team when others with far more experience failed."

Chase's gaze dropped to the floor as if he were embarrassed. It was kind of endearing. He was muscular but wiry, and had a boyish face. But he'd been with Raptor longer than Josh, so he must be in his late twenties. Trina had once mentioned that Raptor didn't hire operatives below the age of twenty-one.

"Did you bring the knife?" Josh asked Chase.

He nodded and pulled a blade from the bag by his feet. It was about the size of an eight-inch chef's knife, but meaner looking.

Chase handed the blade to Josh, who held it up for their audience to see. "This is a special demo knife. The cutting edge is blunt and covered with an ink-filled pad. It releases red dye on anything it touches. He ran the blade over his open palm. Red ink dripped down his palm as if he'd been sliced.

Chase handed Josh a towel. He wiped his hand clean, then nodded to Chase. "You ready?"

The younger man nodded, and they faced each other and bowed, fist in palm.

They circled each other, Josh wielding the knife. Then there was a blur of motion. Chase kicking and dodging, Josh jabbing and twisting. It was a masterpiece of choreography as the two men danced a deadly tango.

Then, in a flash, Josh was on his back on the mat, Chase loomed above, and the knife was now in his hands.

Josh kicked out and hopped to his feet in a show of athleticism that she would ask him to perform later, in private. Then he was dancing with Chase again, but this time, he was unarmed. He dodged and weaved and tried to take the knife back, but Chase was always one step ahead, his hands moving at lightning speed.

Finally, Josh struck the weapon from Chase's hand just as the taller man slammed him back to the floor. Josh looked up at the victor. He was breathing heavily as he said, "You *let* me knock the knife away."

"You looked like you were getting tired," Chase said, speaking for the first time, without the slightest hint of being winded.

Several onlookers—including Maddie—laughed.

Josh gave a rueful grin as Chase pulled him to his feet. Josh then turned in a full circle, arms in the air, so everyone could see the red lines on his forearms and staining on his yellow shirt across his stomach. There was even a red streak across his cheek and another short mark on his neck.

Chase raised his arms and spun in a circle as well. He didn't have a spot of red on him.

"And that, my friends, is why Chase made Falcon team at the age of twenty-two, without any military service or training."

Several people cheered, and Chase blushed. He was kind of adorable.

"How did you do that?" someone called out.

"I—I..." He took a deep breath, and Maddie realized he suffered from stuttering. "I've studied martial arts s-s-since I was a toddler. My dad was a karate instructor." He seemed to settle in and the stutter disappeared. "I'm here to teach you defensive techniques when fighting with an assailant armed with a knife."

"Damn, where were you two weeks ago?" Desmond asked. "I coulda used your tips then."

There were several loud barks of laughter.

"Yeah," another man said. "All we had was Josh over there, and he's all striped up like a red-and-white zebra."

Josh laughed. "Hey, you want to take on Chase? I guarantee you won't come out as good as I did."

"I kind of do," another man said. "But I get the knife."

Chase shrugged. "Sure. Bring it."

What followed was twenty minutes of guys trying to get the best of Chase. None of them lasted more than thirty seconds, and Josh was right, no one fared as well as he had.

Chase never got a drop of red dye on him.

"Impressive," Maddie said as she stepped up beside Josh while Chase demonstrated some of the defensive moves in slow motion to a rapt audience.

Josh glanced her way and smiled, then returned his attention to the center of the room. "Chase is the best at armed hand-to-hand combat. I wasn't sure if we were going to be able to get him out here for a lesson, but the contract with Nielsen clinched it. We get him for six weeks."

"He flew in this morning?"

"Yeah. I got the call that he was on his way right after I dropped you off. Present from Keith."

Last night, she'd gotten a very private glimpse into his friendship with Keith. She was damn happy Trina had landed a good one.

She leaned close and whispered, "Is Chase the one… Trina told me about?"

Josh nodded. "He's a different man than he was last fall. A year ago, we only got glimpses of moments like this. He was competent, but not confident. Look at him. He's got over seventy-five people paying rapt attention, and he's already got four trainees stepping up and doing demonstrations for smaller groups. He's a born teacher."

"I thought Falcon team was operatives, not teachers?"

"They're both. Each compound has their own Falcon team. The Alaska compound, where Chase was originally hired, doesn't go on missions or handle private security. Their business is training. But even so, each member of Falcon needs to be operation ready at all times, in case they're needed elsewhere."

"Chase will be part of C-IV's personal security team?"

"Yeah, until we get it figured out. We don't have any specs from him on what he wants yet for his personal security. And then there are the mines and plants he's got here and abroad —I have no clue what he wants there. He said he'd send me papers during his flight, but all he's sent so far was a picture of us in the *Oregonian*."

"Oh? I haven't seen that yet. How'd we look?"

"You look gorgeous. Fortunately, the photographer got at least one picture before I answered my phone, so I look decent." He gave a lopsided smile. "The article isn't about the fund-raiser, though. It's about Nielsen Steel's plan to hire Raptor."

"Is that sort of thing really *news*? I mean, who would care beyond other security firms?"

"Nielsen wants to milk the association with the work I'm doing here." Josh nodded toward the gym full of people. "Kinda makes me wonder how bad his family's Nazi history is that he's going full court on this right after you started digging in the archives."

"Good point. He and I never had a chance to talk about my research last night."

"If you hear from him while he's in Japan, I want to know everything he says. Keith is fine sinking money into landing this contract on the chance it's legit, but neither of us is entirely convinced. Nielsen has an angle he's working."

Chapter Fifteen

Josh tucked his phone away and nodded to Ava. It was time to leave. The training had ended twenty minutes ago, and he was ready for some down time after yesterday's emotional ride and today's ongoing workout. Chase was staying behind to do an hour or two of one-on-one sessions with Desmond and a few of the others who wanted it, then he'd be taking over the guest room at Josh's house. Maddie had left the gym already, and now, at last, he could take Ava home and spend some quality time with his niece.

He'd missed her over the weekend. Much as he'd enjoyed his R&R time and had been eager for a first real date with Maddie, he'd missed Ava's energy and wit. Missed being able to give and receive the affection she so desperately needed.

"I vote we order pizza and binge-watch TV for the rest of the day," he said as he hit the button to unlock the SUV. "How about every *Spider-Man* movie, starting with Tobey Maguire."

"No way, it's Tom Holland or it ain't *Spider-Man*." She

chewed on a thumbnail, then said, "I think we should watch every movie that features a female superhero as the lead."

He settled behind the wheel. "*Wonder Woman, Captain Marvel*, what else?"

"*Incredibles 2* is all about Elastigirl, so that counts. *Birds of Prey* counts too."

"What about *Catwoman?*"

"Um. No. Definitely not."

Josh laughed and started the engine.

"I'm going to add *Black Panther* to the watch list, because the women in that movie are so badass, I don't even care that the main superhero is a guy. Plus, Chadwick Boseman and Michael B. Jordan are both crazy hot."

"No objection from me. I could watch Lupita Nyong'o all day." Thinking about the beautiful Black actress brought Trish to mind. He put the SUV in Reverse, but kept his foot on the brake. "Did Maddie tell you about my friend Tricia?"

Ava nodded. "How is she doing?"

"Better. Sean is making arrangements to fly her back to DC tomorrow, along with the other survivor, in Raptor's jet."

"She's still in a coma?"

"Yeah. Medically induced. There'll be a doctor on the flight, but keeping her out is probably best for the long flight."

"I'm so sorry she was hurt, but glad she's alive." Ava reached out and placed her hand on his biceps.

He covered her fingers with his. "Thanks. Me too."

"You were…supposed to go to that conference, weren't you?"

He nodded.

"And you didn't. Because of me."

He gave her a half smile. "Owen, actually. His start date at R&R made being here a priority."

"Is it…wrong that I'm glad it wasn't you?"

"Honey, you've had enough loss. Not wanting to lose one more doesn't make you a bad person."

"I don't want you to get hurt, Uncle Josh. I—I need you. To be my dad. But also because I love you."

Tears came to Josh's eyes lightning fast. She'd never said that to him before. "I love you too, kiddo. I hate how it came about, but moving here, being your"—he stumbled, because he'd never dared to use the D-word before—"dad-like person is the best thing I ever did."

"There's something I have to tell you. You aren't going to like it."

Unease slithered down his spine, but really, what could she say that would be a problem? That she wanted him to find a different job because his work was dangerous? Give up training the volunteers? He could understand her reasons for feeling that way, and he would never tell her her feelings were wrong.

"Can it wait until we get home?"

"No. I might chicken out."

He put the SUV in Park. "What's up?"

"I—I know about Trina. That you moved here because you wanted to get away from her."

All the blood in Josh's body went straight to his gut. His deepest darkest secret. His greatest shame. Said aloud for the first time by his niece.

*M*addie was sore everywhere. The training session in the gym had worked out muscles she'd only known existed in theory after intensive study of the human skeleton. She knew the insertion points on the bone, knew where they resided under her skin, but until today, they'd never made themselves felt.

They burned now, angry at being woken from their life-long slumber. And if experience was any guide, tomorrow would be even worse.

She stopped at a Fred Meyer on the way home to pick up groceries and bath salts for sore muscles. She was driving back to the Painted Hills tomorrow and hoped the salts would ease the soreness before the long drive.

Next to the checkout was a stack of newspapers. She picked up the *Oregonian*, wondering if the photo of her and Josh with C-IV had made the print edition. She tossed it in the cart, just in case.

She probably wouldn't see Josh again until Wednesday. Disappointing, but he needed alone time with Ava, and now he had Chase to take care of too.

The man couldn't not be a caretaker. Although Chase appeared to be doing just fine. Much further along the healing spectrum than Owen had been. But Trina had given only the barest overview of what Chase had been though, and Maddie suspected what Trina had been allowed to share was only the tip of the iceberg of what the operative had suffered.

She was in her car, nearly home, when her cell phone buzzed. With the phone in the dashboard holder, the caller was easy to read without taking her eyes off the road for a full second.

Portland Police Bureau.

She spotted a gas station on the right and pulled into the lot, then answered the call.

"Ms. Foster, this is Officer Leahey with the Portland Police Bureau," a woman said. "Your alarm service alerted us to check on your address, and we discovered a break-in. How soon can you get here to assess the damage and inventory what was stolen?"

Her stomach had plummeted at the officer's first words.

Her beautiful little rental house. She felt a sharp sense of violation and fear, and she didn't even know if anything had been taken. She managed to form the necessary words. "I'm —I'm f-five minutes away."

"You're driving?"

"I'm pulled over at a gas station."

"Stay there. I'll send a patrol car to pick you up."

"No. I'm okay. I can drive. I just…" She trailed off. She wasn't sure if she was feeling adrenaline or panic or both.

"Give yourself a few minutes, then. Buy a soda if the station's got a convenience store. We're guarding the property, and will be here when you arrive."

"Okay."

She took the officer's advice and entered the store, grabbing the first sugary drink she could find. Back inside the car, she sipped it slowly and tried to sort her thoughts. Her hands were still shaking. She wasn't quite ready to drive.

She dialed Josh's number. Her call rolled to voicemail, and she left a message, telling him the scant details she knew. She waited a few minutes to see if he'd call back. When he didn't, she took several deep breaths and held out her hands. The trembling had lessened.

She put the car in gear and headed home, dreading what she would find there.

***

Josh's phone buzzed as Ava's words hung in the air. He glanced at the screen. Maddie.

No way could he take her call now, not when Ava had just laid that bombshell. He sent the call to voicemail.

"Talk," he said to Ava, a harder edge to his voice than he

intended. It was a gut punch that Ava knew his secret. The only way she could possibly know was if she'd read the damn letter. The one he'd intended to burn after getting it out of his system.

But for some damn reason, he'd kept it. Hadn't been able to destroy it because rereading it had helped him come to terms with the guilt and shame. He'd have put it in the gun safe at the house, but that was Raptor property. Not only did it feel weird to store it there, but Owen, Chase, and any other visiting operative could've found it.

He should have bought his own damn document safe.

"I—I—I'm sorry, Uncle Josh."

"First, I came here for *you*. That letter was me processing something that has nothing to do with you. Second, it hurts that you would go through my things. I would never violate your privacy in that way."

"It—it wasn't me."

She wasn't making sense. "What do you mean? How could it not be you?"

"When Maddie took me home yesterday to grab clean clothes for my sleepover at Marcus's house, I found her in your room, going through your nightstand drawer. I was shocked. I told her that I was going to tell you. She said you'd never believe me. Because I've already made it clear I don't like her and I'd do anything to get rid of her. Even lie. Then she gave me the letter and said, 'You should know he didn't come here for you. You were his excuse.'"

Every word from Ava's mouth was a sucker punch. It didn't sound like Maddie at all. Ava had to be lying.

But if he called Ava a liar and she was telling the truth… He'd lose everything he'd built with her.

And how well did he really know Maddie?

Sure, the sexual attraction was there in spades, but what if that was based on her resemblance to Trina? What if their chemistry came from nothing more than a shared taste in wine?

No. Hours on the phone with her said his feelings went deeper than that. He *knew* Maddie. She wouldn't violate his privacy, wouldn't cut Ava's growing confidence by saying something so awful.

But Ava loved him. Needed him to be her dad. Why would she hurt him by making up such a story?

Last night, when Tisdale mentioned Maddie's resemblance to Trina, Maddie had stiffened. He'd had a flash of worry that somehow Maddie knew, but that was impossible.

Except now he knew it wasn't.

Maddie *had* known.

His eyes burned. One of the two women who'd become the center of his world in a very short time had just hurt him deeply. And he wasn't a hundred percent certain which one.

Chapter Sixteen

It could be worse.

Maddie stared at her office. She'd lost her old desktop computer, but the files were backed up to the cloud. She'd had her laptop with her, safely locked in the trunk of her car, and it held all her recent work. They'd left her printer and TV—both items were likely too large for a quick break-in, especially with the alarm blaring.

She wore gloves provided by the officer, but even so, she plucked a pen from her purse and slid it behind the top desk drawer handle and pulled it open. She didn't keep much in the drawer. Post-its, her favorite pens, a north arrow scale for photographs. And portable USB storage drives. *Shit.* They weren't there. "They took my thumb drives. All of them." She tried to remember what was on them. Photos and work files. She rubbed her temples. "My accounting software backup file is on there. They'll have all my account numbers."

"Was the accounting file on the desktop computer?" Officer Leahey asked.

"No. I have a cheap laptop I use only for accounting."

She took the desk key from her purse and unlocked the large bottom drawer. The laptop was still there. The thieves hadn't bothered to waste time prying open the desk.

Thank you, Josh, for making me get a high-end, loud security system.

But her financial data was still on the thumb drives. She'd call her bank and credit card companies the moment she was done with the inventory with the police. This was going to screw up all her autopayments. If they managed to get her Social Security number, she could find herself having to deal with the fallout for years.

Oh goody.

"What about jewelry?" Officer Leahey asked. "Or other valuable items?"

"Jewelry is in my bedroom upstairs." She led the way upstairs, passing another officer on the way down.

"No sign anyone made it upstairs, but we'll need you to confirm," the officer said.

She nodded, afraid to hope.

She checked the jewelry box first—it was small and held a few of her favorite—and relatively inexpensive—items. All necklaces, bracelets, and earrings were there.

She then turned to the closet and pulled down a large, dusty hatbox from the top shelf. "I don't keep the valuable stuff in the jewelry box. It's too obvious, and these items are sentimental."

She pulled out the wide-brimmed red hat with black netting that had been her grandmother's and revealed the candy tin beneath. She opened the tin, and there was her maternal grandmother's gold watch and diamond earrings.

And the engagement ring Maddie had worn for eight months.

"Gorgeous ring," Officer Leahey said. The uniformed

white woman was probably close to Maddie's age, and she'd been kind throughout the unsettling process.

"Honestly, I kind of wish it were stolen."

"Ouch. I take it it's not an heirloom."

"Nope. Bad breakup."

"Good for you in not giving it back," she said.

Maddie probably would have given it to him, but then he said he needed to sell it to buy his new fiancée a ring. And well...*fuck that*. The ring was hers, even if she'd never wear it.

She put her grandmother's watch on her wrist. It was time to stop storing it and actually use it. It could have been stolen today, and she never would have enjoyed having the piece that connected her to a woman who'd always believed in her. Grandma had worked in factories during World War II and fought for women's equality for nearly six full decades after the war.

She put the rest of the jewelry back in the tin and hat box and returned it to the shelf. "It looks like the only thing they took was the computer and flash drives."

"Which is pretty targeted—but they were also in a hurry. We were on the scene within five minutes of the alarm going off."

The thieves had smashed through the back door. They'd likely parked on the street parallel to hers and jumped the rear neighbor's fence coming and going.

As they headed back down the stairs, Maddie's cell phone vibrated with a text.

Probably Josh. She felt a rush of warmth. She knew he was planning a movie night with Ava, but maybe he'd let her come over for a bit and just hold her. She needed a little comfort after her home had been violated.

At the bottom of the stairs, she pulled out the phone and frowned to see a message from Ava. Two words: *I'm sorry.*

What was that about?

She tucked the phone away.

"Given that this theft appears to be targeted, did anyone know you were going to be out today?" Officer Leahey asked.

"Anyone who knows I'm dating Josh Warner might have guessed I'd be at the training today."

"He's the Raptor guy who's been training counterprotesters? In consultation with the Bureau?"

Maddie nodded.

"And how many people know you're dating?"

"Well, it was sort of in the paper today."

"So basically, everyone. And especially people who are watching Warner—all officers received a briefing from the chief after he was doxed. And yesterday, there was an attack at his house."

Maddie nodded. "Yes. I was there."

"You know," the officer cocked her head, "you probably should have led with that. It changes everything."

"But my address isn't a matter of public record. *I* haven't been doxed. No one knows where I live, and as you said, this looks pretty targeted at my computer."

"You're certain you haven't been doxed? You just said your relationship with Mr. Warner was in the paper."

She pulled out her phone as her brain raced to remember which website had doxed Josh. She never went to the nut-job sites. Ever.

She was about to google it when a message popped up on her phone. Not from Josh.

KEITH

Voigt Forum doxed you three hours ago. We were busy with medivac arrangements for Tricia, or we'd have caught it sooner. Raptor is setting you up in a hotel. Will text with reservation confirmation.

She showed the officer the message on her screen.

"Damn," the woman said. "I'll call the chief. You pack a bag. I'll escort you to the hotel."

"I need to make arrangements to fix my back door. I can't leave the house wide open like this."

"We'll nail a board over it on the inside. You're going to need a new door, and that'll take a few days. Take everything valuable, including the stuff hidden in the hatbox. Anyone who wants in will get in." She nodded to the phone. "Go to the hotel, and we'll get the detective investigating last night's tear bomb attack to follow up with you there. This could be random, thanks to the doxing—but why did they go for the computer and nothing else? *That's* not random."

Maddie's brain raced as she took in the officer's advice. Move to a hotel. Her home wasn't safe for the foreseeable future.

And…why hadn't Josh been the one to call her? Why Keith?

She checked her messages. Nothing from Josh since she'd called to say her house had a break-in. But she did have a message.

AVA

I'm sorry.

Her stomach clenched. What had Ava done?

MADDIE

Why?

"Go pack," the officer ordered.

Maddie headed back up the stairs, staring at her phone.

She was in her bedroom with her suitcase open on the bed when her phone vibrated again.

AVA

I told Uncle Josh about the letter.

That was good news. Josh would be upset, but once Ava explained how she felt scared having a man she barely knew as her guardian, he'd understand. They'd clear the air and be stronger for it.

Her phone buzzed again.

I told him the truth. How I caught you snooping in his nightstand drawer yesterday. I'm sorry, but you shouldn't have done it.

Maddie closed her eyes as pain sliced through her. Pain for Ava. Pain for Josh. Pain for herself.

Her anger at Ava left her breathless, but she reminded herself Ava was a brokenhearted, struggling girl who was trying desperately to keep the attention of the one adult in her life—a man who collected strays like he walked around with raw meat in his pockets—focused on her.

Ava could share Josh with Owen. She could share him with Chase. But Maddie was a threat in that she didn't *need* Josh the way the others did. He just made her happy. And she made him happy.

Ava's lie could well have destroyed that. For good.

Josh was in an untenable position. If he accused Ava of lying, he could break the fragile bond they'd found. But if he didn't believe it was a lie…what did that say about their nascent relationship?

He couldn't *really* believe it, could he? And did it really matter?

The first night they'd met, he'd stated in no uncertain terms that Ava came first. He'd reiterated it the second time.

How much would it gut him to hear Maddie claim Ava

had lied? Would he think she was trying to drive a wedge between them, that she was jealous of Ava's place in his heart and life?

This was a no-win situation all around.

If Josh reached out and said he knew it was a lie but he had to bide his time to get Ava to admit it so they could heal without making things worse, Maddie could accept that. But the longer her phone remained silent—in the aftermath of doxing and a break-in, no less—the longer she was certain that Josh wouldn't make that call.

Which meant on some level, Josh believed Ava. And there was nothing Maddie could do to change that.

Chapter Seventeen

Josh stared at the TV, not seeing the action on the screen. Hell, he'd be hard-pressed to name the film they were watching. Beside him, Ava laughed and nibbled on her pizza.

Her phone lay on the coffee table. He'd seen the texts to Maddie on the screen when she set it down earlier to go to the kitchen for a soda.

He'd noted Maddie's lack of response. No replies that called out Ava for lying. But of course, Ava could have deleted the replies before she placed the phone on the table.

He could call Lee Scott, have him hack Ava's phone and provide a full transcript, but that violated every ethic he had and would be a gross abuse of Lee's skills.

What if everything he saw in Maddie was an illusion? What if he'd been so desperate to break the lock his obsession with Trina had on his heart that he'd fixated on Maddie and saw only what he wanted to see? What if she wasn't the warm, caring person he'd believed her to be?

Keith hadn't said a word when Josh asked him to inform

Maddie about Voigt Forum, but he knew his best friend had questions.

He couldn't face Maddie right now. Not when his stomach churned at the idea she might have thrown his feelings for Trina in Ava's face.

Bad enough to read his letter. But to weaponize it?

He wanted to believe it was all a cruel lie on Ava's part. But was his niece that vicious? Did she not want Josh to be happy?

She'd practically called him Dad and said she loved him. They were making *progress*, dammit. She wasn't conniving enough to use those words to manipulate him, was she?

Ava was too straightforward for that. Like the first night, when she said she was afraid Josh would fall in love with someone horrible and she'd be squeezed out—she'd been honest. And later, when she'd been rude to Maddie's face. It hadn't been pleasant, but it had been Ava unfiltered.

She'd said on Thursday night that she kind of liked Maddie. If that was true, why would she lie now? None of it made sense.

All he knew was his heart hurt, and the person he wanted to turn to, Maddie, was the cause of the pain.

And he sure as hell couldn't tell Keith, the other person he'd always confided in. *Hey, man, I wanted to bang your wife for years. And I wrote a letter about it. And either Ava or Maddie found it. And either Maddie was snooping and cruel, or Ava lied to hurt us. And in the meantime, I was doxed and so was Maddie, and I'm just trying to keep us all from getting swatted. Plus, I've got a billionaire yanking my chain with a big contract, and by the way, how is Tricia?*

He picked up his beer from where it sat next to his ignored pizza and drank half of it. He'd planned to allow himself only one drink tonight, but Chase would be here as backup. He could have two.

"You okay, Uncle Josh?"

He turned to Ava and tried to figure out how to answer. His dad would never have showed emotional weakness. But then, his dad was about the worst example of fatherhood imaginable. Unfortunately, he was the only example Josh had when it came to teenagers. Lee and Curt were good dads, but their kids were toddlers.

He didn't know Matt Clark very well, but he knew the guy was devoted to his adopted son. But Julian was only six or seven. You didn't unload your heartache on innocent seven-year-olds.

But what about potentially lying seventeen-year-olds?

He sighed. "No. Not really."

"Is this about…Maddie?"

He gave a clipped nod.

"You…really liked her."

"I don't want to talk about it, but yes. I did."

"I'm sorry."

He waited, hoping she'd add more, but she didn't.

"Did you…love her?"

He picked up his beer and finished it off. Then he stood. "I don't want to talk about it. Sorry, Ava. I'm not in the mood for a movie. Chase should be here soon. Maybe he'll keep you company."

He retreated to his bedroom, sat on the edge of the bed, and dropped his face into his hands.

Ava had lied to him. She must have.

But…what if she hadn't?

*Maddie powered through Sunday night, canceling credit cards and putting a fraud alert on her bank accounts. She turned on the ringer on her phone, determined not to miss Josh's call, if it should come.

She woke Monday with a heavy heart, her phone having remained silent except for texts from Trina checking on her.

God. She wished she could talk to Trina. After she'd lost her closest friend last year, she'd found herself turning more and more to Trina, finding the distance didn't matter when they had FaceTime. But sharing this heartache with Trina would be a massive violation of Josh's privacy, and no matter how much she was hurting, no matter how angry, she'd never do that to him.

The drive to the Painted Hills was every bit as painful to her sore muscles as she'd feared, but at least she was working, staying busy.

Her privacy had been stolen by the doxing, but she hadn't begun to wrap her brain around that. There were too many questions, starting with: did she need to move? Followed by: would they just dox her again?

It could all be futile.

She was nearing her destination—a parcel of land in the middle of a checkerboard cut out of tribal land. The parcel had been along a railroad line, and Otto and Sally Kocher had been invited to dig there by none other than Clifford Nielsen the first, whose steel company was a big investor in the railroad and later ended up acquiring the line and half the checkerboard.

Checkerboarding—which looked on a map exactly like it sounded—was the method by which the federal government had leased and sold land in many western states. Government lands were divided into squares, and only nonadjacent squares were sold to private companies, like railroads, which could only purchase half the squares along the line, or settlers. This way, there were federal—or tribal—lands amidst private property. It was seen as a way to encourage invest-ment in the private holdings between government land as well as a way to destabilize tribal communities on and off the reservation.

She hoped to determine if the Kochers had been digging in a government-owned square *before* the square was sold to Nielsen Steel.

She'd found references to the dig in the Nielsen Steel archives, and it matched a note card from one of the vaults. Today, she'd hike out to the area and see if there were artifacts on the surface and would fill out a site form to file with the state. Having the remains tied to a recorded site would make it a lock for returning to the proper tribe, and add to her preponderance of evidence.

Today, she would focus on *that*. She'd do her job and see to it the remains were returned and reburied. She would not think about Josh or Ava or heartache.

Her cell phone rang. Caller ID indicated it was an international call. What were the odds it was an extremely wealthy steel magnate?

She didn't usually take calls while driving, but the road was straight and empty, so she tapped the screen.

"Maddie, it's Cliff. I heard you had a break-in yesterday."

"Your knowledge of my life is getting a little creepy, Mr. Nielsen."

"I've told you to call me Cliff."

"That doesn't make it less creepy."

He laughed. "I have contacts at the police department and asked them to keep me informed if your name came up. Your relationship with Warner puts you at risk."

She bit her tongue from telling him the relationship was history. Their relationship status didn't matter. She was in danger. "Your concern is flattering."

"I'm sure Warner will do an excellent job seeing to your protection."

Okayyy. So he *wasn't* concerned. Good to know. "Yes. Raptor is taking good care of me." That was true enough.

"Excellent. I look forward to working with them. My question for you is, I understand your computer was stolen. Were my great-grandparents papers on that computer?"

She pulled over to the side of the road, realizing her vision had narrowed to the degree that she would probably miss a road train in the oncoming lane.

"Really, let me repeat, your concern is *flattering*."

"I could waste both our time on platitudes, but I'm a busy man."

She rolled her eyes. "Yes. Photos of your great-grandparents' papers were on the computer. It loads all my photos from the cloud."

"I would like an inventory of all the documents you photographed."

"I provided that with my documents request last week." She sighed. "Cliff, what is your issue here? What are you afraid of?"

"Nielsen Steel is an American company with a hundred-and-twenty-five-year history. We've made mistakes, but we worked to right them. We played an important role in the war effort during World War II, and we're about to embark on an ad campaign highlighting that history. If you should come forward with papers indicating my great-grandparents were Nazi sympathizers, we're going to have a problem."

"I can't speak to your great-grandparents' sympathies because I wasn't researching that. You should check your own archives if you have that concern. Now, sir, like you, I am a busy person and need to get to work. I hope your business in Japan is going well. Goodbye."

She hung up and took a deep breath. *What the hell?*

Why was this man pestering *her*? The papers were in *his* archives. He could answer his own damn questions. Clearly, he wanted to intimidate her, and she'd bet he planned to use the Raptor contract to silence her if she found anything damaging to the family legacy.

Unlucky for him that she wasn't feeling too charitable toward Ava right now—who would be the direct beneficiary of the contract in the form of college money.

Not that Maddie would be so petty as to sink Josh's deal, but she also wasn't going to bow to pressure when it came to doing her *job*.

It didn't even make sense. Her job had nothing to do with exposing the Nazi history of Portland businesses. But Nielsen was clearly afraid of something.

So afraid he'd had her computer stolen?

Maybe.

*M*addie was out of cell phone range for the majority of the day as she hiked across rocky desert ground to locate the areas where Kocher had excavated just under ninety years ago. The day's work was a success, though, as she located and recorded three archaeological sites, which, her gathering evidence indicated, included no fewer than fourteen burials, and all had been government land in the 1930s. Today, one parcel—which included one archaeological site—was probably owned by Nielsen Steel. Thankfully, she didn't spot any "No Trespassing" signs as she crossed from public lands to private. She would confirm ownership when she reviewed county tax records next week.

The moment she hit cell tower range as she drove back toward Portland, her phone chimed with missed calls and texts. Unable to help herself, she pulled over to the side of the road to see if Josh had called.

Her heart sank upon seeing he hadn't.

Deep down, she'd been hoping he'd come to his senses. Or that it was all a big mistake. She found she was able to spin a hundred wild fantasies that explained his ghosting her, and every single one started with an apology.

But there was no apology, and her eyes burned.

Alan had called, but not the man she'd been steadily falling for.

Her finger hovered over her brother's name on the voice-mail list. Might as well make a crappy mood worse. It wasn't as if Alan could hurt her more than Josh had.

"Hey, Maddie. I…think we should talk. Seeing you the other night, and then reading in the news that you were doxed…I'm worried. And I miss my baby sister. Will you call me? Please?"

Alan sounded genuine. But then, he was a politician, and he practiced sounding genuine. But he was also the only brother she had, and she was feeling particularly alone right now. She couldn't even call Trina.

She took a deep breath, quenching the threatening tears, and hit her brother's cell phone number in the address book. He answered on the second ring. "Hey, sis. I'm so glad you called me back."

His voice was warm and reminded her of the big brother who would swoop into her life on breaks from school and take her out for ice cream. How she missed that Alan.

But she needed to keep her barriers in place. "What's up?"

"I know you're mad at me because of the campaign."

She remained silent. She'd been clear on her hurt for months, him acknowledging her upset changed nothing.

The silence stretched on, and finally, Alan sighed. "You aren't going to make this easy for me."

"No. Why should I? You have never given a thought to my feelings, so I'm not going to consider yours."

"Ouch."

"Yes. The truth does hurt."

"Maddie. You know I don't believe it. You know it's what I have to say to get elected. But once I'm in office…"

"No, Alan. You don't have to say it. Call me crazy, but I think a politician running for office should only advocate for what he actually believes. For what will actually be pursued once he, she, or they are in office. When you say you think I should have been forced to die instead of getting the medical care I needed, I will believe that's the policy you'll pursue if you're in office."

"But that's not how politics work. I can't come from the center. I have to work the extremes to get elected. Once I'm in office, I can do what I want."

She let out a bark of laughter. "Right. Sure. Because it's never about the next election cycle and donors. Do you really think I'm that naïve?"

"Trust me, Maddie. I won't let you down. I just need to get in office, and then we can fix this crazy world. You want health care? I'll fight for it. You want equal pay? I'll make it a priority. But I can't do any of that without votes. And I won't get votes in the middle."

"You'll tell any lie to get elected. Is that what you're saying?"

"No! I'm…listen, no one is going to deny a woman surgery to save her life from an ectopic pregnancy. So it's a safe area for me—I can *say* I disagree with the practice to get elected, but it's not a change that's going to happen. I look good to the voters I'm courting without risking anything."

"And you think *I'm* naïve. Alan, women die all the time because they can't get the medical care they need. Maternal mortality rate in the US is appalling compared to other First World countries, and it's worse for Black women and other minorities."

"I promise, Maddie. I won't let you down. I'm not a monster. I just… There is no other path to victory for me. I need to take a stance my opponent won't touch to get votes. Something needs to set me apart."

"Have you considered running again later? Against a different opponent you don't have to work so hard to differentiate yourself from?"

"I'll be fifty in a few months. If I want to run for president, I need to make the jump from congressman to senator now."

She closed her eyes. Alan had always joked about running for president one day, and much as she loved him, she'd always known he didn't have the charisma for it. Too much hunger for power and not enough selflessness.

The best leaders made sacrifices and took leadership roles because it was the right thing to do. Because someone had to step up, and if they didn't, a power-hungry monster might fill the void.

Josh was that kind of man. The person who stepped up to do the right thing, risking himself so someone else wouldn't have to. So someone without a moral compass wouldn't end up in charge.

Josh would make a great senator, come to think of it.

She closed her eyes against the pain. She still had a long drive ahead of her. "Listen, I need to go."

Alan sighed. "You're still mad."

"Yes, Alan. I'm mad. And hurt. And…" She huffed out a sigh. "I've got a lot on my plate right now. This contract I'm working on is huge, and Troy Kocher is doing his best to scare me, and now I've got Cliff Nielsen the fourth on my back."

"Cliff is powerful. You need to play nice with him."

"No, I don't. I'm not a politician. I'm a NAGPRA specialist."

"Do it for your boyfriend, then. I saw the news about Nielsen hiring Raptor. Surely you don't want to screw it up for Warner?"

Was that the reason Alan had called in the first place? Had C-IV reached out to her brother and asked him to lean on her to get her in line? She ran a hand over her face. She needed to remember that Alan always had an agenda.

The big brother who used to take her out for ice cream was long gone. In his place was a man who wanted power above all else. And she wasn't certain she would ever understand why.

<h2 style="text-align:center">Chapter Eighteen</h2>

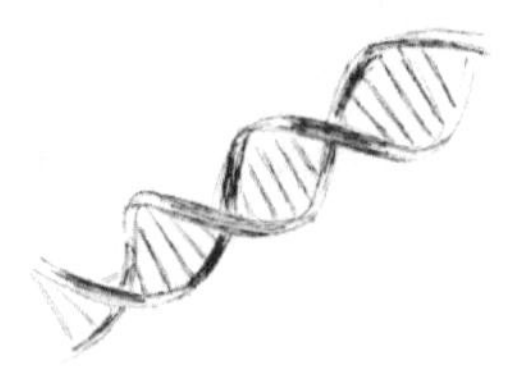

Thursday evening, Josh slid his credit card across the counter at the check-in desk of a hotel in downtown Portland. Bulletproof windows and other security measures were being installed in the house, and it would take a few days. He, Ava, and Chase would call this hotel home until the work was complete.

"I have you in two connected rooms, one standard king, and the other a standard double," the clerk said.

"Any chance the double can be upgraded to a suite?" He didn't mind sharing a room with Ava, but they'd both be more comfortable if they had a little separation.

"I'm sorry, sir, all our suites are booked for the next four nights."

He'd have shopped around for something more comfortable, but this was the hotel Raptor had negotiated corporate rates with, so this was where they were staying.

The clerk gave him their key cards and Wi-Fi instructions. "Don't forget, you can unlock your door with the app," she said as she pointed him toward the elevators.

"Thank you." He picked up the keys and crossed the

ornate lobby to the couches in the middle, where Ava sat with Chase. Ava was distracted by her phone, while Chase scanned the lobby like the operative he was.

His eyes narrowed. "Brunette in the bar vestibule. Weren't you talking to her in the gym on Sunday? She looks a lot like Trina Sorensen."

Dread settled in Josh's gut. He'd known she'd be here, but the hotel had over four hundred rooms on sixteen floors. It shouldn't be hard to avoid her. He turned and got both a jolt and a kick in the nuts.

She was hugging a beautiful Asian woman. The woman cupped her cheek like a lover and said something that made Maddie shake her head.

Had Maddie moved on that quickly?

He caught the low sound of her voice, but not the words. Then the Asian woman kissed Maddie on the lips and headed toward the revolving door at the front of the hotel. Maddie watched her leave. Josh couldn't see her expression. Sadness? Longing? From her posture, he guessed she wasn't happy.

She turned, head down, as she dug in her purse and pulled out a key card. She looked up and caught Josh's gaze.

She froze. She remained utterly still for a heartbeat, and Josh could swear the entire lobby went silent, but it was probably temporary deafness due to his brain no longer sending signals as needed. Their gazes locked, and he saw the hurt in her eyes. Then her gaze flicked to Ava, and her nostrils flared, but her expression didn't otherwise change.

Ava let out a soft gasp, and suddenly, he could hear all the ambient noise of the lobby. People rolling suitcases across the polished floor. The clink of glasses and conversation in the restaurant. A preseason football game playing on the TV in the bar. The honk of horns on the street.

The only thing he couldn't hear was Chase's words as he asked Josh something. Well, he could hear it, but the words themselves might as well have been the *waahhh waaa wahhh* of the adults in a *Peanuts* holiday special.

Maddie's expression didn't change as she lifted her chin and headed toward the elevator. She disappeared into the alcove, and Josh took a deep breath.

For the first time in days, he had clarity. He realized, far too late, what he couldn't have fathomed before: he should have called her Sunday night.

"Who was that?" Chase asked, probably for the second or third time.

"Uncle Josh's girlfriend," Ava said.

He glanced down at the girl he loved with all his heart but at the same time feared had done the unthinkable.

"You have a girlfriend?" Chase asked. "And I'm just hearing about it *now*?"

"*Had*. Sort of. It's complicated."

"What's she doing here? Is she stalking you? Is she a suspect in any of this? Does she have anything to do with the tear gas attack?"

Josh ran a hand over his face. It had been shitty of him not to tell Chase, but he hadn't been able to talk about it Sunday night. He'd braced for questions, assuming Keith would mention Maddie and the doxing. But Keith hadn't, which meant Keith was keeping his secrets, even if Keith himself didn't know what they were. "Grab your bags. We'll head up to our rooms, and I'll explain after we order room service. I'm starving."

He was relieved to find she wasn't in the elevator alcove when they got there. Alone with Chase and Ava in the elevator heading to the fourteenth floor, he said, "She was never really my girlfriend. It was a convenient excuse." He knew Ava wouldn't dare correct him on this…blurring of the truth.

"Oh. Wait. She's Trina's friend. Madison. Or Maggie?"

"Close. Madeline. Goes by Maddie."

"Something go wrong between you two? And why is she in the same hotel?"

"She was doxed Sunday night because our picture was in the paper on Sunday morning."

Chase's eyes narrowed. "You've been holding out on me, Warner. Someone else was doxed, and I'm just hearing about it *four* days later?"

Josh flicked his gaze to Ava. "We'll talk about it in your room." He gave Chase the key to his room with the king bed. Their rooms were connected to provide extra protection for Ava should someone figure out where they were staying.

Ten minutes later, he grabbed two beers from the honor bar in his room and knocked on the connecting door. Chase opened the door on his side. Josh turned to Ava, "Don't answer the front door for anyone. If you hear a knock from the hall, get me. Room service should take about forty-five minutes."

"Sure," she said. Her tone was subdued, not at all the girl who'd been excited a few hours ago at the idea of staying in a posh downtown hotel for a few days.

In Chase's room, he closed and locked the connecting door. He didn't want Ava barging in on this conversation.

"What's the deal with Maddie Foster?" Chase asked.

"Can you let me open the beers first?"

"You can open and talk at the same time."

He set the beers on the counter above the minibar and found the bottle opener. "Maddie was with me Saturday night when the teargas grenades were tossed through the window." He handed Chase one of the beers. "We were, uh, fooling around."

"Way to bury the lede, man. I still can't believe you're just telling me this now."

"Sunday afternoon Ava said she caught Maddie going

through my personal papers when they were in the house alone the day before. And she said something very hurtful to Ava."

Chase frowned. "What did Maddie say when you asked her about it?"

"I didn't ask her."

"You didn't ask her," Chase said with growing disbelief. "But didn't you say she was doxed? You must have talked to her then."

Josh shook his head. He took a swallow of beer, then said, "She, uh, also had her house broken into while she was at the gym with us on Sunday."

"So this chick you'd been fooling around with on Saturday night, who then was hit with a tear gas grenade and doxed because of you, and, we can only assume had her house broken into because of you…and you haven't *talked* to her? Because your insecure, jealous niece said she did something wrong. Shit, man, and people say *I'm* messed up in the head."

Josh nearly choked on his mouthful of beer. "No one says—"

"We're talking about your dumb ass right now, Warner, not me."

"You don't understand. Maddie reacted to something said on Saturday that…kind of confirms what Ava accused her of." Hell, he'd begun to wonder if Maddie had told her brother about the letter and that was why the guy had mentioned the resemblance. Like, maybe the whole brother rift was a lie.

His brain had traveled a lot of dark roads in four days and three hours. Not that he was counting.

"What did she do?" Chase asked.

"I can't. It's…I just can't."

"If you aren't going to talk to Maddie, you should talk to someone."

"You know how delicate my relationship with Ava is. If I talk to Maddie, she'll think I don't believe her. Ava needs to be my focus."

"You're being manipulated by a seventeen-year-old girl. She's sweet. And troubled. I'm not dissing on her. I like Ava a lot. But she's manipulating you just the same, because she knows you're terrified of fucking up your newfound fatherhood. News for you, Josh. All fathers screw up. Even the best ones make mistakes. Dads are human too."

"But I don't get the luxury of making mistakes, Chase. Her real dad already made them all. She turned seventeen a month after I took over all the parenting jobs. I've got less than two years to undo all the damage her parents did in the first sixteen years and eleven months of her life."

"Josh, she's a person, not something you can *fix*. Just like you can't fix me. Or Owen. You are a great friend. An amazing mentor. You're one of the best people I know. I respect and admire you and I love you like a brother. But you can't fix the damage other people did to me. All you can do is provide a safe space for me to express what I'm processing now. The rest has to come from me. I have no doubt you're the best dad Ava has ever had—"

"That's not saying much."

"But you can damn well bet for Ava, it's everything. She loves you so much, she's terrified of losing you. It's a demon that's controlling her, and through her, you."

"You don't even know what she said Maddie did."

"I don't need to. I saw the way you looked at Maddie and she looked at you. There was enough pain going back and forth, I got a contact gut punch." He shook his head. "Go talk to her, man. Tell her you're sorry. Tell her you're a dipshit."

"I can't. It will screw things up with Ava."

"Josh, it's not like you to be such a chickenshit. What did Maddie supposedly read in your papers that has you too scared to face her?"

He looked at Chase sharply. "I'm not afraid."

"Bullshit."

And it hit him, another damn blow to the nuts. Chase was right. He hadn't been able to face Maddie knowing she'd read the letter in which he poured out his heart and all the pain of wanting someone he could never have, especially knowing the woman in question was one of her closest friends and Josh's best friend's wife.

It was too much for a relationship that had barely started.

He met the younger man's gaze. Chase, who'd been tortured and brainwashed—twice. Chase, who had spent years under the control of an evil bitch who'd fucked with his brain as a scientific experiment.

Josh had made it his personal mission to help Chase in his recovery, but he never considered that the guy was way ahead of him in emotional intelligence. He sat on the edge of Chase's bed, the wind knocked out of him. "There's nothing wrong with your brain. Don't let anyone tell you otherwise."

"Aw, hell, man, I've got a bag of cats playing with knives in my head. It's *you* I can see clearly."

Josh let out a pained laugh. He liked this Chase, who was nothing like the man he'd worked with before last October. "I've really fucked up, haven't I?"

"Dude, this one is epic. I don't know Maddie, but I know Trina. If Trina says Maddie's one of the good ones, she is." Chase fixed him with a knowing look. "I take it you like her. You weren't just fooling around to blow off steam."

Josh thought back to Saturday night, when they'd stood in his garage and held each other. *"I'm crazy about you,"* he'd said, when what he'd been thinking was, *am I falling in love?*

"Yeah," he said to Chase.

"Then get your ass to her room and talk to her."

"I can't leave Ava alone."

"*I'm* here for Ava. I'll leave the connecting door open."

"I don't have her room number, and at this point, I doubt she'll give it to me."

Chase shook his head. He pulled out his phone and tapped the screen, then held it to his ear. "Rico, hey, it's Chase. Listen, we just checked into our hotel and want to check on Maddie Foster and don't have her room number. Yeah, probably in the shower or something, because she's not answering texts. I know Raptor booked her room. Do you have the number in the file on her case?" He smiled and paused. "1420? Ha. Same floor. Makes it easy. Thanks, man. Have a good night."

Chase hung up, then looked at Josh. "She's just down the hall. No more excuses."

"I'll tell Ava—"

"*I'll* tell her. You go. Now." He pushed Josh toward the door to the hallway.

He stepped out and glanced at the numbers. Maddie would be down the hall and around the corner.

He reached the corner and paused.

Get a grip, man. You used to be a SEAL.

He squared his shoulders and marched forward until he stood in front of Maddie's door.

The knock shouldn't have startled Maddie. She'd half expected it after seeing Josh in the lobby, but still, it did. It wasn't as if she'd given him her room number.

Like that would stop a Raptor operative.

She sighed and reached for the door. Might as well get it

over with. She wasn't quite braced for the gut punch of seeing him again. But there he stood, broad shoulders, stiff, almost military stance. Rigid. So handsome, it made her guts ache.

His expression was neither hot nor cold. But upon closer look, she could see something, some spark of emotion in his eyes. She just wasn't sure *which* emotion.

She waited, saying nothing. He closed his eyes as if searching for a place deep inside that would tell him what to say.

"There's only one thing you can say to me right now, and if it's not the first words out of your mouth, you can leave now."

"I fucked up."

"That's actually pretty close, but not it." She shut the door.

"I'm sorry!" Josh shouted. "I'm so, so sorry, Maddie."

Her heart pounded as she stood next to the closed door. Should she open it? Should she hear him out?

"Please, Maddie," he said, his voice suitably pleading. "Please let me apologize. Let me explain."

Slowly, she pushed down on the bar and opened the door a crack.

"Can I come in?" he asked.

She pulled the door open wider and stepped back, allowing him to enter.

He stepped into the room and turned to close the door. With his back to her, he repeated, "I'm sorry."

"Face me when you say that."

He turned as she commanded. His face was flushed, and his eyes burned with intensity. "I'm sorry. I fucked up."

"Yes. You did."

"You aren't going to make this easy for me, are you?"

"No. Why should I?" She crossed her arms. "Do you believe Ava?"

"Honestly? I think I did, but never a hundred percent. I just believed it was *possible* she was telling the truth. With that in mind…I—I didn't know what to do."

He ran his hands through his hair. "I told you the night we met that she has to come first. Ava has to be the number one on my priority list, and if there was any chance that you said what she claimed, I had to be there for her. She needs me. Needs one adult to count on."

"She also needs discipline. And letting her manipulate you is about the worst lesson you can teach her. But aside from that, I don't really know what she said about me. So as much as I'm sympathetic to your reasons and maybe might even understand a little bit, I'm not quite there. The time for you to confront me with this was Sunday night."

She took a deep breath and turned to pace the room. She couldn't keep staring at him and maintain her sanity. "When I offered to take Ava for a few days to help you both out, I told you there was nothing she could say that would hurt me. And that was true. She can't hurt me, because I understand her. The only one who hurt me is *you*."

She paused before the window. Evening was settling in, and the city was lighting up. "And if you still believe her, why are you even here? Why are you saying sorry? I have work to do, and I don't need you wasting my time if you're just here to tell me why you ghosted me and then walk away again."

That was the crux, the very heart of her pain. Right when she'd needed him, he'd ghosted her. This man who spent his life taking care of others wasn't there for *her* the moment she needed him most. Her anger spiked, and she turned to face him. "I was doxed and I was robbed, and you *ghosted* me. Do you have a clue how that made me feel? I *needed* you. And you abandoned me."

Her voice broke on the last sentence. She couldn't help it. She did not want to cry over this man, and yet here she was, not only crying over him, but in front of him.

She couldn't stop the tears, so she would defend them. "You abandoned me less than twenty-four hours after I told you how I feel abandoned by my family. After I shared with you how much it hurt to be betrayed and abandoned by my fiancé and best friend."

He dropped to his knees and reached out, placing his hands on her thighs just above the knees and pressing his face into her jeans. "I am so sorry, Maddie. I'm ashamed." His shoulders rose like he'd let out a sob, but he didn't make a sound.

He released her, and she stepped back. She dropped to the edge of the bed and willed him to look at her. She wanted to see his eyes. To see if this could be some sort of act.

"Chase talked some sense into me. He made me see something that I didn't want to. I think I shut down the moment Ava said you'd read the letter about Trina." He took a deep breath and finally looked up. His eyes were damp. "I —I was afraid to face you. I was so ashamed. I've never told anyone, but in a moment of desperation, I wrote it all down, what I would say if I could. Hoping to exorcise my demons. Maybe if I put the words out there, the feelings would go away. It wasn't healthy, and I hated myself for it. Moving to Portland was an escape from everything I hated about myself. An escape from the daily reminder I was obsessed with my best friend's wife."

He rose to his feet and began to pace. "But it's not why I moved here. I moved here for Ava. I've worried about her since the day I first held her in my arms. I worried about my brother following in the abusive path of our father. And I *still* don't know if Ari ever hit her. I trusted Lori to protect her. I told her if she ever needed me for anything, I'd be there, and

I meant it. I have loved that girl from the day she was born, and her whole life, I've wanted to save her from the shitty family she was born into, because I, more than anyone, know exactly who my brother is.

"My greatest fear is I'll screw up with Ava. That I'll lose her to drugs or depression, like she lost Lori, so you reading that letter represents my deepest shame and my greatest fear all rolled into one horrific package. And there I was, sitting in a car, and my niece tells me she loves me and needs me and wants me to be her dad, and the next minute, she tells me the woman I'm crazy about told her about Trina and said I'd only moved to Portland to get away from Trina."

Maddie couldn't hide her jolt at his words. All of it. Her emotions went into overdrive. The accusations. The heartache. The shame. It was too much.

He was supposedly crazy about her, but his behavior this week denied that. But maybe he was running scared because of his deepening feelings. He certainly seemed to believe he couldn't prioritize Ava and care about someone else at the same time.

Maddie had never found love of any kind to be a finite commodity, but then, she hadn't grown up in an abusive household, which Josh had just hinted at.

No wonder he had a driving need to take care of people.

But she wasn't one of the people he was interested in taking care of. He'd proved that by ghosting her. And while she didn't *want* to be taken care of, she did want a partner who would consider her feelings. That shouldn't be too high a bar.

If she forgave him now, what would happen the next time Ava lied? He needed to deal with her, to set a boundary that didn't allow for any more lies, before Maddie could even consider a future with him.

"That's a lot to take in," she finally said. "I'm sorry about your father and your brother. And you have no reason to be ashamed about Trina, because you never put the burden of your feelings on her. You respected her, her marriage, and your best friend. We can't always control whom we develop crushes on. Would that it were that easy." She gave him a sad smile. "I'd give anything not to have feelings for you right now."

He flinched, but didn't interrupt.

"I'm not going to defend myself when it comes to what Ava said. It hurts that you took her word unquestioningly, but it's not my responsibility to change your mind when I'm the accused. The burden of proof is on her. One thing I know, if you don't set boundaries with Ava now, she will learn nothing from this and things will only get worse. Thank you for your apology, but you need to deal with her before your words will mean anything to me. Come back to me after you've gotten the truth. Come back to me when you can one hundred percent say you know I didn't do what Ava claimed. You're not welcome in my room or in my life until then."

She swiped at the tears that slid down her cheek and crossed the room to open the door. She turned and faced him. "Goodbye, Josh."

Chapter Nineteen

There was no getting out of it, Maddie had to return to the Kocher Mansion. Notes from the Nielsen archives indicated that at least one of the woven baskets in the main display room was a funerary object and should be returned to the tribe along with the bones in vault 73. But she needed to inspect the basket to be certain it was the one described. And she wanted to take a second look at the remains in vault 138 again. The red staining on the clavicle and scapulae nagged at her.

She should have looked for soil or organic material adhered to the bones instead of just noting the possibility. Pollen analysis might explain the odd staining.

After everything that had happened, she should ask Josh to go to the house with her. Kocher was openly a White Patriot, and he had strong motive to hinder her work. She'd been doxed and robbed, and he could see that as an opportunity to attack her and shift the blame. It would be beyond dangerous to go to the mansion alone at this point.

She would call her boss and ask for advice, but Sienna had given birth to a baby girl two days ago, six weeks early.

Mother and baby were doing fine, but the baby needed to be in NICU until her lungs were ready for the world. The last thing Sienna needed was to be bothered with the situation Maddie had managed to get herself into with a rotten client.

After some consideration, she texted Josh and asked if Chase could accompany her to the house late afternoon or early evening.

JOSH

I can take you.

MADDIE

No. Is Chase available?

The three dots appeared and disappeared. A full minute passed. Finally, he replied.

He is.

Great. Please give me his number so we can make arrangements.

A moment later, she received a text from an unknown number.

CHASE

Hi Maddie. Nice to finally meet you. Sort of. Good job playing hardball with Josh. He's an idiot.

She laughed.

MADDIE

I like you already.

I'm really quite charming. Don't let my reputation scare you.

She stared at the words, cupping the phone. This was his acknowledgment that she likely knew some of his history.

MADDIE

I only know the public version. And I know Trina trusts you with her life.

CHASE

Trina is good people.

One of my very favorites.

So what do you need?

It only took a few minutes to arrange their late afternoon excursion, then Maddie was able to return to her notes, which were spread all over the hotel room bed.

She'd printed copies of the Nielsen papers and the Kocher papers. Now she sorted them by date, merging the collections together like a deck of cards. She didn't have any letters to Otto and Sally from the Nielsens—she highly suspected the Kochers had burned the correspondence because it was incriminating.

Thankfully, the Nielsens hadn't been so careful. They had Kocher's letters and their own journal entries that described the digs. It appeared Clifford Nielsen the first was in it for the glory of the find. His personal notes indicated he was interested in the objects they found, but over time, he'd begun to read reports from archaeological excavations in Greece and Egypt and wondered why Otto didn't document his finds like other archaeologists.

She guessed he'd expressed this in a letter to Otto, because Kocher sent a reply that stated Greek and Egyptian society were worthy of studying due to their written languages and technology. Indigenous Americans were accorded no such respect from him.

It made her stomach ache to think of the racism her profession had been built on. Many in archaeology and anthropology still used their studies to justify racism.

She studied the stack of documents she had yet to read and braced herself. It was time to dig deeper into the founder of the Nielsen empire. Maybe she'd find whatever it was that C-IV was so afraid of.

An hour into reading photographs of really bad handwriting, she sat up straight and rolled her aching shoulders, causing joints to crack. Nielsen's thoughts and writings showed a deeper interest in scientific method, and in one journal entry, he stated clearly that with a little more due diligence on Kocher's part, they could prove that white people had been in the Americas since 4004 BC, when the world—according to one group of Christian theologians—began.

Nielsen was clearly a religious man, but he also had to know about geology—after all, he owned a steel company that was mining iron ore from several places around Portland—but he didn't reconcile the two. For starters, he disagreed with the estimated age of the fossils in the John Day Fossil Beds National Monument. Of course, it hadn't been a national monument then, but researchers had been studying the fossils in the area as early as the eighteen nineties.

Nielsen, it appeared, believed the Painted Hills were a mark from God. The vibrant colors were unnatural—except, of course, geologists knew the colors were the ultimate in natural, but Nielsen didn't truck with that—and a sign that the area was blessed. A homeland for the Aryan people who were meant to occupy the space.

And there it was. He encouraged Kocher's digging because it "removed the stain." Maddie closed her eyes against the horrible words on the page, then took a deep breath and forced herself to keep reading. Nielsen wanted both living and dead indigenous people removed from the

Painted Hills so the whites could claim it, as was their right, having been chosen by a Christian god.

This had to be what Nielsen was afraid she'd find. And yeah, it would be a problem, even more than having a Nazi history.

Nielsen was gung-ho for active eradication of Native Americans. In addition, he'd used the purchase of checker-boarded lands to seize what he could of tribal property, pushing indigenous people onto smaller and smaller reservations.

After that, he'd gone on to fight the state's purchase of parcels in the Painted Hills for establishment of a state park in the thirties. He'd wanted the land for himself.

She sat back on her heels. What did this evidence mean, beyond that Nielsen was a raging bigot? The land had been stolen from the tribes a hundred years ago, and the theft had been government sanctioned.

Nothing here could overturn the old land grants and sales. Tribes had tried. For decades. At worst, this was a public relations headache for C-IV, but that was all.

She glanced at her watch. She had several hours before she needed to meet Chase in the lobby to head to the Kocher Mansion. The hotel was walking distance to Nielsen Tower. Had C-IV banned her from the archives? She wanted to see the property records from the twenties and thirties. How much land had Nielsen managed to acquire in the Painted Hills region?

The archives were open by appointment only on Fridays. She called the appointment number, and, after navigating an irritating phone tree, she finally got a human on the phone. "I think one of our archivists is digitizing files today and will pass on your request. I'll call you back with a response in twenty to thirty minutes."

She expected the receptionist would run the request by

Nielsen himself and hoped the time difference with Japan quashed that from happening. And maybe it did, because thirty minutes later, she had an appointment with the archivist at one fifteen.

She swept her hair up in a messy bun and donned a professional pantsuit, sadly giving up the yoga pants that were her favorite work attire. She could face pushback. The more professional she looked, the better.

At one o'clock on the dot, she was in the lobby, walking past the fountain with copper flowers where Josh had kissed her and she'd met C-IV the first time. Had that really been ten days ago?

And yet, given all that had happened since then, had it really *only* been ten days ago?

The lobby was as busy today as it had been then, a hive of activity even on a sunny summer Friday. She crossed the large ornate space, heading to the information desk to sign in.

A blonde woman in a blue blazer stood behind the counter. Nielsen Steel owned the high-rise, but they rented several of the lower floors to other businesses. Blazered lobby staff worked for the building management, a subsidiary of Nielsen Steel that was a large property management company in their own right.

Nielsen was deep in the real estate business—between properties they purchased a hundred years ago for mining, right down to redevelopment of old smelting factories into posh rental space for trendy restaurants with artsy loft living space above. They were all part of the Nielsen family and the reason the steel empire had lasted so long.

Moss doesn't grow on stainless steel. But then, the Nielsens always seemed to know when to diversify.

She should probably go to the real estate office next, but she'd start with the archives because she wanted to know how much of the checkerboard C-I had managed to acquire in his quest to establish an Aryan homeland eighty-five years ago. Land he'd asked his friend and fellow Aryan Otto Kocher to remove all human remains from.

How many of the skeletons in the vaults had come from the horrific "clearing" of land Nielsen owned or planned to purchase?

She reached the desk and gave her name, just as a door to offices behind the wide reception desk opened, and there was Josh.

Dammit. Why hadn't it occurred to her that Josh would be here? He must be inspecting the building specs and systems as C-IV had mentioned Saturday night.

Josh looked just as surprised to see her, but said nothing and let the blonde do the talking. "ID, please," the woman said. Maddie knew the drill. No one was given an elevator pass for floors ten and above without signing in and leaving a copy of their ID.

Josh stood back, arms crossed, apparently there to observe procedure. That had to be a boring job. After all, this was an office building, not a bank. But job security was job security, and he was doing this for Ava.

Maddie signed in on the computer touch screen, the process swift given that her name and ID were already in the system and her appointment had been validated. Her gaze landed on the address, which she hadn't bothered to update when she was here ten days ago. She hadn't yet changed her address with the Department of Motor Vehicles, so it hadn't been necessary.

Today, her address was accurate, listing her rental house. Who had updated it, and why? How closely was Cliff Nielsen watching her?

"It says here, Ms. Foster, that you're required to leave your phone and any external cameras or scanners at the front desk."

Damn. Nielsen must've left instructions—or he *had* been reached in Japan.

"I can't leave my phone. How can I trust it'll be here when I get back?"

"We have a safe. Under the desk, just for this type of thing. In some offices, we have proprietary technology that could be observed by visitors."

She sighed. "Fine."

"Is this a common request for the archives?" Josh asked.

The woman's smooth brow furrowed. "I couldn't say."

That was a nonanswer if ever there was one.

"I'll escort Ms. Foster to the twenty-first floor."

"That's not standard procedure," the woman said.

"Maybe it should be." There was an edge to Josh's voice.

Maddie wondered if this woman would have to answer to him if he landed the security contract for the building. Probably.

"Fine," she said, clearly not happy with the break in protocol, but not foolish enough to argue with a potential boss.

Maddie handed over her phone, and it was duly logged in to the system. A minute later, she and Josh were alone in the elevator together.

"You look beautiful today," he said softly.

She flushed. She hadn't expected him to say anything personal. He was at work, and so was she. This wasn't the time or place. "Thank you," she said.

He said nothing more, and they settled into silence. At last, the elevator doors slid open, and he led her down a short corridor and turned the corner. When they reached the middle of the long corridor, he stopped and said, "We're in the middle of a camera dead zone. No surveillance of this ten-foot segment of hall." He then slipped something into her hand.

Flat, and rectangular. A glance confirmed it was his smartphone.

"You can take pictures without unlocking it, but the code is 3-4-7-1 if you need it."

It kind of shocked her he was trusting her with his code, but she imagined he was making a point with that. She slipped the phone into her purse, hiding it in the liner pocket where she kept sanitary napkins. "Won't someone notice you don't have your phone?"

He touched his headset. "This is a Raptor headset. It works as a phone and a radio, and it's what Chase and I have been using all day. They won't know. Find me before you leave to return the phone."

She nodded. "Thank you. I just want to look at old property records."

"Why?"

"I'll explain later."

"Will you? Will you talk to me tonight?"

She cocked her head. "At this point, that really depends on you."

He nodded and gave her a half smile. Like he had some kind of plan brewing.

She felt a strange flutter of hope, but resumed walking as if the man didn't have the power to crush her heart.

She noted the security camera mounted to the ceiling as they stepped within its range. She'd have to find the cameras in the archives and be careful taking pictures. She wouldn't bother with the camera unless she found something important. She didn't want to trigger alarm bells unnecessarily.

The archivist behind the desk was a man Maddie hadn't met before. But then, Maddie had never visited on a Friday afternoon.

Josh left without a goodbye, and she smiled at the bearded

man behind the counter. "Maddie Foster. Thanks for taking my appointment on such short notice."

He smiled warmly. "I was here anyway, digitizing documents. Jennifer told me about your visit last week. I hope you found what you needed."

"I did, but it only raised more questions."

"The curse of research."

"Exactly."

He gestured to the tablet on the counter with the digital catalog. "You know the drill. Click on the years and boxes you'd like me to pull. Unfortunately, the twenties and thirties papers haven't been digitized and the inventory is incomplete, but there are a few keywords to help you decide if it's what you need."

She scrolled through the listing and checked off the boxes. The system had recorded which boxes she'd searched already, making the process even easier. She sent the records request to the archivist's tablet and said, "That should do it."

He glanced at the list of boxes and dates. "This should only take a few minutes for me to pull. In the meantime, would you like a cup of coffee? Just made a fresh pot."

"I thought all archives have a strict rule about no food or drink in the reading room?" She gave him an easy laugh.

He winked at her. "It's just you and me here today, and you're an archive pro. I trust you." He nodded toward the full pot behind the counter. "Help yourself."

"If only you had a shot of booze to add to it."

"That kind of week?"

"Worse."

"Sorry, can't help you there, but I do have caffeine. Grab a mug from the cupboard above the coffeemaker. I only ask you use a lid. My willingness to bend the rules has caveats."

"That's fair."

He disappeared into the climate-controlled storage room.

She rounded the counter and poured herself a cup of coffee, then, after scanning the room for cameras, chose a table in the back corner that might be on the edge of the dome-covered camera's range.

The coffee was too hot to drink, but she was a rule follower and left the lid on, knowing it would take that much longer to get to drinkable temperature.

While waiting, she opened her notes for a refresher on which dates and land parcel descriptions to look for. Her search today would have to be fast—no time to read the documents. She would scan each page for keywords. Before she left the hotel, she'd printed samples of Nielsen's hand-writing with the words she was looking for: Painted Hills, dig, burial, Aryan, homeland, master race. With her handwriting swatches, the keywords should jump from the page as she flipped from one document to the next.

A few minutes later, the archivist pushed a cart loaded with boxes through the room, weaving between reading room tables. He parked the cart in front of her. "This should keep you busy for a while." He looked at her mug and added, "I forgot to tell you there's half-and-half in the fridge."

"No, thanks, I prefer it black." She lifted the mug and took a careful sip. "Still too hot." It was a little odd, how solic-itous he was being with the coffee given that beverages that could stain were generally a big no in the archive world, but she wasn't about to question it. She was glad to have a pick-me-up for what was certain to be a long, boring afternoon.

She cracked open the first box and began going through pages, having to force herself not to read but to scan for the keywords she had identified. Her coffee cooled, and she took a sip, pleased with the rich brew. She wasn't a coffee snob, but she also wasn't a fan of weak or overly strong coffee, and this mug hit a spot that would make Goldilocks happy.

Twenty minutes in, she was starting her second box. She

had yet to pull out Josh's phone to take any photos, but she had twelve more boxes and was familiar with the process of useless box after useless box before hitting pay dirt. Patience was key.

She finished the coffee at the same time she finished the second box. She pushed back from the table and stood to return the box to the cart and grab the next one, but she must've moved too fast, because the room spun. Did she forget to eat lunch today?

No. That wasn't it. She'd indulged in room service while she worked. So why did she feel…lightheaded?

She reached for her purse, which hung from the back of the chair, but somehow she missed it and knocked over the coffee mug. It landed on the papers, and she cursed, but nothing spilled. The lid. And she'd finished it.

Her brain was muddied.

Why didn't her hands work?

The archivist was running toward her. Yelling because of the overturned mug? She couldn't tell. His face blurred as he loomed over her. Was she on the floor looking up at him?

His mouth contorted. Was that a smile? He held up the mug, and finally, his words made it through to her muddled brain. "Good to the last drop."

Oh shit. The coffee.

Chapter Twenty

Josh gave in to temptation and decided to text Maddie. She might not see it if she had the phone hidden away, but it was worth a shot. He was doing a walk-through of the upper floors of the tower and intended to drop in on the archives when he got to twenty-one, unless she objected.

He tapped the button on the earpiece and dictated the text. He was still waiting for a response as he descended another flight of stairs to walk the next floor.

He'd told Ava he'd gone to see Maddie, and she'd flinched as if she was waiting for Josh to call her out. And he'd wanted to, but he didn't think pushing would work when it came to his niece.

Ava would come clean. He knew it. But until she did, all he could do was pine for Maddie.

He was a damn evergreen tree, considering how he felt about her. Hell, he was even impressed with her dignity as she told him off.

It gutted him to realize just how deeply he'd hurt her by abandoning her right after she'd told him of her heartbreak with both her family and fiancé. But still, she'd stood up for herself with magnificent steel in her words and spine. Maddie knew what she was worth, and he didn't think he'd ever known anyone who was quite so rational and clear and yet still so able to live in their emotions as Maddie did.

Josh had spent his whole life regretting where he came from and believing he couldn't have a relationship because he'd repeat the patterns of his father and brother. He'd spent his adult years wishing he could fix his brother and childhood years wanting to save his mother. He probably even wanted to fix his father, but he'd always known he was a lost cause. Still, Josh had blamed himself for those failures.

He'd found himself in the Navy and the SEALs. Hell, he had an ego as big as any of them, but ego wasn't the same as centeredness, and Maddie was a perfect dot in the middle of the most perfect sphere.

He didn't deserve her. Not at all. But he wanted her just the same, and for once in his life, he wasn't going to get in his own way. Or, at least, he'd stop getting in his own way, considering he'd already screwed up royally. But he'd get her back. Convince her he was worthy, even though he didn't believe it.

All those years he'd thought he was in love with Trina? That had been a fantasy. He'd idealized her in the extreme, probably because she was unobtainable.

Safe.

She couldn't reject him, so he could never be hurt.

Plus, since he couldn't have her, he could never hurt *her*. Not in the way Ari hurt Lori or his father hurt his mother.

And those feelings for Trina were nothing compared to how Josh felt about the very human and attainable Maddie.

He walked two more floors, noting potential security flaws, getting the vibe of the employees and building. He'd bring in ten guys to do the initial security work, then slowly roll in new hires as they worked out the kinks and patched the holes.

There were a ridiculous number of holes in this company's security. Josh had managed to hack the computer system on his lunch break, which meant they'd have to start with a tech upgrade. He'd get Mothman here to comb through the system and weed out the backdoors. They'd standardize the name badges and RFID tags. Get rid of the app that unlocked doors and allowed elevator access to the upper floors. The app was a piece of crap that could be hacked by a bored fifteen-year-old or a security consultant while enjoying a pastrami on rye.

Simon Barstow and Apex had gotten dangerously lax. No wonder C-IV wanted a new private security firm. Josh might even be able to poach a few of Apex's better employees in the process. They weren't all bad, and Josh needed guards who knew the building and business.

Rav and Keith would get a kick out of that, after all the employees Barstow had poached from the Alaska compound a few years ago. Turnabout was fair play.

Josh glanced at the floor number. Twenty-one, at last. He couldn't suppress a smile as he walked the floor as he had all the others. When he reached the archive suite, he came to a dead stop.

The lights behind the glass panels that flanked the door were off. The room was dark.

Closed-for-business dark.

Maddie couldn't have left. She still had his phone. She could be waiting for him in the lobby, but Chase would have spotted her and radioed. Unless she gave Chase the phone and took off?

Which was entirely possible. Even reasonable.

But his gut offered up a hard *no*.

The back of his neck tingled. There was something off

here. He'd entered the archives, and the guy behind the desk —who must be the archivist—had immediately turned, dropped his head. Like he was grabbing something behind the counter that was urgent.

What the hell could be urgent for a guy whose job it was to guard boxes of old papers? Had he been hiding his face?

And why the hell hadn't Josh picked up on that before?

Because his focus had been on how good Maddie's ass looked in that pantsuit, and he'd never considered a pantsuit hot before. He'd screwed up because he was thinking with the wrong head.

He tapped his headset to make a private call to Chase. "Chase, has Maddie passed through the lobby in the last hour?"

"Not that I know of."

"Check and see if her phone is in the safe at the check-in desk."

"Will do."

Josh swiped his key card through the reader to unlock the door. He had a master key that would open every door except C-IV's office. He'd get that key once he was officially hired.

The door didn't unlock.

He swiped it again. Nothing.

He radioed Gretchen at the front desk. "My master key isn't unlocking the archives."

"That's odd. It should work."

Worry coursed through him, and he had to bite his tongue to keep from snapping at her. "Unlock it from the console. Use the emergency code."

"I'm not authorized to do that unless it's an actual emergency."

"It is an emergency."

"Mr. Warner, I know you might take over security, but you aren't in charge yet, and I would be remiss in my job if I unlock that door without proper authorization. For all I know, this could be some sort of test you've devised and if I open the door, I fail."

She wasn't wrong. Dammit.

"Josh," Chase said, "I'm at the desk, and Maddie's phone isn't here."

To Gretchen, Josh asked, "Did Madeline Foster collect her phone and sign out?"

Her words sounded as if they were directed at Chase, but she answered his question just the same. "She must've taken it, because it's not here."

"But the log doesn't show her signature. That scribble could be anything. Did you give her the phone?" Chase asked.

"She must've gotten it when I was on break. One of the security guards covered the front desk."

"Who?" Josh asked.

"Karl Hoffman."

"Where is Hoffman now? I need to talk to him."

"His shift was over when my break ended. He left."

Josh wanted to bash his head against the wall. He tried his key one more time in the reader. Nothing. He turned and bolted for the elevator, choosing the service one because it was closer and faster with less traffic.

Two minutes later, he was in the lobby. He went straight into the security room behind the front desk and shouted orders. "I want to see video feed for the twenty-first floor for the last hour, and the front desk for the same time period."

The man monitoring the bank of screens cocked his head. "Is this some sort of test?"

"No. Every camera on twenty-one. From the moment I left Madeline Foster in the archives, on the left bank of monitors. The front desk and lobby entrance for the last hour on the right."

"I'll watch the front desk videos," Chase said.

Josh watched six screens while Chase watched four.

"Pause front desk," Chase said, adding, "Hoffman is alone at the desk."

"Pause all screens," Josh said so he could watch the video of Karl Hoffman. "Rewind front desk to when Hoffman first takes over."

They watched the video at triple speed. A few minutes after Gretchen left, Hoffman reached under the desk and remained bent over long enough to retrieve something from the safe.

"He took the phone," Chase said.

Josh nodded. "And there, he's scribbling on the tablet, logging her out."

"Resume twenty-first floor feed." Several minutes in, the video showed the archivist pushing a cart carrying a giant box through the entrance to the archive. Cameras tracked his progress to the same freight elevator Josh had taken minutes ago. His entire body went cold. "Maddie's in that box." He turned to see Gretchen in the doorway. "What can you tell me about the archivist?"

She stepped closer to the screen. "For starters, that's not the archivist. That's Peyton Hoffman, another security guard. He's Karl's brother." She shook her head. "Shit, I didn't think Ben—the archivist—was working today. I was surprised when he responded to my message, agreeing to the appointment with Foster."

"Were Karl or Peyton at the front desk when Maddie's request to research in the archives came in?"

"Peyton wasn't working today."

That explained why Josh hadn't met him yet.

"But he looks familiar," Chase said. "I've seen him before."

"Was Karl at the desk?" Josh persisted.

The woman closed her eyes in thought; finally, she nodded. "I think so."

"So Karl could have heard the request and sent his brother a message to come in and pretend to be the archivist for an hour. With his security credentials, he could breeze right through after Karl changed the access code to block my master key card from working on the archives."

She nodded. "But why would he do that? What's the point?"

"Josh," Chase said, "I know why." He held up his cell phone. On the screen was a news article about the White Patriots rally from weeks ago. Peyton Hoffman was right there, next to Troy Kocher.

Chapter Twenty-One

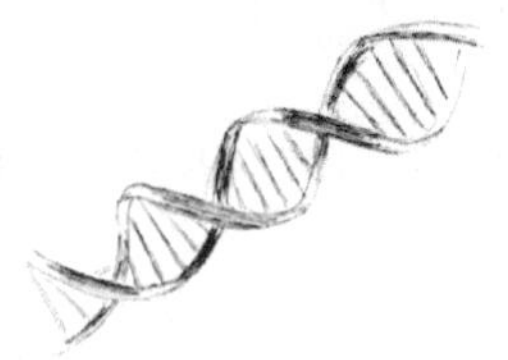

$\mathcal{E}$verything ached. Her head, her back, her hips. Why was she contorted into such a tight position?

Understanding came several steps slower than consciousness had.

She was in a box, if the scent of cardboard and the texture against her cheek were any indication. Her hands were bound. Zip tie? Maybe. It didn't feel like metal or rope fiber.

Her feet were bound too, and the restraints for both were tied together at her front. She was trussed tight in a box, and the sounds and vibrations told her she was in a moving vehicle.

Panic swamped her the moment her brain wrapped around these facts. The archivist had drugged her, put her in a box, and now she was in a car going who knows where.

Why? What did he want with her?

Hundred-year-old land records weren't *this* important.

She felt around in the box for her purse. It wasn't there.

Damn. She had a pocket knife that would've made quick work of the ties.

At home, she had a bracelet she wore in the field, in case of emergencies. Braided paracord with tools hiding in the weave, including a razor blade.

If she survived today, she'd never take that damn bracelet off again.

Her eyes teared at that.

If I survive.

Another wave of panic hit. *Breathe deep. One step at a time.*

First, hurdle, the box.

She'd put on nice pumps to go with the pantsuit. They weren't exactly stilettos, but the heels did have a reasonably narrow point.

Trussed as she was, she had to shift her entire body to get the leverage required to jab at the cardboard. It wasn't an archive box—she was too large to fit in one of those—thankfully, because the cheap cardboard split easily.

She broke through the side, then wriggled and twisted until she was free of the box. The difference between inside and outside the box was minor, given she was in a pitch-black trunk.

But trunks also had tools in them. Jacks, tire irons. She could find them under the floorboard if she was lucky.

But first she needed to get untrussed. She felt along the seam of the trunk lid and the body of the car. There had to be some sharp edge somewhere. After a minute of rolling and slithering to get her hands and feet as close to the rear of the car as humanly possible, she found her edge. Plastic housing—maybe for the tire changing tools?—had cracked. It was just thick enough to have an edge to it and jagged enough to provide a hint of serration.

She ran her joined hands and feet over the spot, feeling the plastic on plastic catch. With the added tension of pulling the binding tight, it finally snapped under pressure.

She could now straighten her legs, almost full-length.

Sometimes being short was convenient, like when trapped in the trunk of a moving vehicle.

She worked on her wrists next, but the jagged plastic was now worn down. She scooted back and tugged at the edge of the plastic housing, hoping to remove the cover to a cache of tools.

The car made a sharp turn, and she hit her head on the trunk lid. In grappling to steady herself, she caught the edge of the carpet beneath her, and it pulled free.

Under it, she felt a metal rod.

Pay dirt.

She managed to work it free even though it was partially beneath her and found herself the proud holder of a small crowbar-shaped tire iron, complete with a flat, sharp end for crowing. Or barring. Or prying.

She might use it for all of those things, but first, she'd use it for cutting.

With a real blade, it took only a moment to free hands and feet.

At last, she was unbound—still trapped, but no longer trussed—and she lay on her back in the trunk, gasping for breath, her body soaked in sweat.

She hadn't even realized how hard she'd been breathing or how much she'd been sweating. But then, she was in an oven of a trunk. And she'd been drugged and abducted. So yeah, she was breathing and sweating like she'd just finished a marathon.

The problem was, she still had at least twenty-four more miles to run. This marathon wouldn't be over until she was safe in her hotel room with several kinds of alcohol and five pounds of something chocolate.

She took several deep breaths as she tried to remember everything she'd ever heard about being trapped in a trunk.

Like, wasn't there an emergency latch to pull to open it? Weren't they required by law?

Would opening the trunk help her? It *felt* like they were going fast. But how could she know? And what if she opened the trunk and there were no other cars around, no one to see her and call the police? The archivist would see the open trunk in the rearview, and she would have lost her chance to catch him off guard.

She struck "open the trunk with interior latch" from her list of actions. If the car stopped, she might add it back.

Next abduction fun fact: hadn't she read somewhere that when abducted and in a trunk, kick out the taillights?

Drivers and passengers in the cars behind the abduction mobile might see the taillight fall out and realize what was happening. She had nothing to lose with that technique.

She groped the edges of the vehicle and found the housing that covered the taillight, and used the pry edge of the tire iron to remove it.

Someday—maybe tonight, maybe next week—she would have a full-on breakdown about this experience and the fear that threatened to swallow her.

But right this minute, she had to take it one panicked breath at a time. In through the nose, out through the mouth, try not to cry.

She would definitely cry later. She'd put a whole week of crying on her calendar. But right now, in the thick heat of the trunk, crying would paralyze her.

She jabbed at what she hoped and assumed was the taillight case with the tire iron.

Her hands hit the fresh broken plastic and sliced her skin. There was a reason kicking out the lights was recommended, but her shoes, while great for kicking through cardboard, weren't up to the task of taking on plastic, metal, and wiring.

The short tire iron was her best bet.

The sound of plastic cracking and giving way was muted by the road noise. She hoped the sound was louder in the trunk than in the passenger area.

She paused. Many sedans these days had rear seats that folded down, allowing access to the trunk while inside. Could she slip through the opening and bash the archivist with the tire iron?

Considering she was in the moving vehicle too, that seemed like a risky move. And what if he wasn't alone?

She returned to her task of destroying the taillight. Cutting her hands with abandon. Between her sweat and blood, her DNA was all over this trunk. It was a morbid, horrifying thought that her blood and sweat might be the only way she was identified when all this was over.

She bashed at the light with renewed vigor, and it popped free, opening a hole of light in the dark trunk. A hole through which the bloody, slick metal rod that was her only weapon slipped through and disappeared.

"Chase, use the Rap App to find Maddie's phone."

"Already on it," Chase said, not looking up from the device in his hand. "Got it. The phone is…heading to our hotel."

Josh felt the blood drain from his body. Ava was there. Alone.

Chase met his gaze. "I'll get Ava. You stay here and find Maddie."

He closed his eyes. "Before you go, I need you to search for my phone."

"Right. Thank God." Chase must have realized why Josh was asking him to do all the searching. He tapped a few buttons and showed Josh the screen. "It appears you're heading west, into wine country, or maybe the coast."

He closed his eyes against the small wave of relief that it appeared she still had the phone. "That's where I'll find Maddie."

Gretchen tilted her chin toward him. "Why does Miss Foster have your phone?"

"I gave it to her. She's in danger after being doxed. Leaving her without a phone was a risk I wasn't willing to take."

"Bullshit. You gave her the phone so that she could take photos in the archives. When Mr. Nielsen learns of this, he won't be pleased his new security team subverted his orders."

"I don't really give a damn, considering she was abducted from Nielsen's archive and if I hadn't given her the phone, we wouldn't know where she is." He turned to Chase. "Let's go."

On his way out the door, he said, "Gretchen, call the police and report Madeline Foster was abducted by White Patriots. Show them the videos. They'll want to see video from the parking garage cameras too." There was no way she could defy the order. Doing that would implicate her in the abduction, and he didn't really believe she was involved.

He turned and ran for the parking garage. The only thing that mattered now was catching up to Peyton Hoffman and finding Maddie.

Chase took off in his rental car for the hotel, and Josh slid behind the driver's seat of his Raptor SUV. He opened the Rap App on the dashboard computer and locked onto his phone, which was headed west outside the city, as Chase had said.

Chase spoke to him through the headset. "What do you think they want with Maddie?"

"Either it has to do with her research into the Nielsens, or they want to stop us from going to the rally on Sunday." After all, threatening Ava or Maddie was the only thing that would convince Josh to stand down.

Another wave of fear ripped through him. This wasn't a combat mission with Keith and the rest of their SEAL team. This wasn't a Raptor operation extracting hostages from places the US government couldn't go. This was his family being targeted. "Tell me when you lay eyes on Ava."

"Will do." After a long silence, Chase spoke again. "Why was Maddie at the archives?"

"She said she wanted to look at property records. I don't know why, but it has to do with her Kocher contract."

It was his own damn fault he didn't know why she was here. He'd ghosted her the day she'd been doxed. Now he didn't know what was going on with her project.

He hadn't known he was capable of being such a first-class asshole. He wasn't even sure what had come over him, how he could dig in and sink so deep.

It made him realize he was neglecting his own mental health, pretending he didn't have a problem, while Chase and Owen dealt with their issues openly and without shame.

He respected the hell out of both men and needed to tell them that. Later. After he had Maddie back in his arms.

He hit the gas, breaking several traffic laws as he wove through downtown streets heading to the nearest freeway entrance. But the map on the computer indicated the freeway was a traffic snarl of cars inching along, which meant whoever had taken Maddie hadn't taken the freeway or they'd still be downtown. Portland on a Friday afternoon was a nightmare of gridlock.

He would stick to surface streets. If a cop stopped him, all the better. Then he'd have a car with sirens to run down Peyton Hoffman.

From the red dot on the map, Josh guessed the guy had a thirty-minute head start, but Hoffman probably hadn't realized Maddie had a phone that could be tracked and was taking his time. After all, he didn't want to draw attention from police.

Josh called Gretchen with his headset. "What kind of car does Peyton Hoffman drive? Did you get video of him in the garage?"

"There's video of him rolling the cart through the garage and loading it in the trunk of a sedan."

"Vehicle make and model?"

"We don't have that. He parked as far from the cameras as possible, and it's dark—it looks like the ceiling lights are out in that area."

That made sense. Both Hoffmans worked security; they knew all the blind spots and how to make them wider by taking out lights. Their caution told Josh the men weren't fools. They might have seized a surprising opportunity, but they'd been methodical in execution.

"No hope you got a license plate, then?"

"None. We can't even be sure of the color, but it's dark—gray, maybe blue."

"Do you have a vehicle on file for him?"

"Yes. A red pickup truck."

"Thanks, Gretchen."

"Mr. Warner," she said, reverting to his last name for the first time since they'd met this morning. "I'm sorry I didn't understand the seriousness of this earlier. I spoke before it really sank in what had happened."

"Thank you, Gretchen. Duly noted." Josh had no idea if he'd take this job with Nielsen or not, but if he did, this apology told him it would be possible to have a decent working relationship with the woman who ran the front desk during primary business hours.

He clicked off from the call and tapped the gas, darting between vehicles and earning honks from other drivers, but his sole focus was catching up to Peyton Hoffman and Maddie.

He reached a six-lane highway and was able to push his speed up to seventy for short stretches as he darted and weaved.

Chase's voice came over the headset. "Ava's fine. She's with me. She wants to talk to you."

"Thank God. Tell her I can't talk right now, but I love her. Pack our things and Maddie's. We'll move to another hotel until we can arrange a safe house for all of us." He clicked off and pressed the accelerator again. Knowing Ava was safe freed up another part of his mind.

He was closing the distance between him and Hoffman.

"I'm coming for you, Maddie." The words were a whisper. A solemn vow. "Believe in me. Hold on to hope. I will find you."

Chapter Twenty-Two

The car took a sharp turn at speed, causing Maddie to bang her head on the rear panel as she was tossed about. The vehicle slowed, but the new road didn't seem to be paved and was rutted with sizable potholes if the jerky motions of the car were any indication. She tried to brace herself in place with a hand pressed to the hood above her, one hand on the driver's side panel, and her feet braced against the passenger side panel, but she was no match for a bumpy road and a speeding driver.

Where was he taking her, and why?

Had Josh even realized she was missing?

Josh. She'd turned him away when he apologized. She'd assumed they'd have time to work things out. Regret pummeled her along with the bumpy ride.

She tamped down those thoughts. She needed to focus on what she could do, not actions that were out of her hands.

She'd been in the trunk for at least an hour and thanked her decision to wear her grandmother's watch for having any concept of time. Once she'd kicked out the taillight, allowing light to seep in, she'd contorted herself to put the antique wristwatch in the faint shine and read the tiny Roman numerals.

Her struggle to read the time had made her wonder where her glasses had gone. She'd worn them in the archives. Her vision was adequate without glasses—she had progressive lenses that she wore for driving and work situations like archives and creepy crypts—so she wasn't crippled without them, but wondered if the archivist had taken them hoping to disable her with lack of vision.

And really, what was the purpose of all this? What did he hope to gain? Did he think no one would notice she was gone?

She'd been doxed after being photographed with Josh and Cliff. The article had mentioned her brother was Congressman Alan Tisdale. Could this have to do with Alan and his Senate run? Or was this about her work, or to stop Josh from doing his? If she was still missing on Sunday, would Josh and his team from Bond Ironworks be at the rally?

If it was to stop Josh, she hoped they failed. She didn't want Josh to cave because of her. If he did, then Ava would be next. They'd go after everyone who mattered to him. Hell, they'd probably expand to Raptor as a whole, and Trina would be in danger too.

Well, that was a hornet's nest they'd be sorry they stirred. Raptor was basically a private army of special forces operators, and from what Trina had told her, they protected their own.

She held on to that thought as the car bounced along the rutted road. Even if Josh didn't claim her, Trina did. She was one of Raptor's own by association. A close friend of the CEO's wife.

She would survive this. She grabbed that hope and held

on to it, envisioning it like a ball of blue fire she could hold in her hands, beautiful and light and warm.

If she was going to get through these next hours, she needed hope more than anything, because otherwise, she'd fall into panic.

The car came to an abrupt halt, and the hope slid from her grasp, no longer light and fire, but a slippery hand-caught fish determined to be free.

Had they arrived wherever it was they were going? What would happen to her now?

A car door opened and slammed. Footsteps sounded alongside the car.

As panic threatened to suffuse her, she remembered the plan she'd formed after she lost the tire iron, and found the trunk release. She might not have a weapon, but if she timed this right, she could still have the upper hand.

She had to act fast, before he realized what the broken taillight meant. As the footsteps reached the rear of the car, she pulled the cord and shoved the hood up, then launched herself as best she could from her position on her back, thankful for the lessons she'd gotten on Sunday.

She cleared the trunk, and her body hit the archivist, causing him to fall back, but she couldn't get her feet beneath her in time and stumbled to the ground.

He landed on his ass a few feet from her, glared at her, then seemed to remember the gun in his hand. He raised it, pointing the short barrel at her head.

The car was a dark gray Ford Taurus. Late model. In his first glimpse—miles before it turned off the highway and onto a rutted private road—even from a distance, he could see the right taillight was flapping in the wind, hanging by the thick connecting cable.

A quick call to Gretchen confirmed that the taillight had been intact in the garage video. They didn't have footage of the vehicle leaving the parking garage because, not surprisingly, the camera monitoring the employee section had been shut off at the source. Karl had probably disabled it when he did his rounds in the garage about twenty minutes before his brother arrived.

It appeared the Hoffman brothers expected to get away with this crime and had covered their tracks accordingly. They'd probably planned to plant Maddie's phone in her hotel room and make it look like she'd disappeared from there. No one had expected Josh to discover her missing so soon—nor had they expected her to have Josh's phone—which begged the question, did they somehow know that Maddie and Josh had been estranged this week, or did they just assume Josh would focus on his job of going over all the building systems and not pay attention to Maddie's presence in the building?

Whatever their thoughts had been, they'd been careful, but fools to think Josh wouldn't check on Maddie.

Once he'd seen the dangling taillight, he'd dropped back, trying to figure out what to do. He could hardly ram the car with Maddie in the trunk, and any maneuver designed to run Hoffman off the road could injure her. She might still be bound, but she had enough movement to kick out the taillight.

His Maddie was brave and smart. She had to be utterly terrified, but she'd been able to take action anyway.

Now that the car had left the highway, he had to wonder if Hoffman had spotted Josh on his tail, or if his destination was at the end of the road. The map offered little informa-

tion, but the team at Raptor were diving into their databases
and digging up what they could.

Josh turned onto the road and tucked his vehicle into the
trees while he waited for intel. Chasing Hoffman down the
road blindly could get Maddie killed.

Police were scrambling to join this hunt, but they
wouldn't come sirens blaring. No one wanted to tip off
Hoffman unnecessarily. That could turn into a standoff.
Better to catch the asshole unaware and extract Maddie, then
arrest Peyton Hoffman.

Maddie came first. The hostage always came first.

"Okay, Warner," a tech at Raptor HQ said, "it appears
the road connects up with an old logging road that may or
may not be passable. If it is, it in turn connects to a road on
the other side of the foothill and meets up with a highway
that offers a straight shot to the coast or north to the
Columbia."

"Logging road," Josh said, repeating the word that had
stuck out in his mind. "When was it logged?"

"Decades ago, as far as we can tell. It was replanted but
never harvested again because the logging company went
bankrupt."

"Who owns the land now?"

"The state, I think, but only parts. It was
checkerboarded."

Josh knew about checkerboarding from growing up near a
reservation in eastern Oregon. The government kept some
parcels, and either the tribe or railroad or logging companies
got the rest.

"How much you wanna bet the logging company was a
subsidiary of Kocher Lumber Mills?" Josh said.

"I don't have that information," the tech said, "but I
wouldn't bet against you."

If Kocher's family once owned this land, Troy would have

old maps and data. He might even know of old abandoned— or not abandoned—buildings that were perfect for White Patriot meetings.

Had Peyton Hoffman led them right to the heart of the White Patriot group?

Why bring Maddie here?

Josh stared at the red dot on the satellite map in the middle of a sea of evergreens, no hint of road visible from space. "The car has stopped," he noted aloud.

"Yeah. Thirty seconds in the same spot. Could be a big pothole he can't get around."

"Or they've arrived at their destination." His gut churned. He had a feeling this stop wasn't good for Maddie.

On the screen, the red dot disappeared.

Shit. What happened to the signal?

"I'm going in," he said.

"The police ordered you to wait and let them handle it."

"Duly noted." It was the tech's job to remind him of legalities. Covering Raptor's ass. Right now, Josh only cared about one thing: Maddie.

He hit the gas. The Taurus was a mile and a half down the rutted road. It would take several minutes to drive that distance in these conditions. He shouldn't have played by the rules and waited for so long to follow.

Maddie was in trouble. He knew it just like he knew Earth was round. Like he knew he was falling in love with her. The feeling went all the way to his bones.

And he might have hesitated too long. With his heart and with her life.

*G*et up and start walking, bitch." The archivist's eyes were hard and angry, and Maddie had no doubt he wanted to pull the trigger.

What had she done to make him so angry? Aside from knocking him to the ground, of course. But he'd drugged and abducted her, so he really didn't have room to complain about that.

She rose to her feet slowly. Resisting his commands would only hurt her. She'd bide her time, look for an opportunity. Maybe she could get her hands on a branch or a rock and bash him in the head.

He gestured with the gun toward a path that disappeared into the forest. "Walk."

"Where are we going?"

"The fuck away from here. Your Jew boy managed to track us. You weren't supposed to have a fucking phone."

He must've had her purse with him in the car and found it. That would explain his anger. "Your anti-Semitism is showing," she said.

"Like I give a damn."

"How long have you worked in Nielsen's archives?"

He let out a bark of a laugh. "You still think I'm the dumbass archivist? Hell no, that twat is a fucking—" He used a slur no white person should ever say.

This man owned his racism in a chilling, outward way that triggered primal fear. He had no pretense to uphold, which made her think he didn't plan for her to live through this. He probably expected to get away with the abduction altogether. But Josh had given her his phone, and Raptor had tracked them.

That meant help was coming.

But it also meant whoever this man was, he needed to get

rid of her. And they were heading deep into an overgrown forest. She stumbled as her heels caught on a root.

"Take your shoes off."

"No," she said. The shoes were terrible for walking in, but bare feet would be worse.

He gripped her arm and swung her around to face him, then backhanded her. Her head snapped to the side as pain exploded across her cheek. "I said, take your fucking shoes off."

She was dizzy, her head swimming, likely from the combination of blow to the face and whatever drug he'd put in the coffee. She needed to clear her head. Plan.

Josh was on his way. The closer she stayed to the car, the faster he'd find her. Her blurry gaze landed on her feet and the prints in the dirt. Her heels left distinct tracks in the woods. Plus they slowed her walking.

She remembered what the instructors had said about taking blows at the rally—that part of the lesson hadn't been for her and Ava, but she'd listened just the same.

She pressed a hand to her throbbing face, then spit on him. "And I said no."

He backhanded her again, and this time, she moved with the blow as she'd been trained, letting it knock her to her ass.

They were only a hundred feet from the car. Josh was coming. He would find her.

"Get up and walk."

Maddie reached for a thick branch, at least five feet long, that lay on the ground just inches from her hand.

A kick to her ribs sent her face-first into the ground. "Leave it and get up."

"I need it. It's the perfect size for a walking stick. I'll be able to walk faster in the heels with support. Barefoot or in heels, I can't walk fast in this forest."

He glared at her, but finally said, "Fine. No sudden moves."

No worries there. Her goal was to move as slowly as possible. She'd move backward if she could get away with it.

She clutched her ribs as she got to her feet. In truth, they didn't hurt much—he'd likely muted the blow because he feared disabling her. She might not be tall, but she was solid, with more pounds than her small frame needed. Even a man at peak strength like Josh would have trouble hauling her on the uneven terrain, and this man looked strong, but he wasn't in Josh's league.

With her right hand, she planted the stick in the ground, testing the feel of it. It was a little heavy and thick for a walking stick, but just right for a club. She broke off a few thin branches that jutted out, hoping they'd leave nice, sharp barbs on the shaft. Slowly, she walked, planting the stick, then moving her feet, as if she'd been injured by her fall and his kick, when really, it was her cheek that still stung from being backhanded. The rest of her was fine.

"Get moving!" her abductor said.

She picked up her pace a little. "What's your name?" she asked.

"None of your fucking business."

"Actually, I think it is, considering the situation."

He just grunted.

"How did you know we were tracked?"

He was silent a moment, then he said, "Warner said he gave you his phone, and the other Raptor guy was able to track you with it."

"How do you know this?" She wished she could see his face, but they walked single file, with her in front. She stumbled on purpose so she could look back at him. "Well?" she said, prompting him.

He shrugged and gave her a nasty grin. "We've got

another partner in security, tipped us off to everything Warner knows, including the fact that he knows who I am now, so once you've served your purpose, you're going to disappear."

That sent another jolt of fear through her. The look in his eyes said he meant every word. So this man wanted her alive today, but tomorrow was anyone's guess.

"You know, at first, the phone thing was a major fuckup, but then my boss said it was good. We can use the phone to hack into Raptor. They'll think they're using it to hack into us, but they have no idea what we're capable of. I should thank you."

He still had the phone on him? She couldn't keep the spark of hope from her face. Josh could track them, even in these woods. Josh had told her he had a high-end hybrid smartphone that could switch to satellite when there wasn't cell coverage.

"Don't get excited." He reached into his pocket and pulled out a small black rectangle, then gave her yet another awful grin. "I removed the battery. Need to keep it off until I get it to my boss's tech guru."

Shit.

This man wasn't dumb. He wasn't the boss, but he also wasn't a fool.

He put the battery back in his pocket and pointed the gun at her face. "Get moving."

She turned to the path ahead. The canopy grew thicker as the trees got taller, and the forest darkened. She'd always loved hiking in Pacific Northwest forests, yet never before had the moss-covered trees seemed so ominous. The smell of earth and pine now carried the scent of fear.

There were supposed to be sasquatch in these woods. The name sasquatch came from a British Columbia tribe, and in her work recording Traditional Cultural Properties, she'd interviewed tribal members in Oregon and Washington who'd seen the creatures.

She wasn't a believer herself, but she had no doubt the men and women who'd shared their stories had seen something, and who was she to say they were wrong?

Today, she wanted to believe in sasquatch. She wanted a bigfoot to spring from the trees and save her from the real monster in these woods. Today, she'd look for hope wherever she could find it, be it Josh or *Harry and the Hendersons*.

She gripped her stick and planted it with her next step. It was a worthy club, even if a bit unwieldy. If she couldn't find hope from without, she'd make her own. She'd find her moment and bash the bastard with the barbed tree branch.

Minutes passed as she trudged through the woods, looking for an opening. A branch snapped with a loud crack in the trees nearby, and she turned, expecting to see a deer or other critter, but there was nothing there.

Was that Josh?

But with his training, Josh wouldn't make a sound like that unless he wanted to.

She kept walking, using her peripheral vision to scan the ground for tree roots, keeping her gaze straight ahead. She spotted a root and let it catch her heel before she'd planted the walking stick. She let out a loud scream as she pitched forward, the hard, damp earth racing toward her.

She rolled with her fall and swung the stick around, slamming it into her captor's arm, just above the elbow, with all her strength.

He maintained his grip on the gun, but now it was pointed to the sky, so she pulled back and hit him again, this time catching his hand and hitting his head as the branch arced down.

He dropped the gun, his hands moving to cup his head.

He'd been caught by a barb, and there was an open gash on his face.

She scrambled forward and grabbed the gun. She pointed it at him and said, "Now it's your turn to get up and walk, asshole." If Josh and/or sasquatch weren't in these woods to help her, she'd march him back to the car and wait for the police. They had to be nearby.

Cold blue eyes glared at her. "Bitch. No fucking way I'm taking orders from you. You'll have to shoot me."

"You think I won't? You drugged me and put me in a trunk! You hit me and held me at gunpoint."

"And now you've hit me and are holding me at gunpoint. Let's call it even."

"You're insane."

"No. I'm walking away from here." He rose to his feet, hands in the air. Blood dripped down the bloody gash on his face. He turned, presenting his back to her, and set off into the woods, leaving the trail. "Go ahead, shoot me in the back."

Her hands shook wildly as she pointed the weapon at his retreating form. Could she shoot him? He wasn't threatening her. He was leaving. She'd never even fired a gun before. Could she shoot a human being who wasn't actively threatening her?

Could she pull the trigger at all?

Maybe the gun had no bullets and that was why he wasn't afraid to walk away. Maybe he realized she'd figure that out and he could no longer scare her with the useless weapon. She raised the pistol, pointing it at the forest canopy, and wrapped both hands around the handle. She tried to squeeze the trigger but couldn't do it. Was the safety on? She didn't see one. She put her left index finger over her right one, both crossing the trigger. This had to be terrible shooting form, but with pressure from both fingers, she managed to squeeze the trigger.

The report of the bullet echoed through the forest. The recoil made her arms jolt upward, and she wobbled on her heels.

Her abductor was now thirty feet away. He glanced back, and the asshole *laughed* at her. "Your aim is a bit off." And then he turned and kept walking, disappearing between the trees.

She backed up, pressing her spine against a large tree. Tears slid down her face, and her arms shook, still clutching the gun in a death grip pointed toward the patch of trees in which he'd disappeared.

Chapter Twenty-Three

The crack of the bullet echoing through the woods sent a sharp, fresh wave of fear through Josh. He gave up on stealth and ran down the path full bore, easily following Maddie's spike-heeled footprints along with Peyton Hoffman's size twelve hiking boots.

"Maddie!" he shouted. If she'd been shot, she needed to know help was on the way.

"Josh!"

Her responding shout sent relief through him. "I'm coming!" He used his headset to update the police officers who were somewhere behind him, then increased his speed, running as fast as the terrain allowed, the ground a blur beneath his feet.

He rounded a bend, and there, in the shadows of the forest, he saw her pale pantsuit as she stood pressed against a tree. She held a gun pointed into the forest to his left. She jerked and turned the pistol in his direction.

He held up his hands, pointing his own gun into the air. "It's me, Maddie. Where is Hoffman?"

She jerked the gun back to his left. "Hoffman? Is that his name?"

"Yes. Peyton Hoffman. He and his brother are security guards at Nielsen Tower." He jogged toward her. Tracking the line of the pistol with his eyes, he said, "Did he go that way?"

She nodded. "He walked away when I got the gun." She let out a heaving breath. "I couldn't shoot him in the back. I wanted to. But I couldn't. I've never shot a gun before. What if I killed him instead of just wounding him so he couldn't escape?"

He reached her and saw the tears tracking down her cheeks. Her face was red on one side and her skin and clothing streaked with dirt. She didn't lower the gun or take her gaze off the forest where her abductor had disappeared. He pointed his own gun in that direction with one hand, and gently lowered her outstretched arms with his other hand. "I've got this, honey." She resisted for a moment, then dropped her arms, keeping a firm grip on the gun with one hand, and slumped back against the tree.

She let out a sharp, deep sob that wrenched his heart. "He got away."

Every muscle in Josh's body wanted to chase after the man who'd hurt Maddie, but instinct had him reaching toward her and pulling her to his chest, even as he kept his gun trained outward, ready to fire. She needed him by her side more.

She curled against him, pressing her red cheek to his chest, and her body shook with sobs. He stroked her back. "You're amazing, Maddie. You fought him and escaped all by yourself. It doesn't matter that he got away. What matters is you're safe."

"Am I? He's still out there."

"But we know who he is. His life as he knows it is over.

His brother's life is over. They'll be caught. Police officers are only a few minutes behind me on the trail. They'll catch him."

He pressed the button on his headset and gave the officers in the forest an update, then cupped her face with his free hand. "You did an amazing job. Kicking out the taillight. Leaving an easy to follow trail in the forest. How did you overpower him and get the gun?"

"I hit him with my walking stick."

He'd noted the addition to her tracks on the trail and had suspected she'd picked up a stick. "I'm impressed." In truth, *impressed* didn't begin to describe how he felt.

She studied the gun in her hand. It was noticeably shaking.

"Careful with that. The first pull on that kind of gun is hard—it's basically like the safety. After that, the gun is cocked and easy to fire."

Her hand wobbled, and he took the weapon from her, removed the magazine, and ejected the round from the chamber. He then tucked the gun and magazine in his jacket pocket.

"He still has your phone," she said.

He smiled. "Even better."

"He said his boss wants to use it to hack Raptor. He thinks their hackers can outsmart your system."

"They'll be in for a nasty surprise, then." He tapped his headset and called the home office. After informing everyone Maddie had escaped her captor and was safe with him, he said, "Keith, we're going to need Mothman to work his magic. The next time my phone is powered up, we need to run the Vampire protocol."

"Hoffman got away with your phone?"

"Yes."

"Damn, that's a nice stroke of luck."

Maddie looked at him, head cocked in question, and mouthed, *Vampire protocol?*

"We let them hack through a few layers to get to a dummy network. Make them think they're safe in our system, when really they're just inviting us in so we can invade theirs." He tightened his arm around her back and couldn't help but smile. Impulsively giving her his cell phone had a domino effect, and they'd yet to reach the finale.

Shouts sounded in the distance, and Josh called out to let them know their position. Within minutes, the woods were flooded with officers, several of whom went off in search of Peyton Hoffman.

Josh reluctantly let go of Maddie so she could give the officers her account. Under armed escort, they returned to the main road, and paramedics whisked her inside an ambulance to examine her. She refused transport to the hospital, claiming she was fine, and much as he wanted to be certain there were no lingering effects of whatever agent had been used to drug her, he was glad she wasn't whisked away, out of his reach and protection.

He never wanted to let her out of his sight again.

She emerged from the back of the ambulance in her torn, dirty clothing, looking more beautiful than he'd ever seen her. It could be the way the evening sun cut through the scant canopy by the side of the road and landed on her delicate features. Her cheek remained bright red, but she was stunning just the same.

Madeline Foster was it for him, and he'd been a fool to let confusion get in the way. She probably wasn't traditionally beautiful. He couldn't possibly know because all he saw when he looked at her was perfection. Lovely eyes, clear skin, pert nose, high cheekbones. Once upon a time, he'd looked at her face and seen a distorted version of Trina Sorensen, but now he only saw Madeline. He could come up with a list of a hundred ways the women were different physically, and could no longer understand why he'd ever thought them similar.

He knew Maddie now. *Maddie.* And he was fairly certain he was falling in love—really in love, not infatuation—for the first time in his life.

Ignoring the officer who was questioning—and berating—him, he crossed the distance to the most beautiful woman he'd ever met and pulled her into his arms. He planted his mouth on hers and kissed her. A savage kiss, he plundered her mouth with his tongue. Everything he took, she gave. She threaded her fingers into his hair and pulled, even as she bit his lips and sucked on his tongue.

The heat of the kiss rocked him. Probably rocked her. It was primal and unlike anything he'd ever been a part of.

He raised his head and met her gaze. They were surrounded by at least a dozen people, but the only person in this sphere who mattered was Maddie.

"Get me out of here," she said.

He pressed his lips to hers then said, "As you wish."

*M*addie leaned her cheek against the cool glass of the passenger window. "I want a shower. Now. Ten minutes ago. I feel gross." The plea came without premeditation. The words—the need to be clean—were primal. She usually enjoyed the smell of salt and sweat on her skin. It was an achievement. A hike to a beautiful summit. A virtuous workout. Amazing sex.

But this was none of that, and she felt itchy and dirty.

"Chase is searching for a secure hotel and is hitting snags. It's going to take a few hours."

"Take me to my house, then."

"Your house keys were taken from your purse. We need to have all the locks changed."

"Your house?" she asked, feeling a little desperate.

"The window-replacement project hit a snag. Totally unsecure."

"Take me to a cheap motel, then. I'll pay for it."

The rhythmic clicking of the right-turn signal filled the cab of the SUV. "How 'bout we go to Bond Ironworks? There'll be at least a dozen bodybuilders there ready to protect you to the ends of the earth."

"Works for me," she said.

Ten minutes later, they entered Bond Ironworks through the front door. Josh led her straight to the unisex/multigender/accessible/private shower, a ten-by-fifteen-foot room with a toilet, sink, large curtained changing vestibule, and wide shower stall.

"I'll find you some clean clothes," Josh said before leaving her alone in the tiled room.

She stripped slowly in front of the full-length mirror, examining her body for bruises and other imperfections.

She was so far from being anyone's ideal of womanhood, but she couldn't help think she should be appealing to *some* men or women. She wasn't skinny in any sense of the word—not like Trina—but that meant she had curves. More than Trina had, that's for sure.

And damn, if it didn't suck that she was comparing herself to a woman she loved and held dear as one of her best friends and confidantes.

She wasn't in competition with Trina. How could she be? Trina was happily married, and they lived on opposite coasts. But it was there, planted in her brain. Would Josh Warner find her more sexually appealing than Dr. Trina Sorensen?

She was far more not-like Trina physically than she was like her. Trina was skinny like a rail. Which was sexy in its own way. Maddie was curvy. Too curvy for Josh's tastes? But she'd never felt insecure about her proportions before, and she hated that she felt it now.

But then, Josh had rattled her when he didn't trust her. And really, that was the core of the issue. Why had he been so ready to take an insecure seventeen-year-old's word without even minimal due diligence?

Probably because he didn't really care about her. She was a substitute for Trina. Nothing more.

But there was that hot kiss by the ambulance. The possessiveness of his mouth. The intensity and passion. That was for her and her alone. But she was afraid to believe in that kiss.

She stepped into the spray of the shower, and it was gloriously hot. The steam filled the small room, too much for the bathroom fan. The scalding water pummeled her body, cleansing her skin of Peyton Hoffman's brutal touch. Of the panic and fear she'd felt in the trunk. Of the musk and dirt she'd picked up in the forest.

It was a cleansing spray that left her stripped of natural oils and inhibitions.

She stood in the steaming, bracing shower, naked of everything except her soul. She'd just suffered through and survived the most terrifying experience of her life, and all she wanted in this moment was for Josh Warner to want her.

Chapter Twenty-Four

Josh hung up the landline phone in Arthur's office. He ran his hand over his face as he processed the latest development. Both Hoffman brothers were on the loose. The FBI had just missed nabbing Karl Hoffman at the hotel. Peyton had done a decent job of erasing his trail in the forest and escaped before dogs could be brought in to track him.

But neither man could return to work at Nielsen Tower without facing consequences, so that was a small win. Very small, in the scheme of things, but he'd take it as a victory.

Chase and Ava had settled into connecting rooms in a hotel by the Willamette River. Josh had a double bed waiting for him in Ava's room, and Maddie had a king room on the same floor.

The thought of Maddie splayed on her large bed had him hot with want. She could be taking a bath right now in the large tub. But instead, she was showering in the gym unisex bathroom, the only place he could think of that was safe and private.

It was his fault she'd been doxed. His fault she'd had to

fight Peyton Hoffman in the forest. His fault she had that red mark on her cheek. His fault she'd probably have nightmares for the rest of her life reliving the experience of waking up to find herself bound and in the trunk of a moving vehicle.

He shook himself, as if that could dislodge the guilt so he could deal with it later. He rose from behind Arthur's desk and went to the closet, where the gym owner stored sweatpants and T-shirts sporting the Bond Ironworks logo. He grabbed a pair of medium women's sweatpants and a T-shirt and hoodie, then opened a pack of socks and grabbed two pairs. Maddie probably wouldn't want to wear shoes taken from the lost-and-found bin, so two pairs of socks would have to do until they got to her hotel room, where Chase had moved her stuff.

She was on her own for undergarments too. It was too bad Arthur didn't have a line of branded sports bras, but the gym's clientele leaned heavily male.

He dropped several twenties on the table to pay for the clothes. Arthur had told him to take what he needed and not worry about the cost, but Josh paid his debts, and this was definitely on him.

He left the office, locking the door behind him, and walked along the back wall, passing the men's and women's locker rooms on his way to the private unisex shower where Maddie was. There were a dozen people working out on the main floor, some lifting, some on the rowing machines, one guy doing pull-ups with the vigor that came at the start of a rep.

He nodded to Arthur, who stood to the side talking with one of the trainers, then ducked into the alcove in front of the unisex shower. He could just hear the sound of running water through the thick walls. He knocked on the door. "Maddie, I've got clothes. I'm coming in." He used his key to unlock the door and stepped into the bathroom thick with white steam. "I'll just leave these on the counter and go."

She shut off the shower. "No."

"No? You don't want the clothes?"

"No. I don't want you to go."

His heart stuttered, but then he realized she was probably afraid. "You're safe here. I promise. Arthur and I are the only ones who have keys, and the door is thick and the walls made of cinder block."

"That's not what I meant." She pulled aside the curtain and stepped from the vestibule. She had a towel around her hair and was in the process of drying her torso with another towel, slowly sliding the blue-and-white-striped cloth down the front of her body and along her arms and legs until it dropped to the floor and she faced him, fully, beautifully nude.

He couldn't stop his surprised—and admiring—gasp.

She flicked her gaze to the doorknob beside him. "Lock the door."

He hesitated. "I don't think this is a good idea."

"It's a spectacular idea. I want you, Josh. I have for weeks."

"I don't want to take advantage. You've just been through an ordeal." Hell, ordeal didn't begin to describe it.

"But *I* want to take advantage of *you*. I want to feel. To forget. To escape. You once promised me selfish pleasure. I want to be selfish with you."

He shouldn't do this. She was wrecked and might regret it later. "I—uh—could just make you come."

She shook her head. "Do you have a condom?"

"Yes."

"Good. Give me what I need, Josh." It was the low, sexy plea in her voice that broke him. And the fact that she slid her fingers into the dark curls between her thighs as she added, "Please."

He turned and flipped the dead bolt to the locked position, then set the clean, dry clothes on the counter by the sink. He pulled out his wallet and plucked a condom from what was supposed to be a credit card slot. He set both wallet and condom on the counter.

She stepped in front of him and pressed a hand to his chest. "I want you inside me. I *need* you inside me. Like I need air."

Her words and touch made his cock thicken. He wanted to give her everything she needed. Wanted the selfish sex he'd described in her ear that night as they stood with her pressed up against the side of his garage.

Her hand slid down his body and found his fly. She undid his belt, button, and zipper and reached inside his boxer briefs and wrapped her hand around him, stroking the length of his penis. He groaned as his cock thickened even more in her hand. Her touch was everything.

She kissed him as she stroked him, long, slow pulls that banished all thought from his brain. He placed one hand behind her neck and the other on her ass as their tongues explored and tasted.

He'd lost track of how many times he'd kissed her, but each time, it felt new. As if the pleasure of mouths joining was something he'd never adequately explored before. He stroked her tongue with his, enjoying the texture, taste, and sound of her.

In her hand, his cock was hard and aching.

She pulled back from the kiss. "I don't want foreplay. I don't even want you naked. I don't want anything but your cock inside me right now. I want to feel. I want this." She ran her thumb over the tip of his penis, spreading precum to punctuate the last sentence.

He grabbed the condom from the counter. "But you might not be ready for me."

"But that's part of what I want too. I don't care if I'm not ready, because it will make me *feel*. And that's what I need. I want to get out of my head and just feel. Feel you. Feel me."

She took the condom from his hands and opened the packet, then rolled it down the length of him. "This is slippery enough."

Once he was sheathed, he scooped her up with his hands beneath her ass and carried her to the blank expanse of wall next to the shower vestibule. A large vertical rail was mounted to the wall for accessibility, and she gripped it with one hand and wrapped the other around his neck. She leaned her head against the cinder-block wall, and he noted the towel wrapped around her hair would offer some padding.

He positioned the tip of his cock at her opening and held her gaze in a moment of exquisite anticipation.

"Do it," she whispered.

He penetrated her with one smooth, glorious thrust. Lubrication was not a problem as he filled her and she clenched around him. Holy hell. He'd needed this feeling as much as she did.

His brain shut down as pleasure flooded him. With each thrust, he chanted her name in his mind. *Maddie. Maddie. Maddie.*

He pounded into her, thoughtless of the steamy room, the gym outside the locked door. All he could focus on was the sound of her moans, the feel of her slick and hot around him, the tightening of her thighs around his hips.

There was nothing sweet about this coupling. It was hot and furious and superb. He felt her clench around him as she let out a cry of release. And to his ever-loving satisfaction, she kept making that sound, as if her orgasm was endless. He slid a hand between their bodies and thumbed her clit, and she cried louder, a guttural sound that would be the end of him.

His orgasm drew ever closer, and he thrust harder, faster, driving into her. He closed his eyes as he tipped over the precipice and came inside her, likely straining the limits of the condom reservoir.

He leaned forward, supporting her weight with one arm under her. He moved his other hand from between their bodies and gripped the handrail as he caught his breath.

He opened his eyes to see Maddie's face, eyes closed, jaw slack in a serene expression he'd put there. All the primal feelings he'd been feeling about her today converged and sprang from his throat. "You're mine, Maddie Foster, and I'm never going to let you go again."

*M*addie's eyes shot open, the languid pleasure of postorgasm interrupted by Josh's words. The problem was, she didn't know if she liked his words or not. Part of her got a little thrill at his declaration, but another—bigger—part hadn't forgiven him for abandoning her.

Guilt swamped her. She'd used him for sex just now, with no thought for his feelings, what it would mean to him.

She shifted in his arms, and his penis slid from her body. She unlocked her ankles from behind his back and lowered her feet to the floor. She looked down, unable to meet his gaze. "Thanks. I. Uh. That…was great."

Great didn't begin to describe it, and yet her tone made it sound like she was lying.

He placed a finger under her chin and gently raised her gaze to his. "It was better than great, and you know it. And I know I messed up, and that's still between us."

She nodded. "Sex doesn't change anything in that regard. Not for me."

"That's fair. But *I'm* changed. I care about you, Maddie. I want more than a quickie in the gym shower."

"I don't know if I can give you more. You hurt me, Josh. And you're giving me whiplash with your hot and cold. Hell, the first few times we saw each other, you gave me a lecture on how this couldn't happen, then you kissed me senseless."

She nudged at his chest so he'd step back, giving her a clear path away from the wall. "I respected your boundaries every time you told me we couldn't be together. And every time *you* kissed *me*. You asked *me* out. I feel like I'm riding a yo-yo. I *never* made the first move until a few minutes ago." She steeled her courage and met his gaze. "And I realize I shouldn't have done it. Shouldn't have used you. For that, I'm sorry."

His eyes were warm as he gave a small earnest smile. "I'm not, Maddie. Not even a little bit."

She closed her eyes, glad for that. She didn't want to hurt him. She nodded, then without a word stepped into the shower and turned on the spray, rinsing sweat and the smell of sex from her body. She stepped out of the shower and grabbed a fresh towel from the rack, drying off in front of him. She resumed talking as if she hadn't paused to clean up. "Okay, then, thank you for the sex, but I can't give you more until you figure out what it is you want. Until you and Ava work out your issues. I'm done being jerked around."

She pulled the tags off the sweatpants, the plastic strips cutting into her skin as her mother's voice played in her head, warning her she'd damage the fabric. But the plastic snapped, and the pants survived. She pulled them on her damp legs, the soft interior sticking to her skin. She'd have to go commando because she didn't want to put on anything she'd worn in the forest today, ever again.

She hit the floor pedal to raise the lid on the garbage can and saw the condom and wrapper. A glance over her shoulder showed Josh had cleaned himself while she'd rinsed. He was tucked away, belt buckled. Ready to face the world, and, as always, so damn handsome.

She dropped her formerly favorite bra into the can, followed by her underwear, heels, and pantsuit. The only item she'd worn today that she would keep was Grandma's gold watch, which she fastened to her wrist again before pulling the T-shirt over her head. Her order of operations was skewed, probably, but so was her brain.

She noted the T was tight on her bust, and without a bra, it was downright indecent. She raised an eyebrow at him. "What is this, a kid's size?"

He gave her a sheepish grin. "Honest mistake. But it looks good on you."

She pulled on the hoodie, and Josh stepped in front of her, grabbing both sides of the zippered opening. He slid the pin into the box at the base and pulled up on the zipper tab, pulling her toward him gently as he did so.

Her heart pounded at his nearness. They'd just had sex, and yet *this* felt intimate?

"I'm going to work out my crap with Ava. And I'm going to win you back. You can't scare me off now, if that's what you're trying to do, because I'm crazy about you, Madeline Foster."

She wanted to believe him. But she needed to protect her heart. "How do you know you don't just want me because I look like Trina?"

It was a hard, cutting question, but he didn't even flinch. "You think I haven't considered that? I did. That first night. That first week. But Maddie, I got to know you. I know you better after three weeks than I know Trina after four years.

Honestly, I can't even remember what Trina looks like when I look at you. I'm crazy about *you*."

Did she dare believe him? Or was he lying to them both?

She had one more weapon in her arsenal, and she had to deploy it. "Okay, then. What if you only want me because after what happened today…I'm just another person you can try to fix? Isn't that what you do, Josh? You take people in and try to save them?"

This time, his nostrils flared. She'd hit him where it hurt.

"It might be what I do, but that's not why I want *you*." His grip on the closed hoodie tightened. "I get that you can't believe me right now, but you're not going to push me away that easily. Listen, I'm out of pride. I'll take whatever you want to give me. If that means you just want a screw in the gym bathroom to forget your troubles for a few minutes, I'm your guy.

"If you want me to hold you all night long because you've been through an ordeal, I'll do that too. You want a punching bag for your anger? I've earned that role. I'm here for you, however you'll have me. Not because I want to fix you, but because I think you're amazing just the way you are."

She rose on her toes and brushed her lips against his. She hesitated for a moment, then took the kiss deeper, a brief touching of mouths and tongues, then pulled back. "Okay. I'll keep that in mind. Now, let's go to our new hotel, because I'm both exhausted and starving. I want to order room service, then crawl into bed and fall asleep while eating."

He smiled and cupped her face between his palms. "Thank you for not shutting me out."

"Thank you for finding me in the forest. For coming after me."

"I'm sorry I didn't stop him before he abducted you. That I didn't get there sooner."

She pressed her fingers to his lips. "Don't apologize for things beyond your control. I don't hold you responsible."

"But I do. I should have recognized him from the rally. Should have known you were in danger the moment you set foot inside the building. You were doxed because of *me*."

"I was doxed because of Troy Kocher, probably. Or because Cliff Nielsen insisted we attend the museum event. Those were both due to my work, not yours."

Josh's gaze narrowed. "Do you think Kocher is trying to stop you from finishing your job?"

"Maybe, but it doesn't make sense. Technically, he's the client. They're paying me to do this inventory, and they can't sell the house until I'm done. So what's in it for him to stop me?"

"But you're also identifying artifacts that will be repatriated—what did you call them? Funerary objects?"

She nodded. "You'll also find them referred to as 'grave goods,' but most tribes find that term offensive."

"Could there be something that's funerary that Kocher is worried you'll identify? Something really valuable?"

She shrugged. "Real archaeologists—not looters like the Kochers—don't put a value on artifacts, so I really couldn't know or imagine how an item in the collection could be worth so much, it would be worth having me abducted."

Josh nodded. "Still, it's something worth considering." He kissed her forehead, then released her, stepping back. "You ready to get out of here?"

She nodded. "Take me home. Wherever that is today."

Chapter Twenty-Five

*J*osh had finally slipped into a light sleep when he heard the creak of the other mattress in the room. He tried to ignore the sound, assuming Ava was using the bathroom, but instead of her light footsteps retreating, he felt the bed shift as she sat on his mattress.

He opened his eyes to see her silhouette in the dark room. She'd pulled her knees up to her chin as she sat on the bed and wrapped her arms around her legs. "Uncle Josh, I—I'm sorry. I did a horrible thing." Her voice was quiet, difficult to hear above the air conditioner, but he'd been waiting for this, and even though he'd been asleep a moment ago, he was now fully alert.

"I've been wanting to tell you for days," she continued, "but I've been so scared you'll put me in foster care for what I did. Even now, I kind of hope you're sleeping and aren't hearing this."

"I'm awake, Ava." He kept his voice gentle. He didn't want to scare her into stopping.

She sniffed. "I did it," she said.

He waited.

After a long pause, she said, "All of it. Everything my dad accused me of."

This startled him. He'd expected her to confess to lying about Maddie. "What do you mean?"

"I got him arrested on purpose. I knew the stuff in the garage was stolen. I was so mad he said I couldn't be friends with Marcus anymore. We had a big fight, and I told him I hated him. He said all sorts of horrible things about trans people. I told him he was the monster, not Marcus. Then he —he called my mom a slut. Said she didn't love me enough to stick around. Said it was my fault she was dead. He said I was lucky he hadn't abandoned me, because I could be living in the streets. Nobody would ever love me."

Josh's heart broke for about the fifteenth time in the last twelve hours.

"I told him *you* love me. You said you would take care of me. So he went into my bedroom and grabbed the expensive drone, the one you sent me in January."

He knew the one. It had been signed by the chief AI engineer, Leah Ellis. Leah was his friend and coworker Nate "Hawk" Sifuentes's girlfriend. Josh and Leah had celebrated Hanukkah together a few nights. Later, Leah had managed to get a drone for Josh to give to Ava after they'd been sold out everywhere.

"He smashed it. He destroyed my drone and said he'd do that to you if you ever came near me. That he'd beat up Marcus if he ever came to our house again." She sniffled. "So, the next day, I called his work and played dumb. I didn't think it would work. Didn't think he'd get arrested. And then you had to move here to take care of me, and I felt so awful I'd ruined your life too."

Josh sat up and pulled her into his arms. "You didn't destroy my life, Ava. Being here with you is exactly where I want to be." He did marvel that it had never crossed his mind that she'd intentionally gotten her father arrested. He squeezed her tighter. Props to her for being more cunning than anyone—well, except Ari—realized.

He leaned back on the pillows, keeping one arm around her. She rested her head on his chest like it was the most natural thing in the world.

"After I read your letter to Trina—"

He stiffened. He wouldn't push her about snooping through his papers now, but he'd definitely revisit that point at a future time.

"I—I got more worried. You didn't come here for me at all. I was just a burden to you. You're probably counting the minutes until you can be rid of me."

"None of that is true, Ava." He stroked her back. "I've loved you since you were a baby."

"Yeah. Right."

"I did."

It was time to tell her everything—even the parts about her dad that he'd hoped she'd never have to hear.

"I lived in Portland, not far from your parents' apartment, when you were born, and your dad and I still tolerated each other then. I was twenty, and you were the first baby I'd ever spent time around. Your mom was sweet and kind and so damn young when you were born, just a year older than you are now. She grew up in the same small town as us in eastern Oregon, and I'd known her since middle school.

"Our moms were friends—there were only a handful of Jewish families in the community, and since my dad wasn't Jewish and, I later realized, a raging anti-Semite—we some-times observed the High Holy Days and Passover with Lori's family. My mom wasn't super observant, but she wanted Ari and me to know our history. Your mom's family was very observant. I learned a lot from your grandma." He smiled, thinking of what a relief it had been to have the Passover

Seder with Lori's family, away from his father's insidious cruelty toward his mother.

"I don't understand. If Grandpa is anti-Semitic, why did he marry Grandma?"

"I don't know if my dad was anti-Semitic before he moved to eastern Oregon and became friends with a guy who was openly white supremacist, but my guess is the seeds were there. His views intensified when my mom decided she wanted to teach Ari and me about Judaism. Your grandpa was emotionally and physically abusive to Grandma, so it was another part of the cycle of violence."

Josh had done a lot of reading about power and control and abuse to try to understand both his parents.

"But back to *your* parents. I think your mom had a crush on Ari since she was a freshman in high school and he was a senior. Ari moved to Portland after graduation, but he came home for Passover the year Lori was a junior. They started dating, and the following fall, a few weeks before her eighteenth birthday, she got pregnant."

"My dad said she—they—waited until they were married to have sex. He said anyone who doesn't wait is a slut."

"Honey, your dad lied to you. And he's dead wrong when it comes to slut shaming."

"Maddie said the same thing. About slut shaming."

His heart squeezed. It wasn't time to talk about Maddie yet. Ava needed to know her own history first.

"Your mom dropped out of school and moved to Portland with your dad. She got her GED, and after you were born, she wanted to take classes at the community college. But your dad…let's just say he wasn't big on helping take care of you. When you were six months old, I started babysitting you three times a week so your mom could sneak off to class. You and I had great adventures on those afternoons. I'd stack the blocks, and you'd knock them down." He could remember her laugh. The squeals of joy. The zest for life of a nine-month-old who'd just learned to crawl was a power to behold.

"We spent three days a week together for nearly eighteen months. I remember your first words, first steps. All of it."

Maddie had said he was a caretaker and was concerned he wanted to fix her. Thinking back, he realized Lori was probably the first person who brought out the caretaker in him. Ava's mom was also his biggest failure.

"Then I joined the Navy. I tried to stay close to you and your mom after that, but you know how your dad feels about the military. Your mom sent me pictures of you, though, and I sent her money for you, until your dad found the letters."

"Dad said you had an affair with my mom. He said I might even be your daughter, and I'm lucky he stuck around all these years raising your bastard."

"I'm not your dad, Ava. I never touched your mother. We were friends."

"I wish you were. My dad, I mean."

What could he say to that? Sometimes, in an abstract way, he'd wished he was her father too. But if he'd fathered a child at twenty, he never would have joined the Navy. Never would have been a SEAL. He'd had his own path to follow.

But on his path, he'd abandoned this girl to a depressed mother and abusive father. Did his service to his country matter when he couldn't even help those closest to him?

"After your dad found the letters, your mom wrote me one last time. She said not to send money anymore. If he found another note, he'd hurt *you*. You were six years old, and I was in Afghanistan and there was nothing I could do. I thought I was protecting you by letting you go. But I was abandoning you and your mother to a man I suspected was the same kind of monster I grew up with."

Tears slid down his cheeks as he held Ava, remembering

the crushing pain of reading that email. The hopelessness, heartache, and fear. He'd had an op to prepare for, a dangerous scouting mission deep in Taliban-held territory, and he'd had to shut off his mind and heart to Ava and Lori, or he'd be a danger to his team and the mission.

His mom had suffered a stroke and died the year before. Without her or Ava and Lori to visit, there'd been no reason for him to return to Oregon. He'd never communicated with Lori again. Hadn't reached out to his brother at all until eight years later, when a Google alert told him Lori had committed suicide.

He should have gone back to Portland after the Afghanistan deployment was over. He should have kicked his brother's ass and moved Lori and Ava to Norfolk, where he was based. He should have gotten CPS involved when he received the threat to Ava.

Lori always swore Ari didn't hit her, but there was more to domestic violence than physical abuse, and knowing Ari, it was only a matter of time until the abuse escalated from emotional to physical.

"I failed your mother, Ava. I failed you. And I will live with that shame for the rest of my life. But I can promise you now, I will never fail you or abandon you again. There is nothing you can say or do that will make me turn my back on you."

Ava let out a heart-wrenching sob. "I was so scared. Maddie said I had to tell you, and I started to because I knew she was right, but then…I saw the look on your face, and I was afraid you'd decide I'm not worth it. That you'd throw me away."

She pulled back and looked at him. He could see the tears streaking down her face in the dim glow of the alarm clock and LED lights from the electronics on the desk. "When I was small—I'm not sure how old I was, but I think I was in kindergarten—Mom was gone for a few days. I think she'd gone home to see her parents, and she didn't bring me. Maybe it was when Grandma was sick, I'm not sure. Anyway, it was fun to have Daddy to myself for a bit. He got me McDonalds. Let me eat ice cream right out of the container. I could watch as much TV as I wanted, and it wasn't all stuff for little kids. Then I did something wrong. I—I don't even remember what it was. I talked back to him, or maybe I spilled juice on the couch. I don't know. But he suddenly got all mad. Said I was such a pain in the ass. He then told me that it's okay to throw away bad kids, and I needed to always be good, or he could throw me away and nobody would care.

"He wanted me to know what that was like, so I'd never be bad again, and he put me in the stinky, huge dumpster behind our apartment complex. It was empty—I guess it had just been dumped—and the walls were slick and slimy. I was too small to reach the lid, and I couldn't climb out. I don't know how long I was in there, but it felt like hours. A neighbor finally found me. I'd lost my voice from screaming, and my knuckles were bloody from punching the metal walls. They helped me out and brought me to my dad. He was playing Nintendo on the TV, claimed I'd been playing hide-and-seek with one of the neighbors and must've gotten stuck."

Josh went cold, his body rigid with horror. He could picture it all in his mind. Her screams. Ari's indifference as he played video games. He might wonder if Ava was lying to garner his sympathy, given that she'd lied before, but that detail, it was so Ari.

"I still have nightmares about that dumpster. I can still smell it. Feel the slime of the walls on my skin. I hear the sound of a garbage truck, and I panic. My biggest fear was that a truck would come and I'd be emptied into the bin and be crushed to death."

"My God," Josh said, barely able to breathe. "Have you told your therapist about this?"

She hugged herself as she shook her head. "For years, I'd wake up screaming, but Dad must have convinced Mom it was just a nightmare, because she would just pat my head and tell me it was nothing but a dream that couldn't hurt me. Eventually, she stopped coming to my room when I screamed. Nobody believed me. I guess I didn't see the point in telling a therapist."

"Honey, therapy only works if you tell them the things you're keeping locked inside."

"But what if she didn't believe me? What if she thinks it's all in my head? Just a nightmare, like my mom always said?"

"I believe you," Josh said.

"You do? Even after I lied and said Maddie found and read your letter?"

"I do. I know Ari is capable of being that cruel. And I even understand why you felt compelled to lie about Maddie. But that doesn't mean your lies won't be punished. Doesn't mean you can get away with hurting people like that."

She backed away from him. "Punished?"

"Of course. You can't lie like that and not suffer consequences." He saw stark fear in her eyes. "Ava, what do you think I mean when I say *punish*?"

"A few weeks after Mom died, when we were still living in the third-floor apartment, Dad took all my books and burned them, then he locked me in my room—without any electronics, paper, pens, or anything to do—for twenty-four hours. No food. No water. I couldn't escape out the window. I had to pee in the trash can."

Holy hell, she was telling him all this *now*? But then, he sort of understood. She was so afraid he'd reject her, she'd held back from telling him just how messed up her life had been. Again, he had to consider she might be lying to garner sympathy, but also again, his brother's actions over the years gave her words the ring of truth.

"Okay, so to start with, I think we're going to forgo the word *punish* in favor of discipline. Discipline is about learning, while punishment is about retribution. Your dad deserves retribution. You need to be disciplined. You lied to me, and I took you at your word because I didn't want to hurt you by not trusting you. Your lie hurt not just me, but a woman who has been nothing but kind to you."

"I don't want to like her," she said under her breath. "But she's okay."

Josh reached out and pulled her back to his side. "I didn't plan or want this thing with Maddie—I mean, I want it, but the timing is bad, for you and me. But I'm all in now. I'm crazy about her. I want her in my life. And I'm all in on being your dad too. You're stuck with me, for better or worse. So you're going to have to apologize—and *mean it with all your heart*—to her, or none of us are going to be happy."

"That's it? Just…apologize?" Ava's voice was hopeful.

"Uh. No. You're also grounded for two weeks, no going out with friends, no computer or video games except for schoolwork—all to be carried out when it's safe to do so. Living in a hotel does not count as part of your grounded time. You also are going to start opening up to your therapist about everything that went on with your dad, and you and I are going to start doing joint sessions so we can work through our issues together."

"I guess that's fair," she said softly.

"You're going to have to try with Maddie," he added. "If she'll even take me back. I abandoned her right after she'd been doxed and robbed." *And opened herself up to me.*

"I'm so sorry. I—I didn't know. But that shouldn't matter. I shouldn't have lied at all."

"Don't lie to me again, Ava. I need to know I can trust you, or all the therapy in the world won't help us."

"Does Maddie hate me?"

"Before any of this ever happened, she said there's nothing you could do or say that would hurt her. And she meant it. It's what *I* did that hurt her. She's angry with you, yes. But she's a compassionate person and knows this was more about you and me and our messed-up communication. I think she might be willing to forgive you but you've got to earn her forgiveness."

"I was so scared when Chase said she'd been kidnapped."

"I was too, Ladybug."

"I like it when you call me that. It reminds me of my mom."

He hugged her tight and leaned back against the pillows. For the first time, he was glad the hotel put an insane number of pillows on each bed. He'd been too exhausted to dump them on the floor before crawling into bed, and now they made a decent nest for him and Ava. He closed his eyes, one arm around her. "Your mom loved you very much. She'd be proud of you."

"Would she? I mean, I got my dad arrested. Lied about Maddie…"

"Your dad got himself arrested—he's the one who committed the crime, and you were protecting yourself. He should have been arrested for what he did to you and your mother years ago. So yeah, she'd be proud. I mean, not about the snooping and lying part, but you're a good kid, Ava. You're owning what you did wrong—now I *am* talking about the snooping and lying part—and that's an important step. Absolutely everyone makes mistakes. It's how we respond to those mistakes that shows who we are at our core."

"Thanks, Uncle Josh."

"We should get some sleep."

"Can I—can I stay here for a few more minutes? Marcus won't hug me now that he's a guy—not because I care, but because everyone watches us weird. Like they expect our friendship to be different. So I guess it is. My mom used to hold me like this sometimes. I miss it. Being hugged."

"Sure, Ladybug. But you'll probably sleep better in your own bed."

"Just a few minutes."

He was dozing when, sometime later, her voice cut through the darkness. "Uncle Josh?"

"Hmmm?"

"Does Desmond have a girlfriend?"

He jolted, physically, mentally, at the shift in conversation. *Oh, to be a teenager…*

"I don't know."

"If he…asked me out, would you let me go?"

He did *not* want to be having this conversation in the middle of the night. But apparently, that was when Ava did her best talking. "I don't know. I mean, it depends on the whole doxing situation, really. People are after him because of his role in the rally. People are after me, and by extension, you, for the same reason. It wouldn't be safe."

"It's not because he has a police record?"

Josh let out a bark of a laugh. That was the very least of his worries. "Not in this case." He'd looked into it, and the charges against Desmond had been bogus. Plus, the young man had more than proven himself. "It's more about the fact that he's nineteen and you're barely seventeen."

"It's legal for us to date in Oregon. I looked it up."

He didn't correct her by saying, *legal for you to have consensual sex,* which was an entirely different thing, but no point in planting that thought in her mind. It was probably already there.

"Did Desmond ask you out?"

"No. But I want him to."

"Tell you what. I'll invite him over for dinner one night. You, me, Chase, Desmond, and Maddie—if she'll come—and no hitting on him or making him uncomfortable, but it'll give you two a chance to talk. See if you like each other."

"*Everyone* will be there?"

"Everyone. I can invite others from the gym too…"

"No! Then they'll all hang out together, and no one will notice me."

Josh highly doubted a bunch of nineteen- to twenty-one-year-olds would fail to notice Ava, but he kept his mouth shut on that point, not thrilled at the idea of some of the older guys giving her attention. A two-year age difference, he could handle. Four was out of the question. Not until she was eighteen and, legally, he had no say.

Damn, he had his work cut out for him to prep her for making good decisions when she was a legal adult.

"All right, Ladybug, we'll keep the dinner small. Now scoot. We both need to sleep."

She climbed from his bed. "And you can't call me Ladybug in front of Desmond."

He smiled at that. "But you *like* being called Ladybug."

"Uncle *Josh*—"

There was a very normal teenage whine in her tone, and his heart squeezed. God, he loved this girl, and she was going to thrive, dammit.

Strangely, it was because of Maddie that they were finally on the right track. If this thing hadn't happened this week, and if Maddie hadn't insisted he address it with Ava, he'd probably be in Maddie's bed right now, not available for this middle-of-the-night talk.

He'd wanted to be in Maddie's bed, had hoped she'd change her mind, and not because he wanted sex, but because he wanted to comfort her in the wake of her abduction. But she'd refused, and now he'd had the most revealing and rewarding conversation with Ava since he became her de facto father.

"We'll negotiate endearments later," he said with a laugh.

Her blankets rustled as she settled back into her bed. He was drifting off to sleep when he heard her whisper, "I love you, Uncle Dad."

Chapter Twenty-Six

Thank goodness for bathtubs. After an early and exhausting morning being interviewed at the police station, Maddie had earned a long, quiet soak in the big hotel room tub. She'd dumped at least a cup of fancy salts in the bathwater, and now, as she floated in the deep tub, she willed her mind to go blank and forget everything that had come to pass in the last week.

But even bath salts couldn't quiet her mind, and slowly, she began to go over what she'd learned during her interview with the detective on her case. She'd easily picked out her abductor in a photo lineup, and he confirmed the man was the Nielsen Tower security guard, as Josh had said.

She'd watched video taken at the White Patriot rally three weeks ago and spotted Peyton Hoffman without difficulty. She'd spent time studying his brother Karl's face, in case she came across him in the hotel or any other place she frequented.

Both men were at large, and with her firm identification along with the footage from building security, their faces were likely plastered all over the news right now as wanted men.

Hence the tub.

Part of her wanted to turn on the TV or check the internet. But the rest of her knew that would only be a rabbit hole. She knew how these things went. The first comments would be supportive. There would be retweets and likes and shares and hashtags like #JusticeforMaddie. And then the White Patriots and Voigt Forum would launch their bots, and the questions would start. She'd be blamed. Then she'd be called a liar. Then they'd claim a false flag, and before long, #JusticeforPeyton would be trending.

After that, the rape and death threats would roll in.

She'd already deleted her Twitter and Instagram accounts and locked her Facebook, deleting all but her family and closest real-life friends from her profile. She'd have deleted Facebook altogether, but there were a few professional groups she was in that she needed to keep access to. She could see what she wanted on Twitter without a login.

After cinching down social media, she'd made a call to her boss and had spoken with Rhys, Sienna's husband. She begged him not to worry Sienna with the news—they had a sweet, beautiful, preemie newborn to take care of—but suggested either they pull the company website down for a few days or get rid of the contact information, as Aubrey Sisters Heritage Preservation was bound to face attacks from the alt-right.

Rhys had been kind and understanding—he was an assistant US attorney and knew the connection between criminal investigations and social media fallout—and said he'd take care of it. He'd suggested she take a few days off from work, but she didn't want to. Troy Kocher was part of this. She'd seen him talking to her abductor in the rally videos. It felt like taking time off was letting those bastards *win*.

They'd already stolen her home from her. Her sense of safety. It wouldn't be right to let them take her job too.

For that reason, in the late afternoon, Chase would take her to the Kocher Mansion to reexamine the bones and artifacts she'd planned to review yesterday. She needed to look at the basket and red-stained bones. But she had hours to kill before then. Chase needed to be here at the hotel, guarding her and Ava, while Josh was at the gym, running the final training. When Josh returned, Chase could take her to the mansion.

She did not look forward to seeing Troy Kocher. She had no doubt he would be among the first to call her abduction a false flag.

Her hands and feet were prunes when she pulled the plug on the tub, slightly more relaxed than when she'd gotten in, but still something of a mess. Chase had taken her to the police station for the early morning interview, which was a relief because she wasn't mentally prepared to face Josh yet.

She didn't know if she wanted to beg him for sex again or tell him to get lost, so it was best to avoid him altogether.

She'd barely slept the night before, wishing he'd been there to hold her, as they'd done after the terrifying news about Tricia Rooks followed by the assault with tear gas.

Trina had told her Tricia was back in the US, in a hospital in the DC area. She'd had at least one surgery since her return and remained in a medically induced coma. But still, her prognosis was good, her body healing.

Maddie had been heartened by the news and instantly wanted to call Josh and tell him how happy she was. And then she'd wanted to rip her hair out for being so pathetic.

She'd called *him* a yo-yo. What did that make her?

She toweled dry, then wrapped herself in the fuzzy hotel robe. She could get used to this life of room service and freshly laundered robes. But her days of luxury were almost at an end. Chase told her Josh was working on finding a safe house for the four of them, and when he did, she'd have to move out of the hotel. Raptor wouldn't continue to pay her hotel bill if she refused to move to the safe house, but she couldn't see how she could live with Josh and Ava.

Maybe Chase would agree to be her new bodyguard. The boyfriend ruse was no longer necessary. She could find a new house. Her landlord wouldn't argue if she broke her lease given that she was a liability as a tenant now.

But then that could make it hard to find a new place to live.

How did her life get so messed up? Where had she gone wrong? She ate her vegetables and exercised. She donated to charities and did work that was meaningful to herself and others. And still, somehow, everything had gone topsy-turvy.

Was it because of her job?

Was it because of Josh?

Did it have something to do with C-IV? Or was it because of her brother?

She went to the minibar and checked the contents. There was a decent chilled pinot gris for only twice what it was worth. She closed her eyes and considered her bank account. With all the other unplanned expenses, could she afford this indulgence?

She sighed. Not really.

She closed the bar and reached for the overpriced bottle of fizzy water in the fridge. At least she could afford that.

She settled on the bed with the bottle of water and wished she had her cell phone. The police had recovered it last night. The theory was Karl Hoffman had planned to enter her hotel room and leave it inside to thwart suspicion that she was missing, or possibly leave it in her car in the hotel parking garage. But cameras monitored every garage entrance, and he hadn't been able to get her room number before the hotel was swarmed with police, so he'd ditched it in the bushes and bolted.

Thankfully, she hadn't left her room key tucked in the little pouch with the room number, and the phone app that unlocked the room didn't store the number. The police believed at some point between her being drugged but before they left the city, the brothers had met up and they'd unlocked her phone with her fingerprint and then run a program that prevented it from locking again, because there was no way to change the fingerprint without a passcode.

The only items missing from her purse were her house and car keys, her hotel key card, and Josh's cell phone. It was possible they'd planned to ditch her phone at her house if Karl couldn't get to her car or hotel room, but once he saw the police, he must have panicked and known her house would also be monitored and the phone in his possession was being tracked, so he chucked it and disappeared.

Police were searching the forest surrounding the old logging road for signs that Peyton Hoffman had some sort of destination in mind—that he wasn't just taking her deep into the woods to kill her.

That was a chilling thought. What if the motive had been nothing more elaborate than murder? He'd spoken of a boss and orders, but that didn't mean they wanted her anything other than dead.

Would Josh have been a no-show at the rally if Maddie had been murdered?

She knew he'd gone on fighting when he'd lost a teammate on an op, but…this wasn't combat.

There was another avenue she needed to explore, and she'd spoken with the police about it this morning. Would her brother halt his campaign if something happened to her?

She had no clue.

The police only knew White Patriots were involved because Josh had discovered she was missing within twenty minutes of her being hauled from the building. If the phone had been planted, it could have been hours. With her phone unlocked, they could've read the exchange with Chase and known about her plans to go to the Kocher Mansion. They could have sent a text to Chase canceling the trip, and twenty-four hours could have passed before anyone knew she was gone. The search for her would have started with the hotel, not Nielsen Tower.

In that scenario, who would the abduction have been pinned on? A group backing her brother's campaign, or the incumbent senator who was the opposing candidate?

Any rando who felt she had it coming because she'd been photographed with C-IV and Josh?

Was it possible Troy Kocher believed taking her out would mean the artifacts and human remains would go to the museum and not be repatriated? But Oliver Shields was a curator with a degree. He knew better. But he'd also asked for a valuation of the collection, and he knew better than that too. Then again he would also know how to obscure the provenience of artifacts, so if he altered her initial inventory, and she was unable to dispute it, a number of items in the collection could quietly disappear and no one would be the wiser.

Her thoughts had chased all her bath-time serenity away, and now she was getting a headache. She rubbed her temples and reached for her phone…which was where this whole thought nightmare had started. The phone was now evidence. She might get it back. Someday.

Last night, Josh promised to get her a replacement, but none had been delivered yet. She studied her laptop. She could download desktop versions of apps so she could access her books. There was a podcast series on the rise of white supremacy movements in the US she'd started listening to last week. It was difficult listening, but it wasn't like she could enjoy something on the fun side right now.

She settled on her bed, wishing she had her earbuds, but her purse was also evidence now. Peyton Hoffman had gone through her stuff, touched her credit cards. It all had to be processed. She'd spent an hour canceling cards and resetting autopayments—*again*—this morning.

She hit Play on the podcast and got up to pace the room as she listened to a woman and a man discuss the factors that led not just to white supremacist beliefs, but what made them form groups to take violent action.

Ten minutes in, there was a knock on the door. She tapped the Pause button and padded softly to the door to gaze through the peephole. Her heart clenched at seeing a very nervous Ava through the fish-eye lens.

She closed her eyes, not sure if she had the mental capacity to deal with Ava right now, but she'd promised herself that when the girl was ready to talk, she'd be ready to listen.

Unless Ava was about to spew more lies, showing up at her door took a lot of courage. Maddie couldn't throw that effort away. She suspected Ava had a more difficult childhood than even Josh knew. Part of her even thought he'd done the right thing for Ava in showing he trusted her, that the girl needed that kind of blind faith from him.

It had just hurt so damn much that he couldn't *also* have reached out to Maddie and said he recognized the lie but would wait the girl out.

Maddie flipped back the bar that prevented the door from opening even with a key, then unlatched the dead bolt. She opened the door to admit Ava, and, without a word, she placed the "Do Not Disturb" sign on the hallway knob before closing the door.

"Is this a bad time?" Ava asked, waving her hand at Maddie's robe.

She shrugged. "I didn't feel like getting dressed. The robe is…comforting."

"I'm sorry," Ava said abruptly.

Maddie held her gaze. When the girl said nothing more, she said, "For…?"

Ava closed her eyes, and tears rolled down her cheeks. "Uncle Josh said I had to apologize to you, and he said I really have to mean it with all my heart. And the thing is, I do. I have since I found out you were doxed too…"

"When was that?"

"Thursday, when we saw you in the lobby."

Maddie felt a twinge of pain, but gave the girl a faint smile. "So you haven't felt sorry since Sunday?"

Ava's eyes popped open. "Would you rather I lied about that?"

"I suppose not. But also, I do have feelings, and your honesty stings because deep down, in spite of what you did, I kind of thought you'd started to like me."

More tears poured down the girl's face and they were genuine. "I did! But—but Uncle Josh is all I have."

Maddie nodded toward the couch. "C'mon. I'll order us some tea."

Ava settled on the couch while Maddie called room service, paying a premium for extra-fast delivery. She then grabbed yoga pants and a jog bra tank from the dresser and changed in the bathroom. Being naked under the robe might be comfortable when she was alone, but it wasn't the right attire for tea with Ava.

Ava's head was down, thumbs on her phone when Maddie stepped out of the bathroom. Knowing they'd be interrupted by room service, Maddie didn't want to begin now. She stepped to the window. She had a corner room with a view of the Willamette River and the riverfront park. The nearest bridge that spanned the river had been built over a hundred years ago, probably constructed with Nielsen Steel.

With the exception of her college years, she'd lived in the Portland area her whole life. She loved the crazy, weird vibe the city had cultivated, the nude bikers and hippies that had never faded away as the rest of the country moved through the decades.

With the exception of her work with tribes, however, she'd been largely blind to the racist underbelly of her hometown until the White Patriot rallies began. She knew Oregon's racist history, of course. There had been laws passed to prevent Black settlers from moving to the territory, while "sundown towns"—communities that made it known nonwhites had to be outside the town before sunset or they'd face dire consequences—were established west of the Cascades after statehood.

At the same time, east of the Cascades was like a different country. Not the lush green of the west, but desert plateau. Dry and wide-open spaces. Oregon-trail wagon-wheel ruts remained visible in the ground. Settlers had arrived in their wagons and taken native land. Then the government sliced and diced it into a checkerboard and stole indigenous children from their families and forced them to go to boarding schools hundreds—even thousands—of miles away. At the same time, the Kochers and Nielsens were cutting down trees and extracting the iron ore from the ground, taking the bounty from land indigenous people had lived on for thousands of years.

Tomorrow, the park that ran along the riverfront just feet from the hotel would be filled with White Patriots. She'd be able to watch from this very window, as Arthur, Josh, and Chase would be down below with upwards of seventy volunteers in an effort to wrest this city from its racist foundation.

One rally couldn't bring about the end of a hundred-and seventy-five-year history of systemic racism on this one patch of American soil, but at least the counterprotesters could make their statement. She wanted to join the volunteers and do her part, but understood why being there would not help the cause.

There was a knock on the door, and her shoulders tensed. Intermission was over. It was time to talk to Ava.

She'd ordered the high tea service, complete with finger sandwiches and petit fours. Maddie had never had high tea before and figured why not? The server rolled the table into the room and positioned it in front of the couch. The table was covered in a white tablecloth, and in the center was a delicate, flowery, gilded ceramic teapot and two matching gold-rimmed cups. And naturally, since they were in the heart of the Rose City, there was a small vase on the table with a perfect salmon-colored rose.

The table was picture perfect, the kind of setting one would expect for royalty wearing elaborate fascinators, and now Maddie wished she'd taken more than her jewelry from the hatbox in her closet at home.

The server lifted the silver cover from the sandwiches and cakes, and Ava let out a gasp when she saw the small, pink-frosted treats. Then she started to cry.

Shit.

The server cocked his head to ask if he should pour the tea. Maddie gave a quick shake of her head and walked him to the door. She quickly signed the check, adding extra to the already included tip, then locked the door behind him.

She returned to the couch and poured two cups of tea before asking gently, "What's wrong?"

"For my eighth birthday, my mom took me and Marcus to high tea. I loved the little cakes so much. My mom gave me an American Girl Doll at the tea, and she had her own cake. But later at school, Missy Fisher said my doll was a cheap fake from Target, not like hers. She had a real Kit doll. And I pushed her off the swing and got sent to the principal's office, but my mom didn't punish me because she said Missy was a brat and every doll deserves love and cake, just as much as every girl can be a princess if she wants."

Maddie felt her own eyes burn. There were so many emotional ups and downs in that burst of speech. She had a feeling Ava carried a cauldron of memories she'd been forced to tamp down with her father. Memories she hadn't been ready or even knew how to share with Josh, but still, not the kind that would come up in a therapy session either.

Sometimes pink petit fours were a trigger—for both good and bad.

"I wish I'd known your mother."

Ava grabbed a cake and popped the whole square into her mouth. She smiled and said, "Raspberry," with a small hum of pleasure. She swallowed and met Maddie's gaze. "I think my mom would have liked you, but you'd have intimidated her."

She'd never considered herself very intimidating to other women, so she asked, "What makes you think that?"

"You're a professional with a high degree. Aren't you like a doctor or something?"

She shook her head. "I have a master of arts, not a PhD. But yes, that's a graduate degree."

"My mom didn't graduate high school. I just found out last night she took community college classes when I was a baby. I never knew that. She always said she wished she'd gotten a degree, wished she had skills. My dad wouldn't let her work. Said she had no skills and would never make more than minimum wage, and someone needed to take care of me, so why bother?" Ava's mouth tightened. "I think that's why she didn't leave him. She had no way to support us."

She let out a heavy sigh. "She didn't like the other moms at my schools. Well, except Marcus's mom. Ms. Collins is cool. But the other moms were all older and judgy. My mom was an uneducated hick in their eyes, too young to be a mom. They didn't think she might know anything about raising a child. She had me when she was eighteen."

Lori Warner must have been in so much pain. Trapped in an abusive marriage with a small daughter. Maddie didn't know much about Ava's parents, but she had no doubt the woman had suffered from emotional abuse, at a minimum.

Maddie took a sip of her tea. "I know your mother suffered from depression, and I suspect her marriage to your father played a major part in that, but I also feel confident in saying you were the light and joy in her life, Ava."

Tears tracked down Ava's face. "Then why did she leave me?"

Maddie put her hand over Ava's on the table. "Because depression lies. It makes you believe life is too hard, or you're not good enough. Because your father fed her depression instead of trying to help her. Because she lost the battle with her own mind. But honey, none of that was because of you. You're probably the reason she stayed around as long as she did."

"You can't know that."

"No. I can't and don't. I'm just guessing. What does your therapist say?"

"She says my mom loved me."

"What does your heart say?"

Ava shrugged. She mopped her face with the cloth napkin, then took a sip of tea. The hand holding the cup shook as she set it down. "Maddie, do you think you can ever love me? Even after what I did?"

She'd asked herself the same question these last few days and hadn't known the answer, but now, faced with the tearful girl who was so clearly remorseful, so deeply troubled, the answer rang out loud and clear. "Oh, honey, I think I already do."

Chapter Twenty-Seven

According to Chase, Ava had been in Maddie's room for hours. Josh paced his small hotel room. He trusted Maddie to be gentle with Ava, but still, his heart clenched, given what he now knew about Ava's childhood. Should he check on them?

The package that had just arrived from DC gave him the perfect excuse. He could bring Maddie her new Raptor-issued cell phone and help her download her phone backup from the cloud. But it would be lousy of him to interrupt if she and Ava were working things out.

They were working things out, right?

What if, somehow in this mess, he lost them both?

He ran a hand over his face. Sometimes he missed military life. When he'd been in the Navy, he'd always known what he had to do. He'd kept his emotional life simple—leaving toddler Ava behind had been bad enough. He wasn't about to fall in love and have his own kids.

Still, he'd been envious of the guys with families. Someone to go home to. He couldn't see Ava and Lori without endangering them, so he'd done his best to turn off his heart. He screwed around when Stateside, but never, ever got emotionally attached.

His team was all the family he needed. Then Owen had been injured in Somalia, and when he was Stateside, Josh did his best to help the guy. He ended up leaving the service a year before Keith so he could monitor Owen, who was living with his aunt in the DC area. During that year, he'd done consulting work for the Navy, sometimes at the Pentagon and other times at the Washington Navy Yard.

One day, he'd been in the cafeteria at the Yard and he'd seen Dr. Trina Sorensen with a group of friends having lunch. He'd later learned she'd been with Erica Scott and Mara Garrett, but at the time, he'd had no clue who any of the women were. It was just clear that they were more than three coworkers having lunch. They were friends, the kind that might even be closer than family.

He'd felt a pang of longing for his SEAL team, who were God knows where at the time. He'd suddenly missed Ava and Lori, and even Ari.

Trina's laugh had carried across the room, and he'd been…mesmerized. He'd watched her and had felt the cold vise that had gripped his heart for years loosen a bit. It dawned on him that he no longer had to hold back from getting involved. He wouldn't be gone for long stretches of time anymore and could make his own family.

He saw Trina a few more times in the cafeteria in the following months. He was thoroughly infatuated, but never tried to speak with her, never sought her attention. He didn't even know if she was single or liked men, for that matter. It was safe to want her. Wanting a nameless woman didn't cut into his ability to monitor Owen. Didn't make demands on his time or his heart.

He risked nothing, but had a reason to look forward to

the days when he was at the Navy Yard. Strangely, he felt less alone.

Then Keith left the Navy and moved to DC to help out with Owen, and Josh felt some of that burden lift. He received an email from an historian asking about the Somalia op, and that was the one event he could never speak of. He replied, telling her he wouldn't speak with her, and deleted her email.

Then one early August night a few weeks later, Keith called and said he wanted to introduce his best friend to his new girlfriend—the historian who'd been researching the Somalia op.

Nothing had prepared Josh for walking into that bar in Adams Morgan and seeing Keith with his Navy Yard crush. And the two were obviously crazy in love.

He and Trina had become genuine friends after that, and she lived up to the person he'd created in his mind as he'd admired her from afar, which had left him wondering what would have happened if he'd sent a different reply to Trina's initial email. What if *he* had met her first?

He was happy for his best friend. Happy for them both. But that lingering question had haunted him.

Now, with the clarity of meeting Maddie, he figured he could guess what would have happened: absolutely nothing. Trina was an infatuation made deeper by being totally off-limits. There'd never been a spark between them, not like the pure chemical combustion he felt with Maddie.

He'd wasted years hating himself and closing his mind and heart from others because of that strange twist of fate that had gotten in his head.

He had no doubt it was all wrapped in with his abusive father and skewed sense of self-worth. Before he'd even joined the Navy, he'd convinced himself he'd never have a relationship without repeating his father's and brother's patterns, so later, when he decided maybe it was time to attempt a real relationship, he fixated on a woman he couldn't have.

He'd seen a therapist a few times over the years—the Navy had provided therapists who specialized in special forces operators, and Raptor required it for all employees who worked as trainers—but he'd kept his focus on his military and training work, never delving into his childhood. Now he would make a commitment to not just go to sessions with Ava, but he'd do private sessions to work through his own crap. He'd be no good to Ava—or Maddie—if he didn't prioritize his mental health in the same way he did the physical.

In a way, he supposed that was what Maddie had urged him to do when she told him to take time for himself. Maybe she sensed he'd been nearing his limit between Ava, Owen, Chase, starting up a new office, and taking on the volunteer trainings.

He huffed out a breath and picked up his new phone from the dresser top. He'd already configured the device and transferred his data. It only took a moment to find Ava's therapist's email address. Before he could think twice about it, he sent a message requesting an appointment for him alone before meeting for a joint session with Ava.

His hand shook as he set the phone down. Okay, so talking to a therapist about his family scared him. Good to know.

C'mon, man. You used to raid terrorist strongholds.

But back then, the people he'd cared about most had been raiding the stronghold with him.

He picked up Maddie's new cell phone. Time to face an even bigger fear.

*T*hey were almost to the no-man's-land scene in *Wonder Woman* when there was a knock on Maddie's door.

Ava groaned. "It should be a crime to interrupt this movie now."

Maddie hit the Pause button on the computer. "Agreed. If my brother gets elected, we can ask him to sponsor a bill." She rose from the bed and crossed to the door. She rose on her tiptoes to look through the peephole and spotted Josh.

A new kind of warmth swept through her. The hours spent with Ava had dispelled her hurt more than she'd realized. She understood his protectiveness now, even more than she had before.

She flipped the dead bolt and opened the door.

He looked uncertain. It was sweet, really, the nervousness this big, achingly handsome man showed. "Um, if this is a bad time, I can come back."

"You almost ruined the no-man's-land scene," Ava called out.

His brow furrowed. "You've watched *Wonder Woman* at least a half dozen times in the last two months. How could I ruin it?"

"Maddie promised me she cries every time she watches it, and I wanted to see that. But we had to pause right before the scene. The buildup is gone."

"You cry *every* time?" Josh asked.

"You don't?" She crossed her arms and gave him a teasing smile. "But then, of course you don't. You've always been represented in superhero movies like that. I mean, you were an actual SEAL. They make movies about guys like you all the time."

He held up his hands, and his eyes got big, like a deer in the headlights. "I didn't mean—"

She laughed. "Relax. You ever see a grown woman cry while watching an action adventure movie?"

"Come to think of it, no."

She nodded toward the bed. "Scoot over, Ava. Make room for your uncle."

Ava shifted to the middle, and Maddie took her spot beside her. "You'll have to rewind, or I'll never get in the right mood. Maybe all the way back to the bar scene."

Josh settled on the bed on the other side of Ava and gave her a quizzical look over his niece's head.

Maddie just smiled.

"I've never watched this with a woman before," Ava said. "It's different, having someone to talk to about how it makes you *feel*. As a woman. I mean."

To Josh, Maddie said, "We haven't been watching so much as analyzing—we've both seen it too many times to need to watch closely. Except for the no-man's-land scene. When it starts, you aren't allowed to speak until it's over."

"Any more rules I need to know?"

"No nitpicking or disparaging anything."

"I would never," Josh said in mock outrage. "I mean…it's Gal Gadot."

"*Right?*" she and Ava said in unison.

Josh's eyes widened. "You guys aren't punking me, are you?"

She and Ava shared a look, then they both shrugged, which made Ava giggle. Maddie bit her lip to contain her smile. They still had a long road ahead, but at least they were driving in the same car.

Ava hit Play on the computer, which she held on her lap, requiring Maddie and Josh to squeeze in to see the screen.

As they settled in, he draped an arm over the pillow behind Ava, his hand resting free on the thick pillow next to Maddie's shoulder.

When they reached the trench scene—where they'd been before Josh's interruption—she pressed back into the pillows, bracing herself for both the tears and for letting others see her cry. Right on cue, she felt the pressure in her chest as Diana Prince climbed from the trench.

It was silly, but this moment meant so much to her. The strength and power and beauty of it.

She scooted back on the bed, and bumped into Josh's fingers. He jerked away in response, and she reached up, grasping his hand to let him know it was okay. She gave his fingers a light squeeze, then relaxed her grip but left her hand wrapped in his.

They sat there together on her bed, watching a movie while holding hands, with Ava snuggled between them.

Chapter Twenty-Eight

The tension in Maddie's chest and shoulders had ratcheted up with each mile of the drive to the Kocher Mansion. Now that they were in the horseshoe driveway and she stared up at the gothic monstrosity, she was almost paralyzed by it.

"I usually like this architecture style," Chase said. "But knowing there's a crypt underneath with stolen human remains gives this house an ominous look. Like it belongs in a horror movie or something."

"It's even worse on the inside."

She rolled her shoulders. Time to get this over with. She grabbed her bag and opened the SUV door. Raptor had a thing for big, beefy SUVs, even when it was a rental, and once again, she had to jump down to exit the vehicle. It was a good thing she was wearing sensible shoes, because she landed wrong and stumbled.

She huffed out a breath. She was rattled, and she wasn't even facing Troy yet.

Troy, who had unknowingly changed the path of the last

weeks of her life by creeping her out on the first day, which led to her calling Trina.

A warm glow settled in her chest at the thought of this afternoon with Ava and of the quiet ease with which Josh had joined them. Things weren't settled, but they were on the right track, and she used that feeling to bolster her so she could face Troy.

"You okay?" Chase asked.

"Fine. Just short and clumsy."

The front door to the mansion opened, and there was Troy. He hadn't been happy with her request for a meeting after her no-show yesterday, but then, he wouldn't have been happy either way. "You're all over the news," he said, and the prick had the nerve to *smirk*.

She ignored him as she climbed the front steps to the wide wraparound porch. It really was a beautiful house. Too bad it was hopelessly tainted.

"Who's the new guy?" Troy asked, nodding toward Chase. "Did you dump that dick Warner already?"

She debated whether or not she needed to provide an answer. Given that she was entering his private residence, she was probably contractually obligated to name the person who accompanied her. "Troy Kocher, this is Chase Johnston, my bodyguard."

Neither man offered the other a handshake.

Maddie reached the threshold, and Troy moved to constrict her so she'd have to squeeze by him.

"Step back from the lady," Chase said, his voice hard and cold.

"Lady? She's a Christian girl who's fucking a Jew. She's trash."

Faster than lightning, Chase had the bigger man in a tight hold, Troy's face pressed to the door panel and his arm wrenched behind his back.

"You can't do this," Troy said, his voice cracking with pain as Chase torqued his arm. "This is my house."

"I can do whatever I want if I think Maddie is threatened. Did you miss the part where I'm her bodyguard?"

"I didn't threaten her."

"I didn't like your tone. Or your words." His voice went really low. "After what Maddie's been through, the cops will believe me over you, especially given that there are photos of you with her abductor for all the world to see."

"I didn't have anything to do with that! Hell, for all we know, she made it up."

Chase wrenched Troy's arm higher. "Let me tell you something, *Troy*." The name sounded ominous the way Chase said it. "I might look like a nice guy, but deep down, I've got a shit ton of rage, and I've been looking for an excuse to let it all out. So don't fuck with me."

He released Troy and stepped back. Without missing a beat, he turned to Maddie. "Which way to the crypt?"

Maddie had seen him in action in the gym and knew he was fast and formidable, but even then, the sparring had been friendly, with no intent to hurt. His boyish face *did* make him look like a nice guy. But all traces of that were gone now. This was a different man altogether, and he was powerful. And he hadn't been kidding about the banked anger.

She felt like she'd just glimpsed Bruce Banner's inner Hulk, and she was so very grateful to have both versions of Chase as her bodyguard right now.

She smiled, said, "This way," then led him to the interior crypt entrance.

Troy followed, but unlike before, he did not ride her or Chase's heels down the narrow staircase, and he even gave her room to breathe once they were in the crypt.

Maddie went straight to vault 138 and opened the iron door and removed the box that contained the contents. She set it on the work table, donned her gloves, and then laid out the bones as she'd done weeks ago.

"You already did that. Why are you looking at this one again?" Troy asked.

She ignored him. It went against her natural instinct to be rude like that, but Troy had lost his right to respectful treatment even before his anti-Semitic words today.

"Is something wrong with those bones?" Troy asked.

She continued to ignore him. She flipped on the switch for the light on the large magnifying glass, picked up the left clavicle from the bones, and studied it under the bright light of the magnifying glass.

There were a few tests she was allowed to run, and pollen analysis fell within that category. If she could get a sample, maybe she'd get an idea of what the reddish staining was.

The clavicle didn't provide any soil, but she had many bones to go over—cranium, long bones, pelvis, scapulae, a few ribs, and a half dozen vertebrae. She frowned looking at the right ulna. If she remembered correctly, it had been in two pieces when she documented this skeleton weeks ago. She pulled up her notes on her phone and searched on the burial number.

As expected, the right ulna had been broken with both parts present. She lifted her gaze and turned to Troy. "What happened to the distal end of the right ulna?"

Troy's jaw clamped tight and his nostrils flared, and she'd bet he was trying to decide if he could get away with a lie.

"This skeleton is missing part of a bone. That will go in my report, and I will go through all two hundred and thirty vaults again to see if other bones are missing. If it's determined that you knowingly destroyed or withheld remains after they were inventoried, we'll have documentation of your violation of the Native American Graves Protection and

Repatriation Act, and restitution will be required. These remains do *not* belong to you."

"No. They belong to Shields now. He took it," Troy said.

Shock rippled through her. "What? Why would he do that?"

"He did his own inventory of all the remains, to make sure you do it right."

"Oliver Shields lacks the expertise to conduct a NAGPRA inventory. And his conflict of interest means he cannot double-check my work." This would only harm the curator in the long run. What was his agenda here?

Troy shrugged. "I don't care. He wanted to look, so I let him. Like you, he thought that skeleton was weird. He took the bone because he wanted to run a DNA test."

Rage shot through her. "Those tests *destroy* the bone. DNA tests are strictly forbidden to prevent further harm to the remains. It's another desecration."

Now Troy gave her a full smirk. "What are the tribes afraid of, that we'll discover the truth?"

"Truth?" she asked, although she had a feeling she knew what he was about to say.

"Yeah. The truth. That white people were here first. That this isn't really *their* land. It's ours. Oliver Shields took that bone because he thinks that skeleton looks Caucasian. He sent it in to a lab to prove that the idea that Indians were the only people here before 1492 is a lie. We're going to prove it and take our land back."

In the car on the way home, Chase said, "When you were arguing with Kocher, you said something about Kennewick Man, but I didn't quite follow what you were talking about. Kennewick is that old skeleton found about twenty-five years ago in Washington State, right?"

"Yes. The remains—which tribes call 'The Ancient One'—are one of the most complete Paleoindians ever found, and the remains date to about nine thousand years BP —before present. The archaeologist who first examined The Ancient One described the skull as having Caucasoid features, which set off a lot of the controversy around whether or not scientists had the right to study it versus the tribes' rights to rebury the remains without study as is required under NAGPRA. Along the way, others weighed in, including a group that was white-identity, and which might have neo-Nazi leanings. They joined the lawsuit for the right to study the remains because they wanted to prove white people were here first and undermine treaty rights, et cetera."

"But you told Kocher that the DNA tests proved the tribes' claim?"

"Yes. After the lengthy court case, the tribes lost the fight for immediate reburial without examination, and the remains were studied extensively by several experts, and eventually, a DNA test was run which proved the tribes' assertion all along: the remains were closely related to several Pacific Northwest tribes. The remains were finally returned to the tribes a few years ago, and The Ancient One was reburied in an undisclosed location."

"So why would Kocher and Shields pull this stunt now? What's in it for them?"

"I have no idea. Yes, the remains are different from the others, but it's ludicrous for them to think a DNA test will get different results from that of Kennewick Man. And I'm going to see to it that Shields's museum will pay a steep price for stealing a bone. It's immoral and unethical, not to mention just plain stupid. If it wasn't a Saturday, I'd be on my way to see the State Historic Preservation Officer right now."

"The skeleton was taken from the Painted Hills area?" Chase asked.

"As far as I can tell. The sample I took today will be sent off for pollen analysis, which might give us more information. It's actually one of the burials that was mentioned in correspondence between the Kochers and the Nielsens. There's some discussion of funerary objects that were found in association, which Otto Kocher gave to Clifford Nielsen the first. I wonder if those items are in C-IV's possession. If I could get a pollen sample to match from the artifacts, it would be a slam dunk provenience-wise. Unfortunately, artifacts are usually cleaned differently from bones, so it's unlikely pollen would remain. But still, a girl can dream."

"From what I've heard about Nielsen, there's slim chance he'll give you access to his family's collection."

"He seems so eager to own a senator—if my brother is elected, maybe he can put pressure on him."

Chase laughed. "You'd pimp out your brother that way?"

She shrugged. "I disagree with my brother on almost every major political issue. The least he can do is use his power to provide closure of sorts for the tribes."

"Would your brother do it? Put pressure on Nielsen?"

"I doubt it. But it's always worth a try."

"Do you get along with him?"

She shrugged. "It's hard. We can't talk politics, which is pretty much his life, but he's also fifteen years older than me, so we've never really been close. I worshipped him when I was a kid. I miss the man he was before he got into politics."

"What did he do before?"

"He was an attorney. He had a lot of clients, but really made a name for himself representing the timber industry."

"Did he ever represent Kocher Lumber Mills?"

"No. KLM closed down thirty years ago."

"But someone bought their land and assets, right?"

"Yes. Evergreen Timber Resources bought most of their assets."

"Were they one of your brother's clients?"

"Probably."

"Is there any chance Troy Kocher knew you were related to Alan Tisdale before you were doxed?"

"Actually, yes. Alan said Troy was complaining about me at the reception Josh and I went to last Saturday. I thought it was odd at the time, but forgot in the wake of hearing about Tricia."

It was all so convoluted. Yesterday, Hoffman had brought her to a forest that had once been harvested by Kocher Lumber Mills. And what was Nielsen Steel's role? The Hoffman brothers worked for Nielsen, not Kocher.

She rubbed her temples. "I think all this is going to break my brain. Plus I'm still so angry at Kocher and Shields, I want to scream. They might not suffer any consequences from this stunt. NAGPRA is a process, and it's not set up to be punitive."

By the time they reached the hotel—after a lengthy surveillance detection route—Maddie's temper had cooled. She was tired and hungry, having consumed the tiny tea sandwiches and cakes far too many hours ago. Before she and Chase left Ava and Josh, they'd all agreed to order room service for dinner and dine in Chase's room so they could discuss the coming rally and come up with a plan for Maddie and Ava's protection.

She was thankful for this preparation because the food had already been delivered by the time they reached Chase's room, and it smelled wonderful. Josh and Ava had taken the two chairs from their room, and the four of them took their seats at the small table as if it were a family dinner. Josh poured each adult a glass of red wine.

Maddie met his gaze across the table and felt a flutter of

heat reemerge. They hadn't spoken privately this afternoon, but the ease between them had returned after watching the last third of *Wonder Woman*.

His eyes held an intensity that was just for her. Questioning. Hungry. And hot.

For the first time since Sunday, she knew without a doubt this thing between them was far from over. It hadn't even begun, really.

Chase gave a rundown of their visit to the Kocher Mansion, and Maddie again explained the significance of Kennewick Man.

"We learned about that in school," Ava said. "When I was in eighth grade, my social studies teacher spent a whole week talking about Paleoindians, but I was confused because she said paleontologists study dinosaurs, not paleohumans, and the Paleo diet is something else too."

"Paleo as a prefix comes from the Greek word that means 'ancient,'" Maddie said, "and the definition is 'older or ancient—especially when it comes to the geological past' as well as, 'early, archaic, or primitive' so when used scientifically, it can describe dinosaurs who first evolved two hundred and forty-five million years ago, or nine-thousand-year-old humans like The Ancient One. There are also disciplines like paleobotany—study of fossil plants—or usage for things like the modern Paleo diet, which is based on what humans had available to consume pre-agriculture."

"So paleo can mean both humans and dinosaurs, even though they're separated by sixty-five million years of Earth's history," Chase added. He met Maddie's gaze. "When I was a kid, I had dreams of being a paleontologist. Read everything I could. I could've told you the difference between Deinonychus and Parasaurolophus. It's been a while, but some childhood memories stick."

She wondered what Chase had been like as a child. She

had no clue if he had family beyond the Raptor employees who'd claimed him as their own after his ordeals.

Josh's phone buzzed. He checked the screen and let out a curse, then added, "The gym alarm is going off. I need to go." He met Chase's gaze. "You good with being on duty a few more hours?"

"Always."

"Thanks, man," Josh said and rose from the table, leaving his salmon dinner barely touched.

Maddie felt a pang of disappointment. Tomorrow, Josh would be busy from dawn to dusk with the rally. She'd hoped to talk to him tonight.

Their reunion would have to wait another day.

Josh met Arthur at the building, arriving just minutes after the police. He felt a burn low in his stomach as he took in the damage. Racial slurs and a swastika had been painted on the side of the old warehouse. The front window had been smashed, but bars had prevented the vandals from entering the building.

After the police filed their report, Josh helped Arthur secure two panels of plywood in place. Arthur had the plywood on hand in the storage room in expectation of something like this. There wasn't a lot you could do to a concrete building with bars on the windows.

They painted over the graffiti with powered paint sprayers. Two hours after the alarm had sounded, the damage was covered. There might be more attacks in the night, as word had gotten out that the number of volunteers expected at tomorrow's rally could be as high as a hundred. And that was just the volunteers who would protect the counterprotesters.

With such a large number of protectors, it was expected that there could be as many as four times the number of counterprotesters—they might even outnumber the White Patriots. For sure, many who were on the fence about going to the rally might think twice before marching without a hood when they were clearly in the minority.

Josh felt strangely content as he drove back to the hotel. It was after ten p.m. Ava would still be up, and maybe they could watch a movie together. He doubted she would tell him about her conversation with Maddie, and he wouldn't ask, much as he wanted to know.

His gut clenched as he relived the moment Maddie had gripped his hand as they watched the movie. All the kisses and even the sex they'd shared, and that was the touch that gave him an intense rush. Hope.

Much as he wanted to hurry back to the hotel, he did a full surveillance detection route. Raptor was paying for the hotel through an affiliate—Lee Scott's tech security company—and they were registered under false names, so there were no financial transactions to lead the White Patriots to the hotel where Ava and Maddie were staying. Josh wouldn't jeopardize their security with a sloppy SDR because he was tired and eager to get back to his family.

Family.

It had been a loaded word for him since childhood, made worse when he had to abandon six-year-old Ava for her protection.

His SEAL team and later his Raptor team had become his family. The misfits who lived in the Virginia compound, wounded Owen and Chase—each less damaged now than when they'd first moved in—frustrated Nate, who had fallen in love last winter and moved out of the compound and was no longer dissatisfied with his job at Raptor. And then there was Tricia, saving up for a future that she might not get to have.

Those and others in the compound, along with Keith and his SEAL team, had been the only family he had for the last fifteen years. Now his real and found families were merging.

Would Maddie be part of his family moving forward?

The idea of it made his heart quicken. How was it possible to be in so deep this quickly? But then he'd seen it happen with Nate and Leah and even Keith and Trina. For some people, it happened fast. Then there was Sean and Hazel, who took five years to get off their asses and commit.

He reached his hotel room and knocked. Ava was under orders to have the inside bar latched at all times. She answered the door, opening it as wide as the metal latch would allow. "I want to be alone," she said as she shoved his toothbrush through the gap. "You need to find somewhere else to sleep."

Alarm shot through him. Her voice sounded fine, but he couldn't really see her face through the narrow opening. "What's wrong? Did something happen?"

"Nothing's wrong. I just want to be alone right now. You snore."

He did, in fact, snore, but he didn't think that was the issue.

"I can't sleep somewhere else. This is my room. I need to protect you."

"The connecting door is open. Chase is here. I'm fine. Get another room…or maybe Maddie will let you stay in her room."

"Ava," he said, using his brand-new fatherly warning tone. "What are you doing?"

"Nothing. I just want to be alone. Take your toothbrush. Go. I need to sleep."

She waved the toothbrush in the gap, and it looked like

she was about to toss it, so he grabbed it. The moment the item cleared the door, she closed it, and he heard the lock turn.

He could still get into the room through the connecting door.

He should knock on Chase's door. Should sleep in his own bed. Ava's gambit was cute, but it was up to Maddie to extend the invitation, and she hadn't.

He strode the short distance to Chase's door and raised a hand to knock, then froze, staring at the toothbrush gripped in his other hand.

He *could* go to Maddie's room.

He *wanted* to go to Maddie's room. She…might even welcome him.

There was only one way to find out.

Chapter Twenty-Nine

Maddie startled at the sudden knock on the door. It was late, and Chase had checked on her thirty minutes ago. She was locked and tucked in for the night according to their safety plan. She picked up her phone to text Chase—she'd agreed to text him if anyone other than room service came to her door—when the phone buzzed and a text appeared.

Josh: *It's me.*

She climbed from the bed and crossed to the door. A quick glance in the peephole confirmed the text, and she unlocked the door. "What's wrong? Is Ava okay?"

His lips flattened in a way that showed amusement and annoyance and wasn't quite a grin. "She kicked me out."

She leaned against the frame, concern leaving her in a rush as the dots connected. "Oh, really? What did you do to warrant that?"

"She says I snore."

Maddie nodded. "She's not wrong there." He *had* snored briefly during the one night they'd spent together.

His eyes lit with humor as he held up a toothbrush. "She

gave me this and told me to find another room. Then she suggested I ask if I could bunk with you."

Maddie felt a giggle rise. "Hmmm. But…there's only one bed in my hotel room."

"That *is* a problem."

"I mean, there's a couch, but I'm sure it's horribly uncomfortable. I wouldn't even wish it on my worst enemy."

She took a step back, and he came forward, into the doorway but not entering her room. Her body flooded with heat at his nearness, at his scent. A flash of memory from yesterday in the gym shower as he held her against the wall and gave her what she wanted set her body buzzing.

She'd really done that, demanded sex from him, and he'd given her exactly what she needed.

"I'm not your worst enemy, Maddie?" Her name on his lips was a caress.

"Not even a little bit," she whispered.

"Can I share your room tonight? The couch is fine. I won't ask for more than you want to give."

It was decision time, but now that they'd arrived, it wasn't any kind of decision at all. It was like water flowing down a valley, cutting a natural path, reshaping the landscape to suit the flow. No dams, no channels, nothing to hinder the course of nature.

"You can stay." She grabbed his jacket and pulled him to her, bringing them chest to chest. She pulled him down as she rose on her toes. "And I want you in my bed." Her lips were a centimeter from his as she whispered, "And in me."

He lifted her from the ground even as he kissed her. He kicked the door closed behind him, then turned with her in his arms, his tongue sliding between her lips, and she heard the click of the dead bolt followed by the slap of the interior bar being engaged.

She sucked on his tongue as he carried her to the bed and

set her down on the foot of the mattress. He ended the kiss by standing up straight. She gripped the front of his jacket, tugging at the zipper. Off. He needed all his clothes off.

She had yet to see him fully naked, and she wanted to see just how beautiful his body was, to lick every inch of him.

He smiled as he doffed his jacket, followed by pulling his T-shirt over his head. And there was his chest. His magnificent chest. Honed and chiseled and utterly perfect. She placed a hand on his pec, and he covered it with his own, sandwiching her palm and fingers between his warm skin.

"We've done fast and hot," Josh said, "and it was glorious. But that's not what I want from you tonight. I want slow and sensual and to explore every inch of you. I want to make you come over and over. I want to be utterly selfish with your body. By the time we're done, I want you to fall apart at the mere touch of my fingers, because you know exactly what they can do to you."

She bit her bottom lip and rose on the bed. She licked his nipple, then ran her tongue up over his firm muscle as she ran a hand over the other pec and down to his abs. Her mouth reached his neck, and she traced his clavicle with her tongue, then licked upward until she sucked his earlobe into her mouth.

He shifted, taking her in his arms as his mouth covered hers again. She liked that they didn't need to talk. There was no need to delve into the hurts of the last week. This, right now, was about moving forward. Sunday no longer mattered.

His fingers threaded through her hair as he cupped the back of her head, and the possessiveness, the intensity of his kiss, blew her mind a bit. It made her feel like she'd never been kissed before this moment. Never been possessed quite like this. The only possible exception was in the forest yesterday.

Josh wanted her. Not Trina. Not some ideal woman. *Her.*

And he wanted her with an intense, raw, virile energy that lit up the room and set her on fire.

She tugged at his belt, desperate to get him naked. Desperate to have his bare skin pressed to her. Inside her.

She stopped and scooted back, moving just out of his reach. "I've got an IUD, and I'm clean. I was tested when I found out my ex cheated on me. I haven't been with anyone since."

"I'm clean too. Regular physicals are part of my job, and I always have them run all tests."

She bit her lip, feeling surprisingly nervous. "I want you bare inside me, but if it's too soon for that for you, I've got condoms."

He climbed on the bed, also on his knees so they faced each other. She tilted her head back to see his face as he loomed over her, so beautiful in the dim light of the bedside lamp. "I always use condoms when I don't want more than a casual relationship with my partner."

Flutters traveled from her belly to her heart, which started to pound to her own ears. "And do you want something more than casual with me?"

"I want everything with you, Maddie. I want it all."

She leaned her forehead on his chest, closed her eyes, and took a deep breath, taking in the scent of him, flooded with feelings and overwhelmed. His arm closed around her, holding her tight. Several seconds passed as she reveled in the wash of emotion. Then she raised her head and met his gaze. "Make love to me, Josh."

As promised, he took her slowly. His attention to detail and her reactions guided his touch as he explored her. Undressing her was easy—she wore only a T-shirt, pajama pants, and underwear—but he still managed to take his time with it, giving her breasts all his attention before moving lower to remove her pants and panties.

He moved to go down on her then, but she clamped her legs together. "Strip!" she demanded. She wanted to see and touch him too.

He complied with a laugh and then proceeded to slowly remove his clothes, stopping between each item to caress a new area on her body with his hands and mouth.

She was in a frenzy of need by the time his boxer briefs finally hit the floor and she could see every beautiful inch of him. He stood next to the bed, and she knelt at the edge, rapt with attention. She ran her hands over his body, taking his thick cock in her hand and stroking the smooth length. She was going to have this. She already *had* had it. But tonight would be different.

Yesterday in the gym had been wild. Hot. Frenetic. Perfect for what she'd needed. But this was something else altogether. Today, he was claiming her, and she was claiming him. Her body was his to play with, and she would give as good as she got.

She lowered herself and licked the tip of his penis, then put her mouth over the head. He bucked, and she loved that small loss of control. She'd made him do that.

She slid her mouth down on the shaft until she could take him no deeper, then she licked and sucked and cupped his testicles with one hand while the other wrapped around the base of his cock and stroked him. Her mouth and hands worked his body, his hard flesh sliding along her tongue.

He gasped and wrapped his fingers in her hair, and she reveled in the pleasure of it all, this perfect moment as she had Josh Warner deep in her throat and lost in the pleasure she could give him.

He wasn't worried about anything in this moment. He wasn't taking care of anyone but the two of them. He was taking selfish pleasure. She wanted him to come in her mouth. She wanted to feel him pulse against the back of her throat as she swallowed. She wanted to give him that ultimate selfish pleasure of only receiving.

But he didn't let her. He withdrew from her mouth even as she resisted.

"Later, sweetheart. I promise." His voice was deep and guttural and oh so sexy. He rubbed the tip of his cock across her lips. "I'm going to take everything you want to give me. But right now, I want to give to you, and then I want to come inside you, without a condom."

She gave the tip one last lick, then obeyed his orders to move up on the bed so he could put his face between her thighs. Damn, she realized she really liked being ordered around in this situation. She was one hundred percent on board with this hot, bossy bodyguard in bed.

His tongue was hot and wet on her clit, and it was her turn to buck involuntarily. As he'd done with undressing her, his touches were slow and languid, each stroke of tongue or fingers a precision strike that maximized her pleasure even while drawing it out. He traced her folds and kissed, sucked, licked, and worshiped. It was a slow yet intense buildup to orgasm that tested her sanity.

When she reached her breaking point, he increased the speed and pressure of his tongue, and the delicious friction sent her over the edge. She cupped his face between her thighs, her arms cradling his head as she gasped and groaned, her orgasm coming at her in multiple waves.

She loosened her legs and tugged at his hair, opening her body, urging him to enter her. He kissed her belly on his way up her body, then sucked on her nipples. Finally, his mouth reached her neck. He sucked on her skin at the same time he entered her slick vagina with a sure, hot, deep thrust.

She gasped with the pleasure of being so utterly filled. Joined. Connected. *Claimed.*

But this wasn't hard and fast like in the gym. No. As

promised, he tempered his speed, and each slide of his body in hers was measured perfection. She rode the waves of her ongoing orgasm, the pleasure continuing endlessly.

He rose up on his hands, locking his elbows as he thrust into her. She opened her eyes. As much as she was lost in the moment, she wanted to see his face. His eyes were open as he gazed down on her with such intensity, and she felt utterly claimed. Part of him, as he was part of her.

He increased his speed, ratcheting up her pleasure and, from the look on his face, his too. He closed his eyes and tilted his head back. He was so close, and now she was climaxing again, but she wasn't entirely sure she had stopped coming from the first orgasm yet. One pleasure flowed into the next.

He came, his thrusting punctuated by a guttural groan. He kept up the friction, rocking his hips, and she went over the edge again, taking her long, sensuous orgasm to a new peak. She clenched around him, gripping his back with her hands, sweat glistening on them both.

His breathing was ragged as he held himself above her, then slowly lowered to kiss her, long and deep. A romantic kiss that said so much more than words.

He raised his head and looked into her eyes, and for the first time since this afternoon, she saw the question there.

He still didn't know. Sex without a condom in the heat of the moment wasn't a binding commitment, and yesterday, after she'd gotten the sex she needed from him, she'd rejected him. He'd braced for that to happen again.

She smiled and stroked his cheek, her heart pounding as pure, unfettered feelings for this man flowed downstream, having cut a new, more direct path. "You're mine, Josh Warner, and I'm never going to let you go again."

*J*osh woke with a start, disoriented. For a moment, he feared it had all been a dream, but the cool sheets against his naked skin, not to mention the sleeping woman beside him, reassured him that the previous hours had been gloriously real.

He wanted to pull her against him and breathe her in, revel in having her in his bed—well her bed for now, but that would change in the safe house—and in his life. He didn't want to wake her, though, so he rose on his elbow and stared at her. She was naked, and the blanket had slipped, leaving one breast bare in the dim light of the room.

She was so damn beautiful, from the shape of her nose to the slope of her shoulders to that perfect breast he wanted to tease and suck.

He wouldn't screw this up again.

She shifted, rolling toward him, and said in a sleepy voice, "Are you staring at me, Josh?"

He pulled her to him, and she pressed her face against his chest. "Only a little bit."

"Why?"

"Because I'm happy. Being with you makes me happy."

Her lips pressed to his chest with soft little kisses. "You make me happy too." She raised her head, and while her body was relaxed against him, he sensed she was more awake than asleep now. "This is real between us, isn't it? No more excuses, no more yo-yoing from either of us? We're together, in bed and out?"

He traced her hairline, tucking her hair behind her ear. "I'm all in, Maddie Foster. I'm crazy about you. I've never felt this way before, and I'm pretty sure that's because I've never been in love before."

He could just make out her features in the darkness. He

really should have turned on a bedside lamp before making his declaration. A romantic strategist he was not.

She must've felt the same way, because she pushed him to his back, leaned across him, her chest pressed to his, and fumbled with the lamp to his left until the light snapped on.

He blinked at the sudden brightness as she did the same. "Say that again," she commanded.

He held her gaze, forcing his eyes to adjust to the light. "I'm falling in love with you, Maddie. Head over heels. Ass over teakettle. All those phrases finally make sense, because you've flipped my world upside down, but when I'm with you, I know it's the way the world should be."

Her entire face—eyes, cheeks, brows, mouth—lit with the most beautiful smile he'd ever seen. "I'm crazy in love with you too, Josh Warner."

Chapter Thirty

The heat wave had broken, thank goodness. Today would be a perfect seventy-eight-degree summer day, not so hot that tempers would rise exponentially due to discomfort. Tempers would be bad enough without the added stress of dehydration and sunburn.

A cool breeze courtesy of the Willamette River, which snaked alongside the park, wafted across the wide swath of grass. The grass strip was so long, it intersected with three bridges. Josh and his team had set up at the south end of the park, just below the historic vertical-lift truss bridge, the oldest of its kind in operation in the United States, according to Maddie, who was prone to giving fun facts about historic structures within the city.

He glanced toward the hotel where she and Ava were holed up, but kept his gaze moving, in case White Patriots were watching. He didn't want them to see him pay undue interest to that particular building. He scanned to the area where Portland Police Bureau officers were inspecting volunteers for weapons.

Given that many who'd signed up to protect counterprotesters had a history of confrontations with cops, this act went against their sense of self-preservation, but still, they were here, playing by the rules that Josh had managed to negotiate to keep everyone as safe as possible.

Desmond was back, his cut from three weeks ago now a thin line across his dark skin. Remembering his promise to Ava, Josh would invite the young man over for dinner, except he didn't exactly have a house just yet. And he probably should discuss it with Maddie first, given that the current plan was that they'd all move to a safe house once it was ready.

Maddie.

His body, his heart, heated yet again. Last night had been a new beginning. A restart. A damn miracle. And this morning had been a continuation. He'd woken in her bed to find her hands on him, as if she couldn't get enough, and he'd made love to her again, knowing it was the first of thousands of mornings that would follow the same pattern.

She'd come apart in his arms, his body giving her everything she demanded, and damn if it wasn't a thousand times more satisfying than anything he'd felt before.

He'd been waiting his whole life for this morning and hadn't even known it.

They still had much to work out, and he wasn't foolish enough to believe that it would be smooth sailing with Ava from here on out either, but there was so much he had to hope for.

He focused on the scene before him. He needed to get his head out of the dreamy afterglow of magnificent sex and get his head—the one on top of his body—in the game. He had a job to do.

Cleared by the police, Desmond approached. After his experience at the last rally, he'd been promoted to green T-shirt and could take a place on the front line if he wanted it, but could also choose to hang back, interspersed with the crowd. Josh wouldn't pressure him either way.

"Your niece going to be here today?" Desmond asked in a voice that was so not casual, but clearly trying to be.

Josh couldn't suppress his smile. "Nope. No way. Too distracting for me if she or Maddie were here."

"Maddie's your girl? The one who was with Ava at the gym last week?"

"Yes," Josh said, utterly thankful the relationship was truer now than it had been when Owen joked about it on the radio at the last rally. "She's all mine," he added in a whisper that was only for himself. Every curvy inch of her.

"Good. That they're not here, then. I mean." Desmond's words came out a bit stumbling.

It appeared the interest between Ava and Desmond went both ways. As much as that made Josh happy for Ava's sake, it also filled him with a little dread. Was he ready to deal with the prospect of her dating?

He'd just become a father. He was supposed to have seventeen years to prepare for this moment, and instead, he'd had less than two months. At some point in the future when he could catch his breath, he'd have a stiff drink and assess what bad karma he'd incurred to bring him to this point.

"You want to take the front line, or work the crowd?" Josh asked.

"Front line. No way are those assholes going to scare me off with their bullshit false flag tactics of trying to make it look like we instigated violence."

"Okay, then. Take your spot. Counterprotesters and White Patriots should start arriving any minute, and we need to be ready."

"Yes, sir," Desmond said and went to the line of thin barricades that were supposed to separate counterprotesters from rally attendees on this side of the bridge.

Other volunteers passed inspection and took their places. Slowly, the park began to fill. Josh couldn't stop himself from glancing toward the hotel again. The two women who were his whole world waited, unprotected, but locked in tight until the rally was over and he and Chase could return.

They were safe. They had planned for every contingency. He needed to focus on the men and women who were here on the front lines and protect them as he'd promised.

The park was filling up fast on both sides of the barricades that had been set up to separate White Patriots from Josh's team. She was so damned impressed with his willingness to put his physical body on the front line. That man, who lived his convictions, who volunteered his time so others could do the same, was *hers*.

She glanced at Ava, whose attention was divided between the television and her phone. Local news channels were just beginning coverage of the rally, while counterprotesters were live tweeting from their side of the barricades. Ava was following the hashtag and, Maddie suspected, looking for pictures of Desmond.

The girl had a full-on crush. It was sweet to see, but Maddie also knew Ava was scared for Desmond.

It was impossible not to be worried, given the situation. Josh had been a Navy SEAL, and still Maddie worried. This wasn't an op. These were Holocaust-denying American citizens who talked about taking "their" country back with violence.

And Josh was down there on the literal front line.

It was scary stuff, and just two days ago, she'd been abducted by one of them.

This rally would be bigger than the last. For starters, it

was at a larger, more central park, but also, after the news coverage three weeks ago, even more news organizations had shown up to document every second. The road that fronted the hotel and paralleled both park and river was lined with satellite trucks. She opened Facebook on her laptop to see what was being said about the Portland rally there. There would probably be live videos taken by counterprotestors.

A notification popped up for one of her favorite groups—Archaeologists for Science and Freedom. It was a safe space for roughly five thousand of her colleagues to discuss what was happening in the world and how attacks on the veracity of scientific data and historical facts affected their profession. They discussed the suppression of data on climate change, and academics posted when their universities took action to curtail research at the behest of government or corporations. There were several threads calling out professors for sexually harassing students in the wake of #MeToo.

Failures in NAGPRA enforcement popped up a fair amount, as well as pleas for help when willful destruction of archaeological sites was occurring unchecked. Many landowners believed that because they owned the property, they could destroy sites, but in most states, it remained illegal to knowingly destroy an archaeological site even when on private property. But enforcement of those laws only happened when Cultural Resource Management professionals knew the destruction was happening and it was documented.

The group was a cornucopia of information on what was going on in the world of CRM, mostly in the US, but with contributing members from all over the world. She clicked on the notification, which indicated she'd been tagged in a post, and smiled when she read it. A man she'd worked with several years ago said he intended to go to the rally and was thankful for the Raptor-Bond Ironworks alliance to make it safer for counterprotestors. He tagged Maddie, asking that she thank Josh for him personally, and added concern and support for her abduction on Friday. In the two hours since the post had gone up, there were over two hundred comments from her colleagues, all offering her support and virtual hugs and appreciation for the work she did. Some people knew her, like the original poster, because they'd worked or gone to school together, some were well-known and respected archaeologists who only knew her from the group, and still others were lurkers with unfamiliar names. Her eyes teared as she read them all.

In her rush to shut down social media yesterday, she'd forgotten that in safe spaces like this one, it could also be a comfort.

"Why are you crying?" Ava asked.

"I'm having a Sally Field moment."

"What does that mean? Who is Sally Field?"

"She's an actress who, when she won her second Oscar, gave a really sweet and heartfelt speech about what it meant to be liked by all her peers. And she was mocked for it, but really, her genuine emotion was kind of wonderful."

"Oh. She's the 'you really like me' woman."

"Yes. She's also a brilliant actress."

"And why are you having a Sally Field moment?"

Maddie patted the bed beside her. "Come see. Your uncle is part of it too."

Ava settled on the bed and leaned close to read the post, then she scrolled through all the comments. She'd scrolled through only about a third of them—with more being added every minute—when she put her arm around Maddie in a surprising, spontaneous hug and said, "Oh, wow. This is really cool. You deserve it, Maddie."

Maddie hugged Ava back, fully crying now. This was their

first hug, and Ava had offered it to comfort her, not the other way around. "Thanks, Ava."

"I'm glad you and Uncle Josh are back together," she whispered. "He deserves to be happy too."

She squeezed the girl, out of words for the moment. She was under no illusion that the road wouldn't get bumpy again, but right now, she believed she and Ava could forge their own relationship in which Maddie existed in a space somewhere between uncle's girlfriend and maternal stand-in.

Ava loosened her grip and idly scrolled down the comments. "This one's from Cressida. I've never met her, but Uncle Josh has talked about her. She married another guy from Raptor last year."

Maddie clicked the heart reaction on Cressida's comment. "I met her a year and a half ago, when I was in DC and visited Trina."

"Is…everything okay with the Trina thing? With Uncle Josh, I mean?"

Maddie nodded. "We're fine. I was never worried about his feelings for Trina. After all, I know what it's like to have an unbearable crush on her too."

"You're not jealous?"

"No." Maddie smiled at seeing another familiar name in the list of comments. She'd never met the woman, but she'd heard a lot about her from Trina. She pointed to the name on the screen. "Have you ever watched any of Stefan Gray's marine biology documentaries?"

"I think so."

"That's his daughter, Undine. She used to work with Trina and the others in DC."

Maddie hearted Undine's comment too and kept scrolling. She would email Cressida and Undine a personal note later. Which reminded her, she needed to send all her real-life friends a note telling them what they meant to her.

Josh and Keith had shared their emotions in the wake of nearly losing their friend Tricia. Maddie had been abducted, and, except for Trina, she hadn't reached out to anyone.

She'd sent a quick note to her parents, of course, but hadn't even checked email for a response, and she hadn't given her mother her new cell phone number. Hadn't called her brother at all.

She reached the end of the comments and scrolled down to the next post. She hadn't checked this group in days—maybe weeks? Life had been something of a blur for the last three weeks.

There was a funny archaeology comic posted, followed by a post about global warming and the melting of permafrost in Alaska resulting in the erosion of archaeological sites on the northwestern coast, complete with a sad video taken by an archaeologist on survey for a military project.

The next post was a link to a news article about a twenty-five-hundred-year-old skeleton that had been stolen from a museum in Norway. All that remained of the early Iron Age remains in the museum's storage facility were the smaller bones. The theft had been discovered a week before, and the post had gone up in the group Friday morning. From the comments, it appeared it had been posted, then disappeared, then reposted multiple times. Either Facebook was wonky, or someone in the group was screwing with posts. But it wasn't the technical issues that caught her attention, it was the photo that accompanied the report. Familiar. But of course, she spent her days looking at skeletons and, on a basic level, all skeletons looked alike.

She clicked through to view the larger, higher-resolution image on the news website and couldn't stifle her gasp. Not only was the right ulna broken in two and the femur broken in three, but there was distinctive red staining on the clavicles and scapulae, identical to the remains she'd found in a closet in the Kocher Mansion.

Chapter Thirty-One

So much for White Patriots being scared off by the large number of counterprotesters. Josh supposed it had been a narrow hope, but still, he'd clung to it. Instead, the white supremacist crowd was triple what it had been three weeks ago—so perhaps they'd been galvanized by knowing they were opposed.

It didn't matter, because they were *still* outnumbered by counterprotesters. Josh's group couldn't be contained by the original barricade placement, and so they'd been moved to the north side of the bridge encroaching on the south side of the platform set up for speakers. Counterprotesters lined the roadway, claiming the sidewalk on the far side of the grassy strip of park. These were the most vulnerable positions, and Josh and Arthur made sure there were protectors every twenty feet along that line.

Josh's gaze went to the corner room of the hotel, where Maddie and Ava watched from above. He and Chase had given the women their binoculars, and they'd set up one of Raptor's cameras with a high-powered zoom on a tripod. If they desired, they'd be able to count the freckles on the white supremacist speaker's face, with the added benefit of not having to listen to the speeches.

The men—and all the speakers were men—who took the podium gave speeches that aligned with the beliefs of the activists who took over the Malheur National Wildlife Refuge a few years ago and the ones who staged protests in front of the capitol to regularly shut down state government. Those groups had been emboldened by their successes and acquittals, and Josh hoped the demonstration today would set them back a notch.

He scanned the line and saw a counterprotester step forward, pressing against the hastily strung-up police tape, shouting something at a White Patriot who was jeering from the crowd. Javonte nudged the counterprotester back, and the woman complied. Josh tapped his headset and said, "Well done, Javonte."

The young man gave a thumbs-up without saying a word.

"I've got some WPs encroaching on the north end," another volunteer said.

"Chase, how close are you?" Josh asked.

"On it," the operative said.

The last hour had seen tiny skirmishes and encroachments just like that, but nothing too alarming. Josh kept his eyes on the walkway to the bridge, as at rallies in the past, attendees had tried to seize the bridge and shut down traffic.

A familiar head in the crowd caught his eye, and his stomach dropped.

*A*va was at the window with her eye to the camera's viewfinder, giving Maddie a play-by-play of the movement of the crowd. "It looks like things are getting pretty tense down there."

Maddie hit Send on the email she'd composed for the museum and police in Norway. It had taken a while to write the emails as she'd had to look up her correspondence with Shields, but sure enough, he'd been in Oslo around the time the remains went missing and, most importantly, the day Josh had pried open the *empty* vault, the curator had been on his flight home. Two days later, she'd found the bag of bones in the closet. The bag contained one of Kocher's note cards with the vault number and had been made to look like it had been misplaced after being put on display months or even years before, but had probably been placed there the previous day.

She understood their entire plan now: Shields stole the remains but wasn't able to return to the US in time to fold them into the collection, so Kocher had probably glued several vaults shut, ensuring she would remember the sealed, empty repository, and even offering a reason why the bones weren't put back. After she found the random bag of bones in the museum office—which she was bound to do at any point in the days she was working in the mansion—it was logical for her to return the remains to the empty vault. She'd done the work of folding it into the collection, essentially authenticating it, for Shields and Kocher. Once she'd served her purpose, Shields had taken a bone and sent it off for DNA testing, determined to prove Caucasians had been in North America for thousands of years in an attempt to undermine treaty rights and steal yet more reservation land.

Given that the remains would likely be returned to the tribes—because the original remains in that vault had definitely been stolen from government land—and reburied in a secret location before the DNA analysis came back, it was a perfect, untraceable way to get the DNA results on record without further testing. Plus, the skeletal remains' original origins—Norway—meant the DNA test would come back white as white could be.

But Maddie had seen staining that looked more like iron than copper, which was odd for a Native American burial, and she'd taken a pollen sample from the bones. What story would the pollen tell?

She glanced at the dresser drawer where the sample was stored. She'd mail it today if she could, but it would have to wait for tomorrow. It would be weeks before the pollen analysis would come back, but when it did, it would be further proof of what Kocher and Shields had conspired to do.

"I can't believe how many White Patriots there are," Ava said, pulling Maggie's attention away from her computer.

She rubbed a hand over her face. Reporting Oliver Shields's crime to Norwegian authorities was just about the only thing that could have distracted her from the rally in the street below the hotel.

"I can't either," she replied as she closed the laptop and rose from the bed. "Or at least, I don't want to believe it." At the window, she scanned the thick crowd that filled the park and spilled out onto the street. "Where's Josh?" She searched for his green shirt. It was easy to pick out the volunteers. The color was a distinctive Yale blue, and there were dozens of them along the perimeter of the rally, separating WPs from counterprotesters. With only a dozen green shirts, they were less easy to spot in the large, surging crowd.

"Last I looked, he was near the bridge—by the pedestrian stairs."

Maddie scanned the ramp first, then spotted the stairs Ava mentioned. She picked up a pair of binoculars and zoomed in on that area, easily picking out Josh, whose muscles were on full display in the tight T-shirt.

Hot damn. That body is all mine.

She still couldn't quite believe it.

She dialed in on his profile. She could see anger on his handsome features as he faced off with another man, who wore a surprisingly bulky coat considering it was a warm summer day. "Who's he talking to?"

"Just a sec, I need to find him."

The girl was probably watching Desmond. Maddie had learned today that the two had been texting each other for the last few days. Or maybe they were chatting on Discord. Whatever it was, they'd somehow found each other online, and a friendship—or something more—was blooming.

Ava tilted the camera toward the stairway, and Maddie watched as her delicate long blue fingernails adjusted the zoom. She let out a sharp gasp and jumped back from the tripod. "Oh my God, oh my God. *Ohmygod!*"

Her face showed stark, raw fear.

"Who is it?" But the moment Maddie said the words, she figured it out, and her heart squeezed for the girl.

"My dad," Ava said in a bleak voice. "I guess he's out of jail."

Chapter Thirty-Two

Josh stared at Ari. The older brother he'd once worshiped, although that feeling hadn't survived childhood. By the time he'd left Portland for the Navy, he'd only tolerated the man because of Lori and Ava.

Now they were strangers. Josh hadn't been face-to-face with his brother since the day he joined the military. The intervening years hadn't been kind to him. But then, he'd spent the last five months in jail. Now Ari stood before him with new ink on his neck. The long sleeves of his bulky coat probably hid more tattoos, and Josh's gut clenched to realize they were probably of the neo-Nazi variety.

Their dad had been anti-Semitic. It had been part and parcel of the abuse their mom had tried to shield them from. She'd done the best she could, but it had been impossible to avoid hearing the slurs Dad had hurled and the other subtle and not so subtle ways he'd made it clear her religion made her lesser. Sometime in their teen years, Josh had realized Ari was following in Dad's footsteps. Now his transformation was complete.

This betrayal hurt even more than the others, because Josh wasn't the only victim of Ari's cruelty.

Mom. Lori. Ava.

Ava.

He would not turn and glance at the hotel. Bad enough to know she was probably watching this from above. He wouldn't give Ari a hint that his daughter was witnessing this moment.

And dammit all, no matter how much he wanted to, he couldn't throw the first punch.

"How'd you get out early?" he asked.

"I've got connections, baby bro."

"When did they release you?"

"This morning."

"And the first thing you do is go to a white supremacist rally?"

"My boys helped me in the joint. Figured I should show up and support them."

"That's all you have to say?"

Ari gave an indifferent shrug. "Yep."

Was it his fault Ari had turned into this monster? Would this have happened if Josh had stayed in Portland instead of joining the Navy?

He could hear Maddie in his mind, telling him that Ari's decisions weren't his fault. And yet, he'd *known* this was the path Ari was on. He'd seen him emulate their father until the two were indistinguishable.

Josh had cut off all ties with their father after their mom died. There was no relationship left to salvage and, without Mom, no reason to try anyway.

"Right after this here rally, I'll be getting my daughter back from you. Your services are no longer needed."

"You signed over your parental rights. You have no legal claim."

"I've got myself a kick-ass lawyer who's gonna take care of that."

Bile rose in Josh's throat. His attorney had made it clear that family law could be dicey and parental claims were hard to sever permanently. But given that Ava really had turned Ari in on purpose, she was in more danger from the man than ever. That would help her case if they came before a judge. Add to that the abuse she'd suffered over the years—from being discarded in a dumpster to being imprisoned in her own home—and she had a solid case against being returned to her father's care.

But Ava didn't tell her therapist about the abuse.

Shit. This wasn't the time. He was in the middle of a damn white supremacist rally.

"You'll be talking to my lawyer," Josh said.

"Don't you wanna know who my attorney is?" Ari asked.

"No."

"But you do. You really do. You see, his sister asked him to help me out. Get me outta jail, so I could take my girl off your hands."

Josh turned and walked away. He was done with his brother's bullshit and lies.

"Well, will you look at that. My lawyer is about to speak to the crowd. See, baby bro, you aren't the only one who's got political allies. Ravissant is weak compared to the next senator from Oregon."

Josh's gaze landed on the speaker platform, where a new speaker was being introduced, and his stomach clenched as Maddie's brother stepped up to the microphone.

Shivers took over Maddie's entire body as she glanced from the TV to the window, not quite able to believe her eyes.

Her brother. Her fucking *brother* had aligned himself with White Patriots to get elected.

It shouldn't surprise her. He was far from the first in Oregon or Washington politics to go after that particular demographic, and he'd already showed her he had no ethics when it came to collecting votes. But still, it was a blow.

She'd underestimated his hunger for power by a huge margin. But then, no amount of votes was worth this. There was no justification in the world that could make this right.

"That's your brother, isn't it?" Ava asked.

Maddie nodded. "It appears Josh isn't the only one to be surprised by a brother today."

"So your brother is…he's one of them?"

Maddie nodded. "Apparently so."

"I'm sorry, Maddie."

She took the girl's hand and squeezed. "I'm sorry your dad is here too."

"Family can really suck sometimes," Ava said, squeezing back.

"Sure can." What an understatement. But Maddie was shocked into numbness. This whole thing was surreal.

She should have realized when her brother mentioned he'd spoken to the Kochers at the museum that night that he was involved with White Patriots. Hell, this whole rally could have been planned as a campaign event. His coming out, so to speak.

Jesus. Josh had wondered at the purpose for the frequency of rallies. Was this it? Politics? Was it all a distorted get-out-the-vote campaign to put white supremacists in key government positions?

Would her parents still support Alan after this? Or had her perfect brother finally gone too far?

"*Goddammit*, Alan," she whispered under her breath. Why hadn't she seen this coming? Why hadn't she realized the extent of his hunger for power?

He would do or say anything for a vote.

Her brother's speech was being broadcast by every network covering the rally—free national coverage for a campaign speech—and the crowd cheered as Alan spoke about immigrants stealing the American dream from "real" Americans.

Some might think this was political suicide, but not in the current political climate of Oregon. Several times in the last year, extremist groups had organized protests in Salem that gave elected officials an excuse to run off and not do their duty, effectively shutting down state government. The fires of racism were being stoked on every level. Her brother was just stepping in to reap the benefits of the uncontrolled burn.

She reached for the volume button to shut it off.

"No," Ava said. "We need to hear it. It's important to know the enemy."

She nodded and set the remote down, sighing as she did so. "You're right."

But still, she couldn't watch, so she returned to the window to look at the crowd. Using the binoculars, she quickly spotted Ava's dad, Ari, who remained by the bridge.

Josh was nowhere to be seen.

She frowned again at Ari's thick coat—warm for the August day, but by the river, there would be the occasional cool breeze. He tucked his head down, and his lips moved, as if he were talking into the collar of his coat.

So the guy wore a wire. Nice.

"Are you getting video of this?" she asked Ava, glancing at the camera on the tripod.

"Yeah. If Dad throws the first punch, I'll have proof."

Maddie smiled as she followed Ari's path through the crowd with the binoculars. Clearly, someone had gotten him out of jail to mess with Josh, which was alarming in and of itself. The WPs wanted Josh distracted, and they'd pulled out all the stops.

Was *that* why C-IV had invited them to the historical society benefit? To make sure Josh knew Alan was her brother? To further divide his attention today?

Ari moved out of sight under the bridge, and she watched the other side closely, waiting for him to emerge. He did, finally, but he no longer wore the heavy coat.

Instinct said something was off.

She picked up her cell phone. She needed to tell Josh.

Tisdale urged the White Patriots to take the bridge as a demonstration of how they would reclaim America. The crowd surged toward the bridge in response. It had happened at other rallies here, where one faction or another tried to take over the bridge and stop traffic. In the past, police had even allowed it, but they were supposed to prevent it if possible.

Now, the crowd moved en masse. Josh's team held their line, blocking the curved walkway ramp and stairs on the north side of the bridge, but if the police didn't back them, this could get ugly.

He got a cell call via his headset. The voice ID said it was Maddie. She wouldn't call right now unless it was important, so he accepted the call.

She didn't waste time with preliminaries. "Ari disappeared under the bridge, and when he came out the other side, the heavy coat he was wearing was gone."

"Shit. Thanks for the heads-up. Gotta go." He clicked off without waiting for her response and radioed the team. "I'm checking out something suspicious left under the bridge. Chase, move up to my position."

He pushed his way through the crowd, heading for the pedestrian underpass.

*A*va had joined Maddie at the window, watching the surging of the crowd as they pushed beyond the barricades and swarmed the curved ramp to storm the bridge. "They just...shoved aside the blue shirts," Ava said, distress in her voice. "Why didn't the police stop them?"

Two officers had moved a barricade, essentially welcoming White Patriots to seize the bridge. Once there was a hole in the line, the rest was a blur.

"Did you get a video of that?" Maddie asked.

Ava checked the camera on the tripod. "Yes, video is still running."

"I hope you can clearly see the police officers' faces."

"The news cameras might have gotten it too."

"Not if they were all focused on the stage." Maddie pointed to the TV, which still showed her brother at the podium.

She was *so* not going to family dinner next month or any month after. Not if her brother was invited.

She put the binoculars to her eyes again and scanned the scene in the park below, spotting Josh working his way through the crowd next to the railing that lined the walkway above the Willamette River. He disappeared under the bridge, enveloped in a group of counterprotesters.

Seconds passed. A full minute? The top of the bridge filled with White Patriots. Cars were forced to stop on the

metal grating near the end of the span. Shouts—audible
through the TV—went up from the crowd on top of the
bridge.

Suddenly, a massive boom sounded. The hotel shook. Ava
gasped, and Maddie watched in shock and horror as the west
end of the bridge collapsed.

Chapter Thirty-Three

*N*ausea and dizziness made Maddie sway on her feet as she witnessed the chaos below. She pressed a hand to the cool glass of the window to keep her balance.

"Uncle Josh!" Ava said, her words an echo of the scream in Maddie's mind.

Josh.

He was under the bridge. Under the pile of rubble with dozens of other people.

Josh.

Smoke and dust clouded her view. She could just make out the scene of White Patriots—the ones who'd been atop the bridge—scrambling. Several appeared to be injured.

It looked like the bridge had snapped near where the green arch ended above the pedestrian underpass.

Ava let out a screeching kind of sound that spoke directly to Maddie's soul.

Josh.

Maddie picked up her cell and dialed his number. Her call went directly to voicemail.

She tried to call Chase, but the call wouldn't go through.

Cellular bandwidth was already being tested as sirens sounded in the distance.

What do I do?

They were under strict orders to stay put in the hotel room until Josh and Chase returned.

Did Chase know Josh was under the bridge? Did his headset still work? Was he…? She couldn't finish that thought.

No. No. No. No. *No.*

NO.

A sound behind her penetrated her haze, and she turned to see the door close. Maddie glanced around the room and realized Ava was gone. The girl must've said something—or maybe she hadn't said a word. It was hard to tell given the chaos in Maddie's mind.

Ava had left. To find Josh?

Probably.

But she'd just be in the way of the emergency crews and…if the worst had happened, Ava shouldn't be there to witness it.

Maddie had to put a lid on her own horror and fear. She had to go after Ava. She'd find her and drag her back up here until someone who wasn't suffering from debilitating pain could offer instruction on what to do.

She went to the dresser and pulled out the pistol Josh had given her this morning. It was a tool of last resort if she and Ava were located while Josh and Chase were dealing with the protest. But Ava had left the room, so it seemed wise to take it with her.

Time moved in the strangest way. It had been scant minutes—seconds?—since the bridge collapsed, but Maddie felt like everything was in slow motion. Surreal.

She shoved the gun into her purse and slung it crosswise

over her shoulder. She grabbed the room key and Josh's car key from the dresser and headed out after Ava.

his isn't a flashback. The thought swam through Josh's mind as he wavered in a place between conscious and unconscious.

This isn't Iraq and a firefight in a crumbling building.

It smelled like it, though. Twisted metal and crumbling concrete. The scent of explosives and blood. The shrieks of civilians caught in the crossfire.

Not Iraq.

Portland. Oregon.

Home.

He took a deep breath and coughed. Dust from the shattered concrete permeated the air. He managed to open one eye—his head hurt like a bitch, and the other eye simply wouldn't cooperate. He'd been hit by something.

The bridge. That's it. He'd been hit by a damn *bridge.*

He heard nothing but a high-pitched ringing—his hearing another thing demolished by the blast.

He lay on his stomach in a tight, dark space, the air thick with dust. Just above him, a crossbeam had collapsed and landed on a pile of debris, forming a pocket. He moved his arms and legs and realized he'd been incredibly lucky and wasn't pinned down, but enough debris rained down on him to let him know he needed to get out before his luck ended.

He scooted an inch to the left and touched something warm.

A body.

Living or dead?

He couldn't move to get a fix on the person with his one

good eye, so he felt along the skin and recognized an arm, which he followed up to the neck. He contorted himself to reach and press fingers to the carotid artery and felt a faint pulse.

Alive.

No clue if the person was breathing or not.

Didn't matter. Josh had to get himself and the mystery person out of here before the bridge finished collapsing on them.

He pulled a small flashlight from his minimal utility belt—he wasn't allowed weapons, but this flashlight was too small to hurt anyone—and shone it around the space, spotting crumbled concrete that might be loose enough to move. Maybe he could tunnel them out.

A grinding sound from above—loud enough to break through his muted hearing—warned him he didn't have time to wait for rescue. He guessed the explosive had been TNT or another kind of shock-wave blast. If it had been C-4 or other type of cutting charge, it would have sliced through the bridge cleanly. Boom and done.

But this wasn't clean. The metal had bent to a new shape, and it was now determining if the new form was structurally sound or not. Everything above him could give way in an instant.

He thought of Ava and Maddie. Had they seen the blast? Did they know he was under here? Did they assume he was dead?

He might be. Dead, that is, if he didn't get out of here quickly.

Even though he couldn't hear, and anyone in close range of the blast would be equally deaf, he started shouting. Warning others he was tunneling through. Calling for assistance.

Ava needed him. Maddie wanted him. He loved them both with his whole being.

He pushed at the chunks of concrete that blocked his way, making a hole wide enough for his shoulders. A memory of Ava at eighteen months came to mind. It was the third or fourth night of her second Hanukkah, and just the week before, she'd helped her mom blow out the candles on Lori's birthday cake. That had seemed to lead to a fascination with the lit menorah.

She'd dragged her little stepstool to the window and climbed up. Josh had been about to grab her, but Lori seemed to understand what her daughter was doing, and she put an arm out to stop him.

Little Ava sang her own version of the birthday song, gibberish that included the word Hanukkah, and blew out the candles, one by one, just as she'd done with her mom the week before. Then she turned and faced them, her eyes big and round and full of excitement, and said, "I have cake?"

Josh and Lori had howled with laughter. They both figured she'd wondered why lighting the menorah wasn't followed by cake on the other nights, and had decided that it was because she failed to blow them out properly.

They'd had cake after lighting the menorah every night after that. But they'd had to work to convince Ava to *not* blow out the candles.

He needed to tell Ava that story. She needed to hear about the parts of her childhood that were good and sweet. She needed to know that her mother immediately baked a chocolate cake that Hanukkah night to appease Ava's sense of order. Because her mother had loved her with all her heart.

There was so much he had to tell her.

He'd abandoned her twice already. He wouldn't abandon her again. Not if he could help it.

Chapter Thirty-Four

*A*va had already caught an elevator by the time Maddie made it to the vestibule. She cursed inwardly and debated which would be faster, elevator or stairs. But the stairs were at the other end of the floor, and then she'd have twelve flights down.

She dialed Chase again, and still, she couldn't get a line out.

She kept trying as she paced and waited for the elevator. In her mind, she kept seeing the flash and plume as the bridge collapsed.

She was going to be sick. *Josh.*

The elevator doors opened, and she jumped inside and jabbed at the Lobby button, cursing every time it stopped on another floor to pick up another person. The expressions on the faces of the new passengers were as bleak as her own must be.

The car was full by the time it reached the fourth floor.

When they finally reached the lobby, she was trapped in the back and too short to see if Ava was still in the building while the passengers in front of her were disgorged.

Finally freed, she scanned the lobby. No Ava.

She hurried to the west hotel entrance, which faced the park. But her escape from the building was blocked by hotel staff making announcements that the area around the bridge had been cordoned off for safety.

"Have you seen a young woman—under twenty—tall, with dark hair in a ponytail?" Maddie tried to remember what Ava was wearing, but her mind had gone blank.

Josh. Josh. *Josh.*

"I don't know, ma'am," the man said. "The entrance on the other side of the building is still open, but you won't be able to go to the park."

Maddie turned and ran for the exit on the east side of the building. She stepped out into the street with a dozen other hotel guests. As warned, the street leading to the park was closed.

Had Ava made it through before a police officer was in place? Had it taken her a long time to reach the lobby too, or had she zipped down, ahead of the crowd because she hadn't hesitated?

"Please," Maddie said to the officer redirecting traffic. "My niece is in the park. She's only seventeen. I need—"

"Sorry, ma'am. Only first responders are allowed through."

"But my boyfriend was under the bridge! I need—"

He gave her a sympathetic look. "Sorry. The bridge is unstable, and you'll only be in the way of first responders. Police are having enough trouble clearing out the rally crowd."

"If I can't go to him, I need to find Ava. She's a minor—"

"Ava? Dark hair? Ponytail?"

"Yes! You've seen her?"

A siren on the street behind her that ran parallel to the

one that fronted the hotel and river drowned out all sounds as it crossed the intersection.

"She was here a minute ago," the officer yelled, his voice dropping as the sirens passed by. "Her dad was here." He pointed to the corner to the east, close to the park. "He saw her talking to me and ran up. Said he has a car parked in the public lot two blocks north, in the containment zone. I let her through since she was with him and he was giving her a ride out of here."

"Her father? You're sure?"

"He said he was her father, and she didn't deny it."

Maddie doubted Chase would pass for being old enough to have a seventeen-year-old kid, which meant it really had been Ari. And Ava had used him to get past the barrier. But did she manage to elude him once she was out of sight of the officer? Was Ava in danger from her father?

Maddie's gut said yes. The first night she met Josh, he'd said Ari believed Ava had revealed his embezzling on purpose.

He could want revenge. How had he gotten out of jail early, without anyone notifying his daughter?

"Please. Ava could be in danger from her father. I need to find her."

"Sorry, ma'am. She was eager to go with him. Why do that if she was afraid?"

"To get past you, because she's worried about her uncle, who was under the bridge."

The bridge.

Josh.

Panic threatened to engulf her again.

She thought of the man who'd held her last night and told her he loved her. The man who moved across the country to take care of his niece. The man who'd told her from the get-go that Ava came first and meant it.

Josh would want me to stuff my grief and fear for him and go after Ava.

But how?

Then she remembered. Josh put a tracker in Ava's purse. Had she grabbed her purse on her way out? Probably. Maybe. Hopefully.

Maddie turned on her heel and ran back into the hotel. This time, she opted for the stairs instead of the elevator. It was only two flights down into the underground parking garage. Josh had left her the keys and authorized Maddie's thumbprint on the Raptor vehicle's key fob this morning, just in case something happened and Maddie and Ava needed to leave while Josh was busy with the rally.

She pressed her thumb to the back of the fob and unlocked the door, then hit the power button the moment her butt landed in the driver's seat. The vehicle came to life, the touch screen computer offering a full menu of options.

She couldn't figure out how to get it to find Ava's tracking signal, however, so she pulled out her phone and called Trina, thankful she was able to get a line out this time.

Trina answered right away, "Maddie, I just heard—"

"I need to speak to Keith."

"He's on the phone with—"

"It's urgent. Ava's missing. I think she's with her dad. I need to find her through the tracking device Josh put in her purse, and I don't know how to use the computer in Josh's SUV."

She was desperate to know if there was any news about Josh, but she buried the questions.

Find Ava, then ask about Josh. It's what he would want.

"I'll tell Keith," Trina said.

A moment later, Keith was on the line. "There's a menu on the project screen where you can find phones, computers, cars, and trackers," he said without preamble. "Josh would have set up a project or client under his own name and listed Ava's phone and the purse tracker there." He talked Maddie through the menus, and in seconds, she had a map with a flashing red dot.

"I've got her," she said.

"Good. Where is she? If she's in the park, I can have Chase—"

Maddie studied the map, trying to make sense of it. "She's not in the park. She's…" The map had to be wrong. Why would she be *there*?

"She's in Nielsen Tower," Keith said for her. He must've logged in to his own computer.

"I don't get it. Why there?" The Hoffman brothers' credentials had been revoked. They couldn't get into the parking garage or building. But that didn't mean there weren't more White Patriots on the staff.

Maddie shuddered, thinking of the video footage of her in a box being rolled down the hallway and later crammed into a trunk. That could be Ava this time.

Maddie put the SUV in reverse. "I'm going after her."

"You aren't trained—"

"Someone has to. Chase can't. And Josh—" Her voice cut out. *Josh.*

"No word on him yet, Maddie. Chase hasn't been able to get to the bridge."

"He was under it. I saw him go under, and then it…" She backed out of the parking spot, trying to keep her panic under control.

"I know. Chase had him on the radio."

"He hasn't radioed since, has he?" She should be focusing on maneuvering the parking garage, but she had to know if she could have any reason to hope.

"The radio could be damaged. Or his eardrums busted. He was damn close to the blast."

Damn close meant so close that busted eardrums would be the least of his problems.

No. She couldn't give up hope so quickly. But she'd watched a bridge fall on him with her own eyes.

"I love him, Keith. And I'm going to get Ava back. For him."

"Be careful, Maddie. Josh wouldn't—"

"No promises." Maddie hit the End button and dropped the phone into the center console. She'd promised Josh she'd watch over Ava, and she'd failed. She wouldn't fail him again.

Chapter Thirty-Five

*A*va stared at her dad, who sat in the front passenger seat. He was a White Patriot now. The first thing he'd said once they were out of earshot of the cop was that his being a White Patriot was her fault. If he hadn't gone to jail, he wouldn't have had to join the white supremacists for protection in jail.

She'd argued it was his own damn fault he'd gone to jail, and he'd slapped her.

Her dear old dad was back.

And Uncle Josh was under the bridge.

She held her breath to keep back the tears and focused on the driver. She'd recognized him from photos Uncle Josh had showed her when he warned her about people to watch out for after they were doxed. It was Troy Kocher. The White Patriot who'd creeped Maddie out so much, she'd called Uncle Josh.

How had Troy Kocher gotten mixed up with her dad? And why were they driving into to the parking garage of the Nielsen building where Uncle Josh worked? The place where Maddie had been abducted.

Another deep breath couldn't stop the tears, even though she knew she'd get smacked again if her dad saw them.

Uncle Josh.

She'd had no memory of ever meeting her uncle when he started writing to her a month after her mom killed herself. When the letters started arriving, her dad said awful things about him, hinting that he'd run Josh off because he'd been in love with her mom.

Ava hadn't known what to believe, but part of her had begun to fantasize that the mysterious uncle was really her biological father, and she'd created a new email account so Uncle Josh could email her without her dad knowing.

When he'd moved to Portland to take care of her, and he seemed to genuinely *care* about her, it was every childish fantasy come true. Until she'd read the letter he'd written to Trina, which made her wonder if he really had been in love with her mom too. If he really had been a stalker like her dad had said.

Was that what her uncle did? Fall in love with women he couldn't have?

And then he met Maddie, and a new fear emerged. If he fell in love with a woman he could actually be with, would he still have room for Ava?

The last months with Uncle Josh had been a mix of hopeful confusion. She had an adult who cared about her, who wasn't cruel like her dad, or depressed like her mom. He didn't try to end her friendship with Marcus. In fact, he actively encouraged it.

He didn't freak out about her anxiety issues. Instead, he found her a psychotherapist and made her keep regular appointments so she could get the help she needed, and he didn't shame her for needing medication.

He didn't even turn his back on her when she deliberately

broke his heart. She'd been unspeakably awful, and he'd never wavered in his care for her.

A sob escaped. She couldn't stop it.

She pulled her knees to her chest in the backseat and held her breath to stop the crying.

After her dad had slapped her—right there on a public street!—she'd told him she knew what he'd done, that she'd seen him leave his coat under the bridge, and she would see to it that he would go to prison—not jail—this time, for domestic terrorism.

Her dad had pulled her to his chest as if he was hugging her and said right next to her ear, *"Watch your mouth, little girl."*

She'd screamed and struggled against his chest, but between the sirens and people running to and from the collapsed bridge, no one had paid attention. They were a block away and around the corner from the cop who was stopping all foot traffic to the park, and all the other officers in the area were dealing with the bridge collapse.

"Don't cry, baby," her dad had shouted as he strangled her with a hug. *"Everything is gonna be just fine."*

Then Kocher had appeared, and her dad loosened his grip. She'd thought maybe someone was going to help her after all. But then her dad said, *"We need to take her with us. She's a witness."*

"I'm not a kidnapper," Kocher had replied.

"She's my daughter. It's all legal."

"No, it's not!" She pushed out of her dad's arms and got a look at the guy's face, and that was when she'd recognized him. Her stomach had plummeted. Troy Kocher would never help her.

What have I done?

She was still asking herself that question as the car circled the lowest level of the parking garage, searching for a space. She'd tried to escape the car right after her dad shoved her inside, but the child locks were engaged and the power windows locked. She was trapped.

The garage was awfully full for a Sunday, but maybe they'd allowed White Patriots to park here for the rally. It was a long walk, but parking was limited by the river, and news vans had taken most of the street spots.

Uncle Josh said he wasn't certain what side Cliff Nielsen the fourth was on, but given his family's connection to the Kochers, and the fact that the neo-Nazi driver had some kind of pass that got him into the garage, it didn't look good.

Did that matter now that Uncle Josh could be dead?

But he wasn't dead. *He can't be.*

She had to believe that. She wouldn't lose another person. Uncle Josh had *promised* her.

She gripped her purse. The tracker was still there, inside the lining where Uncle Josh had hidden it. But Chase was probably helping first responders at the bridge. He had first aid training. He told her he'd been an EMT before he'd gone to the police academy and then was hired by Raptor. He was needed there. Maybe he could save Uncle Josh and the others who'd been under the bridge.

Chase wouldn't be able to come after her, and the police were busy at the bridge too.

Only Maddie would realize she was missing, but she had to be worried about Uncle Josh. Maddie was probably helping dig through the rubble, as Ava had wanted to do.

Ava swiped at a tear. She should have stayed with Maddie instead of running off. Why didn't she stay with Maddie?

She didn't even know why. It had just been…impossible to stay in that hotel room one second longer.

Uncle Josh. The dad she'd always wanted.

Now she was stuck with the dad she'd grown to hate. The dad who hated *her*.

Why had she opened her stupid mouth and told her dad what she'd seen?

She'd been in public. She'd never dreamed her dad would be so brazen as to abduct her on a crowded sidewalk. But he had, and no one was coming to save her. She was on her own. She straightened her spine and leaned forward. "Why are we here?"

"None of your business, little girl," her dad said.

"Uh, I'm pretty sure it *is* my business, since you're kidnapping me."

"I'm your father. You're a minor. Your mama's dead. No such thing as kidnapping."

"You signed over your parental rights." She crossed her arms. "You have no legal rights over me. Kidnapping."

Troy Kocher slammed on the brakes, and the car jerked to a halt. "Wait. What? I told you I don't kidnap minors."

Well, that little qualifier sent her creep-o-meter into the stratosphere.

She'd known Uncle Josh had been named her guardian, but that was a temporary arrangement while her dad was in jail. Uncle Josh had never told her that her dad had signed over his rights, but she'd found the papers when she'd been snooping.

Score one point for being nosey, but lose a thousand points for allowing herself to be grabbed by her dad in the first place.

"Don't listen to her. She's lying."

"I don't like this, Warner. This wasn't part of the plan. We were supposed to grab Foster, not the girl."

"Shut up and find a parking spot," her dad said, "or we're going to be late."

The car started rolling again.

"How did you get out of jail?" she asked. "You didn't even serve half your sentence."

Her dad turned in his seat so she could see his nasty smile. "Your uncle's girlfriend wanted you out of the picture, so she asked her brother to spring me."

Ava thought her heart would explode as a rush of horror and pain erupted from the center of her chest. She was dizzy. Shook.

But fresh on the wave of pain, she thought about tea and cakes and Wonder Woman. She remembered a long car ride to the Painted Hills and frank talk of sex and relationships, the kind she'd spent the last two years wishing she could've had with her mom. With a flash of certainty as strong as the pain of a moment before, she settled on the truth.

Her dad always had known how to hurt her. It wasn't surprising he'd guess her relationship with Maddie was a weak point. Her asshole father was lying. Again.

But the thing about Maddie's brother getting him out of jail, *that* had a ring of truth. The guy was a congressman, Senate candidate, and former attorney. He probably could pull strings. And he'd been the featured speaker at the hate rally, so whatever was going on, it was probably Congressman Tisdale's agenda her dad was serving.

But why would Tisdale release her dad?

Her first guess was to derail Uncle Josh from working the rallies. But then she remembered the explosion, and a new theory formed. Her dad had worked in demolition. He knew explosives.

Did he know Uncle Josh had been under the bridge when it collapsed? She wasn't about to tell him. She figured Uncle Josh was the only person her dad truly feared. That he'd feared him all along—after all, he was better, stronger, smarter. He'd been a Navy SEAL and worked for and had the respect of powerful people, including a sitting senator and former US attorney general.

"You're just a politician's tool, aren't you, Dad?"

Her dad stiffened. "Shut your mouth, little girl."

"Why? Truth hurts?" She didn't care if he hit her again. Reaching between the seats would make the blow awkward anyway. She reached for her purse and dug inside for her nail file. It wasn't much, but it was better than nothing. She would fight her father with everything she had.

Unfortunately, Kocher found a parking space right then, and they came to a halt.

New fear settled in. Not fear of her father, but of what was next. She took a slow breath, but air wasn't really filling her lungs. Was this what hyperventilating was like?

Her father opened his door and slipped out of his seat, then yanked open her door. "C'mon, little girl. It's time for you to meet Daddy's new boss."

Chapter Thirty-Six

$\mathscr{M}$addie drove to the employee parking entrance. Josh's vehicle had the RFID sensor that raised the bar without her needing to show ID, and she hoped she'd be able to get into the building with the same ease. She should have gone back to his hotel room and grabbed his IDs. But time was of the essence, and she had no idea where she would find Ava in the thirty-floor high-rise.

The GPS signal could pinpoint X and Y coordinates, but Z was anyone's guess.

She found a parking spot and tapped more buttons on the computer screen, browsing Josh's uploaded content.

Bless his efficient heart, he'd uploaded the building schematic into Raptor's system. Now she just needed to know how to use this information. She called Trina's number again, and Keith answered.

"We've got maps of all the floors at Nielsen Tower," she said without preamble.

"Josh is always thorough. I bet he also looked for ways to exploit the security system from the inside—to find out if the Hoffman brothers still had a way in."

"You think he created a backdoor?"

"I'd put good money on it."

"How do I find his backdoor?"

"I've already got Mothman combing his files to find it. Are there any headsets in the SUV? It would help if you had one."

Maddie checked the glove box and came up empty. She scanned the garage very carefully—feeling a shiver knowing that she'd been placed in a trunk only fifty feet away—and climbed from the vehicle.

She opened the back to find a cardboard box with green and blue T-shirts and the metal lockbox in which he kept his Raptor gear. She lifted the cover over the front latch and found a number pad. "What's the combination for the lockbox?"

"Josh authorized your thumbprint with full access to the SUV. Press your thumb on the reader below the zero."

She bent down, looking closer in the dark space—the rear dome light was disabled—and saw there was a small shiny black square just below the ten-key pad. She pressed her thumb to it, and the box clicked, releasing the latch.

She opened the box and gasped at the assortment of guns and ammunition. "This stuff is all legal?"

"He's licensed and trained with all of it, yes. But you're not, so leave the weaponry alone unless you know how to use it."

"I've got a pistol he showed me how to use."

"Good. Any headsets in the box?"

"Three, actually."

"Good. Put it on and sync it to your phone. You've got a Raptor phone, so once it syncs, the headset will work separately."

She donned the headset, and it powered on the moment it was in place, just like her wireless earbuds. A pop-up on her phone screen invited her to pair the device with her phone, and it appeared this was more than Bluetooth sharing with Wi-Fi calling. This was like a mating or a cloning of the devices. The phone then showed which buttons on the left ear were for cellular versus radio, and which on the right were volume, record, and voice text.

"We'll use sat/cell calling because the team at the rally is on the radio, helping EMS and other first responders."

"No word?"

"None yet, Maddie. I'm sorry."

Tears burned. A week ago, she'd heard this man tell Josh he loved him. Keith had to be in as much agony as she was. "I'm sorry too."

"I haven't given up hope. You shouldn't either. Now that the dust has settled, helicopters flying over the bridge show it's a relatively small section that went down—few marchers were on top because the bulk of the group hadn't reached that point yet—and from the angle of the collapsed section, there's a good chance there are pockets created by the I-beams. If Josh was close to the concrete foot, he could be fine."

"But didn't the concrete foot crumble?" From above, it had looked like it had buckled.

"Hard to say, but something is holding the beams at an angle."

Maddie held on to that thought. There were dozens of people who were working to find and save Josh right this moment. She closed the lid of the lockbox and the rear door of the SUV.

She needed to study the building maps and focus on finding Ava.

*J*osh took a deep breath and immediately regretted it when thick dust coated his lungs. He coughed, making his head throb even more. He needed to get out of here before he suffocated from the dust that filled this tiny air pocket.

He reached back and grabbed the arm of the man—the beam of his flashlight had showed a thick, hairy arm that had to be male—trapped with him and tugged. From the resistance, he guessed a limb was pinned, but he didn't have time to finesse this and used all his strength to pull harder, bracing his feet on the steel beam for leverage.

Had Nielsen Steel made this beam over a hundred years ago? The thought was an irrelevant tangent and a sign of his fractured focus.

Did Ari have anything to do with the bomb that took down the bridge? Did he have TNT in his jacket? He'd worked in demolition, and he had a grudge against his former employers. He could have stolen explosives from them this morning or even hidden a stockpile before he was arrested.

While White Patriots had been on top of the bridge, the group below had been a mix of the opposing groups. Who was the target of the bombing?

He'd promised the counterprotesters he'd protect them. More had attended this rally than the last because they'd believed he and his trainees would keep them safe.

How many had been under the bridge when it fell? In the moments before the blast, Josh had spotted the small backpack tucked up against the I-beam above, next to the concrete foot. He'd shouted, *"BOMB!"*

People ran in every direction at his shout. A moment later, the bomb went off. On instinct, Josh dove for the concrete pillar, knowing next to it would be the safest place if the pillar remained vertical. In buildings during big earthquakes or explosions like this, it was advised to tuck up against the backs of couches or under tables. If the furniture wasn't crushed by the falling ceiling, safe triangular pockets could be created when beams fell across the furniture.

Same concept here, except it was a massive steel beam braced on a crumbling concrete foot.

It had happened so fast, there hadn't been time for Josh to clear out from under the bridge, but others, those on the edges, had made it out, he was sure of it. He'd done that much right, at least.

But this guy next to him hadn't made it, and they would both die here together if they didn't escape from beneath the crumbling structure. Josh carefully rolled to his back in the confined space for better leverage. He braced his feet on the beam again and pushed off, digging in his heels as he tugged on the man's hand, to pull him out from whatever was pinning him down. It was this or death. Josh's muscles strained, and he feared for the man's limbs, but he reminded himself that if they'd been crushed, the damage was already done. The debris that had the guy pinned gave way, and the deadweight inched forward as Josh pulled and wriggled through the first opening he'd created in the rubble.

His ears pulsed with the pressure caused by the blast, giving his breathing a tympanic ring. Remembering his headset, he reached for it around his neck or on his head. Even though he couldn't hear well, he could use it to call or radio. Let someone know he was alive and stuck.

His headset was gone, likely knocked off by whatever had injured his eye, and, from the feel of things, that whole side of his head. That he hadn't noticed pain from the cuts was due to adrenaline mixed with other, bigger, masking pain. Now he noticed smaller aches all along his limbs and back. He'd been pelted by debris, and who knew what else had been damaged given that he'd lost consciousness for a few moments. Or longer.

How many minutes had it been since the blast? Fifteen? Twenty? Surely it couldn't be more than that?

He shoved at another concrete boulder that blocked his way, this one bigger than the last. It didn't budge. This time, he pictured Maddie. The way she'd looked that first time he saw her face—the moment *after* he'd kissed her in his pretend-boyfriend role. She'd looked like a model from the sixties with her clear, smooth skin and hair pulled back with a headband, curling under at the ends. Her eyes had lit with reaction to the casual kiss, and she'd looked so damn adorable. Warm. She'd brightened the dank crypt with her light, and all his protective instincts had risen to the surface. He'd wanted nothing more than to go after the prick who'd freaked her out so much, she'd been compelled to call for help.

From there, his mind went to last night, when he'd told her he loved her, and again, she'd lit up the room with her smile. But that time, her hair had been tousled by his fingers, her lips swollen from his kisses. Her bare chest pressed to his.

He'd followed up his declaration by making love to her again, and he'd kept his eyes open until the last second so he could see every expression on her face as he made her come.

She was everything he'd ever wanted. And he could have her, if he could just get this motherfucking concrete boulder out of his damn way.

He shoved again, and this time, it moved. Two inches at best, but maybe that was all he needed, because now daylight shone through the hole he'd created. He called out, reaching his hand through the narrow gap, into the afternoon sun.

A hand gripped his. Thick fingers, dark skin. The hand of a bodybuilder. Hope surged in Josh's chest. If anyone could move that damn boulder, it was Arthur Bond.

Chapter Thirty-Seven

*A*va couldn't stop shaking. She rode the creepy freight elevator up with the creepy neo-Nazi and the father she'd hoped to never see again, and all she wanted to do was curl up in a ball and cry.

The only thing that stopped her was knowing how much glee her dad would get from seeing her break. Like when he'd finally broken her mom.

In that moment, Ava understood her mom's final, desperate act, and for the first time knew she could forgive her mother.

She'd only had glimpses of her father's awful side before her mother's death. It wasn't until Lori was gone that Ari had turned his full monstrous personality on her.

Mom must have taken the brunt to protect me.

She ached to tell her mom how much she loved her. How much she needed her.

She hadn't gone to the cemetery since the funeral, not even when Uncle Josh went at the beginning of the summer. Tomorrow, if she was able, she'd go and lie on the grass and cry her heart out. Give her mom all the love and grief she'd denied her for two years.

The elevator doors opened on the top floor, and Ari grabbed her arm and yanked her forward, dragging her out of the steel box. She'd decided on the ride up not to call him Dad anymore, not even in her mind. He didn't deserve it.

Her real dad was the man who'd taken care of her when she was a baby so her mom could go to school. Who'd sent money to her mom when he was deployed. Who'd moved to Portland and opened a whole new Raptor office just so he wouldn't have to move her to a new school district.

That was a father's love.

Troy Kocher led the way down the corridor, while Ari kept a firm grip on her arm, walking at a brisk pace.

She still had her purse, and the file was in her jeans pocket. She'd find a way to fight. Troy Kocher was huge, but she was willing to fight dirty. She'd attended several of the evening training sessions last week, and Desmond had taught her some moves that would work if she didn't get squeamish.

After two long corridors, they finally reached the vestibule where the main bank of elevators let out and faced a glass wall that looked into a modern glass-and-steel reception room. Top floor, so this must be C-IV's office.

Troy Kocher waved a key fob in front of the sensor, and the door opened automatically.

Had C-IV's old security team—the one that included the White Patriots who'd abducted Maddie—taken over the building, or was Nielsen part of whatever was going on?

She followed Kocher into the reception area and down the hall to the corner office. Through the windows, she could see the Willamette River, and beyond that, the Columbia. She broke away from her father's grip and ran to the window so she could look down and see the waterfront park.

It was much farther away and down than it had been in

the hotel, and she couldn't make out the details beyond emergency vehicles, collapsed end of the bridge, and clusters of people as small dots on the grass.

She pressed her fingers to the cool glass.

Uncle Josh is alive. Uncle Josh is alive. Uncle Josh is alive.

She would believe it until she was presented with proof otherwise.

"What the hell is she doing here?" a male voice behind her said. "You were supposed to bring my sister."

*J*osh's hearing was improving. The shouts of excitement as another person was found alive in the pile were dulled, as if he were underwater or had earplugs, but he could hear them.

He'd experienced similar hearing loss in the Navy, when an op went sideways and ear protection wasn't in place, but this might be the worst case of temporary deafness he'd had. But then, he'd been way too close to the explosive.

He sat on a gurney in the triage area that had been set up while he was still tunneling out. A medic washed his head wound, and Josh managed to open his eye. Vision was blurry, but he could focus.

"Pupils normal," the medic said. "Looks like you might have skipped the concussion."

That was a damn miracle considering a bridge had fallen on him and he wasn't wearing the Kevlar helmet that had protected him on ops.

One gurney over, the guy he'd dragged from the rubble was being worked on by a team of paramedics. The guy had turned out to be a White Patriot—swastika tattoos and all. Josh had no illusions the man would see the light when he discovered a Jewish man had saved his life, but then, Josh had always hated stories in that genre.

He shouldn't have to save a person's life for them to see him as human. As equal.

If Desmond and the guy with the swastika tattoos were both pulled over by a cop, Desmond had a higher likelihood of getting arrested on a bullshit charge or outright shot and killed than the guy with the actual Nazi symbols on his body, when the hate-monger almost certainly had a violent record. Hate and violence went hand in hand.

Josh didn't regret saving the guy's life—everyone deserved rescue and aid—but he didn't want kudos either.

"Josh!" His name reached his muted ears, and he looked up to see Chase running toward him. It was a relief to see the Raptor operative. Josh hadn't had a chance to debrief with Arthur before he was hauled off on the gurney. And he hadn't really been able to hear what Arthur had to say anyway.

Officers tried to stop Chase from entering the triage area. "Let him through," Josh said in a commanding tone. He had no authority here, but that didn't mean he wouldn't try.

Miraculously, it worked.

Chase wove his way between the gurneys, which held people with varying degrees of injuries from slight scrapes to the unconscious but breathing man one gurney over.

Once Chase was close enough that Josh would be able to hear his answer, he asked his most burning question. "What's the status of Ava and Maddie?" If they'd seen the collapse from their hotel room, they had to be worried.

"Ava's been taken. By your brother. Maddie's gone after her."

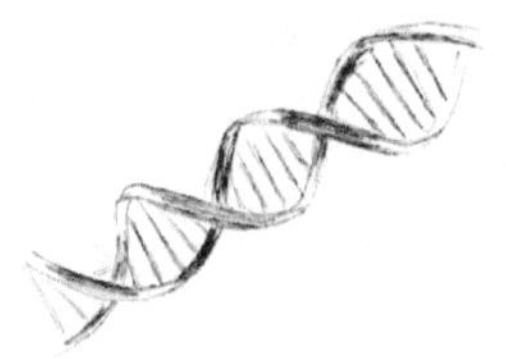

Chapter Thirty-Eight

Maddie typed in the pass code Mothman had provided, and the elevator light turned green. "It worked," she said into the headset.

"Great," Mothman replied. "That's the code that's going to get you through most of the building. The exception is the top floor—Josh wasn't given access to that, and I can't find any overrides he might have tried to gain access."

"Got it." She sighed. "That means she's been taken to the penthouse, doesn't it?"

"That would be my guess," Keith said.

The series of short clicks that Maddie had come to recognize as another person joining the call sounded, followed by a new voice. "Hey, Maddie, mind if I cut in on this conversation?"

Her knees went weak, and the world spun a bit. "*Josh?*"

"Yeah, it's me, sweetheart."

Tears sprang to her eyes. In front of her, the service elevator doors opened, but she was frozen in place. "You're… you're okay?"

"A little battered, slightly deaf, but otherwise fine."

She leaned an arm on the wall next to the open elevator and let out a loud, ugly sob. "I was so scared." She swiped at her tears and straightened her spine, just in case the code Mothman had given her hadn't shut off the garage camera.

"I know, babe," Josh said. "It was a close one."

"I love you." She didn't care that everyone was listening in. Josh was *alive*, and she had to say the words. They were oxygen to her starved lungs.

"It was thoughts of you and Ava that helped me move the rubble in my way."

She let out another sob. *He's alive.* The bridge collapse hadn't been a nightmare she could wake from, but also, talking to him now wasn't a dream. Both were real.

"I love you so much, Maddie." His voice cracked with emotion. "But we've got other priorities right now. Chase brought me up to speed on the situation. Said you're going after Ava."

"I just missed my elevator—"

"Good. Go back to my SUV and lock yourself in. It's bulletproof and locks up tighter than a vault. You'll be safe there. Chase and I are on our way."

"Okay. Hurry." She turned and sprinted toward the SUV, her vision slightly blurry from the tears, her brain foggy with the emotional overload.

Josh would confront his brother and get Ava back. Ari had no legal rights. This was a simple family dispute and would be over quickly. Then they'd get Josh to a hospital to have his wounds looked at, and she and Ava could both dote on him.

She was enjoying that fantasy when she circled the vehicle to the driver's side and came face-to-face with Peyton Hoffman.

He gave her a nasty grin. "Well, well, well. Madeline Foster. Have you missed me?"

Before she could step back or say a word into the headset, his arm swung out. She saw the pistol in his hand just before it hit her temple, pain exploded, then she felt nothing at all.

"Maddie's headset is offline," Mothman said.

Josh swore even as fear ripped through him. What had happened? Two minutes ago, she'd told him she loved him and everything was fine, she was safely on her way back to the SUV. But she hadn't made it.

"Has my SUV been unlocked?"

"No. Still sealed tight. If someone took Maddie, they probably haven't figured out about the thumbprint to unlock it."

Six months ago, it had been possible to unlock a Raptor vehicle without a thumbprint. It was only the engine that wouldn't work without authorization. Then Nate's girlfriend tried to take off in his company SUV. She'd failed, not knowing she needed Nate's thumbprint, but she was a programmer who loved a challenge, and a few weeks later, on a lark, she found a way to bypass the thumbprint using the door lock loophole. Mothman had proceeded to close the loophole, and he'd been damn grumpy that anyone had been able to compromise his security, especially on a lark.

But that closed loophole told Josh something important. Maddie had been intercepted on the lowest garage level, between the service elevator and the SUV within the last two minutes. It was a narrow window of space and time, and thankfully, Chase sped through the garage like a race-car driver.

Josh wished he were at the wheel, but his bum eye was a liability and his ego was far less important than the two women who needed him now.

His daughter and the woman he wanted to spend the rest of his life with.

How had Ari found Ava? It couldn't be a coincidence that he met up with her right outside the only operating hotel exit. He must've *known* where they were staying.

But nobody knew. They'd been damn careful. Ava and Maddie both knew they couldn't tell anyone. Maddie hadn't even told her parents.

Ari had claimed Maddie had orchestrated his release to get Ava out of the way. Josh saw right through that lie, but he didn't doubt Ari had been sprung by Tisdale.

What was Tisdale's role in this, and who had taken Maddie?

"We can override all security, go black everywhere, then take the elevator to the twenty-ninth floor. Stairwells will unlock if you use the earthquake protocol," Chase said.

"I was thinking fire protocol. It's easy to confuse the system by pulling several alarms nearly simultaneously."

"We're only two people. How are we going to do that?"

Josh held out his hand. "Give me your phone." He'd lost his somewhere in the rubble.

Chase complied, and Josh quickly logged in to his Raptor account. "I set up a test for the system yesterday where I can set off alarms one by one from a phone and make it look like I'm on multiple floors, pulling physical alarms."

"Nice. We'll wait until we're on twenty-nine?"

Josh nodded. "Let's suit up."

Chase had the standard gear in the back of his rental car. One M-4 rifle, two Sigs, a Taser, spare headsets, and a lot of bullets in multiple calibers. It would make Troy Kocher's wannabe-security-guard heart envious.

Usually, Josh was against wearing so much hardware, but this wasn't security duty. This was an op.

Armed and ready, Josh and Chase went to the service

elevator. Josh could control it with his phone too, sending different signals as far as floor numbers visited back to the security system. It was appalling how lax Apex had let security go, but Simon Barstow had always been interested in doing the least amount of work possible. He was one step above grifter, in Josh's opinion.

Right now, Josh wanted to thank the guy because, for all intents and purposes, Josh could seize the entire building with the overrides and backdoors he'd added to the system over the last few days. He'd planned to present a list of flaws to C-IV at their scheduled meeting tomorrow.

"Ready?" Chase asked.

Josh looked his friend in the eye. "I'm thankful to have you by my side in this, Chase. You're a damn good operative."

Emotion flashed across Chase's face before he locked it down. "Thank you, sir. Now let's find your family."

Chapter Thirty-Nine

Ava lost all hope the moment one of the Hoffman brothers entered the room and dumped Maddie on the couch. Her body was slack. Lifeless.

A sharp, piercing fear settled in Ava's chest even while her heart raced. She scurried across the carpet to Maddie's side and touched her neck, finding a pulse. She watched her chest and saw a slow rise and fall.

She was breathing, at least.

"What did you do to her?"

"Gave her what she deserved," Peyton Hoffman said.

"Dammit. We need to question her," Tisdale said, without an ounce of real concern for his unconscious sister.

Wow, between her father and Maddie's brother, Ava was suddenly glad to be an only child. Siblings could really suck.

"She'll wake up, and we've got time. Karl has locked down the building. Only the parking garage is open so people who parked here for the rally can get their vehicles. We're safe here."

"You forget that Warner had full access to the system," Tisdale said.

"Warner is probably dead. He was under the bridge when it collapsed," Hoffman said.

Ava couldn't help but jerk at the harsh words, but it was Tisdale's response that surprised her. He turned to her father. "You sonofabitch. You were supposed to draw your brother away from the bridge after you dropped the pack. We needed Warner *alive* if he's going to take the fall for the false flag. What do we do now?"

Uncle Josh had explained false flags to her this week, how a group will do something to themselves—stage an incident—and blame their opposition, claiming they'd attacked first. Like the theory that Russians had intended to shoot down a Russian airliner over Ukraine with the plan to blame Ukrainians, so they'd have an excuse to invade. But it had been a Malaysian airliner that was shot down by mistake.

The purpose of a false flag at a hate rally was to undermine the very groups trying to stop the spread of fascism, racism, and white supremacy by making it look like the anti-fascists, protectors, and counterprotesters were the violent ones. In this instance, she guessed that they'd planned to blame the bridge bombing on Uncle Josh, claiming he was trying to kill as many White Patriots as possible. Make it seem like the Raptor-Bond Alliance was the problem.

Her gaze landed on Tisdale as the truth and horror sank in. Congressman Tisdale had encouraged the White Patriots to take the bridge. He'd known the bomb was going to go off. He wanted it to look like Uncle Josh had set off the explosive, once the White Patriots were on it.

"You're trying to get Raptor labeled as a terrorist organization, aren't you?" Her mind raced with the implications. This was even more than keeping Uncle Josh and Arthur Bond from protecting counterprotesters. This would bring down a sitting US senator and destroy a paramilitary organization—one that would provide resistance if the White Patriots took up arms.

Tisdale's gaze hardened, but he didn't respond, instead he looked to her father, waiting for an answer.

Ari shrugged. "So blame it on Arthur Bond."

"Why would Bond kill his own partner in the endeavor? The association with Raptor is what made it *work*." Tisdale paced. "Jesus. You fucked up everything. First, you bring the girl, not my sister, and you let your brother *die*?" He paused in front of her father, but Ava noted he stayed out of her dad's reach. "I got you out of jail for this. I can send you back to jail just as easily."

Her dad showed zero remorse, and Ava knew why. He simply hated Uncle Josh more than he cared about staying out of jail. He'd probably never intended to do what Tisdale wanted. Her father was loyal to no one.

How had he and Uncle Josh come from the same family?

But then, how had Maddie and Alan Tisdale come from the same mother?

"Listen, Tisdale, we both know you got me out so I'd get nailed for planting the bomb and you'd claim my brother hired me to blow up the bridge. *That* was your false flag scheme, and I wasn't interested in being your patsy. So I did it my way."

Ava shifted Maddie on the couch, repositioning her to a more natural position, then she sat down next to her and scooted and lifted until Maddie's head and shoulders were on her lap. She ran her fingers through her hair, gently probing, and found the growing goose egg that explained her unconscious state.

"What did you hit her with?"

"None of your business," Hoffman answered.

"But it's mine, Hoffman. She's my sister, and you screwed up her abduction and now this."

Ava felt Maddie's shoulders stiffen and wondered if she was waking. Her breathing remained even, and her eyes stayed closed.

"We saw an opportunity to grab her before she learned about the Norway bones and took it. You don't seem to get it, Tisdale, *we* don't need *you* as much as you need us. You haven't done squat for the cause, but you want our votes."

"I'm the one who hacked her Facebook account and saw the post about the skeleton theft and pulled it down several times before she could see it. And when it kept getting reposted, I'm the one who warned you she was going to figure it out. Thanks to Troy"—he glared at Kocher—"making her suspicious." He turned back to Hoffman. "And you *do* need me, because when I'm in the Senate, I'll get the treaties dissolved based on the DNA test. This is a long game, and you know it."

Ava lifted Maddie's hand, adjusting the position of her arm, and felt the slightest squeeze.

She's awake. Thank God.

"I'm sick of the long game. We should have taken over the tribal lands already," Hoffman said.

"Yeah, because that worked so well with Malheur." This was said by Clifford Nielsen the fourth, who entered from a door on the right.

Ava had thought they were in his office, but of course, this room had a table, not a desk, and a comfortable seating area with couches and plush seats, where she was with Maddie now. This must be his outer office, for group meetings.

Had he been in his office the whole time? So much for the fleeting hope that Tisdale and the others were using this space without permission. Nielsen was in this up to the top of his high-rise.

Now it was Nielsen's turn to glare at Hoffman and

Kocher. "Also, unlike Malheur, I *own* half the land. If we can get the treaties dissolved based on the DNA, we can declare our Aryan homeland without the feds coming after us and *then* we'll take the Painted Hills and the rest of the National Monument. It's our land. Our legacy. Our right. But you"—Nielsen jabbed Ari in the chest—"have fucked everything up by getting your brother killed when we needed to use him. The false flag at the bridge won't work now. And when we destroy my archives and torch the Kocher museum, without your brother, we'll have no one to blame. Maddie's disappearance would have been the perfect motive for him to go after the museum. We had him set up perfectly to take the fall for sabotaging everything and erasing all the evidence, including the Kocher family papers and mine, and you *killed* him."

No one was paying attention to her. Ava shifted in her seat as if repositioning Maddie. She slipped the small nail file from her pocket, then stroked Maddie's cheek before again reaching for her hand. She slid the file under Maddie's palm and closed her fingers around it while the men continued talking.

"We can still torch the house," Kocher said. "Maddie didn't photograph the skeleton—NAGPRA wouldn't allow it." He smirked at that. "I've already replaced the skeleton with the real one that was in the same vault."

"That only takes care of the papers," Nielsen said. "Bones won't burn in the brick-lined vaults, and a second DNA test will be demanded after the first results come back."

Kocher shrugged. "The bones will be repatriated and reburied by then. No way would the tribes give us the bones back for a second test."

"Except Maddie contacted the Norwegian museum and police and told them she found the skeleton among the Kocher collection. The bones can't be repatriated now. Not until that investigation is complete."

"When did she do that?" Kocher asked.

"This morning, right as the rally was starting," Tisdale said. "She logged in to Facebook and saw the post in her leftist archaeology group. Between that and Warner's death, we're screwed."

"Then we'll use explosives to make sure the vault doesn't survive the fire and all the bones get mixed together," Kocher said, his voice turning pleading. "No way to know what skeleton to test, then."

"We can't use explosives without someone to pin it on," Tisdale said. "Not when Maddie will have disappeared after reporting a crime." His gaze flicked to his sister. The bastard had the nerve to look regretful.

"Blame it on him, then," Kocher said, pointing to Ari. "He's the one who killed Warner."

She flinched every time her uncle's death was stated as fact.

"Plus he knows explosives," Kocher added.

"Pin it on me, and I'll let everyone know the golden boy here sprang me from jail so I could blow up the bridge for the big false flag show."

Ava assumed the golden boy was Alan Tisdale. She'd looked up things like the Aryan Nation since Uncle Josh started the trainings, and she could see how Tisdale would fit their mold. Unlike Maddie, he was blond and blue-eyed.

"So, are you really super racist, or are you just using the White Patriots to get elected?" she asked.

Tisdale turned his glare on her.

She tightened her grip on Maddie. "She's your *sister*."

His eyes flickered at that. So maybe he had a soul in there somewhere. Not like Ari, who'd wanted Uncle Josh to die under the bridge.

He can't be dead. He can't be.

"Get her out of here," Nielsen said. "It was stupid to bring her here in the first place."

"She said she saw me leave my coat under the bridge."

"So what?" Tisdale said. "That proves nothing."

"I don't like leaving witnesses, and she's ratted me out before."

Ava realized her dad was enjoying this. He really didn't care about Nielsen and Tisdale's agenda. He used them to get out of jail and was making his own rules, such as grabbing her because it suited him.

He took a step toward her, probably seeing his opportunity to use her to get out of the room. "Where am I taking her?"

"Not you," Nielsen said. "Hoffman, take her down to the interview room behind security until we figure out what to do with her."

She gripped Maddie's prostrate form. "I'm not leaving Maddie."

"You really don't get a choice in the matter."

"Hey, we can blame the fire on the girl," Kocher said. "She was so distraught over Warner's death and Maddie's disappearance, she burned the house."

"Then killed herself, just like her mom," Ari added.

She didn't think her father could still hurt her, and yet that little suggestion took her breath away. Literally. She could not breathe.

Nielsen cocked his head. "Does she have a driver's license? Can we make it plausible?"

She gave her father a nasty glare. She didn't have a license because he'd refused to teach her or pay for the school. She had just gotten a permit because Uncle Josh had signed her up for a class in the fall.

"She doesn't have a license, but she knows how to drive."

"Knowing which is the gas and which is the brake doesn't mean I know how to drive."

"But it's enough for an emotionally disturbed girl who has just lost everyone who matters to her," Tisdale said. He directed his next question to her dad. "Has she been seeing a therapist? Someone who can verify she's got issues?"

"Probably. My brother is sucker enough to pay for that shit."

She wanted to launch herself off the couch and scratch both men's eyes out. Her body shook with the rage that pulsed through her.

She did nothing, just gripped Maddie's hand and wondered how the hell she was going to get out of this.

"I like it," Nielsen said. "We'd have to drop the explosives angle so the crypt would survive, but the papers would burn and redirect suspicion. We can stage it to look like she grabbed Josh Warner's car after reading Maddie's farewell letter. Knowing Maddie abandoned her, she goes to the Kocher Mansion and burns it all down, then drives off a bridge and into the river."

"Wake up my sister. We need to know who else she called and if she's done anything with the real estate records so we can start plugging those leaks."

Maddie tensed again, but then her body went slack. Her eyes remained closed and her expression blank. Ava didn't know how she managed it considering her own brother had betrayed her, except maybe it was the simple fact their lives depended on it, so she found a way.

Hoffman crossed to the sofa in front of Ava and reached for Maddie.

Ava held Maddie firmly. "Back off."

"Mr. Nielsen says I need to wake her."

"Don't make this harder on yourself, little girl," Ari said.

Her dad never called her by her name. His placeholder

was very much meant to make her feel small and weak. "My name is Ava, asshole."

"Ava, let Mr. Hoffman take Maddie," Tisdale said. "She needs to wake up."

Hoffman leaned down and yanked Maddie's left arm. Her right shot out in a flash of movement, and Hoffman screamed and grabbed his face, falling backward.

It was like having a catfight on her lap, but ten times worse.

Holy shit, from the blood seeping between his fingers, she guessed Maddie had stabbed him in the eye with the nail file.

Maddie sprang to her feet in a recovery move similar to what they'd been taught at the training a week ago. She charged Hoffman before he could gain any sort of balance and kicked him in the balls.

Ava leapt to her feet, ready to back Maddie up, but she was grabbed from behind by her father.

Hoffman curled over, but attempted to lunge for Maddie. He slammed into her, knocking her back into the couch. He grabbed Maddie by the throat with his bloody hands.

"Enough!" Nielsen shouted. "Kocher, stop him."

Troy Kocher tried to pull Hoffman away, but Hoffman kicked backward, so Kocher reached for his Taser and shot Hoffman.

The man spasmed, but didn't release Maddie, so Kocher pulled the twitching man back even as he held the trigger.

Hoffman fell to the floor, and Kocher released the trigger. Hoffman lay there for a moment, breathing heavily, then he lunged for Kocher, who pulled the trigger again, making Hoffman drop again.

"This thing is fun," Kocher said, pulling and releasing the trigger.

"Stop it," Nielsen said.

He tucked the weapon back in his belt, and this time, Hoffman didn't move.

"She stabbed me in the fucking eye," Hoffman croaked.

"You drugged me and put me in a trunk," Maddie said, calm in spite of Hoffman's bloody handprints that covered her neck. "And today, you hit me and knocked me out." She kicked him in the ribs, and Ava cheered inside.

Maddie was a little more badass than she'd expected.

"Hoffman, go down to security. Your brother can patch up your eye."

"I need a doctor."

"You're wanted for kidnapping by the Portland Police Bureau and the FBI," Tisdale said. "No doctor unless you want to go to prison."

Ari let out a nasty laugh. "You'll like the joint, Hoffman."

The former security guard turned and left the room, her dad's laughter following him out the door.

She wriggled from his relaxed grip and went to Maddie's side. Maddie wrapped an arm around her, and Ava leaned into her and whispered, "I'm sorry I ran off. I was worried about Uncle Josh."

"I know, honey." She raised her gaze and glared at her brother. "I have a feeling we'd have ended up here even if you hadn't run off." She spoke louder, directing her question to Tisdale. "You sent Ari to the hotel to find me, didn't you?"

He shrugged in a way that just confirmed her words.

"But how did you know where I was? I didn't even tell Mom the name of the hotel."

"She was hurt by that, by the way."

"She's going to find out. You can't escape this." Maddie cocked her head. "You found me because I logged in to Facebook today, didn't you? When I logged in on Mom's computer a few weeks ago, you used that to get my password."

"Mom always said you were smart."

"How did you use that to find our hotel? Wait. The login with the hotel Wi-Fi. You managed to get my IP address from my Facebook account once you had access."

"I was starting to worry when you hadn't logged in to Facebook in over a week." He smiled. "But then when you logged in today and I had your hotel, one of our guys was able to use the hotel Wi-Fi to hack all your online activity. I even got your room number from the login. I read every email as I was being driven to the rally. What I don't know are the phone calls you made."

"This was always about the bones, wasn't it?" She looked to Kocher. "Shields stole the remains when he was in Oslo for the curators' conference so I would fold them into the collection—legitimize them—and then you'd run your DNA test and use that to undermine tribal treaties."

Ava had to agree with Maddie's mom. She was smart.

"You said she was the best person to handle the NAGPRA contract, Tisdale," Nielsen said, "because you could control her."

Maddie's gaze jerked to her brother. "You were the reason I got the contract?"

"Yes," Tisdale said.

"And Nielsen was involved from the start." Her gaze turned to C-IV.

"Of course he was," Tisdale said. "I asked him to invite you to the charity event so I could get you and Kocher to smooth things over."

"That failed," Maddie muttered.

"It wasn't my fault you left early," Kocher said defensively.

Tisdale sighed. "But it is your fault she called Warner for help that first day and not me. You were supposed to drive her to her powerful and politically connected brother, not hired muscle."

Ava had to stifle a laugh at how Tisdale saw himself.

"You said come on strong and she'd call *you* if there was a problem. Not my fault she had a boyfriend you didn't know about."

Maddie rocked backward on her feet and landed on the couch, bringing Ava with her. Then she let out a loud, bitter laugh. "I didn't have a boyfriend. I made him up. I didn't call you, Alan, because I knew you would be a condescending ass if I asked for your help." Maddie wrapped her arms around her stomach and laughed. "I wouldn't have met Josh that day if you hadn't told Troy to intimidate me."

She cocked her head. "What was your plan there? Wait, don't tell me. You planned to delve into the political ramifications of the project with me. You were going to push me to request a DNA test. I'm sure your argument would have been to put the debate to rest once and for all—a debate which, by the way, doesn't exist—and when I didn't follow your script, you told Shields to run the test anyway."

"It was our first plan, yes," Tisdale said. "But we knew it was a longshot. The test would have been seen as more valid if you were behind it."

Maddie turned to Nielsen and shook her head. "If I hadn't called Josh instead of Alan, you wouldn't have seen us in the lobby together. He wouldn't have been in Nielsen Tower that day for you to change your mind and decide to hire him."

"I'd have hired him anyway. Once he started coordinating protection for the counterprotesters, I needed control over him. That you knew him was just a bonus."

"Was I supposed to find references to your great-grandparents?"

He shrugged. "We expected it. I wanted to know what you'd found. Your work will back up my claims on the land."

"So you had my computer stolen." She turned to her brother. "And you didn't even need to dox me to do it, because my dear brother gave you my address."

"But doxing made everyone a suspect," Tisdale replied.

Maddie looked like she was going to be sick, and Ava wasn't feeling much better.

"Your plan is insane, you know."

"The only reason Malheur didn't work was because they were rash," Tisdale said. "They didn't have lawyers or politicians on the team. They didn't have money." He nodded toward Nielsen.

"They didn't have the *right*," Maddie said.

Ava thought Malheur was the place where the white supremacists had taken over the wildlife refuge a few years ago, but wasn't certain. It sounded right, given what everyone was saying.

"We're playing a long game here," Nielsen said, "with nothing less than an Aryan homeland at stake. We will create a whites-only country, in the hills touched by God."

"Surrounded by fossils that are millions of years old. Which you don't believe in."

"Don't confuse me with my great-grandparents, Maddie. I believe in science. I mine ore, after all. And I'm going to use science to fulfill my great-grandparents' dream. DNA testing saves the day."

"The evidence is fake. I reported it to the museum and police."

"You can retract that after reexamining the bones."

She turned to her brother. "Do your new friends know you're only doing this to get elected? That once you're in the Senate, you'll turn your back on them faster than you did on me?"

Tisdale faced Maddie and Ava—the others in the room couldn't see his face. Again, Ava saw regret shadow his features. But then he cocked his head and said, "I have always known I am among the chosen ones, as are you, Maddie. It's a shame you don't see and embrace it."

"I know you, Alan. You don't believe that at all. You just want power." She glanced at Nielsen. "And you'll do anything for campaign donations and votes."

Tisdale stiffened. He cocked his head toward Ava. "She's not one of us."

Maddie's entire body went rigid. "The things you'll say and do for power are disgusting. I'm ashamed to be related to you." She rose to her feet and turned her back to her brother, facing Nielsen. "What comes next?"

"One of our guys has already grabbed your laptop from your hotel room and will bring it here. You're going to submit a report that states you submitted the bone for DNA testing after verifying it was a skeleton found by Otto and Sally Kocher in the Painted Hills region on land owned by Clifford and Gladys Nielsen. We will go to the mansion, and you'll log in to all your accounts. The IP address will prove you reviewed the remains again after reading the news report and you discovered you were mistaken in your belief the bones had been stolen from Norway. When that's done, you're going to take off for a few days. Grief over Josh Warner's passing, or some other excuse. You'll write a letter telling Ava you didn't sign on to be a stepmom without Josh in the picture."

"I won't do it."

"Well, that's a shame, then, because if you don't, Troy here is going to use the Taser on sweet little Ava. And if you still don't, he's going to pull out his knife and start carving her skin."

Chapter Forty

Josh paused the video and bolted to his feet. He'd been fast-forwarding through the footage since he and Chase had taken over the security room—pausing only to truss up a one-eyed Peyton Hoffman and lock him in the interview room along with his brother.

The Portland Police Bureau had been notified of the meeting on the top floor of the tower and had access to the recorded files and live feed. The only reason they hadn't surrounded the building was to prevent a full hostage standoff if Nielsen and Tisdale knew they were surrounded. The Bureau had, of course, told Josh and Chase to stand down and wait for them to handle the situation, but given that Josh had control of the tower and was here now, he'd declined to follow their order.

The camera in Nielsen's outer meeting room was supposed to be off along with all the other top floor cameras, but Karl Hoffman had turned it on and had been watching the show when Josh and Chase took control of the security room.

The former security guard had probably turned on the

camera because he wanted leverage should the steel magnate and politician turn on the brothers.

Once they secured the room, Josh had wanted to race to the thirtieth floor, but he forced himself to watch the feed to assess the situation. Now, with the threat to start carving on Ava, he was done.

They were one minute behind real time.

Without a word, he and Chase bolted for separate elevators. Chase went for the service lift while Josh headed for the main bank. He tapped the buttons on his phone to make sure the elevators were ready and waiting with express service to the twenty-ninth floor.

Meanwhile, at the Raptor compound in Virginia, Mothman, Keith, and Nate were watching and listening to the feed from Nielsen Tower, including all the top-floor cameras, which Josh had turned on.

"Shit, Nielsen just tried to radio the Hoffmans for an update," Keith said.

Considering both men were bound, gagged, and handcuffed to a bolted-down table in the interview room, that wasn't going to go well.

"Tisdale wants to take Maddie and Ava to the Kocher Mansion now. Nielsen wants Maddie to write her letter to Ava first, while Kocher is there to threaten Ava."

Josh still couldn't wrap his brain around Tisdale's utter betrayal of Maddie. It was clear the guy intended to have his sister disappear and either blame it on the doxing and her association with Josh, or, if Josh ended up not being dead, framing him for her disappearance, probably because, someone would claim, she supported her White Patriot brother's campaign.

Either way, Tisdale got to run as the grieving brother of a missing sister. He'd paint himself as a victim who'd been endangered by the bridge bombing. And given the current politics of the state and the nation, this gambit could actually work.

Even the crazypants plan to create an Aryan Nation wasn't far-fetched in the current political climate. Oregon state government had been held hostage by racists off and on for the last few years as legislators staged walkouts and extremists held marches in front of the capitol to force or stop legislation. They were getting away with it thanks to the hate rallies that emboldened more to join the ranks.

And Maddie and Ava were in the center of it all.

His elevator reached the twenty-ninth floor, and he exited and headed to the staircase. Chase would be on his way to the other staircase, ready to climb the last flight of stairs, just like Josh.

Josh tripped the fire alarms on the first floor. He'd disabled the alarms and sprinklers on the other floors. The alert wouldn't reach Nielsen's office, but all the stairwell locks released. He entered the stairwell and climbed.

"Kocher is holding a knife to Ava's neck. Maddie is signing some report that Tisdale put in front of her," Nate said. "And your brother is slipping out the side door while everyone is focused on the women."

Josh paused next to the door to the thirtieth floor. "Side door? The floor plan shows the entrance to Nielsen's office and to the lobby. No side door." Josh tried to remember a side door from his meeting, but they'd met in Nielsen's office, not the outer room.

"Floor plan you were given is out of date. There's another door. It's a kitchenette with a pass-through."

Josh closed his eyes and considered the schematic he'd been given last week. "The closet was converted?"

"Looks like it."

"That's the way in, then. Chase, you good with being the decoy?"

"No problem. I'll go to the main lobby. You go in via the kitchenette."

"What about Ari?" Keith asked.

"Is he going to the stairs or elevator?"

"Elevator."

Josh watched the schematic for the penthouse lobby and waited for the green dot to indicate the elevator was there, then pressed a button to open the doors in front of his brother.

"Tell me when he's inside."

"He's in."

Josh sent the elevator down, then counted to three and stopped and locked the box. "He's trapped until Portland Police show up to nab him."

"Damn, Josh, you've been honing your hacking skills," Mothman said.

"I got bored living in the compound." This was true, but he was also taking advantage of a system in place. The elevators were designed to maximize efficiency, with floors being assigned to users based on destination, but the system got overloaded during peak hours, and the fix was to have a human seize control of the system, or no elevators would run. Josh had merely set up his own backdoor into the master control panel.

He pushed down on the handle and entered the thirtieth floor. He knew all the camera dead spots, but he also controlled all the cameras. There was no record of any occupants in the tower other than the penthouse. The building had been locked tight by the Hoffman brothers early this morning—they couldn't show their faces at the rally, so apparently, Nielsen had put them to work—only the parking levels were open to a very limited public.

In short, Josh had little to fear, but still, he stayed off camera and knew Chase was doing the same, just in case

Nielsen had access to a bank of monitors Josh didn't know about. He hadn't been allowed to inspect the top floor last week.

He found the service door to the kitchenette and slipped inside. From there, he positioned himself behind the opposite door and waited for Chase to make it easy.

A minute later, he heard a shout from the front, and caught Chase's whole act on the headset.

"Mr. Nielsen!" he shouted as he banged on the outer glass door. "I got an alert that the building was on lockdown. Some sort of emergency signal sent by the security crew. Since I was just at the park, I thought I'd check it out."

When there was no answer, he pounded again and said, "But there's no one at the security desk. I know we don't have the contract yet, but I figured I should check on you."

Another pause, and he pounded a third time. "Mr. Nielsen! Do you need help? My phone is pinging like crazy, and there's no one in security."

"Warner, go shut him up," Nielsen said on the other side of the door. There was a pause, then he said, "Where's Warner?"

"He left, moron," Ava said, her voice full of teenage sass. Josh couldn't be more proud. Or relieved.

"Kocher, get rid of him. The last thing we need is a Raptor operative in the building. How did he get in anyway?"

"Probably has something to do with you giving him and Josh Warner full access to your system last week." That had to be Maddie's brother.

"I had a plan to use him that would have been perfect if the dumbfuck you freed from jail didn't screw it up."

"We've all made mistakes, but at this point, you're screwed without me, Nielsen."

"Kocher is coming my way," Chase said.

The kitchenette door was on a two-way swinging hinge,

and Josh pushed forward, making a beeline for the biggest power player in the room.

Nielsen jerked with surprise as Josh tackled him and pinned him to the floor, then pulled his gun and pointed it at the big man's forehead. "Tisdale, move away from the women, or I will shoot your boss."

"He's not my boss."

"You really think you can win a spot in the US Senate without Nielsen's backing? You're even dumber than Maddie said you were."

Ava let out a sharp laugh as Josh heard a struggle in the other room. Kocher must've kept the knife he was holding on Ava handy and thought he could play with Chase.

Kocher had no idea whom he was dealing with, and Josh hoped the fight was on camera. He wanted to watch later in slow motion.

"Don't toy with him, Chase. He's not very bright. Show some compassion."

"Hey, I don't want him to be embarrassed."

Josh laughed, but the gun pointed at Nielsen's head didn't waver.

"You can't do anything to me," Nielsen said. "You're nothing. Nobody. My family built this city."

"So did Kocher's, but he's a cheap fraud with a worthless museum he admitted to planning on burning down on camera."

"On camera?" Tisdale said.

"Yeah. On camera." Josh flipped the wealthiest man in the city—possibly state—over and slapped handcuffs on his wrists.

"But the cameras were turned off," Tisdale said.

"And you trusted the Hoffmans on that?"

A sound behind him tipped him off, and he swung out even as he sprang to his feet, catching Tisdale on the side of his head. The man stumbled toward Ava, and she kicked out, sweeping the congressman's legs out from under him. He went down, and Josh tossed Maddie another pair of handcuffs.

She plucked them from the air and handcuffed her brother before the man even realized what was happening.

Ava launched herself at Josh as soon as both men were bound. "I thought you were dead!"

Josh wrapped his arms around her, still crouched on the floor. Still barely able to open one eye, his hearing still muted as if cotton were filtering all sounds. None of that mattered as he wrapped his arms around Ava. "I'm right here and not going anywhere, Ladybug."

"I love you, Uncle Dad."

His eyes burned.

Ava loosened her grip and turned toward Maddie. She let go of Josh with one arm and beckoned Maddie over. Maddie dropped to her knees and joined their hug, the three of them forming a triangle on the floor.

Josh looked toward the dome in the corner that housed the camera and knew they were centered in the screen for everyone watching this display. In a way, this was their first family portrait.

Chapter Forty-One

Maddie sat on a bench in the first-floor lobby, staring at the copper rose waterworks sculpture. Ava was being interviewed by no less than the chief of police, with her guardian at her side at the same time a medic was finishing cleaning Josh's head wound. Meanwhile, on the other side of the sculpture, Chase was being interviewed by two other detectives.

Everything was being done in the open lobby because Ava wanted a line of sight on everyone, and the police chief had agreed.

Maddie had already been interviewed by the detectives who were questioning Chase, and was waiting for her round with the police chief. They would likely be here all night, and she honestly didn't care so long as she could see Josh, battered but walking and breathing, Ava, wound-free on the outside, and Chase, standing tall and whole as he quietly shared his role in the takedown.

Maddie needed the line-of-sight thing as much as Ava.

Her brother and Clifford Nielsen the fourth had been taken into custody and would face both state and federal terrorism charges. The Hoffmans would be charged with her abduction. Ari was going back to jail and would face new terrorism charges that would be a slam dunk once the bomb fragments were recovered. Maddie had already told the police about the video she and Ava had gotten of Ari going under the bridge with his bulky coat on and emerging after an interval without it.

His willingness to testify against her brother and Nielsen for a reduced sentence might be mitigated by the fact that he was going back into a system where his only friends were white supremacists, and testifying against the local leaders of their movement might not make him popular.

Thankfully, they had the video, or charges against both men might not stick without Ari's testimony.

Troy Kocher was also facing charges, but Maddie suspected he'd face the least punishment. He'd threatened Ava with the knife and had admitted on camera to the plan to burn down the mansion, but it would take some doing to determine if he'd played a role in the bridge bombing. A search warrant for Oliver Shields's home and museum was in the works, and when the skeleton was recovered, they'd have both men on antiquities theft and trafficking in human remains, but it wasn't the same as the terrorism charges everyone else faced.

At least for now, Troy was in custody and couldn't return to the mansion to destroy his family's papers, and Maddie still had copies in the cloud even if her laptop wasn't recovered. She had yet to learn if one of Nielsen's men had broken into her hotel room as claimed.

It was such a crazy plan, and yet she could see how it could have worked, especially in the current political climate in Oregon. The federal government was always looking for ways to renege on tribal treaty rights. There were plenty of people in power who would have seized on the DNA test and run with it.

She studied the posh lobby of the high-rise. The architecture was lovely—modern brushed steel and marble. It was light and airy, with massive windows that went all the way up to the high ceiling.

Nielsen owned this building and had real estate holdings across the state and mines all over the world. He had a mansion, a jet, and, she would imagine, a fleet of vehicles. Probably a mega yacht. And it wasn't enough for him.

He'd coveted more land and wanted to exclude others. As if a white colony would be some sort of utopia.

It would have been a bastion of hate that would have collapsed in short order because white supremacist systems only worked when there were people to suppress.

What would happen to Nielsen Steel now?

Wounds cleaned, Josh rose from his seat and said something to the police chief and Ava, then crossed the lobby and dropped onto the bench by her side.

"Ava's okay by herself?" Maddie asked.

"Yeah. The chief is being gentle, and Ava gave the okay."

"How are you?"

"I don't even know, really." He threaded his fingers through hers. "Keith told me about how you made the decision to go after Ava. Thank you."

"Of course." Maddie stared at the tall, lanky girl with long dark hair and dark eyes so like Josh's. "She's important to you, but also, she's important to me. She has been all along." She raised their joined hands to her mouth and kissed the back of his hand. "I'm all in with you, and all in with Ava. No one can or should replace her mother, but if she'll accept me in some sort of maternal or aunt role, I'm up for it, and I won't back out, even if things between you and me don't work out."

He shifted, turning to face her, and lifted her chin so he could meet her gaze. "Us failing is not an option."

She smiled. Trust an operative to couch a relationship in mission terms. "I feel the same way. But I wanted to say it, in case you're having second thoughts now or will later. We have no way of knowing what things will be like between us when the world is normal again. I won't abandon Ava, no matter what happens between us."

"I am not having second thoughts, and I can't wait for normal. I want it all. I want to wake up with you every morning and hold you in my arms every night. I want to have scary conversations about things like children and if you want to have them. I want you by my side for all of Ava's milestones like graduation and college, and I'm frankly hoping you'll be willing to teach her to drive, because I'm pretty sure I won't have the patience for that."

Maddie let out a sharp laugh. "No, you'll be too kind and try to make her feel better when she's almost killed you by pulling out in front of a speeding car."

He chuckled at that. "Nailed it."

"Do you want kids?" she asked, feeling a flutter in her belly that they were even entertaining this question. But today was the kind of day that made one seize the moment.

"I do, actually. Always have since Ava was a toddler. But if you don't, it's not a deal breaker. I want *you*."

She leaned into him and whispered, "I've thought a lot about whether or not I want kids since my ectopic pregnancy, and if I can—there's a chance it could happen again—then yes, I do. With the right partner."

"I'd like to be that partner."

She kissed him. "I'm pretty sure you are."

Epilogue

One Month Later
Portland, Oregon

Maddie pulled the roasted chicken and mixed vegetables from the oven and covered it with foil to let it rest. The rice pilaf was ready and the salad was made, but the sounds coming from the other room stopped her from calling everyone to dinner.

Desmond, Chase, Ava, and Josh were having too much fun playing a four-person racing video game. The laughter and shouts were comforting and joyful. Like the ocean when the surf was up, the sound gave her energy.

Dinner could wait. She could reheat it for ten minutes in the oven if need be.

She poured herself a glass of wine and brought the bottle into the family room to top off Josh's and Chase's glasses, then sat on the arm of the couch next to Josh and watched the screen. Desmond and Ava were cutthroat players, while Josh and Chase were more laid-back.

At least, that was how they were in the four-player game.

Maddie happened to know that one-on-one, the two Raptor operatives were fierce competitors.

"Want to play, Auntie M?" Ava asked.

Ava had gone through a string of names for Maddie in the last month as she tried to find a way to show honor, affection, and her own brand of wit, and this week's name was Auntie M, which was probably Maddie's favorite so far.

"No, thanks. I've been crushed enough for one day."

It had been quite a month, since that day that started with a hate rally and ended with a showdown in a billionaire's office suite, but tonight was a bittersweet culmination of sorts, as tomorrow, Chase was flying back to Washington, DC.

Tricia was moving out of the rehab center and back into the compound, and Chase wanted to be there for her in addition to it simply being time for him to return to his life. Chase wasn't needed for the nonexistent Nielsen Steel contract, and Josh had hired and borrowed operators from the Alaska and Hawaii compounds to meet the needs of the influx of clients he'd landed after the events on that wild Sunday in August that had placed him and Raptor front and center in the local news again.

As much as she looked forward to the new normal of life with just Josh and Ava, Maddie would miss Chase, who was sweet, funny, and kind, and absolutely vicious when he needed to be.

Troy Kocher had needed dozens of stitches on at least a dozen wounds. But the guy had been eager to carve a Nazi symbol on Ava's cheek, so a fitting private justice in addition to the prison time he and the others faced.

The video of her brother and C-IV discussing their plans and options had been hacked and leaked and played on the news ad nauseum. There was no way in hell either man could escape without prison time. They'd blown up a bridge, after all.

The White Patriots organization had fractured. Apparently, Nielsen had been behind much of the organizing and funding, but his attempted false flag had put a stain on the organization as the FBI attempted to root out how many were involved. Dozens of conspirators had been rounded up, along with an arsenal of weapons that Nielsen had been stockpiling to prepare for the battle when they seized the Painted Hills.

While there was still a level of threat from the doxing, the White Patriots had their own problems as they were arrested one by one, and Ava, Josh, and Maddie had been able to relax a bit. After the bombing, the city would no longer issue permits for gatherings, so the organized hate rallies had ended for now.

Maddie had dived into her research notes to find more evidence against Nielsen and Kocher and had discovered that some of the papers she'd photographed in the archives had been forged to show the Nielsens had purchased far more land than they had in the 1920s and '30s. Nielsen had intended to destroy the archives to hide the evidence of the forgeries, and use Maddie's photos to authenticate his claim. The bulk of the original land records had been lost in a fire seventy years before, so he would have had a plausible claim.

Likewise, there were papers in the Kocher collection that were equally fraudulent. Nielsen's claim was bogus from the top down.

The pollen test she'd sent out for analysis had come back as a birch variant not found in Oregon—but was common in Norway. This was just further proof the bones she'd examined in the Kocher Mansion were not Native American. Eventually, police had recovered the Norwegian skeleton, finding it hidden away in Shields's museum. That was enough to put the entire private collection into question. A NAGPRA specialist would comb through their holdings, but Maddie wasn't interested in that job. She was just glad that the museum would be closed indefinitely.

The Kocher family members who were not part of Troy's scheme had agreed to repatriate everything stolen by their great-grandparents to the tribes, even the nonfunerary artifacts. This would free them to sell the house and distance themselves from the cousin who'd planned to burn their inheritance to the ground. Maddie would spend the next months going through the collection to determine tribal affiliation for artifacts in addition to the remains. Everything had been removed from the house to an off-site storage facility with supervision from the FBI.

Troy Kocher was in jail awaiting trial as his family declined to pay his bail. He was there alongside his partner in crime, Clifford Nielsen the fourth. Because of his massive wealth and foreign holdings, C-IV was considered a flight risk.

Maddie took great joy at the thought of the almost billionaire locked in a cell, dining on institutional food.

The video game ended, and Josh took first place. Maddie gave him a kiss worthy of the gold cup while Ava groaned in feigned horror at the display.

"You shouldn't have let him win, then," Maddie said.

"Hey! I won fair and square."

"Sure you did, Uncle Josh."

Maddie laughed. "If you're done playing, dinner is ready."

They moved into the dining room, and dinner was warm and fun, with many toasts to Chase. In a way, she felt like she was losing a brother, which was ironic considering she'd only known him for a month, and in that time, she'd lost her actual brother.

But family was a funny thing, the word not as narrowly defined as the dictionary had led her to believe.

There was no legal arrangement between her and Josh. She'd just moved into his house and his bed the moment the security upgrades were complete. She wasn't Ava's aunt or mother, and yet she felt like a cross between both, even though their relationship was just over six weeks old. Josh and Ava were her family now, as she faced life without her parents or brother.

Her mom and dad had seen the video like everyone else, but neither—her mom especially—could cope with the truth. Her mom alternated between accusing Maddie of lying and altering the video and accepting her son was the monster he presented in the video.

It was a yo-yo Maddie refused to ride, and she'd cut off relations with her mom. Her mom needed to accept that Alan had plotted Maddie's and Ava's deaths to cover up crimes he'd committed for the sole purpose of getting elected. Until her mom could see that Maddie was the victim, she could not have a relationship with her mom. Once again, Maddie found herself grieving the loss of her brother and parents, but on a much deeper level than the first time around.

She didn't think she'd ever understand Alan's need for power. He'd always been ambitious, but when had his drive turned pathological?

They moved to the backyard after dinner for ping-pong on the outdoor table. It was a beautiful mid-September evening, and Maddie felt a wave of contentment.

Chase and Desmond were playing a fierce game, with Ava sitting on the stone wall close to the table, cheering on her almost boyfriend. Maddie had it on authority they were taking it slow and weren't using the terms boyfriend and girlfriend, but it was pretty clear they were a couple.

Maddie and Josh sat at the outdoor table closer to the house, slightly removed from the action.

"You okay?" he asked.

She smiled. "It's a perfect evening. With Chase leaving, I've been thinking about found families and real ones…which made me think of Alan."

He took her hand and threaded his fingers through hers. "Yeah. I've been thinking about Ari too, and how my SEAL and Raptor families made up for so much. I want to take Ava to DC sometime so she can meet everyone."

"That would be a great spring break trip. Cherry blossom time."

Another ping-pong game started up, this time with Ava squared off against Chase, and her warm laugh filled the yard.

Josh squeezed her hand and nodded toward the side yard. "Come with me?"

She smiled and rose from the lawn chair. He pulled her around to the side of the house and led her through the gate to the place where he'd kissed her the first night she'd come here and met Ava.

With his hands on her hips, he pressed her to the wall, then placed his hands on either side of her head, blocking her in. "I'm looking forward to this next phase ahead of us. With Chase gone and now that Ava's in school, we'll have more time for just you and me."

Given that they both worked from home most of the time, they'd have a lot more alone time together. She cupped her hand over the back of his neck. "I'm looking forward to that too."

"I want to do something really selfish. Just for me."

She grinned. Josh's kind of selfish totally worked for her. "Yeah, what's that?"

He reached into his pocket and pulled out a small box. "I want to make you mine, forever and for always."

It took her a moment to take in his meaning. Right after it

sank in, he opened the box, revealing a beautiful solitaire stone, and said the words. "Maddie, will you marry me?"

It should be too soon to talk of marriage, and yet, with Josh, it was just right. Because this was right. He was right. And it would mean a lot to Ava too, that it was official, that Maddie was staying.

"Yes. Absolutely." She felt her eyes tear. She'd done that a lot in the last several weeks, but this was pure joy. "I love you, Josh. I want to be your family, and I want you and Ava to be mine."

He slipped the ring on her finger. "You're everything I've ever wanted, Maddie."

"And you're the best, most caring man I've ever known." She stared at the ring, a symbol of their coming legal union, when in her heart, they were already joined.

Never before in her life had she been so utterly certain she was on the right path. She rose on her toes and kissed him softly on the lips. "You're mine, Josh Warner, and I'm never going to let you go again."

Author's Note

This book was in final edits on the day George Floyd was murdered by police in Minneapolis. The protests that have stemmed from that horrific act bring me hope that there is a path to a different kind of policing in our future, as well as leaving me sickened at the brutality inflicted by officers on so many protesters around the country. This story has an idealized version of counterprotesters working with police, with only a mild nod to corrupt officers who aggravate the situation. I did consider revising those portions of the story to reflect reality, but aside from being a major rewrite just weeks before publication, it also would shift the focus of the plot, and this story was intended to be about the danger presented by white supremacists (some of whom are police) and the way they are using our systems to recruit new members and sow discord. After careful consideration, I decided to publish the book with the original intended focus.

Black Lives Matter and anyone who disagrees with that likely hasn't made it to the end of the book, but I want to be clear that I support the movement and the protests, and I'm filled with grief and hope for our country.

The following is a list of names of lives ended too soon by racist violence. It was posted on the website, BabyNames.com with the heading, "Each one of these names was somebody's baby."

EMMETT TILL • ERIC GARNER • JOHN CRAWFORD III • MICHAEL BROWN • EZELL FORD • DANTE PARKER • MICHELLE CUSSEAUX • LAQUAN MCDONALD • TANISHA ANDERSON • AKAI GURLEY • TAMIR RICE • RUMAIN BRISBON • JERAME REID • GEORGE MANN • MATTHEW AJIBADE • FRANK SMART • NATASHA MCKENNA • TONY ROBINSON • ANTHONY HILL • MYA HALL • PHILLIP WHITE • ERIC HARRIS • WALTER SCOTT • WILLIAM CHAPMAN II • ALEXIA CHRISTIAN • BRENDON GLENN • VICTOR MANUEL LAROSA • JONATHAN SANDERS • FREDDIE CARLOS GRAY JR. • JOSEPH MANN • SALVADO ELLSWOOD • SANDRA BLAND • ALBERT JOSEPH DAVIS • DARRIUS STEWART • BILLY RAY DAVIS • SAMUEL DUBOSE • MICHAEL SABBIE • BRIAN KEITH DAY • CHRISTIAN TAYLOR • TROY ROBINSON • ASSHAMS PHAROAH MANLEY • FELIX KUMI • KEITH HARRISON MCLEOD • JUNIOR PROSPER • LAMONTEZ JONES • PATERSON BROWN • DOMINIC HUTCHINSON • ANTHONY ASHFORD • ALONZO SMITH•TYREE CRAWFORD • INDIA KAGER • LA'VANTE BIGGS • MICHAEL LEE MARSHALL • JAMAR CLARK • RICHARD PERKINS • NATHANIEL HARRIS PICKETT • BENNI LEE TIGNOR • MIGUEL ESPINAL • MICHAEL NOEL • KEVIN MATTHEWS • BETTIE JONES • QUINTONIO LEGRIER • KEITH CHILDRESS JR. • JANET WILSON • RANDY NELSON • ANTRONIE SCOTT • WENDELL CELESTINE • DAVID JOSEPH • CALIN ROQUEMORE • DYZHAWN PERKINS • CHRISTOPHER DAVIS • MARCO LOUD • PETER GAINES • TORREY ROBINSON • DARIUS ROBINSON • KEVIN HICKS • MARY TRUXILLO • DEMARCUS SEMER • WILLIE TILLMAN • TERRILL THOMAS •

SYLVILLE SMITH • ALTON STERLING • PHILANDO CASTILE • TERENCE CRUTCHER • PAUL O'NEAL • ALTERIA WOODS • JORDAN EDWARDS • AARON BAILEY • RONELL FOSTER • STEPHON CLARK • ANTWON ROSE II • BOTHAM JEAN • PAMELA TURNER • DOMINIQUE CLAYTON • ATATIANA JEFFERSON • CHRISTOPHER WHITFIELD • CHRISTOPHER MCCORVEY • ERIC REASON • KIONTE SPENCER • MICHAEL LORENZO DEAN • TRAYVON MARTIN • BREONNA TAYLOR • AHMAUD ARBERY • TONY MCDADE • GEORGE FLOYD

We must put an end to this violence, and stop putting white supremacists in positions of power, be they police officers, politicians, prosecutors, or judges.

I wish to express my deepest gratitude to all the protesters who are risking assault and COVID-19 by showing up and making your voices heard.

Rachel Grant
06/09/2020

Are you wondering what happened to Tricia Rooks, or how Owen ended up at R&R?

To find out what happened in Indonesia, read Toni Anderson's *Colder Than Sin*. Visit www.toniandersonauthor.com/books/colder-than-sin for information.

To learn more about R&R, check out Serena Bell's Returning Home Series. The series starts with *Hold On Tight*, where you meet Jake, before he opens R&R. Visit www.serenabell.com/books/hold-on-tight for information.

Acknowledgments

Huge thanks to Paula Johnson, Registered Professional Archaeologist, for answering all my NAGPRA questions before I started writing, inspiring plot twists and making it possible to write this book at all. Paula also read an early draft and patiently set me straight. Any errors, misunderstandings, or misrepresentation of how historic preservation and repatriation laws work together and are enforced are mine.

Thank you to Serena Bell for plotting help and providing much needed critical feedback. Thank you to Darcy Burke for answering all my Portland questions and for plotting help. As always, thank you to Gwen Hernandez for reading the earliest, ugliest draft and helping me make the story beautiful.

As always, thank you to my husband and children. The extra time we've had together these last months has brought joy to social distancing.

About the Author

USA Today bestselling author Rachel Grant also writes thrillers as R.S. Grant. She worked for over a decade as a professional archaeologist and mines her experiences for storylines and settings, which are as diverse as excavating a cemetery underneath an historic art museum in San Francisco, survey and excavation of many prehistoric Native American sites in the Pacific Northwest, researching an historic concrete house in Virginia (inspiration for her debut novel, CONCRETE EVIDENCE), and mapping a seventeenth century Spanish and Dutch fort on the island of Sint Maarten in the Caribbean (which provided inspiration for the island and fort described in CRASH SITE).

She lives in the Pacific Northwest with her husband and children.

For more information:
www.Rachel-Grant.net
contact@rachel-grant.net

www.ingramcontent.com/pod-product-compliance
Lightning Source LLC
Chambersburg PA
CBHW061543190726
48289CB00004B/1151